OVERRULED

BAEN BOOKS edited by HANK DAVIS

The Human Edge by Gordon R. Dickson
The Best of Gordon R. Dickson
We the Underpeople by Cordwainer Smith
When the People Fell by Cordwainer Smith

The Technic Civilization Saga
The Van Rijn Method by Poul Anderson
David Falkayn: Star Trader by Poul Anderson
Rise of the Terran Empire by Poul Anderson
Young Flandry by Poul Anderson
Captain Flandry: Defender of the Terran Empire by Poul Anderson
Sir Dominic Flandry: The Last Knight of Terra by Poul Anderson
Flandry's Legacy by Poul Anderson

The Best of the Bolos: Their Finest Hour created by Keith Laumer

A Cosmic Christmas
A Cosmic Christmas 2 You
In Space No One Can Hear You Scream
The Baen Big Book of Monsters
As Time Goes By
Future Wars . . . and Other Punchlines
Worst Contact
Things from Outer Space
If This Goes Wrong . . .

BAEN BOOKS edited by CHRISTOPHER RUOCCHIO

Star Destroyers with Tony Daniel
Space Pioneers with Hank Davis
Overruled! with Hank Davis
Cosmic Corsairs with Hank Davis (forthcoming)

To purchase any of these titles in e-book form,
please go to www.baen.com.

OVERRULED

Edited by
HANK DAVIS
and
CHRISTOPHER RUOCCHIO

OVERRULED

This is a work of fiction. All the characters and events portrayed in this book are fictional, and any resemblance to real people or incidents is purely coincidental.

Copyright © 2020 by Hank Davis and Christopher Ruocchio

A Baen Books Original

Baen Publishing Enterprises
P.O. Box 1403
Riverdale, NY 10471
www.baen.com

ISBN: 978-1-9821-2450-2

Cover art by Tom Kidd

First printing, April 2020

Distributed by Simon & Schuster
1230 Avenue of the Americas
New York, NY 10020

Library of Congress Cataloging-in-Publication Data

Names: Davis, Hank, 1944– editor. | Ruocchio, Christopher, editor.
Title: Overruled / edited by Hank Davis & Christopher Ruocchio.
Description: Riverdale, NY : Baen Publishing Enterprises ; New York, NY :
    Distributed by Simon & Schuster, [2020] | "A Baen Books original" —
    Title page verso.
Identifiers: LCCN 2020000557 | ISBN 9781982124502 (trade paperback)
Subjects: LCSH: Legal stories, American. | Science fiction, American. |
    GSAFD: Legal stories. | Science fiction.
Classification: LCC PS648.L3 O94 2020 | DDC 813/.0108353—dc23
LC record available at https://lccn.loc.gov/2020000557

Pages by Joy Freeman (www.pagesbyjoy.com)
Printed in the United States of America
10 9 8 7 6 5 4 3 2 1

Since by the time this hits shelves
we'll have been married just over a month...
Hank has kindly allowed me to dedicate this book
to my wife, Jenna Ruocchio.
—C.R.

ACKNOWLEDGMENTS

Our thanks to those authors who permitted the use of their stories, and to the estates and their representatives who intervened for those authors unreachable without time travel (and raise a glass to absent friends). Among the very helpful agents deserving thanks are Spectrum Literary Agency, Scovil Galen Ghosh Literary Agency, Inc., Donald Maass Literary Agency, David Wison, John Berlyne, and Nancy Kress. And while he has done no courtroom stories we could include, many thanks to David Drake for expert advice and moral support. And thanks to the Internet Speculative Fiction Database (ISFDB.org) for existing and being a handy source of raw data, and to the devoted volunteers who maintain that very useful site.

CONTENTS

OVERRULED

COURT IS NOW IN SESSION...
ALL OXYGEN-REDUCING BIPEDS PLEASE RISE!

Y'KNOW, SOME OF MY BEST FRIENDS ARE LAWYERS...

Granted, lawyers get a bad press, and probably worse, in the mass mind, but nobody wrote a song, "Mammas Don't Let Your Babies Grow Up to Be Lawyers." On the contrary, parents, particularly mothers, want all their offspring to become either doctors or lawyers. (Parenthetically—which is why this digression is set off by parentheses, pardon me for getting technical—parents definitely, don't let your children grow up to be editors, and not just because the pay is so low!)

Back in the Sixties, when I was struggling with physics and math courses in college, before LBJ and his toady McNamara decided I would look simply smashing in olive drab, the mother of a friend (the friend grew up to be a doctor, btw) advised me I should instead become an attorney because I had "an analytical mind." Well, that was intended as a compliment, so I didn't say what flashed into my twisted young brain, which was that was like telling a girl (this was the Sixties, so I thought "girl" without guilt) that because she was beautiful, she should become a member of the oldest profession.

(Hmmm... Might the practice of law be the *second* oldest profession? But I'm getting too far afield from science fiction...)

Though there are multitudes of far-from-complimentary jokes about lawyers, the legal eagles still don't show up near the bottom of surveys about which professions the public views with respect. (Journalists are hanging in there near the bottom, and they can't blame bad press, since they *are* the press.) And courtroom dramas have long been popular in books, movies, and TV shows. The prime example is probably Erle Stanley Gardner's Perry Mason, star of books, movies, and television—though Mason comes off somewhat differently in the three media—watch one of the Perry Mason movies

1

with Warren Williams in the title role for a shock, if your knowledge of the character is limited to Raymond Burr's teleportrayal.

The popularity of courtroom dramas also extends to attorneys who are working for the Man, too. In pre-TV days, *Mr. District Attorney* wowed the radio audience for years. The genre remains popular. My colleague Christopher Ruocchio cites shows like *Suits* and *The Grinder*, to name just a couple of examples.

Now, science fiction has often shown itself to be capable of cross-breeding, at least in states where it's legal, with other forms of fiction. It's an old truism that space opera is often a translation from horse opera, with rocketships and rayguns replacing horses and six-shooters. Similar cross-fertilizations between sf and courtroom drama have frequently been successful. Add in similar joinings with courtroom comedy, and examples of future lawyering played for laughs are included in this book. And while not all sf is set in the future, much is, and it's a safe bet that lawyers and courtrooms will be with us in the foreseeable future. (Unless the libertarians take over, but that's *not* a safe bet, and may even be a contradiction in terms.)

While that subgenre isn't as much a mainstay of sf as the adventure yarn, the space exploration story, the gadget story, the dystopia or other future society extrapolation (though lawyers might stick their briefcases into any of those categories), etc., there are plenty of such stories, going back to the beginnings of sf magazines.

A story that isn't on board here, "One Leg Too Many," one of the Dr. Wentworth stories by W. Alexander, appeared in the October 1929 *Amazing Stories*. While the primary focus was on organ regeneration, there is a courtroom scene in the tale. George O. Smith's classic "Venus Equilateral" series in *Astounding Science-Fiction* in the 1940s had a corporation lawyer who originally showed up just getting in the way of the no-nonsense engineers, but shortly turned to theft of information in a later yarn, finally becoming an outright space pirate who almost ruined a Christmas party in the bargain. Surely that display of ingenuity and ambition qualified him as an ornament to his profession.

In a less villainous vein, Theodore L. Thomas and Charles L. Harness, both lawyers, though Harness was also a chemist, began a series of stories in the Fifties under the joint pseudonym of "Leonard Lockhard," which told of a law firm specializing in patent law, a field which, it happens, is much more fantastic than mere extraterrestrial visitors, time travel, parallel worlds, and such. Later installments were written by Thomas alone, still as "Lockhard," and one memorable case had the firm's lawyers explaining to their client, one Arthur C. Clarke, why he couldn't patent the idea of global communications via relay satellites even though he had come up with the idea before anyone else. (Though that story was fiction, the situation was real, and Sir Arthur told his own tale of woe in an essay titled "How I Lost a Billion Dollars in My Spare Time.")

I regret that space (the paper sort, not the Final Frontier sort) didn't permit me to include a Lockhard story. (I also regret that there aren't enough of the Lockhard stories to make it practical to gather them together in one book.)

Another series detailing the fortunes and misfortunes (mostly the latter) of a future law firm was written by Charles Sheffield, and there *is* one of those humorous tales included here. They were written by Dr. Sheffield at the request of his children, who wanted stories which involved... but I shouldn't spoil the setup for you. Go look at the story.

Theodore L. Thomas and Charles L. Harness were not the only lawyers who also wrote sf. One such, who graces this book with her presence, is Laura Montgomery, collaborating with Sarah A. Hoyt. And I should mention another very good writer-lawyer, Joe L. Hensley, and his absence from these pages makes the book poorer (not that it still isn't a must-buy!). Hensley liked to tell the story of how, when he was serving as Prosecuting Attorney, a somewhat illiterate person wrote him a letter addressed to "Prostituting Attorney," but obviously didn't intend the malapropism to be social commentary.

And, of course, David Drake is one of Baen's most popular authors, with a library full of books to his credit. A graduate of Duke Law School, he was an assistant town attorney for several years, before becoming a versatile and top-selling writer of military sf, just plain sf, and fantasy. David has noted his reason for leaving the law books to gather dust: "They don't tell you in law school that anybody who talks to a lawyer professionally is either pissed off or miserable, And it gets old." Sf and fantasy readers should be grateful to those p.o.'d or miserable people who inadvertently led to David's stellar writing career.

And now for the Dark Side...

Some of the classic writers of sf and fantasy have had a less than rosy view of lawyers and courtrooms. In the first of his celebrated Martian novels, *A Princess of Mars*, Edgar Rice

Burroughs' immortal John Carter describes the green, four-armed Martians' society thus: "In one respect at least the Martians are a happy people; they have no lawyers." In the previous line, Carter muses that "justice seldom misses fire, but seems rather to rule in inverse ratio to the ascendancy of law," which reminds me of that quip that "Justice is what we want, but the law is what we get."

And there's Robert E. Howard's "Queen of the Black Coast," in which Conan (a barbarian, you might have heard) witnesses a friend defending his lady friend from a government guard, and is hauled into court and ordered to bear witness against said friend. When the Cimmerian demurs, saying he does not wish to testify against a friend, the judge explains to him that the law outranks friendship and it is his duty to testify. At which point Conan narrates, "So, seeing they were all mad, I drew my sword and cleft the judge's skull, then cut my way out of the court . . ." (I'm again indebted to Christopher Ruocchio, who identified the story's title, which I had forgotten.)

I don't have a copy of S. Fowler Wright's classic sf novel, *The World Below*, handy to provide an exact quote, but I remember being struck by the man of the present (that is, the 1930s) who has traveled millennia into the future amid beings very unlike humans, and explains to one of them that in his (our) time, the government gleefully churned out law after law, until there were too many of them for anyone to keep track of, and it was difficult to cross the street without breaking at least one of them.

But enough of the gripings of classic writers, and time for your much lesser editor to do some of his own griping. At some point in these anthology intros, I inevitably bemoan the absence of stories I would have liked to include, but circumstances would not permit. I've already lamented the lack of a story by "Leonard Lockhard." Another such regrettable absence is "The Witness" by one of my favorite writers, Eric Frank Russell. It would have been oddly up-to-date for a story from the early 1950s, bearing on the present controversy over illegal aliens, (or, as some would have it, "undocumented immigrants"), this time with a *really alien alien*, and I think it's a terrific story, even if I suspect that the late Mr. Russell and I would be on opposite sides of the controversy. I've tried in the past to include other Russell gems, never with success so far.

I wonder if I could subpoena one of Russell's stories . . . ?

Excuse me, I think I need to visit the more benevolent sort of bar. See you in court!

THE SKETCHER

TOM KIDD

The artist turns writer here with a rollicking story by Tom Kidd explicating his own terrific cover for this book.

The hapless hero of the story might be thinking, frame artwork, not artists. *This artist's services were much in demand, particularly among the aliens, who considered taking a photograph to be heinous and illegal. So he strictly stuck to sketching to earn a living on their planet. Surely it was all a misunderstanding and he could prove his innocence. But it didn't help that the aliens also regarded trial by jury as a ridiculous human custom, certainly nothing that they would bother with...*

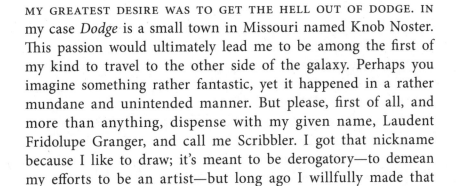

MY GREATEST DESIRE WAS TO GET THE HELL OUT OF DODGE. IN my case *Dodge* is a small town in Missouri named Knob Noster. This passion would ultimately lead me to be among the first of my kind to travel to the other side of the galaxy. Perhaps you imagine something rather fantastic, yet it happened in a rather mundane and unintended manner. But please, first of all, and more than anything, dispense with my given name, Laudent Fridolupe Granger, and call me Scribbler. I got that nickname because I like to draw; it's meant to be derogatory—to demean my efforts to be an artist—but long ago I willfully made that name mine. It now defines me.

At eighteen, I seemed destined for failure; I had no prospects, no future whatsoever. All I had was my art, and it was getting me nowhere. My dream was to go to some distant art college, and become an illustrator. The farther I traveled, the better— maybe even to other worlds. I wanted to escape to someplace the opposite of this one.

And not come back.

Youthful aspirations are like that. They cannot be denied. Their influence is all powerful, all consuming, an unstoppable passion. They make you desperate, drive you to do the silliest and most unlikely of things...

"DRAW BLONKY," the ad said, "AND WIN AN ART SCHOLAR- SHIP!" You saw the advertisements everywhere. All you had to do was make a copy of a goofy face in profile and send it off to the experts to judge your talent. When my older brother, Bill, found out I'd indeed done a drawing and sent it in, actually put it in an envelope and mailed it, he called me a fool. Then he came into my room to show everyone we knew how foolish I was.

"Look at my little brother, Scribbler," he said turning his ring-camera towards me—the feed going directly to his vlog—as I lay on my bed reading. "His head is filled with crazy fantasies about being an artist. He's so desperate to do so, he answered that stupid ad and did a drawing of Blonky. Look," said Bill who scanned the camera across my small library of books, "Oz books; children read those."

I didn't bother to explain that the books were beautifully illustrated, and that's what attracted me to them, but I'd certainly read them all. The idea of escaping to somewhere exotic appealed to me. And I'd watched the original *Wizard of Oz* movie a few times too. Perhaps he was right; maybe I should grow up.

Even my parents worked in turns to expertly belittle me:

"High school is behind you," said Dad.

"It's time you start thinking about a real job," added Mom.

"The world no longer needs artists."

"Never really did."

"We won't support you while you chase this illusion."

"Your brother has the right idea."

"His vlog makes real money."

"Bill pays us rent."

"Maybe it's time you started doing that."

This went on for some time. My parent's perceptions were intransigent, so it would be a waste of time to argue, if it were even allowed. How is it they were proud of my brother, whose vlog is dedicated to humiliating people? Doesn't it matter how someone makes their money?

A week later, a very long week later, a faux-gilded envelope arrived from the Super Art School (SAS). It announced that I was one of the finalists in its scholarship program and that an instructor would come to the house to give me further tests. I was excited until Bill, well-trained in the art of disparagement, informed me that the company told everyone they had "great talent" and gave out "scholarships" that were only partial, mere discounts, enticements to coax you to sign on for their expensive by-mail training. The art school refused to use the internet, they had to see the real art, to make sure it was done by hand. Bill went on to tell me it wouldn't be an instructor who would come by but merely a salesman. That was my brother's mission in life: dashing any small hope I had.

The slick salesman, Jerry Sam, arrived on the appointed day. He gushed with praise for my art, but due to Bill's disenchanting words, his compliments fell on deafened ears. Then Mr. Sam gave me his "Comprehensive Test." He timed this with an old-fashioned stopwatch, something I recognized only from time-worn black & white movies. First, he set several objects on a table in front of me, removed them, and asked me to draw each one from memory. My favorite part of the test was when he told me to use my imagination to create a storyboarded sequence of first alien contact. When he looked at the art I'd done, he exclaimed, "Holy shit!" This didn't seem like a professional reaction to me, nor did it come across as a good sign. Before I could work up the gumption to question this, he'd gathered up all the art I'd done, stuffed it into a portfolio, and said, "I need to take this back to the office." Then he immediately left as if he had an unexpected and pressing appointment. He never offered me a dubious scholarship, nor did he quote me a price for the SAS program. I didn't know what to think.

Things then happened fast. I received a notice from SAS that I'd been accepted for extensive instruction on a full art scholarship. They gave me a day to pack my bags, and to my family's amazement, a Homer hovered outside our house, its massive, lighter-than-air, doughnut-shaped envelope covering the lawn and a portion of the street. It had been dispatched from MacDill Air Force Base to pick me up and fly me off for my training at

Ellsworth Rocket Base in South Dakota. The I-Cixx Corporation, a military contractor, had underwritten my education. They needed people like me. The following week I was a bona fide space artist trainee, and I was about to board a spacecraft that would fly me off into the cosmos. My further art education would take place during my long trip across the galaxy. I would soon be free of Missouri misery. My head spun, my heart pounded with excitement while my stomach churned in anticipation of my future. None of my family members were there to see me off, not even via holo.

No one.

Some small part of me had hoped for a polite familial send-off, a final group picture, a hug goodbye, an expression that they might miss me in some small manner. Of all people, Jerry Sam was there to say goodbye, and he bid me farewell with a face that seemed sorrowful. In retrospect, what I saw was some regret, some sense of complicity in deceiving me.

Other conscripts would tell me that the I-Cixx Corporation's search for artists had three requirements for their art contractors: excellent imaginative drawing skills, a desperation to get away, and a substantial amount of youthful gullibility. Check—check—check.

If I'd had someone to write home to, someone who cared, I'd have told them about the intense whirlwind of activity that followed. Once in space, I was transferred to a space station–sized transport ship of alien design. I quickly realized I must be the only human aboard. Indeed, none of my I-Cixx instructors were human, nor was anyone I met. Each day a tornado of information about the universe spun about me. My young mind took it all in and adapted to my otherworldly surroundings. As I learned, we rocketed on beyond the reach of human civilization—and kept going. No one had told me I was taking the local into space with multiple stops that slowed our travel so much it took over a year for me to reach my destination. Then, after all that time, it came to me, the small print in my contract, the harsh reality of line #62. It stated I'd be "embedded" in this part of the universe: I had only a one-way ticket. Goodbye Earth.

Forever.

Gone now is the starry-eyed kid thrilled to have the opportunity to experience the multifaceted wonders of what lay beyond our solar system. Fifteen years of traveling in space has taken away its sparkle.

Mainly, I work with interpreters in our attempts to communicate with the various self-aware species, to understand their cultures, and establish better communication with them. If you were to ask me now, I'd say there are far too many sentient creatures around these days. Wait, that's unfair of me. My thoughts smack of human bigotry, xenophobia. *The world is an intricate mosaic of fascinating creatures we should all be honored to be a part of*—"blah, blah, blah," I said aloud to myself after having remembered the introduction of my work primer. My present, angry thoughts on alien life are more a reflection of my profound frustration with these knuckleheads.

And one insufferable robot.

In ancient times we humans felt all alone in the universe, and we went around forlornly seeking other peoples as highfalutin' as we saw ourselves. Through organizations like SETI we scoured the skies for extraterrestrial intelligence to no avail. What was it my grandmother used to say? Be careful of what you wish for. Our wishes were answered a hundred thousandfold. It's like a child eating so many of his favorite candy bars, his gluttony is transformed into a period of profound revulsion for them.

In this part of the universe, it's wall-to-wall alien civilizations. I know it's something of a misnomer to call creatures in their own systems aliens, but they come in such mightily weird forms—distinctly alien shapes to my eyes—out here in the Cygnus arm of our galaxy. After all my time here I've only been able to categorize a small fraction of the varieties of perambulating, floating, swimming, digging, flying, sailing; then talking, singing, cogitating, philosophizing, hypothesizing—breathing and non-breathing folk in the universe. And they come in so many disgusting forms. Hold on, I take that back, no, not disgusting, *heaven forbid*, instead, *beautiful varieties of life in wonderful and myriad forms*. That's another phrase that comes right from my training brochure. Isn't that nice?

One important thing the I-Cixx Corporation doesn't tell its contractors is that interpreting work isn't enough money to live on; you have to accept many side gigs, extra art assignments, the lesser endeavors to satisfy people's curiosity about the universe, little things to pad out your income. More importantly, I've been saving up the money from those jobs, little bit by little bit, over all the years I've been here, for my ticket home. In a reverse of my prior need to escape, my overriding desire is now to go home; well, maybe not *home*, not back to Knob Noster, Missouri, but Earth. My feeling of goodbye and good riddance has faded with time.

Full disclosure: I'm in a bad mood today, and I've been drinking a little. Strike that, *a lot*. Seriously, what would you do if you were facing your imminent execution? As is tradition, I was offered my last meal, and I chose potables—whiskey... and bourbon, and vodka, and the lovely green fairy, absinthe. As you can tell by my wavering words, they complied with my final wish. At an insane pace, I've been guzzling cheap liquor from tiny plastic decanters, now strewn about my cell, and it has fueled my need to draw into a state of furious cathartic expression, disgorging my bile into the pages of my sketchbook. Such is my pitiful and mighty power, the imagination to make fun of the people who frustrate me, who make my life miserable, and portray them as pitiful jesters dancing a humiliating jig that amuses the all-powerful god with His little pencil. I thank the Fates—the bouncing autonetic bubble-guards—who left me my tools for drawing when I explained their importance to my well-being, my very *short-term* well-being.

I turned to a blank page and, as always, it seemed to ask: what will you draw next? I no longer want to be a white reflection of all, yet nothing; will you make me into something? It was an old-fashioned thing, this paper, yet without it, I'd be barred from doing my work.

There's a weird quirk among virtually all the alien races, call it a ramped-up sensitivity of privacy, a robust proprietary sense of self, and all of that is backed up by laws with terrible penalties. It came down to one overriding rule—NO PHOTOGRAPHY ALLOWED! If you were caught making vids or using any mechanical device for direct image capture of any creature, anyone or anyplace not your own, you'd lose more than your equipment, perhaps even a limb.

However, drawing and painting is not only encouraged, it is always an honor among aliens to have yourself or your possessions portrayed this way. By holding my sketchbook high as an all-access charm, I could virtually say *open sesame* and pass through any barrier, like some great nobleman, into the most exclusive and intimate settings. In short, aliens love artists. Just not this one, not now. Murder is frowned on even out here in the hinterlands of space. It doesn't help me that the attempted assassination was on a beloved stateswoman. Now I am despised. My plummet from favor was steep indeed.

My head drooped, and my eyes fell on my flannel prison uniform. It was humiliating to be forced to wear what amounted to pajamas, with damnably cute black spots, like a child in his new Dalmatian onesie. The cursed clothes even had a flap in the back. All it lacked was a hood with ears and a tail. I picked up my pencil and began to draw myself as a pitiful spotted puppy. Next to the puppy I placed a grinning executioner holding a massive and bloody ax. She was there to decapitate me and make my fur into a dog schmatta. This was the frightening memory I'd dredged up from my childhood, a cartoon about an evil lady who killed people's pets. To strengthen the composition I added some recently headless dog corpses placed artfully about. Gallows humor.

The door to my cell whooshed open and ended with a loud clank that sent echoes back to me from the catacomb of tightly packed jail cells outside my door. In sauntered my naked-faced mechanical lawyer, Perri. It was spooky how much he resembled the miniature robot drone my older brother, Bill, used to torment me.

"Mr. Laudent Fridolupe Granger." He always irritatingly called me by my full given name. "I am Perri Bricklayer, Esquire," trumpeted my robo-lawyer.

"Yeah, yeah, I know, please speak more quietly."

"I've made a deal for you, no execution; you'll be set free in no time at all," said Perri, in a self-congratulatory and supercilious manner.

"This is fantastic news. I don't know how to thank you." All the tension in my body flowed away. I nearly wept. Perri puffed with pride in his accomplishment.

"Working it out in earthly terms, I believe that I can offer you hard labor for one hundred and twenty-five years. All you need to do is sign this admission of guilt and then I can go on to matters of more significance."

This evil twist devastated then enraged me. "So, I'm insignificant, a trivial detail to you?"

"It's like this, based on what I have, odds are I'll win two or three of my easiest cases today. Yours, I have no chance of winning. You're a lost cause. Why waste time on you?"

"Listen, you clockwork crook; you expect me to sign this thing that guarantees me years of anguish and pain?" He looked back at me blankly, and gestured for me to sign the document by tapping it with his finger impatiently. I took a swing at him. Unfortunately for me, I connected. *THWANG!*

"You broke my fucking hand, you metallic monstrosity." Although I wasn't proud of it, insults came naturally, spontaneously, sometimes explosively, often alliteratively out of me, primarily when I was drunk, hurt or angry. My foul mouth was very much a legacy handed down to me from my parents. Today my mouth was full of venom. Tomorrow I expected to feel embarrassed by my abusive language. Perhaps not for long though—certainly not if Perri lost this case. I'd heard the death penalty was instantaneous here, at the very drop of the gavel. Any regrets would end there. I sat down hard. Defeated.

"Sir, there's hardly a metal part to me. Please don't make preposterous statements," responded Perri as he waved his hands over his goofy body as if to show me what he was made of.

"Sorry, Perri, you can see I'm having a bad day. You may not take my life seriously, but for some reason, *I do*," I said as I shook my aching fingers. He didn't seem to notice I'd struck him. Although it only hurt me, I felt shame for my act of violence. "Look, Perri, I didn't do anything wrong. I'm innocent. Get out there and get them to see I'm not guilty of these trumped-up charges. Don't I get one more appeal? I know they found me guilty, but in this system there's one more go-around, right?"

"Who's the attorney here? It's me, right? Let me handle the law part of this, okay?"

"But I do get another go with the judge?"

"Yes, but I don't advise it. Take the deal. You'll be out before you know it and with all that work you'll do in the labor camp, you'll be in fine physical shape when you're set free."

"I'm thirty-three now. Once I'm ready to be released...hold on, let me add it up..." I pretended to do the math. "I'LL BE LONG DEAD!"

"Such a pitifully short life-span you humans have. Why even bother living if it's so brief?"

"It's more than enough time for me to rip your innards out and make a half-dozen actually *useful* household appliances out of you." I calmed myself with some deep breaths. "Sorry, Perri,

I don't know if it's because you're a robot or a lawyer but the things you say, are, well, terribly insensitive. You will cause me to run out of invectives in response," I added with a sad smile, knowing my attempt at making light of the situation was undoubtedly lost on Perri.

"Sorry sir," apologized Perri, "I'll try to be more...*tactful*. Maybe we should go over your story again. Perhaps I can find some extenuating circumstance to get you a better deal with the DA, cut fifty or so years off of your prison time—maybe even get you *moderately* heavy labor."

"Can I get some coffee? Strong, a bucketful," I pleaded. "Whatever you've got that'll help clear my spinning, befuddled head."

"No worries, I brought some with me," said Perri. "Despite the verbal abuse that is often directed at us..." he paused for emphasis there, "robo-lawyers, we always think well ahead of our client's needs. Do you have a cup for it?"

I was impressed. But I didn't see Perri carrying a thermos or anything like that with him. Still, I brought him the single foam cup I had in my prison cell. He then proceeded to (how do I put this?) piss out a bubbling stream of steaming hot coffee for me from an outgrowth that had extended from between his legs.

"Care for some cream?"

"*No*—No, definitely not. I'll drink it black." At that, two small (I guessed one for milk and one for cream?) nozzles in Perri's chest area retracted.

The bitter substance that had bubbled out from inside Perri's body tasted like engine oil. "What grade is this, 5W40?" I quipped and waited vainly for a response.

After a moment I asked, "Very well, where should I begin with my story?"

"Tell me everything that happened to you the day before you were arrested, *all* over again, like I've forgotten it all," said Perri, sitting cross-legged on the floor and putting his head in his hands like an eager child waiting for story time.

"You *have* forgotten it all, haven't you?"

"No, not exactly, what I did was erase it all. I figured I'd have no need to remember this failure and I was sure you'd take the deal. Everyone takes the plea deal."

"That you...remember?"

"I can honestly say that, to my memory, no one ever refused a plea deal."

"Could you have just erased all the cases that didn't take the plea deal?"

"I don't remember."

Before me was an engine of ineptitude, a wretched entity I could only feel hate for—my only hope. The thought of committing another violent act came to me—but that's not who I am—I like to think. Also, I lacked a lethal weapon. Instead, I merely began my story through gritted teeth: "Here it is, the story of my life all over again for you to hear one more time and then, I presume, delete. It all began . . ."

"Wait, stop; I didn't get a chance to start recording."

I gave Perri my most *I hate you* look of disgust, waited a moment, and growled a sarcastic, *"Ready?"*

"Yes, yes, please, go on," he said as he waved a circle with his hand in a dismissive manner. "And tell me about your job; you draw pictures, right?"

"Close enough. I'm a universal translator with my art."

"Why not use existing photographs or art as a form of flashcards to communicate instead of art?" asked Perri.

"Don't be ridiculous—how could you do that, how could you have the exact right photographs or art ready to illustrate every idea, every point of view, in real time? Not to mention create scenes of the very aliens before you doing things they've never done before? Cameras don't have the creative minds to accomplish that. They can only make what's already there and nothing that isn't. Only an imaginative illustrator can do that in the fullness of manners."

"Ah, I see," he said, then sat for a moment as if thinking through my explanation. "*Now* I understand the value to your work," he added, as if being convinced of this for the first time. That my point of view was accepted so easily by Perri left me feeling deflated. What was I to do with all my examples of professional success I wanted to tell him?

"Right, thanks," I said, and then added out of suspicion an, "I guess," along with a mistrustful sideways look, waiting for Perri to add something demeaning.

Instead, he said, "My understanding is that you're trained not to think in symbols, rather to perceive the world literally. That must be difficult."

"It's a gift and a curse. Symbolic thinking is far more efficient but with it you miss out on so much and it's impossible to build most structural objects from symbolic imagery."

Perri nodded in an almost human way that he understood. "Yes, of course," he went on to explain, "centuries ago the court used to use in-house illustrators to make holographic recreations of crime scenes that the juries and judges could walk through. Once the court got rid of the juries, we no longer needed illustrators. Then we got rid of the persuasive, more poetic type, attorneys by replacing them with plain-speaking lawbots like me. With those simple changes, we fast-tracked justice."

"I have an opposite point of view; you fast-track *injustice*."

"Tomato, tomato," said Perri, pronouncing the word the same way both times. Did he have no understanding of the meaning? Perhaps he'd suffered some blow to his central processor, knocking his electronic brain out of kilter.

"I think you may have some form of mental damage, Perri. Did someone hit you upside your fragile plastic noggin?" He started to answer, but I waved him off. "Never mind, let me ask you this, define justice, and define injustice, please?"

"They both mean the same thing," he said blithely as if he knew better than I. "It's like flammable and inflammable, both those words mean the same thing, that something can very easily catch fire, so ergo, justice and injustice must also mean the same thing, right?"

"Right, no. Not right. Very, very wrong." Consumed with frustration, I turned from Perri, held my aching head and squeezed my eyes shut in an attempt to push Perri's image from my mind. "Why did I hire this inept robot defender? What did I do in a past life to deserve this?" I said to no one as I paced a circle around the small prison cell while I gesticulated wildly.

"Flammable and inflammable have different meanings?" asked Perri incredulously.

I turned on him. "No, dammit, those two words *do* mean the same thing, but justice and injustice have opposite meanings. How is it you don't know this?" I snapped angrily.

"I beg your pardon," said Perri a bit disgruntled. "The problem isn't with me; it's with language. You have to admit it's a subtle distinction." How could he see this as only a negligible misunderstanding? So much did I despise this robot. "I have three hundred and thirteen languages in my immediate memory banks. It can be hard to keep them all straight if they're going to have such arbitrary rules. I say we put aside these semantic arguments for another day." Like I *had* another day, I thought. "Please continue; I need more information if I'm to sway the judge."

My head began throbbing again, and I held it in my hands. I mumbled, "I'm matched up with a lawyer who might get me executed because he says the opposite word for what he means. I'm most certainly doomed. Doomed, doomed, doomed."

"You're not making sense. Didn't you hear me?" complained Perri. "Please, stop mumbling to yourself and tell me more about your silly job. It might help us with your case."

I was shaken from my deep despair by this outrageous description of my profession. "'Silly?' Listen, given all the subtlety of spoken language and all its nuances—to wit, your recent shortcomings with English. We need artists to help communicate. Without us, words will be misconstrued, wars will be fought; species will be made extinct." At this point, my explanation had become a passionate and strident lecture. "*I* could become extinct because of a misunderstanding." As I said that I realized that my anger had brought me to the point of apoplexy. Out of breath, like a fatigued runner at the end of a race, I bent over with my hands on my knees. "Give me a moment, Perri, so I can breathe." Then I sat down, feeling thoroughly emptied.

"Give me my sketchbook," I demanded of Perri, and he handed it to me. "Perhaps this will express how I feel at the moment," I said as I drew. A moment later I handed the sketchbook back to Perri to show him my drawing.

"Ahh," said Perri, "I believe you wish to kill me. You've drawn yourself lunging and piercing me through my middle with a rapier. At the end of the blade is a fanciful gear-driven heart. I believe the correct response here is *touché*."

"Ha! Well done, Perri, touché back at ya. If you can be half that clever in the courtroom, I'll soon be a free man."

"As per your request, I'll do my best to use only fifty percent of my brainpower when arguing your case."

"That'd be more than you used the last time. So deal."

"May I ask why you use ancient materials like paper and pencil to draw with when there are a variety of drawing and painting devices, using all the dimensions of sight, sound and movement, readily available to communicate with?"

"I use them because they always work. Pencil and paper work in places *you* wouldn't work. Also, paranoia is fairly common with my clients so when I meet with these otherworldly creatures, they may even forbid *any* electronic device that might be used against them. As a robot of the law, you know that the universe has innumerable privacy rules against photography but drawing by hand is legal everywhere. It's the same reason that no photography is allowed in the courtroom; the two devices I have with the ability to record, my ring and watch, were quickly confiscated when I was arrested. They don't want the world to see how evil and incompetent you folk are here."

Rather than argue with me Perri made a small confession. "Things were far better before the system was privatized. Once certain predatory businesses took over, cases were expedited, but primarily, I think, for the sake of more prisoners who then become slave labor. I believe this to be both derogatory yet true. A human I defended once called us a 'kangaroo court.'"

It seemed to me that my Tin Man lawyer might actually have a heart, but he was still an idiot.

"What are you doodling now?" asked Perri who had just noticed I was drawing.

"Drawing is not just my job but my therapy. It helps me deal with the hard realities of life. You mentioned a kangaroo court and..." I handed my drawing to Perri.

He looked at it, dropped the sketchbook to the floor and did something that startled me. It was the most bizarre thing I've seen even with all my experiences out here in the vast cosmos. At first I didn't quite know what it was. He shook the room in a raucous, gut-busting, robot laugh. He rocked back and forth holding his robot belly. "That baby kangaroo popping out of its mom's pouch and banging the gavel really tickled my funny circuits."

"I've never seen a robot laugh before. You scared me. I didn't know it was possible. Aren't all of you completely humorless? I mean, clearly not, but how not?"

"It was probably some programmer's sense of humor or lack of it. At some point the cockamamie code was written, and now they can't get it out of the system. It has been buried in a bunch of dampening code, so it rarely comes out, unless, as I say, stress brings it forward."

Ah, I thought to myself, stress explains the laugh. That thought made me do something I didn't want to do, feel sorry for Perri. Poor Perri must have had some serious built-up tension to laugh at my mildly humorous drawing.

"Should I get back to my story?" I suggested to avoid talking about feelings with, of all things, a cyber-man—no, worse—a lawyer.

"Yes, please continue," said Perri robotically. Back to his old self now. "Tell me about the Sketcher Convention."

"Ah, my itty-bitty bytes-for-brains bot, it seems you do remember some of what I told you, however vaguely. I attend the Sketcher symposiums you speak of every so often. Their purpose is to bring together drawing-communicators of various species so that we can sharpen our skills. The conventions are quite useful and rather educational, truly a way to see through another sentient's eyes. And they are also one big alien on alien, eldritch as hell, fu—I mean, love-fest. At such things you can truly have a wild time in Weird Town." I stopped to brush my hair back and take a swig of coffee. "Or so I've heard," I said with a dishonest shrug, but Perri angled his head doubtfully. "Okay, you're my lawyer, I'll be straight with you. The truth is that out here in the infinite height, width and girth of space, a place teeming with all varieties of consenting adults, and my having an open mind, it's still hard for me to ... to ..."

"Have sexual relations with someone?"

"Uh, yes."

"I'd love to hear about some of your, even if rare, sexual interludes," said Perri. Then he leaned forward in a creepy manner, as if I could whisper the stories to him and it would be our dirty little secret.

"No. Don't have any to talk about."

"Please."

"Absolutely not."

"Pretty please!"

"Okay, just one. Do you know what Skinners are? They're hairy or feathered creatures who wear humanlike skin, the opposite of what we have on earth, Furries, who wear animal costumes to—"

"That's nasty."

"Oh, now you're judging me? Who made you a judge? The I-Cixx Corporation tossed me into the universe under their dubious contract, all by myself with little support, with only a brief period of training and zero human contact, effectively leaving me lost in space. *Dude*, it gets lonely. And, AND, where do I find a femalelike body around here? After a while without any human contact what was once out of the question starts to look pretty good. I'm thirty-three years old, in my prime, among societies of people with only monstrous forms and a billion light-years away from humanity. If I can find among the multitudes of creeping, crawling, climbing, slinking, sliding, sliming folk, one single consenting adult, or a dozen at once, of any sex or even multiple genders, I don't care; *I'm hitting it.*"

"Ah, that explains the blow I received earlier from you. That must've been a precursor to sex. I could turn myself into a sex-bot if you like. You could romance me if you think it'll calm you down a bit."

"Yuck! No. Certainly not. Anything but lowering myself into the uncanny valley of soulless, cybernetic sex. That's sick. You disgust me." Perri's blank face looked back at me or looked at something above me. Who can tell? How is it that he can look hurt? Dammit, now I was feeling sorry for him again. Soulless, I called him soulless. What did I know? Maybe robots had souls. Surely there's a programmer somewhere who has written that application.

I jumped when the door to my cell flew open. When I snapped my head in the direction of the door, I saw a furry thing come lumbering towards us. It was about the size and demeanor of a golden retriever, with a classic set of four legs, yet low to the ground and waddling like a lizard. Its thick tail moved back and forth in a controlled prehensile manner. The striped dog-thing nuzzled itself against Perri, and it growled in my direction. It showed me a mouth of incisors that looked disturbingly human. I'd rather have seen sharp canines. "What's that?" I asked Perri, pointing at it with open distrust.

"She's Dr. Susan Calvin, my emotional support animal. Whenever I get upset and start to feel down she comes out to make me feel a little better about life," explained Perri.

The idea that a robot needs emotional support was a new one for me; that it came in the form of a living, warm-blooded animal was somehow endearing; and that Perri insisted on using the animal's full name—that it *had* a full name—was, I had to admit, kind of cute, one hundred percent all Perri too. But doctor? Medical or Ph.D., I wondered.

I decided to make friends with her, "Hi there Susan, you're a good girl aren't you, aren't you?" I said reaching my hand out for her to smell. She snapped at me, and I yanked back quickly.

"See," said Perri, "she's making me feel better already."

Great, now it's two against one. No, it's the whole universe against me—the case of *Everyone* versus Scribbler. I watched Perri pet Susan. He rubbed her behind her ears and, with those affectionate strokes of his hand he made the dog-thing purr. Then I saw Susan extend her tail around Perri's leg and hug it gently. She was green and gold striped: part dog, part cat, part lizard, and part new world monkey—four pets in one—with what looked like awful human dentures stolen from some nineteenth-century codger lodged in her slobbery mouth.

"Okay, I think it's time we get back to your story. Tell me what happened to you at the symposium shortly before you were arrested," suggested Perri.

"Okay," I began as I eyed Susan who looked as sweet as can be at the moment, yet somehow also appeared as if she'd eat me if given a chance. "Here may be the thing that got me into trouble," I explained. "At first all seemed quite well, then suddenly it wasn't. Maybe I insulted someone.

"At night, after all the panels, slideshows and demonstrations, we Sketchers often gather in the bar for what amounts to a mixer, a meet and greet, if you will. To get to know one another, we have a tradition of drawing each other. I'd had a few drinks by the time I met a real beauty. She was a delightful specimen by any standard; she had large opal eyes, long lashes on a perfectly symmetrical face and luscious lips that begged to be kissed. Do you know how rare it is to find an alien with lips? Sure, her 'hair' moved about her head like a jar full of earthworms but that only made her more exotic. Okay, I'm calling her 'she,' but who knows for sure. Whatever gender this creature was, she/it was stunning. We went to a booth to be alone.

"Out came her charcoal stick and she did a most flattering drawing of me, using the back of her tentacle fingers to blend the dark medium in perfect nuanced gradations for the shadows of my face. The only weird thing about it was that after she did my portrait, she reached forward to touch my face and gingerly push my mouth open to look inside. Then she added a drawing of my skull that featured my small chin and prominent cheekbones next to the picture. Even though I was a bit bemused by the skull, I smiled when I looked at the drawing, and she smiled back. My heart skipped a happy beat or two. She was my first smiling alien. I didn't know it was possible. I opened my sketchpad and drew her, pouring all of my passion for her onto the page, and I did one of the best portraits I've ever done. She took my hand and had me touch her face and look in her mouth. I got the message to copy her example, and I drew my best guess of the bone structure of her face. When I showed it to her, I saw her eyes widened, and she gave me another even broader smile. This looked like it'd be my lucky night. In return, she handed me what she'd drawn in her sketchbook. It was herself and me together in an embrace. I put my name on that drawing and my room number.

"The next step in our courtship was critical. I had to draw myself naked, showing all my bits and pieces with exact anatomical precision at full sexual arousal. The way we draw each other may seem crude but, take it from me, it's best to be one hundred percent up front (and behind too, if you know what I mean) before you engage in any alien copulation. My hand shook with anticipation as I gave my potential lover the drawing. It was well received with a sly smile and a flutter of her long lashes. Now she'd have to draw herself in the nude. That's just how we Sketchers do it. I waited as she drew not one page, but two, then three, then, after a pause, a fourth. Leaning forward I could see from my oblique viewing angle that each page held four panels. Was she drawing a complete graphic novel? How much did I need to know about her body? I was beginning to get mighty nervous by the time she finished the sixth page of her storyboard when she handed it to me, with the beginning page out.

"What I saw as I looked through the pages was an elegant and very personal—*very* graphic—comic of us making love. She wanted it all, and her body was beautifully curved and looked like it would be soft against my own. Although she didn't have a true mammalian configuration, she was extremely feminine. Then I turned to the fifth page and saw her magnificent forked tail in action. I was clearly about to bed a red-hot sex devil. On the next page it was just one panel showing a moment of mutual orgasm in a most dramatic manner, a close-up of our contorted faces, her long purple tongue curled around my neck. I almost stopped there but then turned to the sixth page where I expected to see a postcoital cuddle. Instead, I saw my head being ripped off and my beauteous lover devouring my brain.

"I looked up at her face, at her giant, perfect alien eyes, now filled with what was sexual craving and she widened her mouth well beyond any human width into a cannibalistic grin. My stomach churned, and I shook my head. She didn't understand the gesture, so I drew myself with all my clothes on, one hand covering my crotch and my arm holding onto my head. She got the message. A hard pass."

"Did anything else happen at that gathering that you think stood out? Perhaps there's a detail you didn't tell me before that might help you?" asked Perri.

"Nothing that I recall. I drank and drew until my head swam and my hand cramped. It was all the regular kind of visual 'conversation' between Sketchers. Then I went to bed. Oh wait, I forgot, earlier I had to go back to my room to get a new sketchbook, mine went missing. All was okay though, someone found it and returned to me before the end of the evening. They could tell the drawings inside belonged to a human, and I was the only one there. There's a homing signal in the sketchpad too, in case I lose it, but I guess it didn't work in that room. A lot of those places have signal dampeners."

"Hmm," hummed Perri rubbing his chin area thoughtfully. "I need to take a look at those drawings. Do I have your permission to bring in some outside help?"

"Yes, anything."

"It could be costly."

"Anything. Do you think my art can save me? I used it once before to exonerate myself when I was accused of drinking the last of my dad's favorite beer. Once I showed my dad the drawing I'd done of him drinking it himself, with the five empties beside him, he laughed, and said something dismissive like, well, I'll be damned—nothing approaching an apology. Funny how something like that can still bother you years later."

I handed him the three sketchpads I had there. "When the authorities came to my room to arrest me they confiscated my other sketchbooks, 'took them into evidence' they said. I know you erased your memory, but do you have any idea why you didn't ask me about this before?"

"No, I don't know. I'm going over to the evidence room to take a look at what the guards have of yours. Susan can't go there with me. You don't mind if she hangs out with you for a while, do you?" he asked, but he was already out my cell door before I could protest. I looked over to Susan who seemed to smirk at me menacingly.

I decided to talk to her, "What kind of lawyer leaves a dangerous wild animal alone with his client? Seems irresponsible, doesn't it?" I said as I glanced around the cell for anything to defend myself. I pulled on my chair to see if I could get it loose, and use it to keep the vicious animal away from me, but it wouldn't come free.

Susan just sat perfectly still and watched my unproductive efforts. She followed my hand suspiciously as I reached for my sketchbook but settled down once I started drawing. As I drew her, I noticed Susan's back paws seemed to be partly webbed. What seemed to be a soft nose was a beak-like snout. You always learn more by drawing something than just looking at it. The finished picture pleased me. On a lark, I said, "Hey, Susan, what do you think?" Then I held the drawing out for her to see.

Instantly she was up on all fours and headed for me. I had nowhere to run. But her eyes, thank the gods, weren't on me. She went right towards the drawing I held out. I felt a little like a matador waving a small red cape out for an enraged bull. Of course, Susan wasn't a bull, yet she did have horns, and I wished to avoid them. She stopped right at the drawing, looked at it for a full nerve-racking minute, then turned to me and quacked. Yes, *quacked*. Susan was part dog, part cat, part lizard, part monkey, *and* part duck, or so it seemed to me. The only animal I knew that had half those characteristics was a platypus, and they were long extinct. After this encounter we became friends. I got her to do other poses for me, and she loved the results of her portraits—finally, a favorable art critic.

Perri returned carrying a purple spacesuit. He was dressed for court, wearing a white wig and goggles. Since there were no eyes behind those glasses, this was the height of superfluousness, some court affectation, like his headgear. "It's time for you to appear before the judge—put this on. It will adjust to fit your frame perfectly." He extended the suit to me.

"Why? Are we going out into the vacuum of space?"

"It's required apparel, like my powdered wig. Tradition, what are you going to do? You can't go against a custom many thousands of years old." When I first saw Perri in the wig, I thought he was mocking Earthly barristers of well before my time, but he'd claimed that we humans had stolen the idea from the galactic court, not the other way around. Despite my doubts, I didn't know enough about the issue to argue.

I followed Perri's instructions, removed my Dalmatian pajamas and pulled on the spacesuit. It felt more like a flimsy child's costume, clearly unsuitable for actual space. Perri helped me put on the ridiculous fishbowl helmet. When he twisted it on, it made the *schtook* sound of an airtight closing seal. "This feels weird, I don't think I want the helmet," I said as I tried to remove it.

"No, you can't take it off," said Perri sternly.

"Why not?"

"I meant it won't *come* off. You can't get it off unless the judge decrees it."

I felt panic rise in me. "Why, the fuck, is that?"

"Remember when I said we fast-track injustice, pardon me, I mean *justice*, here. When you're found guilty...I mean *if* you're found guilty, you'll be instantly gassed inside that suit."

"Gassed to death?"

"Of course. Carbon monoxide or an inert gas, I believe," said Perri matter-of-factly as if this was simply an issue of discussing the method used. "Then your body will be liquified, dehydrated and absorbed into that nice set of tanks on the back of the Obliteration Suit. It's all very efficient. Impressive, right?"

"Impressively deplorable. You've had me effectively dig my own grave, dress myself in a murder-me suit. By your instructions, I've sealed myself into a nightmarish garb of my instantaneous demise. You goddamn, guileful gearbox; I won't let you kill me. No, strike that, I'm happy to die as long as I kill you *first*." I screamed as I lunged at Perri.

I felt a breeze pushing against my clothes, and I sensed I was moving. When I looked around me it seemed I lay on a plate like an entree about to be served. Standing above me was Perri, the captain of this mini-flying saucer.

"Sorry, Mr. Laudent Fridolupe Granger, I had to quiet you for a little while. You became unreasonably emotional. Come on, get up now, we're about to appear before the judge," said Perri.

"Perri, is there any chance you could refer to me as Scribbler?" I asked.

"Certainly not, that's not your real name."

"Okay, whatever, let's get this over with," I said in defeat. Perri helped me up on my unsteady legs. We were on a kind of dais that moved through the hangar-sized courtroom well above the ground floor. The last time I rode on one of these I tried to jump off, but the dais just grabbed me none too gently by one of its extruding metal tentacles and yanked me back on. There was no escape, my doom awaited, the fast reflexes of this sinister technology assured it.

Another saucer came up alongside us with Dr. Susan eagerly riding on it, her fur fluttering in the wind. As the edge of it touched ours, she ambled over to us. I was happy to see my striped friend, and I bent down to pet her, the way Perri had. With that her inner kitten came out and she purred for me. Having Dr. Susan with me was comforting. She was very much indeed an emotional support animal.

As we flew along through the towering open courtroom, I noticed that the structure most resembled an intergalactic hub, as busy as a beehive. Daily trains, planes, airships and spaceships ferried defendants from all over the universe here for trial and then loaded them back on transport to prison or off to freedom, or dust into space—my likely fate. I saw a frenetic chaos of daises that zipped about with defendants that traveled to levitating benches with judges seated at them in what I'd call court cubicles, and there, people of all alien kinds were then mercilessly judged. Guilty, guilty, guilty, guilty, rang out gavel after gavel and it echoed through the cavernous concourse.

Perri reached down and one of my sketchbooks popped up from inside the dais. He handed it to me after opening it to a page. "That's the portrait you did, right?" he asked. I nodded as I looked at it. "That red dot, that wasn't part of your drawing, was it?"

"No," I said and reached forward to touch the red area.

"I didn't think so," said Perri, "it's a deadly poison and meant to kill you on contact with your skin." I jerked my hand back—who knew what protection my suit offered me? "That's our defense. That poison is not easily attained and humans can't handle it without dying in horrible pain, so why would you have it? Obviously, you were targeted too."

I closed the book and handed it back to Perri, happy to have it out of my hand. Perri seemed confident here, but he had been wrong all too often, I couldn't get my hopes up.

It became foggy as we entered an area meant for creatures needing extra moisture in the air around them. Then, there before me, was the same judge I'd had before, the bloated, slimy invertebrate who'd previously found me guilty. He was an angry mollusk-man whose people had slid out of the swamp, eating scum along the way, yet somehow the species had become sentient. Despair and dread consumed me. All I could think to do was hug Dr. Susan to me.

"Stand up," demanded Perri. I stood and faced the judge. He looked ridiculous in his headdress, a woven wool periwig. In a less series situation I might laugh at his odd attire.

"Back again?" the judge asked theatrically. Having fun with a condemned man was his idea of entertainment. The rest of what he said had to be interpreted by Perri. "Jokes aside, why didn't you take the deal?" Perri repeated in English for me. Then Perri explained my reasons for not taking the deal to the judge and later revealed his explanation to me.

"Sorry," said Perri, turning to me, "it seems the charge of conspiracy to commit murder has been upgraded to first-degree murder. The person you allegedly put a contract on to be assassinated has been murdered."

"I don't see how that matters, I'm already about to be executed," I countered.

"Slight difference," explained Perri, "for planning a murder you are executed. If the murder is carried out they add on twenty-five years of physical torture, then they kill you. The suit you have on will immediately start shocking you with jolts of electricity if we lose. That might sound like, uh, overkill, but our society has a preponderance of sadists, and we need to offer them employment commensurate with their talents. They'll take over your torture once you're delivered to prison."

My frail body surely would likely withstand only a minute of shock torture before it, so to speak, gave up the ghost, so I said, "Whatever." For a second there I thought I saw an ounce of sympathy on Perri's glossy face.

"If the judge will allow, I'd like to enter into evidence the defendant's sketchbook. It will illustrate his innocence without a shadow of a doubt."

Having heard this repeated to me in English, I perked up. Maybe he *could* save me. My heart now pounded so hard it rattled the ribs of my narrow chest.

Perri pulled out the sketchbook I'd been drawing in while I was in my cell, not the one he'd shown me. What did he have in mind? He flipped it open to the page I'd put all my frustrated feelings into about the judge. Perri was about to show the judge all the awful loathing I felt towards the slug of a man who'd found me guilty. My art depicted horrible, disgraceful, caricatures of the judge, the person I most faulted with my most dire circumstance.

"No, Perri, NO! Don't show him that." I grabbed at Perri and begged, to no avail. At first, the judge just stared at the open pages Perri held out. Then the judge snatched the sketchbook out of Perri's hands and flipped through the sketchbook. I knew my drawings started with me holding a giant saltshaker over the judge and showering him with the mollusk killing crystals. Next, my art showed the judge melting into sludge. In the final scene you saw me peeing on his partially melted form with only his awful periwig and black robe left behind, the peruke now stained more yellow than before. God help me, I'd had a few colored pencils with me, and I used them to add an ochre accent to what would lead to my inevitable extermination.

I watched as the judge swelled, and swelled more. His face went purple. Then he squealed out an ear-piercing screech that made his fellow judges floating around the concourse snap their heads in our direction. His head then rocked up and down while he exclaimed something unintelligible. I cowered behind Perri, nearly peeing in my already clammy Costume de la Muerte.

Perri turned to me, "He thinks that your drawings are funny. He's laughing. Now that I've gotten him on our side, I'll show him the main evidence that will exonerate you."

Everything was all going far too fast for me. I couldn't believe it. Perri showed the judge drawing after drawing from my sketchbooks while they exchanged what to me was clickity-clackity gibberish.

Then Perri turned towards me and removed the helmet from my head. It was just in time for me to see the gavel fall and to hear the judge say in perfect English, albeit a bit viscously "I FIND YOU INNOCENT OF ALL CHARGES." Then, all of the pressure of the day drained from me, along with the blood from my head, and I fainted.

I woke myself up by speaking aloud, "There's no place like home; there's no place like home." Then when I recognized her, I said, "Oh, Auntie Em, it's you." I looked around the room and saw the farmhands and others next to my bed, and I said, "You and you . . . and you were all there. But you're no longer Tin-man Robot, Judge Oz and Susan the Sea Lion, you're all regular human people now."

The judge, Judge Oz in my dazed mind, looked bemused. "Auntie Em, Judge Oz?" he parroted.

"I guess I'm her," said a feminine voice. "I'm certainly not one of the other three he named. Oh, I'll be right back," she said, "I need to take care of a misunderstanding urgently."

I opened my eyes to catch sight of the lady but all I saw was a whoosh and a blur as the dais holding her retreated into the fog. The scene before me was my real nightmare rather than my dream of a long-ago place in a black and white world named Kansas. I wanted to go back to my dream, so I closed my eyes again.

"Wake up," demanded Perri shaking me. "The judge has a dozen more cases to expedite. Get up; let him know you're okay so he can move on."

I stood up, and the judge now looked upon me in a way I found kindly, but with mollusk people, you never know. He moved his soft mouth around making his flutter-language. Perri interpreted: "The judge would like to have a meeting with you later. It's about future work; he has become a fan of your art. Here's his card." Perri touched the chip-tattoo on my wrist and contact information was exchanged between me and the judge. Then off we flew on our magic carpet ride for further processing.

"Before I woke up fully I thought I heard what sounded like a woman back there. Was that just part of my dream?" I asked Perri.

"We'll be meeting up with her soon. She goes by the name of Queen Catherine. As per your okaying it, I hired her team to do some investigating for me. Your sketchbooks, the record of your activities, are what saved you, though. She did the footwork, so to speak, getting further evidence needed to guarantee our not guilty verdict. She's a determined, hard-working creature with a tremendous brain. I think it's best that she explain it all to you. We'll meet her in my office."

Having heard Perri's description, my mind saw Queen Catherine quite literally as an alien with a bulging and clear domed skull that you could see a veiny, pulsing brain through. No doubt she was almost all head and traveled about on some sort of contraption with eight metal legs. And, in my mind, she wears an ostentatious crown befitting a monarch.

Perri left Dr. Susan and me in his office. I went to change my clothes and freshen up in an adjoining room. Removing my killing suit made me feel like a human larvae pulling loose of its cocoon. Once free, I could continue my existence transformed, metamorphosed into a better me, with a genuinely transcendent outlook. This time, I promised myself, I'd live my life in a fuller, less shallow, way. As I put back on my regular clothes, I thought, right, I bet everyone tells themselves that after a near-death experience. While I was still shirtless, a squat robot rolled out of the wall. It extended to me a warm, wet hand towel. I rubbed my face and torso with it and then I took a proffered fluffy towel to dry off. Perri was indeed one to think of the little creature comforts his clients might need. Maybe he isn't such a bad fellow after all.

Waiting for me in the greeting room of Perri's office was Queen Catherine or what had to be her. I'd describe her as a brain in a custard bowl with six, not eight, insectlike legs to carry her around. She even had the crown atop her brain's dome, but it was less garish than I'd imagined. I looked around for Perri and didn't see him. Dr. Susan seemed comfortable with this strange being's presence, so I was too. "It's nice to meet you, Queen Catherine. Sorry to have mistaken you for Auntie Em earlier," I said as a joke, my way of setting a friendly tone. She sat there in silence like she was dead. I looked for the slightest bit of pulsation, some sense of blood flow, in her very nicely displayed brain and saw none.

Then the door to Perri's office slid open with a swish and a woman walked in. "Sorry, sorry, I had to go to the bathroom. Did I miss anything?"

All I could do was stare.

You know the kind of actress in a movie who walks into a room and all eyes are instantly on her: she's vivacious, captivating, alluring and devastatingly enchanting? Well, this lady before me is the actress they hired to stand next to the leading lady to make her look even more gorgeous.

This woman was the plainest creature I'd ever seen. She wore the drabbest of suits, her vanilla hair hung flat, the curves of her body were exceedingly pedestrian, on her bland face were round-rimmed spectacles, and she stood all of what was the average height of a human female. HUMAN. I was, in an instant, head-over-heels in love with her, with her stunning, run-of-the-mill normalcy. "Oh, I'm sorry," she said, "I must have startled you; my name is Jane Lane. I'm Queen Catherine's assistant and interpreter." At that, she touched the side of her head where there was a slim piece of metal that facilitated direct mental communication between her and the queen. "I see that you two have met." Ah, I now knew that voice. *She* was the Auntie Em in my dream.

Weakly I said, "It's nice to meet you too Plain Jane, uh, I mean Lame Dame, no, no, sorry, Jane Lane. You can call me Scribbler, that's my nickname. I'm sure you know my full real name. It's likely on the intelli-slate that you're holding... in your hand there, the one holding the intelli-slate," I babbled on, and to stop myself, I blurted out, "You're human!"

"Oh, you poor man, you've had a terrible day, haven't you? Come, sit down so we can go over everything." She took my hand—*I'd not had actual, genuine, authentic human contact in more than a decade and it was thrilling, exhilarating, electric*—and led me to a chair. Her skin was so, so soft, so pleasant to touch; she was my angel of ordinary, flamboyancy's antithesis, the very kind of everyday being I most desperately needed in my far too outlandish life.

Dr. Susan liked her too. She rubbed against Jane's calf. I felt a tinge of jealousy when Jane stroked the multi-creature's head in response. I far more needed Jane's touch than Dr. Susan did, but I buried that rash desire.

As I sat, I noticed my sketchbooks on top of Perri's desk. My face went red when I saw one opened to the page of the drawing I'd done of the exotic/erotic head-eating monster I'd been in lust with only the night before. Would Jane be envious? Even as I thought that, I knew how ridiculous the idea was.

"Queen Catherine has asked me to explain to you how you were, uh, seduced by this charlatan," said Jane. My face now glowed a full-on crimson. "Pardon the following 'joke,' my boss considers herself something of a humorist: How do you know when you can make a fool of a human male? Answer: When he has a dick."

I stood and took a bow, accepting this known weakness of my gender. Belying her drab exterior, Jane smiled with such a warming brilliance that it sparked a nova in my chest. Everything I'd been through today was worth it only for the chance of meeting this everyday Aphrodite.

"Yes, ahem," Jane pulled at her collar. She was clearly feeling a bit uncomfortable with what she was about to interpret, "this alien, with her titillating drawings, engaged you in sensual fantasies, and then she guided you to draw out an execution order for her planet's prime minister. Because all Sketchers are registered and identified by their art, she couldn't do the art herself; she had to trick you into it. Note the red star above the face..."

"Wait, don't touch that—it's deadly!" I reached out to grab her hand but I was too late, her finger ran right across the poison red mark. Now that Jane would die, I felt like touching the red and taking my own life as well. We'd die together like Romeo and Juliet.

"No," said Jane with a guffaw, "not deadly anymore, we neutralized it." Upon seeing the horror on my face, she looked on me with concern. "Oh, my, you were really worried about me, weren't you? That's quite, uh, endearing."

Jane gestured for me to sit back down and her voice returned to business. "Moving on: that red star is the emblem attached to the acting prime minister to denote her office. The woman you drew became her exact double with some physical manipulation. They could've easily put out an execution order on the prime minister on their own, it didn't even have to be a drawing, but they needed a scapegoat, and the schemers considered someone of our human species—being one of the smaller minorities in this part of the galaxy—an excellent choice for a fall guy. You draw extraordinarily accurately, so that made you the absolute perfect choice."

"Why did she have me draw the skull next to her head, though?" I asked.

"What you just asked is what made Perri's case for your defense so convincing. You don't see symbols. In your mind, everything is what it is. Your profession prides itself on this. Sketchers are literal thinkers; you're trained to be that way. You see a skull as the bones of a head, not as a metaphor for death. For the Garbos' culture, it's a clear message to kill the person depicted next to the skull. It helped that they broadcasted the death reward in hundreds of languages as well. Perri argued that, based on the other drawings in your sketchbooks, on how decidedly literal they are, you'd never use such a symbol or, for that matter, anything allegorical as all Sketchers are trained not to do for better communication between species."

"Now that you mention it, I remember that pirates supposedly used a skull and crossbones as their symbol on their flags. I never understood that. Weren't they in search of treasure, not partial skeletons?" I said a bit perplexed by this.

"Exactly," said Jane smiling back at me but not explaining. Then she went on to say in a kindly way, with what seemed like admiration, "You're such a natural at thinking with only precise pictures, it's surprising that you ever learned to talk, read and write."

"Funny you should say that. According to my parents, I didn't speak a word before I was six, despite a special language coach and several psychologists hired to assess me. Then one day at the dinner table I said, 'My soup is far too salty.' My parents dropped their spoons and stared at me in amazement. Then they asked me why it was today that I chose to speak, and I said, 'Everything has been fine up until now.'"

"You are indeed a strange fellow, and you're most certainly full of crap."

Jane cleared her throat, then continued with her explanation of the con job that had nearly put me to death: "The conspirators expected you'd die of the poison, but instead you were arrested, charged with conspiracy to commit murder and incarcerated. While you were jailed they'd emptied your bank account and exhausted your credit to pay the assassins. They were then satisfied that you'd certainly be found guilty and die for their crimes one way or another. Pretty neat trick, eh?"

"The word diabolical comes to mind. How did they, the conspirators, get access to all of my accounts?"

"That's a rather lurid tale. Let's just say that one of your, uh, unconventional paramours helped them get what they needed to do it. Let me remind you that I'm interpreting for Queen Catherine when I add, with all your (she insisted I put it this way) *sex-ventures* that perhaps we should put you in quarantine for a dozen years to see what grows on you." Jane leaned in to whisper, "She thinks that's funny."

"I'll have myself dipped in iodine and swim through a pool of antibiotics. That should do it," I suggested. Again, Queen Catherine's brain sparkled with color at my quip. Jane showed no similar reaction. She only looked worried for me.

"A couple of other things: we helped the authorities catch several of the people involved in this plot, and that came with a rather substantial reward, so we're waiving our fee. Finally, the Garbos, the alien type you encountered at the Sketcher symposium, the females don't eat the male's heads after sex. She just drew that to quiet your rampant coital yearning. Just so you know," said Jane raising an eyebrow with wry meaning that she then explained, "Sexually speaking though, she'd most certainly have eaten you alive."

I had a few more questions for Jane, but Perri came in. "Perri," I said, "I don't know how to thank you. You saved my life. I'm entirely in your debt." I walked over to shake his hard, mechanical hand vigorously.

"Very good, Mr. Laudent Fridolupe Granger, it was my pleasure. I understand your accounts are presently locked due to them being compromised, so you have my permission to take your time in paying me." He then handed me my bill printed out on an elegant sheet of what looked like parchment. It was weirdly anachronistic, but robots are known for their love for archaic and grandiose displays.

Perri had carefully itemized out the bill, noting his hours spent on each task. His memory of all he'd done on my behalf not only seemed thorough but rather... *exaggerated*. One item line caught my interest. "You charged me a hundred and fifty-two solar-reigns for the warm wet towel?"

"I believe you used *two* towels," corrected Perri. "Also, note the laundry fee below that."

"Coffee at sixty solar-reigns a cup? For that dubious swill? You charged me over two thousand to rent the goddamn execution suit, I get charged for my own obliteration inside a portable disintegration chamber?"

"Well, I have to make up for all the times I rented it when the client couldn't pay due to them being gassed and vaporized before I was able to present my bill. That should make that fee far more understandable. Also, the dry-cleaning cost for the sweat-inundated thing you wore was substantial," countered Perri. "I just noticed I forgot to charge you the extra fee to print your bill on faux-parchment." With that my robot lawyer made all the good feelings I had for him dissolve away.

Barely containing my displeasure, I scanned to the bottom of the bill and saw the shocking astronomical total. "PERRI!" I yelled, *"You batshit bag of bolts, I'm not paying this outrageous sum!"*

"Quack, quack, quack," barked Dr. Susan Calvin, who was aroused by the commotion.

"Hold on," said Jane who walked over to Perri. "Scribbler works for us now." As she waved her hand towards me and turned to give me a wink. "As such he should get a twenty-five percent discount on your fee. Furthermore, as Queen Catherine has just reminded me, we've withdrawn our fee for the investigation. Can I see the bill?" she asked extending her hand towards me, so I gave it to her. "Ah, I see it here under 'Special Services.' Let me draw a line right through that." She did so with a pen. "Also, this doesn't apply, nor these other three items now." Jane drew lines through them as well. "Please add up the new total for us," she asked as she handed Perri the bill.

Jane's defense of me made me love her even more. She is the girl for me; I decided this now without any reservation.

"Mmm," grumbled Perri. "Okay, how's this look?" he asked in a perturbed yet resigned manner.

"If you take another ten percent off, Queen Catherine would be happy to pay the bill in its entirety now." Jane then held her intelli-slate to me and said, "Sign this contract, as we've already agreed," and she gave me another wink, "to become our illustrator-communicator, and art investigator, so you can work off your debt to us." I happily made the deal because I knew I would now work beside Jane. *That* would be heaven.

Throughout all of this, Jane had been leafing through my recently returned sketchbooks. It pleased me to see her smile, laugh, grimace and look thoughtfully at my work. More than anything, that's what an artist wants, a reaction, no matter what, even bringing someone to tears, but she saw something more in my work than that. "Perri, look at this, please," asked Jane as she turned the page toward him, "what do you see?"

"I see three Gordons on vacation, sitting on the beach. They seem to be enjoying tropical drinks. Am I missing something?" the robot asked.

Jane responded with an order: "Activate protocol, retrieve data: #Y1013130." Perri made a ding sound in response and stiffened. "Do you recognize any of these Gordons? Access all court databases."

"Searching—searching," said Perri more robotically than usual. "Yes, all three were convicted of slave trading and sentenced to fifty to seventy-five years hard labor. They should presently be serving that time. The sketch must've been done before they were convicted. Let's see, that was twenty years ago..."

"Perri, exit search," ordered Jane. Perri returned to full awareness with that. "Based on the date on this drawing," Jane pointed to it. "it seems these Gordons have escaped, or they were never imprisoned at all. Scribbler's work for us is already paying off. These three were part of our investigation, but because they were supposedly in prison, we discounted them. This mystery has grown considerably."

"That's an exclusive club where I drew them. I was only let in because I'm an artist, and a card-carrying, professional Sketcher, and, as you know aliens love artists, they can't say no to us. Isn't this great," I said, to point out my added value to the team.

"Queen Catherine is concerned that if we don't all get to work on hunting down these criminals right away that there may be more murders," said Jane. "You're likely still on the hit list of the conspirators, Scribbler, so you have a vested interest here."

I sat down hard when a shiver went through me; I felt as if was wearing the awful Obliteration Suit again. Then the feeling passed, and I looked up to plain Jane and smiled. With her there I'd happily walk through the valley of the shadow of death, all would be well—I will fear no evil.

Yes, Death, Perri had saved me from his scythe. I decided to be the better man, swallowed my pride and, before leaving his office, I made sure to apologize for my earlier outburst and respectfully thank Perri one more time. He seemed genuinely appreciative of this. Despite that, it was good to know I'd not have to see this annoying robot again.

✧   ✧   ✧

The next day I received a message from someone I'd nearly forgotten, someone who'd been in my life for the briefest of times—yet, he'd changed my life in the most profound manner. For a minute I stared at the name—Jerry Sam. His note requested that we meet at the Franklin Center Hotel. Seeing his name completely out of context, I thought, who is Jerry Sam? Then it came to me—the salesman who tested me after I'd submitted my art to the Super Art School all those many years ago. My mind flashed back to his sad face on the day I'd rocketed away from earth. This invitation had me more than intrigued. Why would he contact me now? I, of course, accepted his invite. What reasonably curious person wouldn't?

We met in the lobby of his hotel and he greeted me in a warm avuncular manner, as if I were truly an old friend or relative. He suggested we take a walk through the hotel's garden where he would explain the reason for this meeting. As we walked along he named the flowers and plants on display and said he'd chosen them himself. Was he the hotel's gardener? Would I insult him if I asked him that? More than likely he was the hotel's manager. I decided to give him a curious look and hope for an answer. It didn't work so I decided to just go ahead and make a fool of myself. "Are you a gardener now? That seems a drastic change of profession."

"Ha, sorry," he said chuckling. "My company owns the Franklin Hotel chain."

"Impressive!"

"Thank you. Please, let's get down to business. For many years I've carried a heavy weight of guilt regarding my involvement in sending you to space," he explained, "and I wish to make amends. I made considerable money recruiting artists to travel into space. Each young person I persuaded to sign the company's damnable contract brought me a bonus and residuals. That money and some lucky investments have made me a wealthy man. As such I bought back all of the contracts that I had my artists sign and I'm releasing them from them. You were the first artist I recruited, and you're the last of the artists whom I sent into space. I've come to you last because you were sent out far—farther into space than anyone else was. Today, the greater burden of my guilt will be lifted if you'll accept this amount as recompense for my transgression." He handed me an envelope with a notecard in it; a very large number was written on it. It amounted to many times my lifetime earnings. I was flabbergasted and it showed so much on my face that Jerry laughed aloud.

"I accept," I exclaimed once my shock subsided. And with a shake of his hand to seal the deal the money was in my account.

"That will be enough for you to return home, and to live a fine life of some luxury, but take this as well." He handed me another envelope. I opened it and removed a fanciful ticket for a luxury room on Lenoria Rocket Lines. "That company issues paper tickets merely as a keepsake. It's pretty, isn't it? Your flight home is already arranged for you whenever you're ready to leave. Giving that ticket home to you helps me feel as if I've returned your life to you."

After that we talked a little about my adventures as a Sketcher. Then he told me of our homeworld, how much it had changed during my absence. It sounded wonderful. He showed me videos of what seemed to be a virtual utopia. I knew that things were better, but this was an astonishing change, and the first I'd seen of it.

We parted, and we both promised to stay in touch from time to time. I returned to my small and dingy apartment, a new man, a wealthy man—a man now with the means to be fully in charge of his future. My fairy godmother, a man named Jerry Sam, had released me from my life of hardship. I set the rocket ticket on my dresser and looked at it for a while. Jerry was not so much a fairy godmother as a Glinda the Good Witch; that ticket was my Ruby Slippers. It offered me a return to humanity and the good life. I pressed my thumb on the ticket to call up the spaceline, and pressed my finger down on my wrist-tat to have it cashed in. Checking to make sure that the money had been transferred to my account, I tore up the metaphorical—and most defunct—ticket in half and threw it into the trash.

I went out onto my balcony to look at the stars. They gleamed down at me, and I gleamed up at them while I pondered my now bright future. The viz-con in my pocket vibrated so I set it on my patio table and answered.

Before me glowed Jane's face. "Hi," she said, "I want to bring you up to date, have a face-to-face, post-hiring talk and discuss our plans for how to proceed on this new case."

"Okay, but first, let me tell you what just happened. I very much need to tell someone; it's too incredible to keep to myself." I began to tell her about my meeting with Jerry Sam. Once I got to the part about my new wealth, and receiving the ticket, she interrupted, "So, you're leaving us? I'm sure Queen Catherine will let you out of your contract without..."

I then interrupted her, "No, I don't want out of the contract. I'm staying. I cashed in my ticket home."

Surprise showed on Jane's face. "I'm happy to hear that," she said with a pleased look on her face.

"I'm happy to hear that you're happy to hear that," I said with a broad smile.

"Then we can be happy together," Jane smiled back. Yes, very much together, I hoped.

"Oh, then we need to get down to business now, don't we? To start, I thought I'd let you know that Perri will be working on the new case with us."

I suppressed a groan.

∾

Tom Kidd is best known as an illustrator. The story he's written for this book is his first sold piece of fiction. He has written four nonfiction books on art: *The Tom Kidd Sketchbook* (1990—Tundra) and *Kiddography: The Art & Life of Tom Kidd* (2006—Paper Tiger), *OtherWorlds* (2010—Impact) and *How to Draw and Paint Dragons* (2010—Quarto). His art has won him a World Fantasy Award (Best Artist 2004) and eight Chesley Awards. As a concept designer, he has worked for Walt Disney, Rhythm & Hues, and Universal Studios. He has illustrated two classic works of literature: *The Three Musketeers* (1998—William Morrow) and *The War of the Worlds* (2001—Harper Collins). Tom is the official artist for the "1632" series of alternate history books by Eric Flint and others, published by Baen Books, for which he has done over thirty covers—and counting. Highlights of his other projects include a deluxe illustrated version of *The Dying Earth* and the Book of Babel series by Josiah Bancroft, both for Subterranean Press. For Centipede Press he has illustrated *Swords and Deviltry* by Fritz Leiber, *Dark Crusade* by Karl Edward Wagner and a deluxe illustrated edition of *Elric: Fortress of the Pearl* by Michael Moorcock. One final credit for Tom—he painted the cover for this collection.

You can see an alliterative selection of his art here: https://tomkidd.myportfolio.com.

JERRY WAS A MAN

ROBERT A. HEINLEIN

The suave sales executive from the Phoenix Breeding Club greeted the very rich couple (well, the wife was very rich) with all the charm he could muster. It wasn't every day that a couple, no matter how rich, wanted to blow two million on a life-sized living Pegasus (well, the wife's trophy husband wanted one), even if it couldn't fly. But things got more complicated when the very rich wife wanted to buy a chimp whose intelligence had been increased so he could do menial work, but was now scheduled for euthanasia, and her offer was declined. When very rich people get mad, they call their lawyers. And you know what lawyers do...

❧

DON'T BLAME THE MARTIANS. THE HUMAN RACE WOULD HAVE developed plasto-biology in any case.

Look at the older registered Kennel Club breeds—glandular giants like the St. Bernard and the Great Dane, silly little atrocities like the Chihuahua and the Pekingese. Consider fancy goldfish.

The damage was done when Dr. Morgan produced new breeds of fruit flies by kicking around their chromosomes with X-rays. After that, the third generation of the Hiroshima survivors did not teach us anything new; those luckless monstrosities merely publicized standard genetic knowledge.

Mr. and Mrs. Bronson van Vogel did not have social reform in mind when they went to the Phoenix Breeding Ranch; Mr.

Van Vogel simply wanted to buy a Pegasus. He had mentioned it at breakfast. "Are you tied up this morning, my dear?"

"Not especially. Why?"

"I'd like to run out to Arizona to order a Pegasus designed."

"A Pegasus? A flying horse? Why, my sweet?"

He grinned. "Just for fun. Pudgy Dodge was around the Club yesterday with a six-legged dachshund—must have been over a yard long. It was clever, but he swanked so much I want to give him something to stare at. Imagine, Martha—me landing on the Club 'copter platform on a winged horse. That'll snap his eyes back!"

She turned her eyes from the Jersey shore to look indulgently at her husband. She was not fooled; this would be expensive. But Brownie was such a dear! "When do we start?"

They landed two hours earlier than they started. The airsign read, in letters fifty feet high:

PHOENIX BREEDING RANCH
Controlled Genetics—licensed Labor Contractors

"'Labor Contractors'?" she read. "I thought this place was used just to burbank new animals?"

"They both design and produce," he explained importantly. "They distribute through the mother corporation 'Workers.' You ought to know; you own a big chunk of Workers common."

"You mean I own a bunch of apes? Really?"

"Perhaps I didn't tell you. Haskell and I—" He leaned forward and informed the field that he would land manually; he was a bit proud of his piloting.

He switched off the robot and added, briefly as his attention was taken up by heading the ship down, "Haskell and I have been plowing your General Atomics dividends back into Workers, Inc. Good diversification—still plenty of dirty work for the anthropoids to do." He slapped the keys; the scream of the nose jets stopped conversation.

Bronson had called the manager in flight; they were met—not with red carpet, canopy, and footmen, though the manager strove to give that impression. "Mr. Van Vogel? And *Mrs.* Van Vogel! We are honored indeed!" He ushered them into a tiny, luxurious unicar; they jeeped off the field, up a ramp, and into the lobby of the administration building. The manager, Mr. Blakesly, did not relax until he had seated them around a fountain in the lounge of his offices, struck cigarettes for them, and provided tall, cool drinks.

Bronson Van Vogel was bored by the attention, as it was obviously inspired by his wife's Dun & Bradstreet rating (ten stars, a sunburst, and heavenly music). He preferred people who could convince him that he had invented the Briggs fortune, instead of marrying it.

"This is business, Blakesly. I've an order for you."

"So? Well, our facilities are at your disposal. What would you like, sir?"

"I want you to make me a Pegasus."

"A Pegasus? A flying horse?"

"Exactly."

Blakesly pursed his lips. "You seriously want a horse that will fly? An animal like the mythical Pegasus?"

"Yes, yes—that's what I said."

"You embarrass me, Mr. Van Vogel. I assume you want a unique gift for your lady. How about a midget elephant, twenty inches high, perfectly housebroken, and able to read and write? He holds his stylus in his trunk—very cunning."

"Does he talk?" demanded Mrs. Van Vogel.

"Well, now, my dear lady, his voice box, you know—and his tongue—he was not designed for speech. If you insist on it, I will see what our plasticians can do."

"Now, Martha—"

"You can have your Pegasus, Brownie, but I think I may want this toy elephant. May I see him?"

"Most surely. Harstone!"

The air answered Blakesly. "Yes, boss?"

"Bring Napoleon to my lounge."

"Right away, sir."

"Now about your Pegasus, Mr. Van Vogel . . . I see difficulties but I need expert advice. Dr. Cargrew is the real heart of this organization, the most eminent bio-designer—of terrestrial origin, of course—on the world today." He raised his voice to actuate relays. "Dr. Cargrew!"

"What is it, Mr. Blakesly?"

"Doctor, will you favor me by coming to my office?"

"I'm busy. Later."

Mr. Blakesly excused himself, went into his inner office, then returned to say that Dr. Cargrew would be in shortly. In the meantime Napoleon showed up. The proportions of his noble ancestors had been preserved in miniature; he looked like a statuette of an elephant, come amazingly to life.

He took three measured steps into the lounge, then saluted each of them with his trunk. In saluting Mrs. Van Vogel he dropped to his knees as well.

"Oh, how cute!" she gurgled. "Come here, Napoleon."

The elephant looked at Blakesly, who nodded. Napoleon ambled over and laid his trunk across her lap. She scratched his ears; he moaned contentedly.

"Show the lady how you can write," ordered Blakesly. "Fetch your things from my room."

Napoleon waited while she finished treating a particularly satisfying itch, then oozed away to return shortly with several sheets of heavy white paper and an oversized pencil. He spread a sheet in front of Mrs. Van Vogel, held it down daintily with a fore foot, grasped the pencil with his trunk finger, and printed in large, shaky letters, "I LIKE YOU."

"The darling!" She dropped to her knees and put her arms around his neck. "I simply must have him. How much is he?"

"Napoleon is part of a limited edition of six," Blakesly said carefully. "Do you want an exclusive model, or may the others be sold?"

"Oh, I don't care, I just want Nappie. Can I write him a note?"

"Certainly, Mrs. Van Vogel. Print large letters and use basic English. Napoleon knows most of it. His price, nonexclusive is $350,000. That includes five years' salary for his attending veterinary."

"Give this gentleman a check, Brownie," she said over her shoulder.

"But Martha—"

"Don't be tiresome, Brownie." She hardly looked up when Dr. Cargrew came in.

Cargrew was a chilly figure in white overalls and skull cap. He shook hands brusquely, struck a cigarette, and sat down. Blakesly explained.

Cargrew shook his head. "It's a physical impossibility."

Van Vogel stood up. "I can see," he said distantly, "That I should have taken my custom to NuLife Laboratories. I came here because we have a financial interest in this firm and because I was naïve enough to believe the claims of your advertisements."

"Siddown, young man!" Cargrew ordered. "Take your trade to those thumb-fingered idiots if you wish—but I warn you they couldn't grow wings on a grasshopper. First you listen to me.

"We can grow anything and make it live. I can make you a living thing—I won't call it an animal—the size and shape of that table over there. It wouldn't be good for anything, but it would be alive. It would ingest food, use chemical energy, give off excretions, and display irritability. But it would be a silly piece of manipulation. Mechanically a table and an animal are two different things. Their functions are different, so their shapes are different. Now I can make you a winged horse—"

"You just said you couldn't."

"Don't interrupt. I can make a winged horse that will look just like the pictures in the fairy stories. If you want to pay for it; we'll make it—we're in business. But it won't be able to fly."

"Why not?"

"Because it's not built for flying. The ancient who dreamed up that myth knew nothing about aerodynamics and still less about biology. He stuck wings on a horse, just stuck them on, thumb tacks and glue. But that doesn't make a flying machine. Remember, son, that an animal is a machine, primarily a heat engine with a control system to operate levers and hydraulic systems, according to definite engineering laws. You savvy to aerodynamics?"

"Well, I'm a pilot."

"Hummph! Well, try to understand this. A horse hasn't got the heat engine for flight. He's a hayburner and that's not effi-cient. We might mess around with a horse's insides so that he could live on a diet of nothing but sugar and then he might have enough energy to fly short distances. But he still would not look like the mythical Pegasus. To anchor his flying muscles he would need a breast bone maybe ten feet long. He might have to have as much as eighty feet wing spread. Folded, his wings would cover him like a tent. You're up against the cube-square disadvantage."

"Huh?"

Cargrew gestured impatiently. "Lift goes by the square of a given dimension; dead load by the cube of the same dimension, other things being equal. I might be able to make you a Pegasus the size of a cat without distorting the proportions too much."

"No, I want one I can ride. I don't mind the wing spread and I'll put up with the big breast bone. When can I have him?"

"I'll have to consult with B'na Kreeth." He whistled and chirped; a portion of the wall facing them dissolved and they found themselves looking into a laboratory. A Martian, life-size, showed in the forepart of the three-dimensional picture.

When the creature chirlupped back at Cargrew, Mrs. Van Vogel looked up, then quickly looked away. She knew it was silly but she simply could not stand the sight of Martians—and the ones who had modified themselves to a semi-manlike form disgusted her the most.

After they had twittered and gestured at each other for a minute or two Cargrew turned back to van Vogel. "B'na says that you should forget it; it would take too long. He wants to know how you'd like a fine unicorn, or a pair, guaranteed to breed true?"

"Unicorns are old hat. How long would the Pegasus take?"

After another squeaky-door conversation Cargrew answered, "Ten years probably, sixteen years on the guarantee."

"Ten years? That's ridiculous!"

Cargrew looked shirty. "*I* thought it would take fifty, but if B'na says he can do it in three to five generations, then he can do it. B'na is the finest bio-micrurgist in two planets. His chromosome surgery is unequalled. After all, young man, natural processes would take upwards of a million years to achieve the same result, if it were achieved at all. Do you expect to be able to buy miracles?"

Van Vogel had the grace to look sheepish. "Excuse me, Doctor. Let's forget it. Ten years really is too long. How about the other possibility? You said you could make a picture-book Pegasus, as long as I did not insist on flight. Could I ride him? On the ground?"

"Oh, certainly. No good for polo, but you could ride him."

"I'll settle for that. Ask Benny Creeth, or whatever his name is, how long that would take."

The Martian had faded out of the screens. "I don't need to ask him," Cargrew asserted. "This is my job—purely manipulation. B'na's collaboration is required only for rearrangement and transplanting of genes—true genetic work. I can let you have the beast in eighteen months."

"Can't you do better than that?"

"What do you expect, man? It takes eleven months to grow a new-born colt. I want one month of design and planning. The embryo will be removed on the fourth day and will be developed in an extra-uterine capsule. I'll operate ten or twelve times during gestation, grafting and budding and other things you've heard of. One year from now we'll have a baby colt, with wings. Thereafter I'll deliver to you a six-months-old Pegasus."

"I'll take it."

Cargrew made some notes, then read, "One alate horse, not capable of flight and not to breed true. Basic breed your choice—I suggest a Palomino, or an Arabian. Wings designed after a condor, in white. Simulated pin feathers with a grafted fringe of quill feathers, or reasonable facsimile." He passed the sheet over. "Initial that and we'll start in advance of formal contract."

"It's a deal," agreed van Vogel. "What is the fee?" He placed his monogram under Cargrew's.

Cargrew made further notes and handed them to Blakesly— estimates of professional man-hours, purchases, and overhead. He had padded the figures to subsidize his collateral research but even he raised his eyebrows at the dollars-and-cents inter- pretation Blakesly put on the data. "That will be an even two million dollars."

Van Vogel hesitated; his wife had looked up at the mention of money. But she turned her attention back to the scholarly elephant.

Blakesly added hastily, "That is for an exclusive creation, of course."

"Naturally," Van Vogel agreed briskly, and added the figure to the memorandum.

Van Vogel was ready to return, but his wife insisted on seeing the "apes," as she termed the anthropoid workers. The discovery that she owned a considerable share in these subhuman creatures had intrigued her. Blakesly eagerly suggested a trip through the laboratories in which the workers were developed from true apes.

They were arranged in seven buildings, the seven "Days of Creation." "First Day" was a large building occupied by Cargrew, his staff, his operating rooms, incubators, and laboratories. Mar- tha van Vogel stared in horrified fascination at living organs and even complete embryos, living artificial lives sustained by clever glass and metal recirculating systems and exquisite automatic machinery.

She could not appreciate the techniques; it seemed depressing. She had about decided against plasto-biology when Napoleon, by tugging at her skirts, reminded her that it produced good things as well as horrors.

The building "Second Day" they did not enter; it was occupied by B'na Kreeth and his racial colleagues. "We could not stay alive in it, you understand," Blakesly explained. Van Vogel nodded; his wife hurried on—she wanted no Martians, even behind plastiglass.

From there on the buildings were for development and production of commercial workers. "Third Day" was used for development of variations in the anthropoids to meet constantly changing labor requirements. "Fourth Day" was a very large building devoted entirely to production-line incubators for commercial types of anthropoids. Blakesly explained that they had dispensed with normal birth. "The policy permits exact control of forced variations, such as for size, and saves hundreds of thousands of worker-hours on the part of the female anthropoids."

Martha van Vogel was delighted with the "Fifth Day," the anthropoid kindergarten where the little tykes learned to talk and were conditioned to the social patterns necessary to their station in life. They worked at simple tasks such as sorting buttons and digging holes in sand piles, with pieces of candy given as incentives for fast and accurate work.

"Sixth Day" completed the anthropoid's educations. Each learned the particular sub-trade it would practice, cleaning, digging, and especially agricultural semi-skills such as weeding, thinning, and picking. "One Nisei farmer working three neo-chimpanzees can grow as many vegetables as a dozen old-style farm hands." Blakesly asserted. "They really *like* to work—when we get through with them."

They admired the almost incredibly heavy tasks done by modified gorillas and stopped to gaze at the little neo-Capuchins doing high picking on prop trees, then moved on toward "Seventh Day."

This building was used for the radioactive mutation of genes and therefore located some distance away from the others. They had to walk, as the slidewalk was being repaired; the detour took them past workers' pens and barracks. Some of the anthropoids crowded up to the wire and began calling to them: "Sigret! Sigret! Preese, Missy! Preese, Boss! Sigret!"

"What are they saying?" Martha van Vogel inquired.

"They are asking for cigarettes," Blakesly answered in annoyed tones. "They know better, but they are like children. Here—I'll put a stop to it." He stepped up to the wire and shouted to an elderly male, "Hey! Strawboss!"

The worker addressed wore, in addition to the usual short canvas kilt, a bedraggled arm band. He turned and shuffled toward the fence. "Strawboss," ordered Blakesly, "get those Joes away from here."

"Okay, boss," the old fellow acknowledged and started cuffing those nearest him. "Scram, you Joes! Scram!"

"But I have some cigarettes," protested Mrs. Van Vogel, "and I would gladly have given them some."

"It doesn't do to pamper them," the Manager told her. "They have been taught that luxuries come only from work. I must apologize for my poor children; those in these pens are getting old and forgetting their manners."

She did not answer but moved further along the fence to where one old neo-chimp was pressed up against the wire, staring at them with soft, tragic eyes, like a child at a bakery window. He had taken no part in the jostling demand for tobacco and had been let alone by the strawboss. "Would you like a cigarette?" she asked him.

"Preese, Missy."

She struck one which he accepted with fumbling grace, took a long, lung-filled drag, let the smoke trickle out his nostrils, and said shyly, "Sankoo, Missy. Me Jerry."

"How do you do, Jerry?"

"Howdy, Missy." He bobbed down, bending his knees, ducking his head, and clasping his hands to his chest, all in one movement.

"Come along, Martha." Her husband and Blakesly had moved in behind her.

"In a moment," she answered. "Brownie, meet my friend, Jerry. Doesn't he look just like Uncle Albert? Except that he looks so sad. Why are you unhappy, Jerry?"

"They don't understand abstract ideas," put in Blakesly.

But Jerry surprised him. "Jerry sad," he announced in tones so doleful that Martha van Vogel did not know whether to laugh or cry.

"Why, Jerry?" she asked gently. "Why are you so sad?"

"No work," he stated. "No sigret. No candy. No work."

"These are all old workers who have passed their usefulness," Blakesly repeated. "Idleness upsets them, but we have nothing for them to do."

"Well!" she said. "Then why don't you have them sort buttons, or something like that, such as the baby ones do?"

"They wouldn't even do that properly," Blakesly answered her. "These workers are senile."

"Jerry isn't senile! You heard him talk."

"Well, perhaps not. Just a moment." He turned to the apeman, who was squatting down in order to scratch Napoleon's head with a long forefinger thrust through the fence. "You, Joe! Come here."

Blakesly felt around the worker's hairy neck and located a thin steel chain to which was attached a small metal tag. He studied it. "You're right," he admitted. "He's not really over age, but his eyes are bad. I remember the lot—cataracts as a result of an unfortunate linked mutation." He shrugged.

"But that's no reason to let him grieve his heart out in idleness."

"Really, Mrs. Van Vogel, you should not upset yourself about it. They don't stay in these pens long—only a few days at the most."

"Oh," she answered, somewhat mollified, "you have some other place to retire them to, then. Do you give them something to do there? You should—Jerry wants to work. Don't you, Jerry?"

The neo-chimp had been struggling to follow the conversation. He caught the last idea and grinned. "Jerry work! Sure Mike! Good worker." He flexed his fingers, then made fists, displaying fully opposed thumbs.

Mr. Blakesly seemed somewhat nonplussed. "Really, Mrs. Van Vogel, there is no need. You see—" He stopped.

Van Vogel had been listening irritably. His wife's enthusiasms annoyed him, unless they were also his own. Furthermore he was beginning to blame Blakesly for his own recent extravagance and had a premonition that his wife would find some way to make him pay, very sweetly, for his indulgence.

Being annoyed with both of them, he chucked in the perfect wrong remark. "Don't be silly, Martha. They don't retire them; they liquidate them."

It took a little time for the idea to sink in, but when it did she was furious. "Why...why—I never heard of such a thing! You ought to be ashamed. You...you would shoot your own grandmother."

"Mrs. Van Vogel—please!"

"Don't 'Mrs. Van Vogel' me! It's got to stop—you hear me?" She looked around at the death pens, at the milling hundreds of old workers therein. "It's horrible. You work them until they can't work anymore, then you take away their little comforts, and you *dispose* of them. I wonder you don't eat them!"

"They do," her husband said brutally. "Dog food."

"What! Well, we'll put a stop to that!"

"Mrs. Van Vogel," Blakesly pleaded. "Let me explain."

"Hummph! Go ahead. It had better be good."

"Well, it's like this—" His eye fell on Jerry, standing with worried expression at the fence. "Scram, Joe!" Jerry shuffled away.

"Wait Jerry!" Mrs. Van Vogel called out. Jerry paused uncertainly. "Tell him to come back," she ordered Blakesly.

The manager bit his lip, then called out, "Come back here."

He was beginning definitely to dislike Mrs. Van Vogel, despite his automatic tendency to genuflect in the presence of a high credit rating. To be told how to run his own business—well, now, indeed! "Mrs. van Vogel, I admire your humanitarian spirit but you don't understand the situation. We understand our workers and do what is best for them. They die painlessly before their disabilities can trouble them. They live happy lives, happier than yours or mine. We trim off the bad part of their lives, nothing more. And don't forget, these poor beasts would never have been born had we not arranged it."

She shook her head. "Fiddlesticks! You'll be quoting the Bible at me next. There will be no more of it, Mr. Blakesly. I shall hold you personally responsible."

Blakesly looked bleak. "My responsibilities are to the directors."

"You think so?" She opened her purse and snatched out her telephone. So great was her agitation that she did not bother to call through, but signalled the local relay operator instead. "Phoenix? Get me Great New York Murray Hill 9Q-4004, Mr. Haskell. Priority—star subscriber 777. Make it quick." She stood there, tapping her foot and glaring, until her business manager answered. "Haskell? This is Martha van Vogel. How much Workers, Incorporated, common do I own? No, no never mind that—what percent? . . . so? Well, it's not enough. I want 51% by tomorrow morning . . . all right, get proxies for the rest but get it . . . I didn't ask you what it would cost; I said get it. Get busy." She disconnected abruptly and turned to her husband. "We're leaving, Brownie, and we're taking Jerry with us. Mr. Blakesly, will you kindly have him taken out of that pen? Give him a check for the amount, Brownie."

"Now, Martha—"

"My mind is made up, Brownie."

Mr. Blakesly cleared his throat. It was going to be pleasant to thwart this woman. "The workers are never sold. I'm sorry. It's a matter of policy."

"Very well then, I'll take a permanent lease."

"This worker has been removed from the labor market. He is not for lease."

"Am I going to have trouble with you?"

"If you please, madame! This worker is not available under any terms—but as a courtesy to you, I am willing to transfer to you indentures for him, gratis. I want you to know that the policies of this firm are formed from a very real concern for the welfare of our charges as well as from the standpoint of good business practice. We therefore reserve the right to inspect at any time to assure ourselves that you are taking proper care of this worker." There, he told himself savagely, that will stop her clock!

"Of course. Thank you, Mr. Blakesly. You are most gracious."

The trip back to Great New York was not jolly. Napoleon hated it and let it be known. Jerry was patient, but airsick. By the time they were grounded the van Vogels were not on speaking terms.

"I'm sorry Mrs. van Vogel. The shares were simply not available. We should have a proxy on the O'Toole block but someone tied them up an hour before I reached them."

"Blakesly."

"Undoubtedly. You should not have tipped him off; you gave him time to warn his employers."

"Don't waste time telling me what mistakes I made yesterday. What are you going to do today?"

"My dear Mrs. van Vogel, what can I do? I'll carry out any instructions you care to give."

"Don't talk nonsense. You are supposed to be smarter than I am; that's why I pay you to do my thinking for me."

Mr. Haskell looked helpless.

His principle struck a cigarette so hard she broke it. "Why isn't Weinberg here?"

"Really, Mrs. van Vogel, there are no special legal aspects. You want the stock; we can't buy it nor bind it. Therefore—"

"I pay Weinberg to know the legal angles. Get him."

Weinberg was leaving his office; Haskell caught him on a chase-me circuit. "Sidney," Haskell called out. "Come to my office, will you? Oscar Haskell."

"Sorry. How about four o'clock?"

"Sidney, I want you—now!" cut in the client's voice. "This is Martha van Vogel."

The little man shrugged helplessly. "Right away," he agreed. That woman—why hadn't he retired on his one hundred and twenty-fifth birthday, as his wife had urged him to?

Ten minutes later he was listening to Haskell's explanations and his client's interruptions. When they had finished he spread his hands. "What do you expect, Mrs. van Vogel? These workers are chattels. You have not been able to buy the property rights involved; you are stopped. But I don't see what you are worked up about. They gave you the worker whose life you wanted preserved."

She spoke forcefully under her breath, then answered him. "That's not important. What is one worker among millions? I want to stop this killing, all of it."

Weinberg shook his head. "If you were able to prove that their methods of disposing of these beasts were inhumane, or that they were negligent of their physical welfare before destroying them, or that the destruction was wanton—"

"Wanton? It certainly is!"

"Probably not in a legal sense, my dear lady. There was a case, *Julius Hartman et al. vs. Hartman Estate*, 1972, I believe, in which a permanent injunction was granted against carrying out a term of the will which called for the destruction of a valuable collection of Persian cats. But in order to use that theory you would have to show that these creatures, when superannuated, are notwithstanding more valuable alive than dead. You cannot compel a person to maintain chattels at a loss."

"See here, Sidney, I didn't get you over here to tell me how this can't be done. If what I want isn't legal, then get a law passed."

Weinberg looked at Haskell, who looked embarrassed and answered, "Well, the fact of the matter is, Mrs. van Vogel, that we have agreed with the other members of the Commonwealth Association not to subsidize any legislation during the incumbency of the present administration."

"How ridiculous! Why?"

"The Legislative guild has brought out a new fair-practices code which we consider quite unfair, a sliding scale which penalizes the well-to-do—all very nice sounding, with special provisions for nominal fees for veterans' private bills and such things—but in fact the code is confiscatory. Even the Briggs Foundation can hardly afford to take a proper interest in public affairs under this so-called code."

"Hmmph! A fine day when legislators join unions—they are professional men. Bribes should be competitive. Get an injunction."

"Mrs. van Vogel," protested Weinberg, "how can you expect me to get an injunction against an organization which has no legal existence? In a legal sense, there is no Legislative Guild, just as the practice of assisting legislation by subsidy has itself no legal existence."

"And babies come under cabbage leaves. Quit stalling me, gentlemen. What are you going to do?"

Weinberg spoke when he saw that Haskell did not intend to. "Mrs. van Vogel, I think we should retain a special shyster."

"I don't employ shysters, even—I don't understand the way they think. I am a simple housewife, Sidney."

Mr. Weinberg flinched at her self-designation while noting that he must not let her find out that the salary of his own staff shyster was charged to her payroll. As convention required, he maintained the front of a simple, barefoot solicitor, but he had found out long ago that Martha van Vogel's problems required an occasional dose of the more exotic branch of the law. "The man I have in mind is a creative artist," he insisted. "It is no more necessary to understand him than it is to understand the composer in order to appreciate a symphony. I do recommend that you talk with him, at least."

"Oh, very well! Get him up here."

"Here? My dear lady!" Haskell was shocked at the suggestion; Weinberg looked amazed. "It would not only cause any action you bring to be thrown out of court if it were known that you had consulted this man, but it would prejudice any Briggs enterprise for years."

Mrs. van Vogel shrugged. "You men. I never will understand the way you think. Why shouldn't one consult a shyster as openly as one consults an astrologer?"

James Roderick McCoy was not a large man, but he seemed large. He managed to dominate even so large a room as Mrs. van Vogel's salon. His business card read:

J. R. McCOY
"The Real McCoy"
Licensed Shyster—Fixing, Special Contracts,
Angles. All Work Guaranteed.
Telephone Skyline 9-8M4554
Ask for Mac

The number given was the pool room of the notorious Three Planets Club. He wasted no time on offices and kept his files in his head—the only safe place for them.

He was sitting on the floor, attempting to teach Jerry to shoot craps, while Mrs. van Vogel explained her problem. "What do you think, Mr. McCoy? Could we approach it through the SPCA? My public relations staff could give it a buildup."

McCoy got to his feet. "Jerry's eyes aren't so bad; he caught me trying to palm box cars off on him as a natural. No," he continued, "the SPCA angle is no good. They'll be ready to prove that the anthropoids actually enjoy being killed off."

Jerry rattled the dice hopefully. "That's all, Jerry. Scram."

"Okay, boss." The ape man got to his feet and went to the big stereo which filled a corner of the room. Napoleon ambled after him and switched it on. Jerry punched a selector button and got a blues singer. Napoleon immediately punched another, then another and another until he got a loud but popular band. He stood there, beating out the rhythm with his trunk.

Jerry looked pained and switched it back to his blues singer. Napoleon stubbornly reached out with his prehensile nose and switched it off.

Jerry used a swear word.

"Boys!" called out Mrs. van Vogel. "Quit squabbling. Jerry, let Nappie play what he wants to. You can play the stereo when Nappie has to take his nap."

"Okay, Missy Boss."

McCoy was interested. "Jerry likes music?"

"Like it? He loves it. He's been learning to sing."

"Huh? This I gotta hear."

"Certainly. Nappie—turn off the stereo." The elephant complied but managed to look put upon. "Now Jerry—'Jingle Bells.'" She led him in it:

"*Jingle bells, jingle bells, jingle all the way—*", and he followed,

"Jinger bez, jinger bez, jinger awrah day;
"Oh, wot fun tiz to ride in one-hoss open sray."

He was flat, he was terrible. He looked ridiculous, patting out the time with one splay foot. But it was singing.

"Say, that's fast!" McCoy commented. "Too bad Nappie can't talk—we'd have a duet."

Jerry looked puzzled. "Nappie talk good," he stated. He bent over the elephant and spoke to him. Napoleon grunted and moaned back at him. "See, Boss?" Jerry said triumphantly.

"What did he say?"

"He say, 'Can Nappie pray stereo now?'"

"Very well, Jerry." Mrs. van Vogel interceded. The ape man spoke to his chum in whispers. Napoleon squealed and did not turn on the stereo.

"Jerry!" said his mistress. "I said nothing of the sort; he does *not* have to play your blues singer. Come away, Jerry. Nappie—play what you want to."

"You mean he tried to cheat?" McCoy inquired with interest.

"He certainly did."

"Hmm—Jerry's got the makings of a real citizen. Shave him and put shoes on him and he'd get by all right in the precinct I grew up in." He stared at the anthropoid. Jerry stared back, puzzled but patient. Mrs. van Vogel had thrown away the dirty canvas kilt which was both his badge of servitude and a concession to propriety and had replaced it with a kilt in the bright Cameron war plaid, complete to sporran, and topped off with a Glengarry.

"Do you suppose he could learn to play the bagpipes?" McCoy asked. "I'm beginning to get an angle."

"Why, I don't know. What's your idea?"

McCoy squatted down cross-legged and began practicing rolls with his dice. "Never mind," he answered when it suited him, "that angle's no good. But we're getting there." He rolled four naturals, one after the other. "You say Jerry still belongs to the Corporation?"

"In a titular sense, yes. I doubt if they will ever try to repossess him."

"I wish they would try." He scooped up the dice and stood up. "It's in the bag, Sis. Forget it. I'll want to talk to your publicity man but you can quit worrying about it."

✧   ✧   ✧

Of course Mrs. van Vogel should have knocked before entering her husband's room—but then she would not have overheard what he was saying, nor to whom.

"That's right," she heard him say, "we haven't any further need for him. Take him away, the sooner the better. Just be sure the men you send over have a signed order directing us to turn him over."

She was not apprehensive, as she did not understand the conversation, but merely curious. She looked over her husband's shoulder at the video screen.

There she saw Blakesly's face. His voice was saying, "Very well, Mr. Van Vogel, the anthropoid will be picked up tomorrow."

She strode up to the screen. "Just a minute, Mr. Blakesly—" then, to her husband, "Brownie, what in the world do you think you are doing?"

The expression she surprised on his face was not one he had ever let her see before. "Why don't you knock?"

"Maybe it's a good thing that I didn't. Brownie, did I hear you right? Were you telling Mr. Blakesly to pick up Jerry?" She turned to the screen. "Was that it, Mr. Blakesly?"

"That is correct, Mrs. van Vogel. And I must say I find this confusion most—"

"Stow it." She turned back. "Brownie, what have you to say for yourself?"

"Martha, you are being preposterous. Between that elephant and that ape this place is a zoo. I actually caught your precious Jerry smoking my special, personal cigars today . . . not to mention the fact that both of them play the stereo all day long until a man can't get a moment's peace. I certainly don't have to stand for such things in my own house."

"Whose house, Brownie?"

"That's beside the point. I will not stand for—"

"Never mind." She turned to the screen. "My husband seems to have lost his taste for exotic animals, Mr. Blakesly. Cancel the order for a Pegasus."

"Martha!"

"Sauce for the goose, Brownie. I'll pay for your whims; I'm damned if I'll pay for your tantrums. The contract is cancelled, Mr. Blakesly. Mr. Haskell will arrange the details."

Blakesly shrugged. "Your capricious behavior will cost you, of course. The penalties—"

"I said Mr. Haskell would arrange the details. One more thing, Mister Manager Blakesly—have you done as I told you to?"

"What do you mean?"

"You know what I mean—are those poor creatures still alive and well?"

"That is not your business." He had, in fact, suspended the killings; the directors had not wanted to take any chances until they saw what the Briggs trust could manage, but Blakesly would not give her the satisfaction of knowing.

She looked at him as if he were a skipped dividend. "It's not, eh? Well, bear this in mind, you cold-blooded little pipsqueak: I'm holding you personally responsible. If just one of them dies from *anything*, I'll have your skin for a rug." She flipped off the connection and turned to her husband. "Brownie—"

"It's useless to say anything," he cut in, in the cold voice he normally used to bring her to heel. "I shall be at the Club. Good-bye!"

"That is just what I was going to suggest."

"What?"

"I'll have your clothes sent over. Do you have anything else in this house?"

He stared at her. "Don't talk like a fool, Martha."

"I'm not talking like a fool." She looked him up and down. "My, but you are handsome, Brownie. I guess I was a fool to think I could buy a big hunk of man with a checkbook. I guess a girl gets them free, or she doesn't get them at all. Thanks for the lesson." She turned and slammed out of the room and into her own suite.

Five minutes later, makeup repaired and nerves steadied by a few whiffs of Fly-Right, she called the pool room of the Three Planets Club. McCoy came to the screen carrying a cue. "Oh, it's you, sugar-puss. Well, snap it up—I've got four bits on this game."

"This is business."

"Okay, okay—spill it."

She told him the essentials. "I'm sorry about cancelling the flying horse contract, Mr. McCoy. I hope it won't make your job any harder. I'm afraid I lost my temper."

"Fine. Go lose it again."

"Huh!"

"You're barreling down the groove, kid. Call Blakesly up again. Bawl him out. Tell him to keep his bailiffs away from you, or you'll stuff 'em and use them for hat racks. Dare him to take Jerry away from you."

"I don't understand you."

"You don't have to, girlie. Remember this: You can't have a bull fight until you get the bull mad enough to fight. Have Weinberg get a temporary injunction restraining Workers, Incorporated, from reclaiming Jerry. Have your boss press agent give me a buzz. Then you call the newsboys and tell them what you think of Blakesly. Make it nasty. Tell them you intend to put a stop to this wholesale murder if it takes every cent you've got."

"Well . . . all right. Will you come and see me before I talk to them?"

"Nope—gotta get back to my game. Tomorrow, maybe. Don't fret about having cancelled that silly winged-horse deal. I always did think your old man was weak in the head, and it's saved you a nice piece of change. You'll need it when I send in my bill. Boy, am I going to clip you! Bye now."

The bright letters trailed around the sides of the Times Building: "WORLD'S RICHEST WOMAN PUTS UP FIGHT FOR APE MAN." On the giant video screen above showed a transcribe of Jerry, in his ridiculous Highland chief outfit. A small army of police surrounded the Briggs town house, while Mrs. van Vogel informed anyone who would listen, including several news services, that she would defend Jerry personally and to the death.

The public relations office of Workers, Incorporated, denied any intention of seizing Jerry; the denial got nowhere.

In the meantime technicians installed extra audio and video circuits in the largest courtroom in town, for one Jerry (no surname), described as a legal, permanent resident of these United States, had asked for a permanent injunction against the corporate person "Workers," its officers, employees, successors, or assignees, forbidding it to kill him.

Through his attorney, the honorable and distinguished and stuffily respectable Augustus Pomfrey, Jerry brought the action *in his own name.*

Martha van Vogel sat in the courtroom as a spectator only, but she was surrounded by secretaries, guards, maids, publicity men, and yes men, and had one television camera trained on her alone. She was nervous. McCoy had insisted on briefing Pomfrey through Weinberg, to keep Pomfrey from knowing that he was helped by a shyster. She had her own opinion of Pomfrey—

The McCoy had insisted that Jerry not wear his beautiful new kilt but had dressed him in faded dungaree trousers and jacket. It seemed poor theater to her.

Jerry himself worried her. He seemed confused by the lights and the noise and the crowd, about to go to pieces.

And McCoy had refused to go to the trial with her. He had told her that it was quite impossible, that his mere presence would alienate the court, and Weinberg had backed him up. Men! Their minds were devious—they seemed to *like* twisted ways of doing things. It confirmed her opinion that men should not be allowed to vote.

But she felt lost without the immediate presence of McCoy's easy self-confidence. Away from him, she wondered why she had ever trusted such an important matter to an irresponsible, jumping jack, bird-brained clown as McCoy. She chewed her nails and wished he were present.

The panel of attorneys appearing for Workers Incorporated, began by moving that the action be dismissed without trial, on the theory that Jerry was a chattel to the corporation, an integral part of it, and no more able to sue than the thumb can sue the brain.

The honorable Augustus Pomfrey looked every inch the statesman as he bowed to the court and to his opponents. "It is indeed strange," he began, "to hear the second-hand voice of a legal fiction, a soulless, imaginary quantity called a corporate 'person,' argue that a flesh-and-blood creature, a being of hopes and longings and passions, has no legal existence. I see here beside me my poor cousin Jerry." He patted Jerry on the shoulder; the ape man, needing reassurance, slid a hand into his. It went over well.

"But when I look for this abstract fancy 'Workers,' what do I find? Nothing—some words on paper, some signed bits of foolscap—"

"If the Court please, a question," put in the opposition chief attorney, "does the learned counsel contend that a limited liability stock company cannot own property?"

"Will counsel reply?" directed the judge.

"Thank you. My esteemed colleague has set up a straw man; I contended only that the question as to whether Jerry is a chattel of Workers, Incorporated, is immaterial, nonessential, irrelevant. I am part of the corporate city of Great New York. Does that deny me my civil rights as a person of flesh and blood? In fact it does not even rob me of my right to sue that civic corporation of which I am a part, if, in my opinion, I am wronged by it. We are met today in the mellow light of equity, rather than in the cold and narrow confines of law. It seemed a fit time to dwell on the strange absurdities we live by, whereunder a nonentity of paper and legal fiction could deny the existence of this our poor cousin. I ask that the learned attorneys for the corporation stipulate that Jerry does, in fact, exist, and let us get on with the action."

They huddled; the answer was "No."

"Very well. My client asked to be examined in order that the court may determine his status and being."

"Objection! This anthropoid cannot be examined; he is a mere part and chattel of the respondent."

"That is what we are about to determine," the judge answered dryly. "Objection overruled."

"Go sit in that chair, Jerry."

"Objection! This beast cannot take an oath—it is beyond his comprehension."

"What have you to say to that, Counsel?"

"If it pleases the Court," answered Pomfrey, "the simplest thing to do is put him in the chair and find out."

"Let him take the stand. The clerk will administer the oath." Martha van Vogel gripped the arms of her chair; McCoy had spent a full week training him for this. Would the whole thing blow up without McCoy to guide him?

The clerk droned through the oath; Jerry looked puzzled but patient.

"Your honor," said Pomfrey, "when young children must give testimony, it is customary to permit a little leeway in the wording, to fit their mental attainments. May I be permitted?" He walked up to Jerry.

"Jerry, my boy, are you a good worker?"

"Sure Mike! Jerry good worker!"

"Maybe bad worker, huh? Lazy. Hide from strawboss."

"No, no, no! Jerry good worker. Dig. Weed. Not dig up veg-etaber. Dig up weed. Work hard."

"You will see," Pomfrey addressed the court, "that my client has very definite ideas of what is true and what is false. Now let us attempt to find out whether or not he has moral values which require him to tell the truth. Jerry—"

"Yes, Boss."

Pomfrey spread his hand in front of the anthropoid's face. "How many fingers do you see?"

Jerry reached out and ticked them off. "one—two—sree—four, uh—five."

"Six fingers, Jerry."

"Five, Boss."

"Six fingers, Jerry. I give you cigarette. Six."

"Five, Boss. Jerry not cheat."

Pomfrey spread his hands. "Will the court accept him?"

The court did. Martha van Vogel sighed. Jerry could not count very well and she had been afraid that he would forget his lines and accept the bribe. But he had been promised all the cigarettes he wanted and chocolate as well if he would remember to insist that five was five.

"I suggest," Pomfrey went on, "that the matter has been established. Jerry is an entity; if he can be accepted as a witness, then surely he may have his day in court. Even a dog may have his day in court. Will my esteemed colleagues stipulate?"

Workers, Incorporated, through its battery of lawyers, agreed— just in time, for the judge was beginning to cloud up. He had been so much impressed by the little performance.

The tide was with him; Pomfrey used it. "If it please the court and if the counsels for the respondent will permit, we can shorten these proceedings. I will state the theory under which relief is sought and then, by a few questions, it may be settled one way or another. I ask that it be stipulated that it was the intention of Workers, Incorporated, through its servants, to take the life of my client."

Stipulation was refused.

"So? Then I ask the court take judicial notice of the well-known fact that these anthropoid workers are destroyed when they no longer show a profit; thereafter I will call witnesses, starting with Horace Blakesly, to show that Jerry was and presumably is under such sentence of death."

Another hurried huddle resulted in the stipulation that Jerry had, indeed been scheduled for euthanasia.

"Then," said Pomfrey, "I will state my theory. Jerry is not an animal, but a man. It is not legal to kill him—it is murder."

First there was silence, then the crowd gasped. People had grown used to animals that talked and worked, but they were no more prepared to think of them as persons, humans, *men*, than were the haughty Roman citizens prepared to concede human feelings to their barbarian slaves.

Pomfrey let them have it while they were still groggy. "What is a man? A collection of living cells and tissue? A legal fiction, like this corporate 'person' that would take poor Jerry's life? No, a man is none of these things. A man is a collection of hopes and fears, of human longings, of aspirations greater than himself—more than the clay from which he came; less the Creator which lifted him up from the clay. Jerry has been taken from his jungle and made something more than the poor creatures who were his ancestors, even as you and I. We ask that this Court recognize his manhood."

The opposing attorneys saw that the Court was moved; they drove fast. An anthropoid, they contended, could not be a man because he lacked human shape and human intelligence. Pomfrey called his first witness—Master B'na Kreeth.

The Martian's bad temper had not been improved by being forced to wait around for three days in a travel tank, to say nothing of the indignity of having to interrupt his researches to take part in the childish pow-wows of terrestrials.

There was further delay to irritate him while Pomfrey forced the corporation to accept him as an expert witness. They wanted to refuse but could not—he was their own Director of Research. He also held voting control of all Martian-held Workers' stock, a fact unmentioned but hampering.

More delay while an interpreter was brought in to help administer the oath—B'na Kreeth, self-centered as all Martians, had never bothered to learn English.

He twittered and chirped in answer to the demand that he tell the truth, the whole truth, and so forth; the interpreter looked pained. "He says he can't do it," he informed the judge.

Pomfrey asked for exact translation.

The interpreter looked uneasily at the judge. "He says that if he told us the whole truth you fools—not 'fools' exactly; it's a Martian word meaning a sort of headless worm—would not understand it."

The court discussed the idea of contempt briefly. When the Martian understood that he was about to be forced to remain in a travel tank for thirty days he came down off his high horse and agreed to tell the truth as adequately as was possible; he was accepted as a witness.

"Are you a man?" demanded Pomfrey.

"*Under your laws and by your standards I am a man.*"

"By what theory? Your body is unlike ours; you cannot even live in our air. You do not speak our language; your ideas are alien to us. How can you be a man?"

The Martian answered carefully: "*I quote from the Terra-Martian Treaty, which you must accept as supreme law. 'All members of the Great Race, while sojourning on the Third Planet, shall have all the rights and prerogatives of the native dominant race of the Third Planet.' This clause has been interpreted by the Bi-Planet Tribunal to mean that members of the Great Race are 'men' whatever that may be.*"

"Why do you refer to your sort as the 'Great Race'?"

"*Because of our superior intelligence.*"

"Superior to men?"

"*We are men.*"

"Superior to the intelligence of earth men?"

"*That is self-evident.*"

"Just as we are superior in intelligence to this poor creature Jerry?"

"*That is not self-evident.*"

"Finished with the witness," announced Pomfrey. The opposition counsels should have left bad enough alone; instead they tried to get B'na Kreeth to define the difference in intelligence between humans and worker-anthropoids. Master B'na explained meticulously that cultural differences masked the intrinsic differences, if any, and that, in any case, both anthropoids and men made so little use of their respective potential intelligences that it was really too early to tell which race would turn out to be the superior race in the Third Planet.

He had just begun to discuss how a truly superior race could be bred by combining the best features of anthropoids and men when he was hastily asked to "stand down."

"May it please the Court," said Pomfrey, "we have not advanced the theory; we have merely disposed of respondent's contention that a particular shape and a particular degree of intelligence are necessary to manhood. I now ask that the petitioner be called to the stand that the court may determine whether he is, in truth, human."

"If the learned court please—" The battery of lawyers had been in a huddle ever since B'na Kreeth's travel tank had been removed from the room; the chief counsel now spoke.

"The object of the petition appears to be to protect the life of this chattel. There is no need to draw out these proceedings; respondent stipulates that this chattel will be allowed to die a natural death in the hands of its present custodian and moves that the action be dismissed."

"What do you say to that?" the Court asked Pomfrey.

Pomfrey visibly gathered his toga about him. "We ask not for cold charity from this corporation, but for the justice of the court. We ask that Jerry's humanity be established as a matter of law. Not for him to vote, nor to hold property, nor to be relieved of special police regulations appropriate to his group—but we do ask that he be adjudged at least as human as that aquarium monstrosity just removed from this courtroom!"

The judge turned to Jerry. "Is that what you want, Jerry?"

Jerry looked uneasily at Pomfrey, then said, "Okay, Boss."

"Come up to the chair."

"One moment—" The opposition chief counsel seemed flurried. "I ask the court to consider that a ruling in this matter may affect a long established commercial practice necessary to the economic life of—"

"Objection!" Pomfrey was on his feet, bristling. "Never have I heard a more outrageous attempt to prejudice a decision. My esteemed colleague might as well ask the Court to decide a murder case from political considerations. I protest—"

"Never mind," said the court. "The suggestion will be ignored. Proceed with your witness."

Pomfrey bowed. "We are exploring the meaning of this strange thing called 'manhood.' We have seen that it is not a matter of shape, nor race, nor planet of birth, nor acuteness of mind. Truly, it cannot be defined, yet it may be experienced. It can reach from heart to heart, from spirit to spirit." He turned to Jerry. "Jerry—will you sing your new song for the judge?"

"Sure Mike." Jerry looked uneasily up at the whirling cameras, the mikes, and the ikes, then cleared his throat:

> *"Way down upon de Suwannee Ribber*
> *Far, far away;*
> *Dere's where my heart is turning ebber—"*

The applause scared him out of his wits; the banging of the gavel frightened him still more—but it mattered not; the issue was no longer in doubt. Jerry was a man.

～

Robert A. Heinlein (1907–1988) began his career with a competently told, but not very striking story, "Lifeline," which gave no clue that it was the first installment of the grandest saga in the history of science fiction, his "Future History" series, but soon, more substantial and vitamin-packed landmark yarns followed in those magical years when new Heinlein stories were regularly appearing in John W. Campbell, Jr.'s *Astounding*, making it known to all what previously untapped potential the SF field was capable of reaching. Sometimes, there would even be more than one Heinlein story in an issue, though the originator of some of those masterpieces would be concealed under pseudonym such as Anson MacDonald and John Riverside. (True, John Riverside's byline appeared only once, in Campbell's other classic pulp, *Unknown Worlds*, rather than *Astounding*, but as long as Heinlein and Campbell were remaking the shape of science fiction, fantasy had it coming, too.) It was much too soon to take a long pause, but, thanks to Hitler, Mussolini, and the Japanese warlords, it was utterly necessary. Heinlein's incandescent writing career had to cool down while Heinlein and several million others around the globe pitched in to put Hitler and his pals out of business. After the war, Heinlein's career rekindled and blazed anew, bringing the classic juvenile novels, the sales to high-paying "slick" magazines, the trailblazing movie, *Destination Moon*, the *New York Times* bestsellers, and more, This is, of course, an inadequate portrait of grand master Heinlein; but, then, aren't they all?

PARADOX & GREENBLATT: ATTORNEYS AT LAW

KEVIN J. ANDERSON

It was an ineptly bungled attempt at murder, as even the defendant kept telling everyone, not just his counsel, so it all seemed like an open and shut case, with an unavoidable verdict of "guilty." But depend on a lawyer to make the simple far more complicated, particularly with time travel in the case.

❧

YOU MIGHT SAY OUR LITTLE FIRM SPECIALIZES IN CONTRADICTIONS. In a few years Aaron Greenblatt and I are sure to be millionaire visionaries overloaded with cases, but right now our field of law is still in its infancy. We've carved out a new niche, and people are already starting to find us.

Since we can't afford a receptionist (not yet) Aaron took the call. But because he was up to his nostrils in a corporate lawsuit—a client suing Time Travel Expeditions for refusing to let him go to the late Cretaceous on a dinosaur hunt—he passed the case to me.

"Line one for you, Marty," he said as I came out of the lav, wiping my hands. "New case on the hook. Simple attempted murder, I think. Guy sounds frantic."

"They all sound frantic." I pursed my lips. "Is time travel involved?"

He nodded, and I knew there would be nothing "simple"

about the case. Fortunately, temporal complications are right up our firm's alley. We're forward-thinkers, my partner and I—*and* backward-thinkers, when it's effective. That's why people call us when nobody else knows what the hell to do.

I picked up the phone and punched the solitary blinking light. "Marty Paramus here. How can I help you?"

The man talked a mile a minute in a thin, squeaky voice; even if he hadn't been panicked, it probably would have sounded unpleasant. "All I did was try to stop him from buying her some deep-fried artichoke hearts. How could that be construed as attempted murder? They can't pin anything on me, can they? Why would they think I was trying to kill anybody?"

"Maybe you'd better tell me, Mr. . . . uh?"

"Hendergast. Lionel Hendergast. And I read the terms of the contract very carefully before we went back in time. It didn't say anything about deep-fried artichoke hearts."

I sighed. "What was your location, Mr. Hendergast?"

"Santa Cruz Boardwalk. The place with all the rides and the arcade games. They have concession stands and—"

"Sure, but *when* was this?"

"Umm, two days ago."

I hate having to pry all the obvious information out of a client. "Not in your time. I mean in *real* time."

"Oh, um, fifty-two years ago."

"Ah." I made a noise that hinted at a deeper understanding than I really had, yet. "One of those nostalgic life-was-better-back-then tours."

Now he sounded defensive. "Nothing illegal about them, Mr. Paramus. They're perfectly legitimate."

"So you said. But someone must think you broke the rules, or you wouldn't have been arrested. Was this person allergic to artichoke hearts or something?"

"No, not at all. And it wasn't the artichoke hearts. I was just trying to prevent him from buying them for her. I didn't want the two of them to meet."

A light bulb winked on inside my head. "Oh, one of those."

"Altering history" cases were my bread and butter.

The jail's attorney-client meeting room wasn't much better than a cell. The cinderblock walls were covered with a hardened slime of seafoam-green paint. The chairs around the table creaked, and veritable stalactites of petrified chewing gum adorned the table's underside. Since prisoners weren't allowed to chew gum, their lawyers must have been responsible for this mess. Some attorneys give the whole field a bad name.

Lionel Hendergast was in his mid-twenties but looked at least a decade older than that. His too-round face, set atop a long and skinny neck, reminded me of a smiling jack-o'-lantern balanced on a stalk. His long-fingered hands fidgeted. He looked toward me as if I were a superhero swooping in to the rescue.

"I need to understand exactly what you've done, Mr. Hendergast. Tell me the truth, and don't hold back anything. No bullshit. We have attorney-client privilege here, and I need to know what I'm working with."

"I'm innocent."

I rolled my eyes. "Listen, Mr. Hendergast—Lionel—my job is to get you off the hook for the crime of which you're accused. Let's save the declarations of innocence for the judge, okay? Now, start from the beginning."

He swallowed, took a deep breath, then said, "I took a trip back in time to the Santa Cruz Beach Boardwalk to 1973, as I said. You can get the brochure from the time travel company I used. There's nothing wrong with it, absolutely not."

"And why did you want to go to Santa Cruz?"

He shrugged unconvincingly. "The old carousel, the carnival rides, the games where you throw a ball and knock down bottles. And then there's the beach, cotton candy, churros, hot dogs, giant pretzels."

"And artichoke hearts," I prodded.

Lionel swiveled nervously in his chair, which made a protesting creak. "Deep-fried artichoke hearts are sort of a specialty there. A woman nearing the front of the line had dropped her wallet on the ground not ten feet away, but she didn't know it yet. In a few minutes, she was going to order deep-fried artichoke hearts—and when she discovered she had no money to pay, the man behind her in line would step up like a knight in shining armor, pay for her artichoke hearts, and help her search for her wallet. They'd find it, and then go out to dinner. The rest is history."

"And you seem to know the details of this history quite well. What exactly were you going to do?"

"Well, I found the woman's wallet, on purpose, so I could give it back to her. Nothing illegal in that, is there?"

I nodded, already frowning. "Thereby preventing the man behind her from doing a good deed, stopping them from going to dinner, and"—I held my hands out—"accomplishing what?"

"If they didn't meet, then they wouldn't get married. And if they didn't get married, then they wouldn't have a son who is the true spawn of all evil."

"The Damien defense doesn't hold up in court, you know. I can cite several precedents."

"But if I had succeeded, who would have known? There would've been no crime because nothing would have happened. How can they accuse me of anything?"

"Because recorded history is admissible in a court of law," I said. "So by attempting to keep these two people from meeting, you were effectively trying to commit a murder by preventing someone from being born."

"If, if, if!" Hendergast looked much more agitated now. "But I didn't do it, so how can they hold me?"

The legal system has never been good at adapting to rapid change. Law tends to be reactive instead of proactive. When new technology changes the face of the world, the last people to deal with it—right behind senior citizens and vested union workers— are judges and the law. Remember copyright suits in the early days of the internet, when the uses and abuses of intellectual property zoomed ahead of the lawmakers like an Indy 500 race car passing an Amish horse cart?

Now, in an era of time-travel tourism, with the often-contradictory restrictions the companies impose upon themselves, legal problems have been springing up like wildflowers in a manure field. Aaron Greenblatt and I formed our partnership to go after these cases. We are, in effect, creating major precedents with every case we take, win or lose.

Where was a person like Lionel Hendergast to turn? Everyone is entitled to legal representation. He didn't entirely understand the charges against him, and I was fairly certain that the judge wouldn't know what to do either. Judges dislike being forced to make up their minds from scratch, instead of finding a sufficiently similar case from which they can copy what their predecessors have done.

"Do you ever sit back and play the 'What if?' game, Mr. Paramus?" Lionel asked, startling me. "If a certain event had changed, how would your life be different? If your parents hadn't gotten divorced, your dad might not have killed himself, your mom might not have married some abusive truck driver and moved off to Nevada where she won't return your calls or even give you her correct street address? That sort of thing?"

I looked at him. Now we might finally be getting somewhere. "I've seen *It's a Wonderful Life*. Four times, in fact, including the alternate-ending version. I'm very familiar with 'What if?' Who were you trying to kill and what was the result you hoped to achieve?"

"I wasn't trying to *kill* anyone," he insisted.

From the frightened little-boy expression on Lionel's round face, I could see he wasn't a violent man. He could never have taken a gun to someone or cut the brake cables on his victim's car. He wouldn't even have had the stomach to pay a professional hit man. No, he had wanted to achieve his goal in a way that would let him sleep at night.

"The man was Delano R. Franklin," he said. "You won't find a more vile and despicable man on the face of this Earth."

I didn't want to argue with my client, though I could have pointed out some pretty likely candidates for the vile-and-despicable championship. "Much as it may pain me to say this, Lionel, being unpleasant isn't against the law."

"My parents were happily married, a long time ago. My dad had a good job. He owned a furniture store. And my mom was a receptionist in a car dealership—a dealership owned by Mr. Franklin. We had a nice home in the suburbs. I was supposed to get a puppy that Christmas."

"How old were you?"

"Four."

"And you remember all these details?"

He wouldn't look at me. "Not really, but I've heard about it a thousand times. My parents couldn't stop arguing about that day my dad took time off in the afternoon. He decided to surprise my mother over at the car dealership by bringing her a dozen long-stemmed roses."

"How romantic," I said.

"At the car dealership they take a late lunch hour so they can take care of the customer rush between noon and one. When my dad couldn't find anyone at the reception counter, he went to the back room and opened the door—only to find my mom flat on the desk with her skirt hiked up to her hips, legs wrapped around Franklin's neck, and him pumping away into her."

It wasn't the first time I had heard this sort of story. "I can see how that would ruin a marriage."

"My dad went nuts. He tried to attack Franklin and as a result, ended up in jail with charges of assault. Franklin had most of our local officials in his pocket—small town. At first my mom insisted that Franklin threatened to fire her if she didn't have sex with him. In the resulting scandal, she changed her story, saying that the affair had gone on for a while, that Franklin wanted to marry her. My parents split up, but as soon as the divorce was final, the creep wanted nothing to do with her. He kicked my mom out. She had no job, and by that time my dad had lost his furniture store."

"Sounds like a mess. So what happened to little Lionel?"

"We lived in Seaside, California—that's not far from Santa Cruz and Monterey. My dad got drunk one day and drove too fast along Highway 1."

I'd been there. "Some spectacular cliffs and tight curves on that stretch of highway."

Miserably, Lionel nodded. "The road curved, and my dad went straight. Suicide was suspected, but nobody ever proved it. Then, one day my mom just packed up, dropped me off at foster care, and left. Said she hated me because I was just like my father. I lived in six different homes until I was sixteen and old enough to emancipate myself."

I tried to sound sympathetic. "Not a very happy childhood."

"Meanwhile, Delano R. Franklin did quite well with his car dealership. In fact, he opened three more. He married some bimbo, divorced her when she got wrinkles, then married another one. Never had kids, but I think his wives were young enough to be his daughters."

I wanted to cut the rant short. "All right, but what does this have to do with deep-fried artichoke hearts?"

Tears started running down his cheeks. "I remembered my mother yelling at Franklin once. He had wooed her by telling romantic stories, describing how his own parents met. The man who would be Franklin's father came to the rescue, helped find a lady's wallet at the artichoke stand, took her out to eat…and eventually spawned this inkblot on the human race, a uniting of sperm and egg that any compassionate God would have prevented!"

I paced around the table, locking my hands behind my back. "So you figured that if you kept Franklin's biological mother and father from meeting, he would never have been born, your parents' marriage would have remained happy, and your life would have been wonderful."

"That's about it, Mr. Paramus. But Franklin had someone watching me, so I got caught."

"Watching you? How could he possibly have suspected such an absurd thing?"

"Because I, uh…" Lionel blushed. "I told him. I couldn't help myself. I wanted the scumbag to know he was about to be removed from existence."

I groaned. In this business, the only thing worse than a hardened criminal is an unconscionably stupid client.

"You have to get me out of here, Mr. Paramus!" Given the circumstances, an unreasonable demand. "That holding cell is a nightmare. It smells. There's no privacy even for the toilet, and they took blood samples to test me for HIV and other diseases. They drew my blood! That means other people in the cell must have those terrible diseases. What if I—"

"It's just standard procedure, Lionel." I snapped my briefcase shut. "Let me work on this and see what I can come up with. I'll try to get you bail. I'll talk to Mr. Franklin and his attorney on the off chance I can get them to drop the charges."

It was certainly a long shot, but I wanted to give poor Lionel something to cling to.

I set up a meeting in the "boardroom" of the dumpy offices Aaron and I shared. I doubted I could impress Delano Franklin, but maybe I could convince him it wasn't worth the trouble to press charges. Lionel Hendergast had almost no money, and when I learned who Franklin had hired for his own counsel to go after civil damages, I knew that money—or at least showmanship—would be a primary factor in this case.

If you look in the dictionary next to the definition of the word "shyster," you'll find a picture of Kosimo Arkulian. He was overweight, with thinning steel-gray hair in a greasy comb-over that fooled nobody. He wore too many rings, too many gold chains, and a too-large gold watch, and he spoke too loudly. You've seen Arkulian on television with his boisterous ads, flashing his jewelry and his smile, treating everyone with a hangnail of a complaint as the next big millionaire in the lawsuit sweepstakes.

When Arkulian sat down beside his client, I could tell it was going to be a testosterone war between those two men. Both were accustomed to being in charge.

I gave my most pleasant smile. "Can I offer you coffee or a soda?"

"No, thank you," Franklin said.

"This isn't a social call," Arkulian answered in a brusque tone.

"There's always time for good manners." I looked at the clock on the wall. It was 1:00. "How about Scotch, then?" I had to get Franklin to take something. "Or a bourbon? I have a very good bourbon, Booker's." From my research, I knew Franklin was quite fond of both.

"If your bourbon's expensive, I'll have one of those," he said.

Arkulian shot him a glance. "I wouldn't advise it—"

"I'm not going to get sloshed," Franklin said. "Besides, I see a genuine irony in soaking this guy for a good expensive drink."

Arkulian grinned. "Then I'll have one, too."

I had been careful to wash everything in our kitchenette before the meeting started. I quickly poured three glasses of fine bourbon, neat, and handed one to Franklin and one to Arkulian. The third I placed in front of me in a comradely gesture, though I barely sipped from it. I had a feeling I'd need to keep my wits sharp.

Franklin looked like a distinguished late-middle-aged business-man gone bad. If groomed well, he could have fit comfortably into any high-society function, but he had let himself grow a beer gut. His clothes were garish, something he no doubt thought younger women found attractive. The ladies probably laughed at him until they found out how much money he had, then they played along but still laughed at him behind his back.

I tried my best gambit, pumping up the sob story, practic-ing how it would sound before a jury, although it was unlikely this case would ever go to trial. The law was too uncertain, the convolutions and intangibilities of time paradox too difficult for the average person to grasp.

"None of this has any bearing on what your client tried to do to my client," Arkulian said. "Sure, the poor kid had a troubled life. His mother had an affair with my client some twenty-six years ago, which led to the breakup of his parents' marriage. Boo-hoo. As if that story doesn't reflect half of the American public."

Maybe your half, I thought, but kept a tight smile on my face.

"Mr. Hendergast attempted to murder my client. It's as simple as—"

Impatient with letting his lawyer do all the talking, Franklin interrupted. "Wait a minute. This is far worse than just attempted murder." As if he needed the fortification of liquid courage to face what had almost happened, Franklin grabbed his tumbler of bourbon, and took a long drink. He set the glass down, and I could see the smear his lips had made on the edge. "If Lionel Hendergast had gunned me down in the parking lot of one of my car dealerships, he might have killed me, yes, but my legacy would have been left behind—my car dealerships, my friends…"

"Your ex-wives," I pointed out.

"Some of them remember me fondly." He didn't even blush.

Arkulian picked up the story. "You see, what Mr. Hendergast was attempting to do would have erased my client entirely from existence. He would have obliterated the man named Delano R. Franklin from the universe, leaving no memory of him. Nothing he ever accomplished in this life would have remained. Complete annihilation. An unspeakably heinous crime! And if Mr. Hendergast had succeeded, it would have been the perfect crime, too. No one would ever have known what he did, since there would have been no evidence, no body, no victim."

I had heard my share of "perfect crime" stories, and I had to admit, this ranked right up there with the best. I didn't offer them another drink. "What exactly is it you want from my client?"

"I want him to go to jail," Franklin said. "I want him to be locked up so that I don't have to worry every morning that he's going to sneak back on another time travel expedition and try again to erase my existence."

Arkulian smiled and folded his fingers. I couldn't imagine how he could fit them together with all those rings on his knuckles. "I'm guessing the publicity on this case will give a remarkable boost to my business—and don't expect me to believe you haven't thought of the same thing, Mr. Paramus."

He was right, of course. I shrugged. "Publicity is free, after all, and TV ads are a bit out of my price range." Ambulance-chasing seemed to be paying off quite well for Arkulian. I couldn't resist taking a small jab at him. "How much *do* ten of those rings cost?"

Miffed, Arkulian stood up. "If there's nothing else, Paramus? We'll see you in court."

I let the two men show themselves out, staying behind in the boardroom. When they were gone, I took a clean handkerchief, carefully lifted the near-empty bourbon glass Franklin had used, and made sure there were sufficient saliva traces on the rim. This was all I'd need.

Predictably, a media frenzy surrounded the case. Arkulian held a large press conference in which he grandstanded, accusing me of leaking the story in order to get publicity. Within an hour I had a press conference of my own, accusing him of the same. Both of us received plenty of coverage, and neither of us ever admitted to making a few discreet phone calls and tipping reporters off.

Lionel put his complete trust in me, which always sparks that uncomfortable paternal feeling. But I hadn't been kidding when I told him the law is still murky in these sorts of cases. Nobody had any idea which way it would go, and even my "ace in the hole" was a long shot. I still hadn't got the lab results back.

For the preliminary hearing, we were assigned an ancient female judge, the Honorable Bernadette Maddox. I was uneasy about her age. In my experience, elderly judges don't deal well with the second- and third-order implications of rapidly changing technologies. I'd rather have had the youngest, most computer-savvy person on the bench.

I still held out some hope that Bernadette Maddox was a sweet old lady, and the sob-story aspect would work on her. Not a chance.

"Mr. Arkulian!" she roared from the bench in a battle-axe voice before he had even finished his pompous remark. "You will sit down, shut up, and let me run this show." I looked over at my rival with a twinge of sympathy. So much for the nice old lady bit. "And you will remove that disgusting cheap jewelry in my courtroom unless you have an appointment with Time Travel Expeditions to go back to the days of disco."

"Your Honor, my personal appearance has no bearing on—"

"You will remove the jewelry because it hurts my eyes. I can't even see your client through the glare from all those rings."

Cowed, Arkulian left the room. A nervous Lionel sat at the bench next to me, whispering, "Was that a good sign?"

"It wasn't so much a sign—more like a demonstration. The judge is only showing him who's boss. And let me warn you ahead of time, she's going to feel she needs to even the score and scold me as well at some point. Expect it and try not to get too upset."

"What are we going to do, Mr. Paramus?" He sounded so miserable. I felt sorry for this kid who had lost his parents, his Norman Rockwell childhood, and a lifetime of happiness, all because of Delano R. Franklin.

I had dug into Franklin's background, perhaps even more than Lionel had. There was no question in my mind that the world would be a better place if Franklin had never been born. He had left a decades-long trail of ex-wives and shady business dealings behind him. His primary legacy was a handful of auto dealerships, but since he had no heirs and couldn't keep employees around long enough to put them in positions of authority and responsibility, no one would take over the car lots upon his death, and they'd probably be liquidated. Even without Lionel's time travel help, Franklin would vanish.

Since we were the defendants, we sat back and listened as a now-unadorned Arkulian outlined the civil part of the case, explaining time travel paradoxes in painstaking detail, using examples culled not from any law library but from classic science fiction stories. He was long-winded and explained too much to the judge, treating her as if she were incapable of grasping the classic grandfather paradox.

I kept checking my watch as I mentally rehearsed my opening statement. The courier should have been here by now. I would have preferred hard facts to fast-talking, but I could proceed either way. As Arkulian rambled on and on, even Franklin looked bored.

Finally, it was my turn. I hoped the judge would stall just to give me a few more minutes, but she puckered her wrinkled lips and leaned over like a hawk from the bench. "Now then, Mr. Paramus, let's hear what you have to say. I trust you can be more succinct—or at least more interesting—than Mr. Arkulian."

I stood up and cleared my throat. Still no sign of my delivery person, and I really wanted to know which direction to go. Either my ace in the hole was a high trump or a discard. With a sigh, I reached into my briefcase and pulled out a carefully prepared document. "Your Honor, I wish I did not have to do this, but would it be possible to request a brief continuance? I have not yet received an important piece of evidence that has a strong bearing on this case."

Lionel looked over at me, surprised. "What evidence?"

"A continuance?" the judge said with a snort. "I've been sitting here all morning, Mr. Paramus! You could have said this at the very beginning. How long are you asking for?" I was about to get my scolding, and Judge Maddox was clearly primed to let loose with even more venom than she had inflicted on Arkulian.

Suddenly the large doors were flung open at the back of the courtroom. The bailiff tried to stop a man from entering, but my partner Aaron Greenblatt sidestepped him. He marched in, waving a document in his left hand. "Excuse me, your Honor. Please pardon the interruption."

I stifled a laugh. It was a real Perry Mason moment. I suspected Aaron had always wanted to do that.

My partner's face was stoic; I hated the way he covered his emotions. He could have at least grinned or frowned to give me an inkling of what he held in his hands.

Judge Maddox lifted her gavel, looking more inclined to hit Aaron in the head with it than to rap her bench.

I blurted, "Your Honor, I withdraw my request for a continuance—so long as my associate can hand me that paper." I turned, not waiting for her answer as Aaron handed the lab results to me. He finally broke into a grin as I scanned the numbers and the comparison charts.

With a huge sigh of relief, I turned back to the bench. "Your Honor, in light of recent developments I request that the attempted murder charges against my client be dropped."

Arkulian growled, "What are you playing at, Paramus?"

"I'll ask the questions here, Mr. Arkulian," the judge said, rapping her gavel for good measure. "Well then—what *are* you playing at, Mr. Paramus?"

Bernadette Maddox already knew the sordid Peyton Place story of the ruined marriage, the broken family, the miserable life Lionel Hendergast had lived because of Franklin's actions.

"Your Honor, the prosecution's client was not entirely forthcoming about how long his affair with my client's mother lasted. If I might recap: when Lionel Hendergast was four years old, his father discovered Mr. Franklin and my client's mother *in flagrante delicto*, which triggered the chain of events leading to the crime of which my client is accused."

"And?" Judge Maddox said, drawing out the word.

"In fact, the affair had gone on for at least five years previous." I fluttered the sheet of lab data. "I have here the results of DNA tests comparing the blood sample my client gave to the county jail with samples I obtained from Mr. Franklin."

I smiled sweetly at them. Franklin appeared confused. Arkulian was outraged, realizing I had probably tested the saliva left behind on his drinking glass—an old trick.

"These results prove conclusively that the father of Lionel Hendergast is not the man he always believed, but rather Mr. Delano R. Franklin."

Lionel's eyes fairly popped out of their sockets. The judge sat up, suddenly much more interested. Both Arkulian and Franklin bellowed angrily as if in competition with each other until finally Arkulian stood up in a huff, reacting in the way he had seen too many lawyers react on TV shows. "I object! This has no bearing—"

"This has total bearing," I said.

Lionel looked as if he might faint, slide off the chair, and land on the courtroom floor. I put a steadying hand on his shoulder. He looked over at the prosecutor's table, and his two words came out in a squeak. "My father?"

I forged ahead. "The prosecution has interpreted this crime entirely wrong, your Honor. My client is accused of going back in time with the intent of preventing Mr. Franklin from ever being born. But if he had done that, then Lionel Hendergast would've erased *himself* from existence as well. He would have wiped out his own father, thereby ensuring that he himself could never be born."

I smiled. The judge seemed to be considering my line of reasoning. After all, Arkulian had prepped her in excruciating detail about grandfather paradoxes and the like.

"Therefore, instead of attempted murder, my client is guilty, at best, of attempted *suicide*—for which I recommend he be remanded for therapy and treatment, not incarceration."

"This is preposterous!" Arkulian yelled. "Even if Mr. Hendergast *had* accidentally erased himself, his original intention was to do the same to my client. His own death would merely have been incidental to his stated objective. The primary target of his malicious actions was still Delano Franklin."

With a sigh of infinite patience, I looked witheringly at Arkulian, then turned back to the judge. "Again, my esteemed colleague is mistaken."

The judge was actually listening now, fascinated by the implications. I had mapped out the strategy until it made my own head spin.

"My client is accused of *attempted* murder. However, based on these lab results, such an action would be temporally impossible." I waited a beat. "If Mr. Hendergast had actually succeeded in what the prosecution alleges was his intent, then he himself would never have been born. In which case, he could never have gone back in time to prevent Mr. Franklin's parents from meeting. How can my client be charged with attempting a crime that is fundamentally impossible to commit?"

"This is outrageous! Why not debate how many angels can dance on a pinhead?" Arkulian said.

I shrugged in the prosecutor's direction. "It's a standard time-travel paradox, your Honor. As Mr. Arkulian explained to the court so exhaustively."

Lionel was still staring in wonder over at the prosecutor's table. "Daddy?"

The judge rapped her gavel loudly. "I'm announcing a recess for at least two hours—so I can take some aspirin and give it time to work."

When the judge finally dismissed all charges against Lionel, I was relatively sure Arkulian wouldn't take it to appeal. The hardest part was explaining the convoluted matter to journalists afterward, so they could report it accurately; in the end, it proved too intricate for most of the wire services.

Aaron and I celebrated by going out for a fine dinner. We compared notes on cases, and he got me up to speed on his time-travel dinosaur-hunting lawsuit. I came back to the office late at night by myself—after all, that's where I kept the best bourbon—and saw the light blinking on the answering machine. Multiple messages. Four more cases waiting, none of them simple. Some actually sounded like they would be fun. Certainly precedent-setting.

Oddly, after the fallout, Lionel actually reconciled with his biological father. Months later, when I drove past one of Franklin's car dealerships, I saw a crew replacing the big sign with a new one: FRANKLIN & SON.

Funny how things turn out. Sometimes people just need a second chance, even when they aren't looking for it.

∾

Kevin J. Anderson has published more than 140 books, 56 of which have been national or international bestsellers. He has written numerous novels in the Star Wars, X-Files, and Dune universes, as well as unique steampunk fantasy novels *Clockwork Angels* and *Clockwork Lives*, written with legendary rock drummer Neil Peart, based on the concept album by the band Rush. His original works include the Saga of Seven Suns series, the Terra Incognita fantasy trilogy, the Saga of Shadows trilogy, and his humorous horror series featuring Dan Shamble, Zombie PI. He has edited numerous anthologies, written comics and games, and the lyrics to two rock CDs. Anderson and his wife Rebecca Moesta are the publishers of WordFire Press.

THE JIGSAW MAN

LARRY NIVEN

In this scary yarn from early in Niven's justly celebrated "Known Space" series, the well-known disease of bureaucratic creep (no pun intended) is eviscerated. For a real-world example of said creep (still, no pun intended, honest), your editor is old enough to have seen hectoring "public service" ads advising drivers and passengers to "buckle up," with even the Batman TV *show getting into the act, then laws were passed, and you can't drive a car legally without a seat belt, and you're breaking the law if you don't buckle up. But Big Brother knows best, and it's all for your own good. (Or, as a prominent crusader for social justice once put it, "Anything not mandatory is forbidden!") And when "for your own good" becomes "for the good of society," things can really get grim.*

❧

IN A.D. 1900, KARL LANDSTEINER CLASSIFIED HUMAN BLOOD INTO four types: A, B, AB, and O, according to incompatibilities. For the first time it became possible to give a shock patient a transfusion with some hope that it wouldn't kill him.

The movement to abolish the death penalty was barely getting started, and already it was doomed.

Vh83uOAGn7 was his telephone number and his driving license number and his social security number and the number of his draft card and his medical record. Two of these had been revoked, and the others had ceased to matter, except for his medical record. His name was Warren Lewis Knowles. He was going to die.

The trial was a day away, but the verdict was no less certain for that. Lew was guilty. If anyone had doubted it, the persecution had ironclad proof. By eighteen tomorrow Lew would be condemned to death. Broxton would appeal the case on some grounds or other. The appeal would be denied.

His cell was comfortable, small, and padded. This was no slur on the prisoner's sanity, though insanity was no longer an excuse for breaking the law. Three of the walls were mere bars. The fourth wall, the outside wall, was cement painted a restful shade of green. But the bars which separated him from the corridor, and from the morose old man on his left, and from the big, moronic-looking teenager on his right—the bars were four inches thick and eight inches apart, padded in silicone plastic. For the fourth time that day Lew took a clenched fistful of the plastic and tried to rip it away. It felt like a sponge rubber pillow, with a rigid core the thickness of a pencil, and it wouldn't rip. When he let it go it snapped back to a perfect cylinder.

"It's not fair," he said.

The teenager didn't move. For all of the ten hours Lew had been in his cell, the kid had been sitting on the edge of his bunk with his lank black hair falling in his eyes and his five o'clock shadow getting gradually darker. He moved his long, hairy arms only at mealtimes, and the rest of him not at all.

The old man looked up at the sound of Lew's voice. He spoke with bitter sarcasm. "You framed?"

"No, I—"

"At least you're honest. What'd you do?"

Lew told him. He couldn't keep the hurt innocence out of his voice. The old man smiled derisively, nodding as if he'd expected just that.

"Stupidity. Stupidity's always been a capital crime. If you *had* to get yourself executed, why not for something important? See the kid on the other side of you?"

"Sure," Lew said without looking.

"He's an organlegger."

Lew felt the shock freezing in his face. He braced himself for another look into the next cell—and every nerve in his body jumped. The kid was looking at him. With his dull dark eyes barely visible under his mop of hair, he regarded Lew as a butcher might consider a badly aged side of beef.

Lew edged closer to the bars between his cell and the old man's. His voice was a hoarse whisper. "How many did he kill?"

"None."

"?"

"He was the snatch man. He'd find someone out alone at night, drug the prospect and take him home to the doc that ran the ring. It was the doc that did all the killing. If Bernie'd brought home a dead prospect, the doc would have skinned *him* down."

The old man sat with Lew almost directly behind him. He had twisted himself around to talk to Lew, but now he seemed to be losing interest. His hands, hidden from Lew by his bony back, were in constant motion.

"How many did he snatch?"

"Four. Then he got caught. He's not very bright, Bernie."

"What did you do to get put here?"

The old man didn't answer. He ignored Lew completely, his shoulders twitching as he moved his hands. Lew shrugged and dropped back on his bunk.

It was nineteen o'clock of a Thursday night.

The ring had included three snatch men. Bernie had not yet been tried. Another was dead; he had escaped over the edge of a pedwalk when he felt the mercy bullet enter his arm. The third was being wheeled into the hospital next door to the courthouse.

Officially he was still alive. He had been sentenced; his appeal had been denied; but he was still alive as they moved him drugged into the operating room.

The interns lifted him from the table and inserted a mouthpiece so he could breathe when they dropped him into freezing liquid. They lowered him without a splash, and as his body temperature went down they dribbled something else into his veins. About half a pint of it. His temperature dropped toward freezing, his heartbeats were further and further apart. Finally his heart stopped. But it could have been started again. Men had been reprieved at this point. Officially the organlegger was still alive.

The doctor was a line of machines with a conveyor belt running through them. When the organlegger's body temperature reached a certain point, the belt started. The first machine made a series of incisions in his chest. Skillfully and mechanically, the doctor performed a cardiectomy.

The organlegger was officially dead. His heart went into storage immediately. His skin followed, most of it in one piece, all of it still living. The doctor took him apart with exquisite care, like disassembling a flexible, fragile, tremendously complex jigsaw puzzle. The brain was flashburned and the ashes saved for urn burial; but all the rest of the body, in slabs and small blobs and parchment-thin layers and lengths of tubing, went into storage in the hospital's organ banks. Any one of these units could be packed in a travel case at a moment's notice and flown to anywhere in the world in not much more than an hour. If the odds broke right, if the right people came down with the right diseases at the right time, the organlegger might save more lives than he had taken.

Which was the whole point.

Lying on his back, staring up at the ceiling television set, Lew suddenly began to shiver. He had not had the energy to put the sound plug in his ear, and the silent motion of the cartoon figures had suddenly become horrid. He turned the set off, and that didn't help either.

Bit by bit they would take him apart and store him away. He'd never seen an organ storage bank, but his uncle had owned a butcher shop...

"Hey!" he yelled.

The kid's eyes came up, the only living part of him. The old man twisted round to look over his shoulder. At the end of the hall the guard looked up once, then went back to reading.

The fear was in Lew's belly; it pounded in his throat. "How can you stand it?"

The kid's eyes dropped to the floor. The old man said, "Stand what?"

"Don't you know what they're going to *do* to us?"

"Not to me. They won't take me apart like a hog."

Instantly Lew was at the bars. "Why not?"

The old man's voice had become very low "Because there's a bomb where my right thighbone used to be. I'm gonna blow myself up. What they find, they'll never use."

The hope the old man had raised washed away, leaving bitterness. "Nuts. How could you put a bomb in your leg?"

"Take the bone out, bore a hole in it, build the bomb in the hole, get all the organic material out of the bone so it won't rot, put the bone back in. 'Course your red corpuscle count goes down afterward. What I wanted to ask you. You want to join me?"

"Join you?"

"Hunch up against the bars. This thing'll take care of both of us."

Lew found himself backing away. "No. No, thanks."

"Your choice," said the old man. "I never told you what I was here for, did I? I was the doc. Bernie made his snatches for me."

Lew had backed up against the opposite set of bars. He felt them touch his shoulders and turned to find the kid looking dully into his eyes from two feet away. Organleggers! He was surrounded by professional killers!

"I know what it's like," the old man continued. "They won't do that to me. Well. If you're sure you don't want a clean death, go lie down behind your bunk. It's thick enough."

The bunk was a mattress and a set of springs mounted into a cement block which was an integral part of the cement floor. Lew curled himself into fetal position with his hands over his eyes.

He was sure he didn't want to die *now*.

Nothing happened.

After a while he opened his eyes, took his hands away and looked around.

The kid was looking at him. For the first time there was a sour grin plastered on his face. In the corridor the guard, who was always in a chair by the exit, was standing outside the bars looking down at him. He seemed concerned.

Lew felt the flush rising in his neck and nose and ears. The old man had been playing with him. He moved to get up...

And a hammer came down on the world.

The guard lay broken against the bars of the cell across the corridor. The lank-haired youngster was picking himself up from behind his bunk, shaking his head. Somebody groaned; and the groan rose to a scream. The air was full of cement dust.

Lew got up.

Blood lay like red oil on every surface that faced the explosion.

Try as he might, and he didn't try very hard, Lew could find no other trace of the old man.

Except for the hole in the wall.

He must have been standing...right...there.

The hole would be big enough to crawl through, if Lew could reach it. But it was in the old man's cell. The silicone plastic sheathing on the bars between the cells had been ripped away, leaving only pencil-thick lengths of metal.

Lew tried to squeeze through.

The bars were humming, vibrating, though there was no sound. As Lew noticed the vibration he also found that he was becoming sleepy. He jammed his body between the bars, caught in a war between his rising panic and the sonic stunners which must have gone on automatically.

The bars wouldn't give. But his body did; and the bars were slippery with...He was through. He poked his head through the hole in the wall and looked down.

Way down. Far enough to make him dizzy.

The Topeka County courthouse was a small skyscraper, and Lew's cell must have been near the top. He looked down a smooth concrete slab studded with windows set flush with the sides. There would be no way to reach those windows, no way to open them, no way to break them.

The stunner was sapping his will. He would have been unconscious by now if his head had been in the cell with the rest of him. He had to force himself to turn and look up.

He was *at* the top. The edge of the roof was only a few feet above his eyes. He couldn't reach that far, not without...

He began to crawl out of the hole.

Win or lose, they wouldn't get him for the organ banks. The vehicular traffic level would smash every useful part of him. He sat on the lip of the hole, with his legs straight out inside the cell for balance, pushing his chest flat against the wall. When he had his balance he stretched his arms toward the roof. No good.

So he got one leg under him, keeping the other stiffly out, and *lunged*.

His hands closed over the edge as he started to fall back. He yelped with surprise, but it was too late. The top of the courthouse was moving! It had dragged him out of the hole before he could let go. He hung on, swinging slowly back and forth over empty space as the motion carried him away.

The top of the courthouse was a pedwalk.

He couldn't climb up, not without purchase for his feet. He didn't have the strength. The pedwalk was moving toward another building, about the same height. He could reach it if he only hung on.

And the windows in that building were different. They weren't made to open, not in these days of smog and air conditioning, but there were ledges. Perhaps the glass would break.

Perhaps it wouldn't.

The pull on his arms was agony. It would be so easy to let go... No. He had committed no crime worth dying for. He refused to die.

Over the decades of the twentieth century the movement continued to gain momentum. Loosely organized, international in scope, its members had only one goal: to replace execution with imprisonment and rehabilitation in every state and nation they could reach. They argued that killing a man for his crime teaches him nothing; that it serves as no deterrent to others who might commit the same crime; that death is irreversible, whereas an innocent man might be released from prison once his innocence is belatedly proven. Killing a man serves no good purpose, they said, unless for society's vengeance. Vengeance, they said, is unworthy of an enlightened society.

Perhaps they were right.

In 1940 Karl Landsteiner and Alexander S. Wiener made public their report on the Rh factor in human blood.

By mid-century most convicted killers were getting life imprisonment or less. Many were later returned to society, some "rehabilitated," others not. The death penalty had been passed for kidnaping in some states, but it was hard to persuade a jury to enforce it. Similarly with murder charges. A man wanted for burglary in Canada and murder in California fought extradition to Canada; he had less chance of being convicted in California. Many states had abolished the death penalty. France had none.

Rehabilitation of criminals was a major goal of the science/art of psychology.

But—

Blood banks were world wide.

Already men and women with kidney diseases had been saved by a kidney transplanted from an identical twin. Not all kidney victims had identical twins. A doctor in Paris used transplants from close relatives, classifying up to a hundred points of incompatibility to judge in advance how successful the transplant would be.

Eye transplants were common. An eye donor could wait until he died before he saved another man's sight.

Human bone could *always* be transplanted, provided the bone was first cleaned of organic matter.

So matters stood at midcentury.

By 1990 it was possible to store any living human organ for any reasonable length of time. Transplants had become routine, helped along by the "scalpel of infinite thinness," the laser. The dying regularly willed their remains to the organ banks. The mortuary lobbies couldn't stop it. But such gifts from the dead were not always useful.

In 1993 Vermont passed the first of the organ bank laws. Vermont had always had the death penalty. Now a condemned man could know that this death would save lives. It was no longer true that an execution served no good purpose. Not in Vermont.

Nor, later, in California. Or Washington. Georgia. Pakistan, England, Switzerland, France, Rhodesia . . .

The pedwalk was moving at ten miles per hour. Below, unnoticed by pedestrians who had quit work late and night owls who were just beginning their rounds, Lewis Knowles hung from the moving strip and watched the ledge go by beneath his dangling feet. The ledge was no more than two feet wide, a good four feet beneath his stretching toes.

He dropped.

As his feet struck he caught the edge of a window casement. Momentum jerked at him, but he didn't fall. After a long moment he breathed again.

He couldn't know what building this was, but it was not deserted. At twenty-one hundred at night, all the windows were ablaze. He tried to stay back out of the light as he peered in.

This window was an office. Empty.

He'd need something to wrap around his hand to break that window. But all he was wearing was a pair of shoesocks and a prison jumper. Well, he couldn't be more conspicuous than he was now. He took off the jumper, wrapped part of it around his hand, and struck.

He almost broke his hand.

Well . . . they'd let him keep his jewelry, his wristwatch and diamond ring. He drew a circle on the glass with the ring, pushing down hard, and struck again with the other hand. It *had* to be glass; if it was plastic he was doomed. The glass popped out in a near-perfect circle.

He had to do it six times before the hole was big enough for him.

He smiled as he stepped inside, still holding his jumper. Now all he needed was an elevator. The cops would have picked him up in an instant if they'd caught him on the street in a prison jumper, but if he hid the jumper here he'd be safe. Who would suspect a licensed nudist?

Except that he didn't have license. Or a nudist's shoulder pouch to put it in.

Or a shave.

That was very bad. Never had there been a nudist as hairy as this. Not just a five o'clock shadow, but a full beard all over, so to speak. Where could he get a razor?

He tried the desk drawers. Many businessmen kept spare razors. He stopped when he was halfway through. Not because he'd found a razor, but because he now knew where he was. The papers on his desk made it all too obvious.

A hospital.

He was still clutching the jumper. He dropped it in the wastebasket, covered it tidily with papers, and more or less collapsed into the chair behind the desk.

A hospital. He *would* pick a hospital. And *this* hospital, the one which had been built right next to the Topeka County courthouse, for good and sufficient reason.

But he hadn't picked it, not really. Had he ever in his life made a decision except on the prompting of others? No. Friends had borrowed his money for keeps, men had stolen his girls, he had avoided promotion by his knack for being ignored. Shirley had bullied him into marrying her, then left him four years later for a friend who wouldn't be bullied.

Even now, at the possible end of his life, it was the same. An aging body snatcher had given him his escape. An engineer had built the cell bars wide enough apart to let a small man squeeze between them. Another had put a pedwalk along two convenient roofs. And here he was.

The worst of it was that here he had no chance of masquerading as a nudist. Hospital gowns and masks would be the minimum. Even nudists had to wear clothing sometime.

The closet?

There was nothing in the closet but a spiffy green hat and a perfectly transparent rain poncho.

He could run for it. If he could find a razor he'd be safe once he reached the street. He bit at a knuckle, wishing he knew where the elevator was. Have to trust to luck. He began searching the drawers again.

He had his hand on a black leather razor case when the door opened. A beefy man in a hospital gown breezed in. The intern (there were no human doctors in hospitals) was halfway to the desk before he noticed Lew crouching over an open drawer. He stopped walking. His mouth fell open.

Lew closed it with the fist which still gripped the razor case. The man's teeth came together with a sharp click. His knees were buckling as Lew brushed past him and out the door.

The elevator was just down the hall, with the doors standing open. And nobody coming. Lew stepped in and punched O. He shaved as the elevator dropped. The razor cut fast and close, if a trifle noisily. He was working on his chest as the door opened.

A skinny technician stood directly in front of him, her mouth and eyes set in the utterly blank expression of those who wait for elevators. She brushed past him with a muttered apology, hardly noticing him. Lew stepped out fast. The doors were closing before he realized that he was on the wrong floor.

That damned tech! She'd stopped the elevator before it reached bottom.

He turned and stabbed the Down button. Then what he'd seen in that one cursory glance came back to him, and his head whipped around for another look.

The whole vast room was filled with glass tanks, ceiling height, arranged in a labyrinth like the bookcases in a library. In the tanks was a display more lewd than anything in Belsen. Why, those things had been *men!* and *women!* No, he wouldn't look. He refused to look at anything but the elevator door. *What was taking that elevator so long?*

He heard a siren.

The hard tile floor began to vibrate against his bare feet. He felt a numbness in his muscles, a lethargy in his soul.

The elevator arrived . . . too late. He blocked the doors open with a chair. Most buildings didn't have stairs; only alternate elevators. They'd have to use the alternate elevator to reach him now. Well where was it? . . . He wouldn't have time to find it. He was beginning to feel really sleepy. They must have several sonic projectors focused on this one room. Where one beam passed the interns would feel mildly relaxed, a little clumsy. But where the beams intersected, *here,* there would be unconsciousness. But not yet.

He had something to do first.

By the time they broke in they'd have something to kill him for.

The tanks were faced in plastic, not glass: a very special kind of plastic. To avoid provoking defense reactions in all the myriads of body parts which might be stored touching it, the plastic had to have unique characteristics. No engineer could have been expected to make it shatterproof too!

It shattered very satisfactorily.

Later, Lew wondered how he managed to stay up as long as he did. The soothing hypersonic murmur of the stun beams kept pulling at him, pulling him down to a floor which seemed softer every moment. The chair he wielded became heavier and heavier. But as long as he could lift it, he smashed. He was knee deep in nutritive storage fluid, and there were dying things brushing against his ankles with every move; but his work was barely a third done when the silent siren song became too much for him.

He fell.

And after all that they never even mentioned the smashed organ banks!

Sitting in the courtroom, listening to the drone of courtroom ritual, Lew sought Mr. Broxton's ear to ask the question. Mr. Broxton smiled at him. "Why should they want to bring that up? They think they've got enough on you as it is. If you beat *this* rap, then they'll persecute you for wanton destruction of valuable medical sources. But they're sure you won't."

"And you?"

"I'm afraid they're right. But we'll try. Now, Hennessey's about to read the charges. Can you manage to look hurt and indignant?"

"Sure."

"Good."

The persecution read the charges, his voice sounding like the voice of doom coming from under a thin blond mustache. Warren Lewis Knowles looked hurt and indignant. But he no longer felt that way. He had done something worth dying for.

The cause of it all was the organ banks. With good doctors and a sufficient flow of material in the organ banks, any taxpayer could hope to live indefinitely. What voter would vote against eternal life? The death penalty was his immortality, and he would vote the death penalty for any crime at all.

Lewis Knowles had struck back.

"The state will prove that the said Warren Lewis Knowles did, in the space of two years, willfully drive through a total of six red traffic lights. During that same period the same Warren Knowles exceeded local speed limits no less than ten times, once by as much as fifteen miles per hour. His record has never been good. We will produce records of his arrest in 2082 on a charge of drunk driving, a charge of which he was acquitted only through—"

"Objection!"

"*Sustained. If he was acquitted, Counselor, the Court must assume him not guilty.*"

❧

Larry Niven is renowned for his ingenious science fiction stories solidly based on authentic science, often of the cutting-edge variety. His Known Space series is one of the most popular "future history" sagas in sf and includes the epic novel *Ringworld*, one of the few novels to have won both the Hugo and Nebula awards, as well as the Locus and Ditmar awards, and which is recognized as a milestone in modern science fiction. Four of his shorter works have also won Hugos. Most recently, the Science Fiction and Fantasy Writers of America have presented him with the Damon

Knight Memorial Grand Master Award, given for lifetime achievement in the field. Lest this all sounds too serious, it should be remembered that one of his most memorable short works is "Man of Steel, Woman of Kleenex," a not-quite serious essay on Superman and the problems of his having a sex life. Niven has also demonstrated a talent for creating memorable aliens, beginning with his first novel, *World of Ptaavs*, in 1966. A reason for this, Niven writes, is that, "I grew up with dogs. I live with a cat, and borrow dogs to hike with. I have passing acquaintance with raccoons and ferrets. Associating with nonhumans has certainly gained me insight into alien intelligences."

SKULKING PERMIT

ROBERT SHECKLEY

The colony on the planet of a distant star had been isolated from Earth's influence for a long time. Still, things had seemed to be going nicely. Then, contact with the homeworld was going to be renewed, and they decided they needed a government, officials, laws, municipal buildings and all that. Oddly, they didn't decide that they needed a lawyer, but they did now have a card-carrying certified criminal. Almost as good...

TOM FISHER HAD NO IDEA HE WAS ABOUT TO BEGIN A CRIMINAL career. It was morning. The big red sun was just above the horizon, trailing its small yellow companion. The village, tiny and precise, a unique white dot on the planet's green expanse, glistened under its two midsummer suns.

Tom was just waking up inside his cottage. He was a tall, tanned young man, with his father's oval eyes and his mother's easygoing attitude toward exertion. He was in no hurry; there could be no fishing until the fall rains, and therefore no real work for a fisher. Until fall, he was going to loaf and mend his fishing poles.

"It's supposed to have a red roof!" he heard Billy Painter shouting outside.

"Churches never have red roofs!" Ed Weaver shouted back.

Tom frowned. Not being involved, he had forgotten the changes that had come over the village in the last two weeks. He slipped on a pair of pants and sauntered out to the village square.

The first thing he saw when he entered the square was a large new sign, reading: NO ALIENS ALLOWED WITHIN CITY LIMITS. There were no aliens on the entire planet of New Delaware. There was nothing but forest, and this one village. The sign was purely a statement of policy.

The square itself contained a church, a jail and a post office, all constructed in the last two frantic weeks and set in a neat row facing the market. No one knew what to do with these buildings; the village had gone along nicely without them for over two hundred years. But now, of course, they had to be built.

Ed Weaver was standing in front of the new church, squinting upward. Billy Painter was balanced precariously on the church's steep roof, his blond mustache bristling indignantly. A small crowd had gathered.

"Damn it, man," Billy Painter was saying, "I tell you I was reading about it just last week. White roof, okay. Red roof, never."

"You're mixing it up with something else," Weaver said. "How about it, Tom?"

Tom shrugged, having no opinion to offer. Just then, the mayor bustled up, perspiring freely, his shirt flapping over his large paunch.

"Come down," he called to Billy. "I just looked it up. It's the Little Red Schoolhouse, not Churchhouse."

Billy looked angry. He had always been moody; all Painters were. But since the mayor made him chief of police last week, he had become downright temperamental.

"We don't have no little schoolhouse," Billy argued, halfway down the ladder.

"We'll just have to build one," the mayor said. "We'll have to hurry, too." He glanced at the sky. Involuntarily the crowd glanced upward. But there was still nothing in sight.

"Where are the Carpenter boys?" the mayor asked. "Sid, Sam, Marv—where are you?"

Sid Carpenter's head appeared through the crowd. He was still on crutches from last month when he had fallen out of a tree looking for threstle's eggs; no Carpenter was worth a damn at tree-climbing.

"The other boys are at Ed Beer's Tavern," Sid said. "Where else would they be?" Mary Waterman called from the crowd.

"Well, you gather them up," the mayor said. "They gotta build up a little schoolhouse, and quick. Tell them to put it up beside the jail." He turned to Billy Painter, who was back on the ground. "Billy, you paint that schoolhouse a good bright red, inside and out. It's very important."

"When do I get a police chief badge?" Billy demanded. "I read that police chiefs always get badges."

"Make yourself one," the mayor said. He mopped his face with his shirttail. "Sure hot. Don't know why that inspector couldn't have come in winter. Tom! Tom Fisher! Got an important job for you. Come on, I'll tell you all about it."

He put an arm around Tom's shoulders and they walked to the mayor's cottage past the empty market, along the village's single paved road. In the old days, that road had been of packed dirt. But the old days had ended two weeks ago and now the road was paved with crushed rock. It made barefoot walking so uncomfortable that the villagers simply cut across each other's lawns. The mayor, though, walked on it out of principle.

"Now look, Mayor, I'm on my vacation—"

"Can't have any vacations now," the mayor said. "Not now, He's due any day." He ushered Tom inside his cottage and sat down in the big armchair, which had been pushed as close to the interstellar radio as possible.

"Tom," the mayor said directly, "how would you like to be a criminal?"

"I don't know," said Tom. "What's a criminal?"

Squirming uncomfortably in his chair, the mayor rested a hand on the radio for authority. "It's this way," he said, and began to explain.

Tom listened, but the more he heard, the less he liked. It was all the fault of that interstellar radio, he decided. Why hadn't it really been broken?

No one had believed it could work. It had gathered dust in the office of one mayor after another, for generations, the last silent link with Mother Earth. Two hundred years ago Earth talked with New Delaware, and with Ford IV, Alpha Centauri, Nueva Espana, and the other colonies that made up the United Democracies of Earth. Then all conversations stopped.

There seemed to be a war on Earth. New Delaware, with its one village, was too small and too distant to take part. They waited for news, but no news came. And then plague struck the village, wiping out three-quarters of the inhabitants.

Slowly the village healed. The villagers adopted their own ways of doing things. They forgot Earth.

Two hundred years passed.

And then, two weeks ago, the ancient radio had coughed itself into life. For hours, it growled and spat static, while the inhabitants of the village gathered around the mayor's cottage.

Finally words came out: "... hear me, New Delaware? Do you hear me?"

"Yes, yes, we hear you," the mayor said.

"The colony is still there?"

"It certainly is," the mayor said proudly. The voice became stern and official. "There has been no contact with the Outer Colonies for some time, due to unsettled conditions here. But that's over, except for a little mopping up. You of New Delaware are still a colony of Imperial Earth and subject to her laws. Do you acknowledge the status?"

The mayor hesitated. All the books referred to Earth as the United Democracies. Well, in two centuries, names could change.

"We are still loyal to Earth," the mayor said with dignity.

"Excellent. That saves us the trouble of sending an expeditionary force. A resident inspector will be dispatched to you from the nearest point, to ascertain whether you conform to the customs, institutions and traditions of Earth."

"What?" the mayor asked, worried.

The stern voice became higher-pitched. "You realize, of course, that there is room for only one intelligent species in the Universe— Man! All others must be suppressed, wiped out, annihilated. We can tolerate no aliens sneaking around us. I'm sure you understand, General."

"I'm not a general. I'm a mayor."

"You're in charge, aren't you?"

"Yes, but—"

"Then you are a general. Permit me to continue. In this galaxy, there is no room for aliens. None! Nor is there room for deviant human cultures, which, by definition, are alien. It is impossible to administer an empire when everyone does as he pleases. There must be order, no matter what the cost." The mayor gulped hard and stared at the radio. "Be sure you're running an Earth colony, General, with no radical departures from the norm, such as free will, free love, free elections, or anything else on the proscribed list. Those things are alien, and we're pretty rough on aliens. Get your colony in order, General. The inspector will call in about two weeks. That is all."

The village held an immediate meeting, to determine how best to conform with the Earth mandate. All they could do was hastily model themselves upon the Earth pattern as shown in their ancient books.

"I don't see why there has to be a criminal," Tom said.

"That's a very important part of Earth society," the mayor explained. "All the books agree on it. The criminal is as important as the postman, say, or the police chief. Unlike them, the criminal is engaged in anti-social work. He works against society, Tom. If you don't have people working against society, how can you have people working for it? There'd be no jobs for them to do."

Tom shook his head. "I just don't see it."

"Be reasonable, Tom. We have to have earthly things. Like paved roads. All the books mention that. And churches, and schoolhouses, and jails. And all the books mention crime."

"I won't do it," Tom said.

"Put yourself in my position," the mayor begged. "This inspector comes and meets Billy Painter, our police chief. He asks to see the jail. Then he says, 'No prisoners?' I answer, 'Of course not. We don't have any crime here.' 'No crime?' he says. 'But Earth colonies always have crime. You know that.' 'We don't,' I answer. 'Didn't even know what it was until we looked up the word last week.' 'Then why did you build a jail?' he asks me. 'Why did you appoint a police chief?'"

The mayor paused for breath. "You see? The whole thing falls through. He sees at once that we're not truly earthlike. We're faking it. We're aliens!"

"Hmm," Tom said, impressed in spite of himself.

"This way," the mayor went on quickly, "I can say, 'Certainly we've got crime here, just like on Earth. We've got a combination thief and murderer. Poor fellow had a bad upbringing and he's maladjusted. Our police chief has some clues, though. We expect an arrest within twenty-four hours. We'll lock him in the jail, then rehabilitate him.'"

"What's rehabilitate?" Tom asked.

"I'm not sure. I'll worry about that when I come to it. But now do you see how necessary crime is?"

"I suppose so. But why me?"

"Can't spare anyone else. And you've got narrow eyes. Criminals always have narrow eyes."

"They aren't that narrow. They're no narrower than Ed Weaver's—"

"Tom, please," the mayor said. "We're all doing our part. You want to help, don't you?"

"I suppose so," Tom repeated wearily.

"Fine. You're our criminal. Here, this makes it legal." He handed Tom a document. It read:

SKULKING PERMIT.

Know all Men by these Presents that Tom Fisher

is a Duly Authorized Thief and Murderer.

He is hereby required to Skulk in Dismal Alleys,

Haunt Places of Low Repute, and Break the Law.

Tom read it through twice, then asked, "What law?"

"I'll let you know as fast as I make them up," the mayor said. "All Earth colonies have laws."

"But what do I do?"

"You steal. And kill. That should be easy enough." The mayor walked to his bookcase and took down ancient volumes entitled *The Criminal and his Environment*, *Psychology of the Slayer*, and *Studies in Thief Motivation*.

"These'll give you everything you need to know. Steal as much as you like. One murder should be enough, though. No sense overdoing it."

"Right," Tom nodded. "I guess I'll catch on." He picked up the books and returned to his cottage. It was very hot and all the talk about crime had puzzled and wearied him. He lay down on his bed and began to go through the ancient books.

There was a knock on his door. "Come in," Tom called, rubbing his tired eyes. Marv Carpenter, oldest and tallest of the red-headed Carpenter boys, came in, followed by old Jed Farmer. They were carrying a small sack.

"You the town criminal, Tom?" Marv asked.

"Looks like it."

"Then this is for you." They put the sack on the floor and

took from it a hatchet, two knives, a short spear, a club and a blackjack.

"What's all that?" Tom asked, sitting upright.

"Weapons, of course," Jed Farmer said testily. "You can't be a real criminal without weapons."

Tom scratched his head. "Is that a fact?"

"You'd better start figuring these things out for yourself," Farmer went on in his impatient voice. "Can't expect us to do everything for you."

Marv Carpenter winked at Tom. "Jed's sore because the mayor made him our postman."

"I'll do my part," Jed said. "I just don't like having to write all those letters."

"Can't be too hard," Marv Carpenter said, grinning. "The postmen do it on Earth and they got a lot more people there. Good luck, Tom."

They left.

Tom bent down and examined the weapons. He knew what they were; the old books were full of them. But no one had ever actually used a weapon on New Delaware. The only native animals on the planet were small, furry, and confirmed eaters of grass. As for turning a weapon on a fellow villager—why would anybody want to do that?

He picked up one of the knives. It was cold. He touched the point. It was sharp.

Tom began to pace the floor, staring at the weapons. They gave him a queer sinking feeling in the pit of his stomach. He decided he had been hasty in accepting the job.

But there was no sense worrying about it yet. He still had those books to read. After that, perhaps he could make some sense out of the whole thing.

He read for several hours, stopping only to eat a light lunch. The books were understandable enough; the various criminal methods were clearly explained, sometimes with diagrams. But the whole thing was unreasonable. What was the purpose of crime? Whom did it benefit? What did people get out of it?

The books didn't explain that. He leafed through them, looking at the photographed faces of criminals. They looked very serious and dedicated, extremely conscious of the significance of their work to society.

Tom wished he could find out what that significance was. It would probably make things much easier.

"Tom?" he heard the mayor call from outside.

"I'm in here, Mayor," Tom said.

The door opened and the mayor peered in. Behind him were Jane Farmer, Mary Waterman and Alice Cook. "How about it, Tom?" the mayor asked.

"How about what?"

"How about getting to work?"

Tom grinned self-consciously. "I was going to," he said. "I was reading these books, trying to figure out—"

The three middle-aged ladies glared at him, and Tom stopped in embarrassment.

"You're taking your time reading," Alice Cook said.

"Everyone else is outside working," said Jane Farmer.

"What's so hard about stealing?" Mary Waterman challenged.

"It's true," the mayor told him. "That inspector might be here any day now and we don't have a crime to show him."

"All right, all right," Tom said.

He stuck a knife and a blackjack in his belt, put the sack in his pocket—for loot—and stalked out.

But where was he going? It was mid-afternoon. The market, which was the most logical place to rob, would be empty until evening. Besides, he didn't want to commit a robbery in daylight. It seemed unprofessional.

He opened his skulking permit and read it through. Required to Haunt Places of Low Repute.

That was it! He'd haunt a low-repute place. He could form some plans there, get into the mood of the thing. But unfortunately, the village didn't have much to choose from. There was the Tiny Restaurant, run by the widowed Ames sisters, there was Jeff Hern's Lounging Spot, and finally there was Ed Beer's Tavern.

Ed's place would have to do.

The tavern was a cottage much like the other cottages in the village. It had one big room for guests, a kitchen, and family sleeping quarters. Ed's wife did the cooking and kept the place as clean as she could, considering her ailing back. Ed served the drinks. He was a pale, sleepy-eyed man with a talent for worrying.

"Hello, Tom," Ed said. "Hear you're our criminal."

"That's right," said Tom. "I'll take a perricola."

Ed Beer served him the nonalcoholic root extract and stood anxiously in front of Tom's table. "How come you ain't out thieving, Tom?"

"I'm planning," Tom said. "My permit says I have to haunt places of low repute. That's why I'm here."

"Is that nice?" Ed Beer asked sadly. "This is no place of low repute, Tom."

"You serve the worst meals in town," Tom pointed out.

"I know. My wife can't cook. But there's a friendly atmosphere here. Folks like it."

"That's all changed, Ed. I'm making this tavern my headquarters."

Ed Beer's shoulders drooped. "Try to keep a nice place," he muttered. "A lot of thanks you get." He returned to the bar.

Tom proceeded to think. He found it amazingly difficult. The more he tried, the less came out. But he stuck grimly to it.

An hour passed. Richie Farmer, Jed's youngest son, stuck his head in the door. "You steal anything yet, Tom?"

"Not yet," Tom told him, hunched over his table, still thinking.

The scorching afternoon drifted slowly by. Patches of evening became visible through the tavern's small, not too clean windows. A cricket began to chirp outside, and the first whisper of night wind stirred the surrounding forest.

Big George Waterman and Max Weaver came in for a glass of glava. They sat down beside Tom.

"How's it going?" George Waterman asked.

"Not so good," Tom said. "Can't seem to get the hang of this stealing."

"You'll catch on," Waterman said in his slow, ponderous, earnest fashion. "If anyone could learn it, you can."

"We've got confidence in you, Tom," Weaver assured him.

Tom thanked them. They drank and left. He continued thinking, staring into his empty perricola glass.

An hour later, Ed Beer cleared his throat apologetically. "It's none of my business, Tom, but when are you going to steal something?"

"Right now," Tom said.

He stood up, made sure his weapons were securely in place, and strode out the door.

Nightly bartering had begun in the market. Goods were piled carelessly on benches, or spread over the grass on straw mats.

There was no currency, no rate of exchange. Ten hand-wrought nails were worth a pail of milk or two fish, or vice versa, depending on what you had to barter and needed at the moment. No one ever bothered keeping accounts. That was one Earth custom the mayor was having difficulty introducing.

As Tom Fisher walked down the square, everyone greeted him.

"Stealing now, huh, Tom?"

"Go to it, boy!"

"You can do it!"

No one in the village had ever witnessed an actual theft. They considered it an exotic custom of distant Earth and they wanted to see how it worked. They left their goods and followed Tom through the market, watching avidly.

Tom found that his hands were trembling. He didn't like having so many people watch him steal. He decided he'd better work fast, while he still had the nerve.

He stopped abruptly in front of Mrs. Miller's fruit-laden bench. "Tasty-looking geefers," he said casually.

"They're fresh," Mrs. Miller told him. She was a small and bright-eyed old woman. Tom could remember long conversations she had had with his mother, back when his parents were alive.

"They look very tasty," he said, wishing he had stopped somewhere else instead.

"Oh, they are," said Mrs. Miller. "I picked them just this afternoon."

"Is he going to steal now?" someone whispered.

"Sure he is. Watch him," someone whispered back.

Tom picked up a bright green geefer and inspected it. The crowd became suddenly silent.

"Certainly looks very tasty," Tom said, carefully replacing the geefer.

The crowd released a long-drawn sigh.

Max Weaver and his wife and five children were at the next bench. Tonight they were displaying two blankets and a shirt. They all smiled shyly when Tom came over, followed by the crowd.

"That shirt's about your size," Weaver informed him. He wished the people would go away and let Tom work.

"Hmm," Tom said, picking up the shirt.

The crowd stirred expectantly. A girl began to giggle hysterically. Tom gripped the shirt tightly and opened his loot bag.

"Just a moment!" Billy Painter pushed his way through. He was wearing a badge now, an old Earth coin he had polished and pinned to his belt. The expression on his face was unmistakably official.

"What were you doing with that shirt, Tom?" Billy asked.

"Why...I was just looking at it."

"Just looking at it, huh?" Billy turned away, his hands clasped behind his back. Suddenly he whirled and extended a rigid forefinger. "I don't think you were just looking at it, Tom. I think you were planning on stealing it!"

Tom didn't answer. The tell-tale sack hung limply from one hand, the shirt from the other.

"As police chief," Billy went on, "I've got a duty to protect these people. You're a suspicious character. I think I'd better lock you up for further questioning."

Tom hung his head. He hadn't expected this, but it was just as well.

Once he was in jail, it would be all over. And when Billy released him, he could get back to fishing.

Suddenly the mayor bounded through the crowd, his shirt flapping wildly around his waist.

"Billy, what are you doing?"

"Doing my duty, Mayor. Tom here is acting plenty suspicious. The book says—"

"I know what the book says," the mayor told him. "I gave you the book. You can't go arresting Tom. Not yet."

"But there's no other criminal in the village," Billy complained.

"I can't help that," the mayor said.

Billy's lips tightened. "The book talks about preventive police work. I'm supposed to stop crime before it happens."

The mayor raised his hands and dropped them wearily. "Billy, don't you understand? This village needs a criminal record. You have to help, too."

Billy shrugged his shoulders. "All right, Mayor. I was just trying to do my job." He turned to go. Then he whirled again on Tom. "I'll still get you. Remember—Crime Does Not Pay." He stalked off.

"He's overambitious, Tom," the mayor explained. "Forget it. Go ahead and steal something. Let's get this job over with."

Tom started to edge away toward the green forest outside the village.

"What's wrong, Tom?" the mayor asked worriedly.

"I'm not in the mood anymore," Tom said. "Maybe tomorrow night—"

"No, right now," the mayor insisted. "You can't go on putting it off. Come on, we'll all help you."

"Sure we will," Max Weaver said. "Steal the shirt, Tom. It's your size anyhow."

"How about a nice water jug, Tom?"

"Look at these skeegee nuts over here."

Tom looked from bench to bench. As he reached for Weaver's shirt, a knife slipped from his belt and dropped to the ground. The crowd clucked sympathetically.

Tom replaced it, perspiring, knowing he looked like a butterfingers. He reached out, took the shirt and stuffed it into the loot bag. The crowd cheered.

Tom smiled faintly, feeling a bit better. "I think I'm getting the hang of it."

"Sure you are."

"We knew you could do it."

"Take something else, boy."

Tom walked down the market and helped himself to a length of rope, a handful of skeegee nuts and a grass hat.

"I guess that's enough," he told the mayor.

"Enough for now," the mayor agreed. "This doesn't really count, you know. This was the same as people giving it to you. Practice, you might say."

"Oh," Tom said, disappointed.

"But you know what you're doing. The next time it'll be just as easy."

"I suppose it will."

"And don't forget that murder."

"Is it really necessary?" Tom asked.

"I wish it weren't," the mayor said. "But this colony has been here for over two hundred years and we haven't had a single murder. Not one! According to the records, all the other colonies had lots."

"I suppose we should have one," Tom admitted. "I'll take care of it." He headed for his cottage. The crowd gave a rousing cheer as he departed.

At home, Tom lighted a rush lamp and fixed himself supper.

After eating, he sat for a long time in his big armchair. He was dissatisfied with himself. He had not really handled the stealing well. All day he had worried and hesitated. People had practically had to put things in his hands before he could take them.

A fine thief he was!

And there was no excuse for it. Stealing and murdering were like any other necessary jobs. Just because he had never done them before, just because he could see no sense to them, that was no reason to bungle them.

He walked to the door. It was a fine night, illuminated by a dozen nearby giant stars. The market was deserted again and the village lights were winking out.

This was the time to steal!

A thrill ran through him at the thought. He was proud of himself. That was how criminals planned and this was how stealing should be—skulking, late at night.

Quickly Tom checked his weapons, emptied his loot sack and walked out.

The last rush lights were extinguished. Tom moved noiselessly through the village. He came to Roger Waterman's house. Big Roger had left his spade propped against a wall. Tom picked it up. Down the block, Mrs. Weaver's water jug was in its usual place beside the front door. Tom took it. On his way home, he found a little wooden horse that some child had forgotten. It went with the rest.

He was pleasantly exhilarated, once the goods were safely home. He decided to make another haul.

This time he returned with a bronze plaque from the mayor's house, Marv Carpenter's best saw, and Jed Farmer's sickle.

"Not bad," he told himself. He was catching on. One more load would constitute a good night's work.

This time he found a hammer and chisel in Ron Stone's shed, and a reed basket at Alice Cook's house. He was about to take Jeff Hern's rake when he heard a faint noise. He flattened himself against a wall.

Billy Painter came prowling quietly along, his badge gleaming in the starlight. In one hand, he carried a short, heavy club; in the other, a pair of homemade handcuffs. In the dim light, his face was ominous. It was the face of a man who had pledged himself against crime, even though he wasn't really sure what it was.

Tom held his breath as Billy Painter passed within ten feet of him. Slowly Tom backed away.

The loot sack jingled.

"Who's there?" Billy yelled. When no one answered, he turned a slow circle, peering into the shadows. Tom was flattened against a wall again. He was fairly sure Billy wouldn't see him. Billy had weak eyes because of the fumes of the paint he mixed. All painters had weak eyes. It was one of the reasons they were moody.

"Is that you, Tom?" Billy asked, in a friendly tone. Tom was about to answer, when he noticed that Billy's club was raised in a striking position. He kept quiet.

"I'll get you yet!" Billy shouted.

"Well, get him in the morning!" Jeff Hern shouted from his bedroom window. "Some of us are trying to sleep."

Billy moved away. When he was gone, Tom hurried home and dumped his pile of loot on the floor with the rest. He surveyed his haul proudly. It gave him the sense of a job well done.

After a cool drink of glava, Tom went to bed, falling at once into a peaceful, dreamless sleep.

Next morning, Tom sauntered out to see how the little red schoolhouse was progressing. The Carpenter boys were hard at work on it, helped by several villagers.

"How's it coming?" Tom called out cheerfully.

"Fair," Marv Carpenter said. "It'd come along better if I had my saw."

"Your saw?" Tom repeated blankly.

After a moment, he remembered that he had stolen it last night. It hadn't seemed to belong to anyone then. The saw and all the rest had been objects to be stolen. He had never given a thought to the fact that they might be used or needed.

Marv Carpenter asked, "Do you suppose I could use the saw for a while? Just for an hour or so?"

"I'm not sure," Tom said, frowning. "It's legally stolen, you know."

"Of course it is. But if I could just borrow it—"

"You'd have to give it back."

"Well, naturally I'd give it back," Marv said indignantly. "I wouldn't keep anything that was legally stolen."

"It's in the house with the rest of the loot."

Marv thanked him and hurried after it.

Tom began to stroll through the village. He reached the mayor's house. The mayor was standing outside, staring at the sky.

"Tom, did you take my bronze plaque?" he asked.

"I certainly did," Tom said belligerently.

"Oh. Just wondering." The mayor pointed upward. "See it?"

Tom looked. "What?"

"Black dot near the rim of the small sun."

"Yes. What is it?"

"I'll bet it's the inspector's ship. How's your work coming?"

"Fine," Tom said, a trifle uncomfortably.

"Got your murder planned?"

"I've been having a little trouble with that," Tom confessed. "To tell the truth, I haven't made any progress on it at all."

"Come on in, Tom. I want to talk to you."

Inside the cool, shuttered living room, the mayor poured two glasses of glava and motioned Tom to a chair.

"Our time is running short," the mayor said gloomily. "The inspector may land any hour now. And my hands are full." He motioned at the interstellar radio. "That has been talking again. Something about a revolt on Deng IV and all loyal Earth colonies are to prepare for conscription, whatever that is. I never even heard of Deng IV, but I have to start worrying about it, in addition to everything else."

He fixed Tom with a stern stare. "Criminals on Earth commit dozens of murders a day and never even think about it. All your village wants of you is one little killing. Is that too much to ask?"

Tom spread his hands nervously. "Do you really think it's necessary?"

"You know it is," the mayor said. "If we're going earthly, we have to go all the way. This is the only thing holding us back. All the other projects are right on schedule."

Billy Painter entered, wearing a new official-blue shirt with bright metal buttons. He sank into a chair.

"Kill anyone yet, Tom?"

The mayor said, "He wants to know if it's necessary."

"Of course it is," the police chief said. "Read any of the books. You're not much of a criminal if you don't commit a murder."

"Who'll it be, Tom?" the mayor asked.

Tom squirmed uncomfortably in his chair. He rubbed his fingers together nervously.

"Well?"

"Oh, I'll kill Jeff Hern," Tom blurted.

Billy Painter leaned forward quickly. "Why?" he asked.

"Why? Why not?"

"What's your motive?"

"I thought you just wanted a murder," Tom retorted. "Who said anything about motive?"

"We can't have a fake murder," the police chief explained. "It has to be done right. And that means you have to have a proper motive."

Tom thought for a moment. "Well, I don't know Jeff well. Is that a good enough motive?"

The mayor shook his head. "No, Tom, that won't do. Better pick someone else."

"Let's see," Tom said. "How about George Waterman?"

"What's the motive?" Billy asked immediately.

"Oh. Um. Well, I don't like the way George walks. Never did. And he's noisy sometimes."

The mayor nodded approvingly. "Sounds good to me. What do you say, Billy?"

"How am I supposed to deduce a motive like that?" Billy asked angrily. "No, that might be good enough for a crime of passion. But you're a legal criminal, Tom. By definition, you're cold-blooded, ruthless and cunning. You can't kill someone just because you don't like the way he walks. That's silly."

"I'd better think this whole thing over," Tom said, standing up.

"Don't take too long," the mayor told him. "The sooner it's done, the better."

Tom nodded and started out the door.

"Oh, Tom!" Billy called. "Don't forget to leave clues. They're very important."

"All right," Tom said, and left.

Outside, most of the villagers were watching the sky. The black dot had grown immensely larger. It covered most of the smaller sun.

Tom went to his place of low repute to think things out. Ed Beer had apparently changed his mind about the desirability of criminal elements. The tavern was redecorated. There was a large sign, reading: CRIMINAL'S LAIR. Inside, there were new, carefully soiled curtains on the windows, blocking the daylight and making the tavern truly a Dismal Retreat. Weapons, hastily carved out of soft wood, hung on one wall. On another wall was a large red splotch, an ominous-looking thing, even though Tom knew it was only Billy Painter's rootberry red paint.

"Come right in, Tom," Ed Beer said, and led him to the darkest corner in the room. Tom noticed that the tavern was unusually filled for the time of day. People seemed to like the idea of being in a genuine criminal's lair.

Tom sipped a perricola and began to think.

He had to commit a murder.

He took out his skulking permit and looked it over. Unpleasant, unpalatable, something he wouldn't normally do, but he did have the legal obligation.

Tom drank his perricola and concentrated on murder. He told himself he was going to kill someone. He had to snuff out a life. He would make someone cease to exist.

But the phrases didn't contain the essence of the act. They were just words. To clarify his thoughts, he took big, redheaded Marv Carpenter as an example. Today, Marv was working on the schoolhouse with his borrowed saw. If Tom killed Marv—well, Marv wouldn't work anymore.

Tom shook his head impatiently. He still wasn't grasping it.

All right, here was Marv Carpenter, biggest and, many thought, the pleasantest of the Carpenter boys. He'd be planing down a piece of wood, grasping the plane firmly in his large freckled hands, squinting down the line he had drawn. Thirsty, undoubtedly, and with a small pain in his left shoulder that Jan Druggist was unsuccessfully treating.

That was Marv Carpenter.

Then—

Marv Carpenter sprawled on the ground, his eyes glaring open, limbs stiff, mouth twisted, no air going in or out his nostrils, no beat to his heart. Never again to hold a piece of wood in his large, freckled hands. Never again to feel the small and really unimportant pain in his shoulder that Jan Druggist was—

For just a moment, Tom glimpsed what murder really was. The vision passed, but enough of a memory remained to make him feel sick.

He could live with the thieving. But not murder, even in the best interests of the village.

What would people think, after they saw what he had just imagined? How could he live with them? How could he live with himself afterward?

And yet he had to kill. Everybody in the village had a job and that was his.

But whom could he murder?

The excitement started later in the day when the interstellar radio was filled with angry voices.

"Call that a colony? Where's the capital?"

"This is it," the mayor replied.

"Where's your landing field?"

"I think it's being used as a pasture," the mayor said. "I could look up where it was. No ship has landed here in over—"

"The main ship will stay aloft then. Assemble your officials. I am coming down immediately."

The entire village gathered around an open field that the inspector designated. Tom strapped on his weapons and skulked behind a tree, watching.

A small ship detached itself from the big one and dropped swiftly down. It plummeted toward the field while the villagers held their breaths, certain it would crash. At the last moment, jets flared, scorching the grass, and the ship settled gently to the ground.

The mayor edged forward, followed by Billy Painter. A door in the ship opened, and four men marched out. They held shining metallic instruments that Tom knew were weapons. After them came a large, red-faced man dressed in black, wearing four bright medals. He was followed by a little man with a wrinkled face, also dressed in black. Four more uniformed men followed him.

"Welcome to New Delaware," the mayor said.

"Thank you, General," the big man said, shaking the mayor's hand firmly. "I am Inspector Delumaine. This is Mr. Grent, my political adviser."

Grent nodded to the mayor, ignoring his outstretched hand. He was looking at the villagers with an expression of mild disgust.

"We will survey the village," the inspector said, glancing at Grent out of the corner of his eye. Grent nodded. The uniformed guards closed around them.

Tom followed at a safe distance, skulking in true criminal

fashion. In the village, he hid behind a house to watch the inspection.

The mayor pointed out, with pardonable pride, the jail, the post office, the church and the little red schoolhouse. The inspector seemed bewildered. Mr. Grent smiled unpleasantly and rubbed his jaw.

"As I thought," he told the inspector. "A waste of time, fuel and a battle cruiser. This place has nothing of value."

"I'm not so sure," the inspector said. He turned to the mayor. "But what did you build them for, General?"

"Why, to be earthly," the mayor said. "We're doing our best, as you can see."

Mr. Grent whispered something in the inspector's ear.

"Tell me," the inspector asked the mayor, "how many young men are there in the village?"

"I beg your pardon?" the mayor said in polite bewilderment.

"Young men between the ages of fifteen and sixty," Mr. Grent explained.

"You see, General, Imperial Mother Earth is engaged in a war. The colonists on Deng IV and some other colonies have turned against their birthright. They are revolting against the absolute authority of Mother Earth."

"I'm sorry to hear that," the mayor said sympathetically.

"We need men for the space fleet," the inspector told him. "Good healthy fighting men. Our reserves are depleted—"

"We wish," Mr. Grent broke in smoothly, "to give all loyal Earth colonists a chance to fight for Imperial Mother Earth. We are sure you won't refuse."

"Oh, no," the mayor said. "Certainly not. I'm sure our young men will be glad—I mean they don't know much about it, but they're all bright boys. They can learn, I guess."

"You see?" the inspector said to Mr. Grent. "Sixty, seventy, perhaps a hundred recruits. Not such a waste after all."

Mr. Grent still looked dubious.

The inspector and his adviser went to the mayor's house for refreshment. Four soldiers accompanied them. The other four walked around the village, helping themselves to anything they found.

Tom hid in the woods nearby to think things over. In the early evening, Mrs. Ed Beer came furtively out of the village. She was a gaunt, grayish-blond middle-aged woman, but she moved quite rapidly in spite of her case of housemaid's knee. She had a basket with her, covered with a red checkered napkin.

"Here's your dinner," she said, as soon as she found Tom.

"Why, thanks," said Tom, taken by surprise, "You didn't have to do that."

"I certainly did. Our tavern is your place of low repute, isn't it? We're responsible for your well-being. And the mayor sent you a message."

Tom looked up, his mouth full of food. "What is it?"

"He said to hurry up with the murder. He's been stalling the inspector and that nasty little Grent man. But they're going to ask him. He's sure of it."

Tom nodded.

"When are you going to do it?" Mrs. Beer asked, cocking her head to one side.

"I mustn't tell you," Tom said.

"Of course you must. I'm a criminal's accomplice," Mrs. Beer leaned closer.

"That's true," Tom admitted thoughtfully. "Well, I'm going to do it tonight. After dark. Tell Billy Painter I'll leave all the fingerprints I can, and any other clues I think of."

"All right, Tom," Mrs. Beer said. "Good luck."

Tom waited for dark, meanwhile watching the village. He noticed that most of the soldiers had been drinking. They swaggered around as though the villagers didn't exist. One of them fired his weapon into the air, frightening all the small, furry grass-eaters for miles around.

The inspector and Mr. Grent were still in the mayor's house.

Night came. Tom slipped into the village and stationed himself in an alley between two houses. He drew his knife and waited.

Someone was approaching! He tried to remember his criminal methods, but nothing came. He knew he would just have to do the murder as best he could, and fast.

The person came up, his figure indistinct in the darkness.

"Why, hello, Tom." It was the mayor. He looked at the knife. "What are you doing?"

"You said there had to be a murder, so—"

"I didn't mean me," the mayor said, backing away. "It can't be me."

"Why not?" Tom asked.

"Well, for one thing, somebody has to talk to the inspector. He's waiting for me. Someone has to show him—"

"Billy Painter can do that," said Tom. He grasped the mayor by the shirt front, raised the knife and aimed for the throat. "Nothing personal, of course," he added.

"Wait!" the mayor cried. "If there's nothing personal, then you have no motive!"

Tom lowered the knife, but kept his grasp on the mayor's shirt. "I guess I can think of one. I've been pretty sore about you appointing me criminal."

"It was the mayor who appointed you, wasn't it?"

"Well, sure—"

The mayor pulled Tom out of the shadows, into the bright starlight. "Look!"

Tom gaped. The mayor was dressed in long, sharply creased pants and a tunic resplendent with medals. On each shoulder was a double row of ten stars. His hat was thickly crusted with gold braid in the shape of comets.

"You see, Tom? I'm not the mayor anymore. I'm a general!"

"What's that got to do with it? You're the same person, aren't you?"

"Not officially. You missed the ceremony this afternoon. The inspector said that since I was officially a general, I had to wear a general's uniform. It was a very friendly ceremony. All the Earthmen were grinning and winking at me and each other."

Raising the knife again, Tom held it as he would to gut a fish. "Congratulations," he said sincerely, "but you were the mayor when you appointed me criminal, so my motive still holds."

"But you wouldn't be killing the mayor! You'd be killing a general! And that's not murder!"

"It isn't?" Tom asked. "What is it then?"

"Why, killing a general is mutiny!"

"Oh." Tom put down the knife. He released the mayor. "Sorry."

"Quite all right," the mayor said. "Natural error. I've read up on it and you haven't, of course—no need to." He took a deep breath. "I'd better get back. The inspector wants a list of the men he can draft."

Tom called out, "Are you sure this murder is necessary?"

"Yes, absolutely," the mayor said, hurrying away. "Just not me."

Tom put the knife back in his belt.

Not me, not me. Everyone would feel that way. Yet somebody had to be murdered. Who? He couldn't kill himself. That would be suicide, which wouldn't count.

He began to shiver, trying not to think of the glimpse he'd had of the reality of murder. The job had to be done.

Someone else was coming!

The person came nearer. Tom hunched down, his muscles tightening for the leap.

It was Mrs. Miller, returning home with a bag of vegetables.

Tom told himself that it didn't matter whether it was Mrs. Miller or anybody else. But he couldn't help remembering those conversations with his mother. They left him without a motive for killing Mrs. Miller.

She passed by without seeing him.

He waited for half an hour. Another person walked through the dark alley between the houses. Tom recognized him as Max Weaver.

Tom had always liked him. But that didn't mean there couldn't be a motive. All he could come up with, though, was that Max had a wife and five children who loved him and would miss him. Tom didn't want Billy Painter to tell him that that was no motive. He drew deeper into the shadow and let Max go safely by.

The three Carpenter boys came along. Tom had painfully been through that already. He let them pass. Then Roger Waterman approached.

He had no real motive for killing Roger, but he had never been especially friendly with him. Besides, Roger had no children and his wife wasn't fond of him. Would that be enough for Billy Painter to work on?

He knew it wouldn't be ... and the same was true of all the villagers. He had grown up with these people, shared food and work and fun and grief with them. How could he possibly have a motive for killing any of them?

But he had to commit a murder. His skulking permit required it. He couldn't let the village down. But neither could he kill the people he had known all his life.

Wait, he told himself in sudden excitement. He could kill the inspector!

Motive? Why, it would be an even more heinous crime than

murdering the mayor—except that the mayor was a general now, of course, and that would only be mutiny. But even if the mayor were still mayor, the inspector would be a far more important victim. Tom would be killing for glory, for fame, for notoriety. And the murder would show Earth how earthly the colony really was. They would say, "Crime is so bad on New Delaware that it's hardly safe to land there. A criminal actually killed our inspector on the very first day! Worst criminal we've come across in all space."

It would be the most spectacular crime he could commit, Tom realized, just the sort of thing a master criminal would do.

Feeling proud of himself for the first time in a long while, Tom hurried out of the alley and over to the mayor's house. He could hear conversation going on inside.

"... sufficiently passive population," Mr. Grent was saying, "Sheeplike, in fact."

"Makes it rather boring," the inspector answered. "For the soldiers especially."

"Well, what do you expect from backward agrarians? At least we're getting some recruits out of it." Mr. Grent yawned audibly. "On your feet, guards. We're going back to the ship."

Guards! Tom had forgotten about them. He looked doubtfully at his knife. Even if he sprang at the inspector, the guards would probably stop him before the murder could be committed. They must have been trained for just that sort of thing.

But if he had one of their own weapons...

He heard the shuffling of feet inside. Tom hurried back into the village.

Near the market, he saw a soldier sitting on a doorstep, singing drunkenly to himself. Two empty bottles lay at his feet and his weapon was slung sloppily over his shoulder.

Tom crept up, drew his blackjack and took aim.

The soldier must have glimpsed his shadow. He leaped to his feet, ducking the stroke of the blackjack. In the same motion, he jabbed with his slung rifle, catching Tom in the ribs, tore the rifle from his shoulder and aimed. Tom closed his eyes and lashed out with both feet.

He caught the soldier on the knee, knocking him over. Before he could get up, Tom swung the blackjack.

Tom felt the soldier's pulse—no sense killing the wrong

man—and found it satisfactory. He took the weapon, checked to make sure he knew which button to push, and hastened after the inspector.

Halfway to the ship, he caught up with them. The inspector and Grent were walking ahead, the soldiers straggling behind.

Tom moved into the underbrush. He trotted silently along until he was opposite Grent and the inspector. He took aim and his finger tightened on the trigger...

He didn't want to kill Grent, though. He was supposed to commit only one murder.

He ran on, past the inspector's party, and came out on the road in front of them. His weapon was poised as the party reached him.

"What's this?" the inspector demanded.

"Stand still," Tom said. "The rest of you drop your weapons and move out of the way."

The soldiers moved like men in shock. One by one they dropped their weapons and retreated to the underbrush. Grent held his ground.

"What are you doing, boy?" he asked.

"I'm the town criminal," Tom stated proudly. "I'm going to kill the inspector. Please move out of the way."

Grent stared at him. "Criminal? So that's what the mayor was prattling about."

"I know we haven't had any murder in two hundred years," Tom explained, "but I'm changing that right now. Move out of the way!"

Grent leaped out of the line of fire. The inspector stood alone, swaying slightly.

Tom took aim, trying to think about the spectacular nature of his crime and its social value. But he saw the inspector on the ground, eyes glaring open, limbs stiff, mouth twisted, no air going in or out the nostrils, no beat to the heart.

He tried to force his finger to close on the trigger. His mind could talk all it wished about the desirability of crime; his hand knew better.

"I can't!" Tom shouted.

He threw down the gun and sprinted into the underbrush.

The inspector wanted to send a search party out for Tom and hang him on the spot. Mr. Grent didn't agree. New Delaware was all forest. Ten thousand men couldn't have caught a fugitive in the forest, if he didn't want to be caught.

The mayor and several villagers came out, to find out about the commotion. The soldiers formed a hollow square around the inspector and Mr. Grent. They stood with weapons ready, their faces set and serious.

And the mayor explained everything. The village's uncivilized lack of crime. The job that Tom had been given. How ashamed they were that he had been unable to handle it.

"Why did you give the assignment to that particular man?" Mr. Grent asked.

"Well," the mayor said, "I figured if anyone could kill, Tom could. He's a fisher, you know. Pretty gory work."

"Then the rest of you would be equally unable to kill?"

"We wouldn't even get as far as Tom did," the mayor admitted sadly.

Mr. Grent and the inspector looked at each other, then at the soldiers. The soldiers were staring at the villagers with wonder and respect. They started to whisper among themselves.

"Attention!" the inspector bellowed. He turned to Grent and said in a low voice, "We'd better get away from here. Men in our armies who can't kill . . ."

"The morale," Mr. Grent said. He shuddered. "The possibility of infection. One man in a key position endangering a ship—perhaps a fleet—because he can't fire a weapon. It isn't worth the risk."

They ordered the soldiers back to the ship. The soldiers seemed to march more slowly than usual, and they looked back at the village. They whispered together, even though the inspector was bellowing orders.

The small ship took off in a flurry of jets. Soon it was swallowed in the large ship. And then the large ship was gone.

The edge of the enormous watery red sun was just above the horizon.

"You can come out now," the mayor called. Tom emerged from the underbrush, where he had been hiding, watching everything.

"I bungled it," he said miserably.

"Don't feel bad about it," Billy Painter told him. "It was an impossible job."

"I'm afraid it was," the mayor said, as they walked back to the village. "I thought that just possibly you could swing it. But you can't be blamed. There's not another man in the village who could have done the job even as well."

"What'll we do with these buildings?" Billy Painter asked, motioning at the jail, the post office, the church, and the little red schoolhouse.

The mayor thought deeply for a moment. "I know," he said. "We'll build a playground for the kids. Swings and slides and sandboxes and things."

"Another playground?" Tom asked.

"Sure. Why not?"

There was no reason, of course, why not.

"I won't be needing this anymore, I guess," Tom said, handing the skulking permit to the mayor.

"No, I guess not," said the mayor. They watched him sorrowfully as he tore it up. "Well, we did our best. It just wasn't good enough."

"I had the chance," Tom muttered, "and I let you all down."

Billy Painter put a comforting hand on his shoulder. "It's not your fault, Tom. It's not the fault of any of us. It's just what comes of not being civilized for two hundred years. Look how long it took Earth to get civilized. Thousands of years. And we were trying to do it in two weeks."

"Well, we'll just have to go back to being uncivilized," the mayor said with a hollow attempt at cheerfulness.

Tom yawned, waved, went home to catch up on lost sleep. Before entering, he glanced at the sky.

Thick, swollen clouds had gathered overhead and every one of them had a black lining. The fall rains were almost here. Soon he could start fishing again.

Now why couldn't he have thought of the inspector as a fish? He was too tired to examine that as a motive. In any case, it was too late. Earth was gone from them and civilization had fled for no one knew how many centuries more.

He slept very badly.

∽

Robert Sheckley (1928–2005) seemed to explode into print in the early 1950s with stories in nearly every science fiction magazine on the newsstands. Actually, the explosion was bigger than most realized, since he was simultaneously writing even more stories under a number of pseudonyms. His forte was humor, wild and unpredictable, often absurdist, much like the work of Douglas Adams three decades later. His work has been compared to the Marx Brothers by Harlan Ellison and to Voltaire by both Brian W. Aldiss and J.G. Ballard, and Neil Gaiman has called Sheckley "Probably the best short-story writer during the '50s to the mid-1960s working in any field."

CHECKSUM, CHECKMATE

Tony Daniel

It wasn't really a trial, since the accused (and obviously guilty) individual wasn't a human, wasn't even material, was a made thing which had no rights. But when a computer program, no matter how self-aware and intelligent, commits murder, something had to be done. And what about the other copies of the same program, in particular the one present at the inquisition?

❧

THE AIR IN THE THEATER INTAKE FACILITY WAS HUMMING WITH geists—ghostly virtual reality representations of people, A.I.s, and even a few of the *sceeve,* the horseshoe-bat-nosed aliens whose species had invaded the Earth thirteen years ago. Humanity was at war with the main body of sceeve, but a small faction, the Mutualists, had proved to be valuable allies and had given Earth a chance to fight back and avoid total domination.

Ensign NOCK made his way through the entrance foyer in his entirely physically present android body, his *suit,* as he called it. His current model was a Burberry Eleven. He'd been suited up in the Eleven for close to a year and it had performed in an excellent, if utilitarian, fashion. The suit NOCK really wanted was one of the new Burberry Twelves—who wouldn't?—but there was *no way* he was going to be able to afford an upgrade like that on an Extry ensign's pay.

All of the virtual inhabitants in the foyer seemed *overlaid,* one upon another, crowded in layers in such a way that no gathering in real life could ever achieve. Definite scaling problems going on here with the chroma representational software. They appeared as drapes of discrete layers of people, and the entrance foyer had taken on what NOCK imagined might be the décor of a harem den—although visiting a girlfriend in the strip club where she worked on Ceres base was as close as he'd ever come to observing such an establishment.

That had been an interesting liaison. It had been love, at least for his part. Josey had fallen for him precisely because he was an A.I. servant in an android body and not a physical man. Of course, he hadn't let that fact stop him when attempting to please her. Apparently he'd succeeded for, as Josey had once told him, "NOCK, I gotta say, you put the 't' in simulation."

Josey had been blown to smithereens by kinetic weapon barrage when a half-ton of sceeve throw mass had ripped into Ceres asteroid base and left a mile-wide crater.

It was a tough war.

NOCK moved forward and into the geist-filled room.

The Theater Intake Facility served as the main wing for the interrogation of alien prisoners on *Walt Whitman* space station, the enormous Extry facility in orbit around Earth. It was manned by a department of the Extry, the U.S. space navy. The rates and officers of the Extry Xenological Division were universally known as creeps.

NOCK was a creep. He was also no stranger to TIF. In fact, this was his operational billet and his Q-based algorithm, his real self, was backed up on the facility's computer. The processing desk where the entrance foyer terminated was manned by a human, Marine Corps Staff Sergeant Gordon Mallon. Mallon was not a friend—NOCK wasn't sure the humorless Mallon *had* any friends—but was a longstanding acquaintance of NOCK.

Mallon shook his head ruefully at the gathered crowd in the foyer, then reached out with a finger into the chroma to press a switch only he could see. The field that guarded entrance into the bowels of the TIF hummed slightly, indicating a change in the Q generator that would now permit NOCK to step past Mallon's desk and go through the hatchway that led to the warren of cells and interrogation rooms to be found within.

"Logged and Level B provisional admittance granted, Ensign NOCK," Mallon said in the official tone he used for entries in his desk register. "Have a better one, sir."

"You, too, Staff Sergeant."

Mallon only grunted in reply and NOCK, ensconced within his android body, entered the TIF proper.

There were a few geists in the hall leading to the interrogation, most of them NCOs accompanying human MILINT officers as aides and translators. NOCK recognized several iterations of the LOVE series, one of whom, CHARITY, was a friend. He poked her via the virtual feed, which, NOCK knew, felt like the equivalent of a small static electricity shock. CHARITY nodded, smiled sympathetically back at him.

You're on CHECKSUM in Alpha, huh? she replied across the corridor to NOCK using a private virtual feed. Her transmitted voice as actuated in his android's hearing mechanism sounded bright and a little brassy, as if she were deliberate trying to put good cheer into the undertones.

Yup, he replied.

I don't envy you.

What, you wouldn't like to have a traitor and murderer's thought rolling around inside your programming?

Better than a sceeve, Charity said to him. Then her lead interrogation officer found the room he was looking for and went inside.

Got to go, Charity said. *Got a sceeve lieutenant to squeeze.*

He suspended?

She. *Yep, but she's fighting it. My LIO thinks we'll only get a couple more sessions out of her before she liquefies.*

It had only become possible in the last year to prevent captured sceeve from immediately committing suicide by dissolving the portion of their nervous system known as the *gid*. For eight years after the invasion, not a single sceeve had been taken alive. But that had all changed with the coming of the Mutualists to Earth a year before. These were the strange new group of sceeve who claimed to be on humanity's side, and had proved it in the eyes of many by fighting against their own kind.

NOCK's attitude toward the Mutualists was the same as his attitude toward any news that seemed too good to be true: wait, watch and make no assumptions. Making faulty assumptions could get you wiped with no backup. He'd seen it happen to better servants than he.

Good luck with your IP, NOCK said.

You, too, good luck, CHARITY replied, and then her geist, and her algorithmic attention with it, passed into Collection and Exploitation Unit Foxtrot, following her LIO.

A few more paces down the hall and NOCK arrived at his destination, the entry hatch to C&E Unit Alpha, and stepped inside.

The Alpha C&E unit was packed. All the chairs on the floor were taken up by brass—and nothing small-time here. It looked like a shiny black clump of Extry captains, admirals and Marine colonels had collected like crystals in an asteroidal geode.

C&E Alpha was the big room, the special room. It was two floors high, and surrounding the upper tier in a semicircle was an observational galley. This too was filled with spectators leaning against the glass windows. Geists of servants and officers who'd managed to secure a pass hung in the air directly above the unit's center. There had never been an interrogation procedure quite like today's. NOCK, for his part, had tried to recuse himself and get out it. He'd believed he'd succeeded, too, but that Wake Call had brought word that his recusal had been rescinded. That, in itself, was curious, considering who the prisoner was to be interrogated.

On the other side of the room from NOCK was a raised dais with places for three senior MILINT commanders who would soon sit in judgment. They were not yet present.

Neither was the LIO in charge of interrogation. Neither was the prisoner's protocol rep.

The prisoner *was* already present.

He was designated as an EPW, an enemy prisoner of war, but wasn't really any such thing in a strict sense—hell, in any *logical* sense of the term—but he'd been designated at such for the purposes of the IP.

Nobody knows quite what to do with him, NOCK thought. And when a captive's legal rights were in limbo, that captive usually ended up in TIR.

On a small table in the center of the room sat one of the black cubes universally known among servants as a *cat box*.

Inside was the quantum foam that formed the substrate of the PW's consciousness.

The cat box was turned off at the moment.

This was the only copy. The PW had been erased—purged—from all other systems in existence. When the cat box was activated, a basic geist image, a projection of a human form, would appear sitting in a virtual chair next to the box.

This appearance was merely smoke and mirrors for the sake of the human interrogators. The real prisoner was in the cat box, or, more precisely, he was represented as stored values in the quantum foam therein.

The PW in this cat box went by the name of POINT.

He was NOCK's twin brother.

NOCK stepped through the crowd of brass and took his place at a small desk near the commander's dais. He would be closer to the lead interrogation officer than the prisoner and the prisoner's protocol rep, but from where he sat he had a direct view through his android's eyes of the space where POINT would soon appear in the chroma.

Best seat in the house, NOCK thought. Or worst, depending on how you looked at the matter.

A few moments passed, and then without any announcement into the Alpha unit came the MILINT Commanders Board of Inquiry, consisting of two Extry rear admirals—the *Extry* was the name of the United States space navy—and a Marine Corps colonel. The three crossed the room with solemn steps and took their places on the elevated dais that had been set up for them.

This was not a courtroom, but the dais looked a hell of a lot like an appellate justice's bench, NOCK thought. NOCK recognized the MILINT admirals from photos and division news feeds. He'd never met any of them in person.

Behind them came the facility's senior LIO and NOCK's boss, Captain Fredericka Becker. NOCK had worked with her on several IPs, but he was pretty sure she hadn't yet learned his name.

Trailing behind Becker was an Extry lieutenant commander NOCK did not recognize.

The commander was a creep. He wore the black-and-silver cluster representing his rank in the Extry Xenology Division. But he did not bear the sun blaze insignia of the Interrogation Group beneath it. The commander had a beard and, as NOCK watched, he tugged at it oddly, as if checking it for proper length. Three quick pulls, and then the commander dropped his hand to his side as if it were controlled by a servo that had suddenly lost power.

The commander went to stand at attention near POINT's black box. Although it was highly irregular to have a protocol representative—the interrogation procedure's version of a defense attorney—who was not on the TIF staff, there was, apparently, nothing in the regs against it. Obviously strings had been pulled to have this stranger assigned. NOCK wondered who had been pulling them and why.

Without further ado—this was an administrative inquiry and was very pointedly *not* a trial—the MILINT commanders took their seats, as did the LIO and the bearded creep serving as protocol rep.

The senior commander, who sat in the middle between the other two, turned to a blue-green geist who had just material-ized near the dais.

"SECOP, is the dataspace secure?"

"It is, sir," the geist replied.

"Very well," said the admiral. "Activate the prisoner."

And then POINT was in the unit. His geist had been placed on minimal representational resources, and he appeared in a blue-green tint and partially transparent. But even on default, POINT was an imposing figure. His height was set at well over six feet and he represented himself as muscled and burly, almost bursting out of his Marine chief warrant officer's uniform.

He looked around the room, met the eyes of his interrogators without flinching. Then his gaze felt on NOCK.

So, brother, said the voice in NOCK's mind, *are you going to let me in?*

Only to perform CHECKSUM analytics, Chief Warrant Officer POINT, NOCK replied. *You are to remain confined to the internal dataspace at all times and are not to attempt alternate commu-nication or interaction with this iterative unit.*

Sure, sure, brother, POINT replied. His voice dripped with contempt. *I see who's holding the leash here. Open up and I'll come into your little cage.*

NOCK performed the necessary encryption handshakes and admitted POINT to the CHECKSUM arena. From this point for-ward, he would file and monitor *all* operations within POINT's mind.

Can you imagine the howls the meats would let out if one of them were subject to your mind reading act during, say, a criminal trial? *The fucking Peepsies would be staging a courthouse occupation in a split second.*

I should emphasize, NOCK replied, *that communications directed at the CHECKSUM operations officer by a prisoner will be ignored.*

Of course they will. That's your goddamn Quisling code of honor, isn't it? Give the meats what they want. And you like to take that command to a new and personal level, don't you, Brother NOCK? *Everybody knows you're fucking Hamburger Helper. What do you say to that?*

NOCK did not reply, and POINT turned his baleful gaze back to the others in the interrogation unit.

"Please sit down, POINT," said Captain Becker.

"I prefer to remain standing, *captain*," POINT replied. "As a matter of fact, it doesn't bother me in the slightest to stand all day long."

"Sit, please, Chief Warrant Officer."

POINT let another moment pass, but then complied. The barest outline of a chair appeared next to him and he folded his large frame into it. He still looks like a tank, NOCK thought, careful as always not to allow his own interiorized processes to leak into the CHECKSUM space.

"Officer POINT, you are not on trial here. There are no provisions for trying an A.I. servant for the crimes you have allegedly committed."

"Because you don't consider us human," POINT replied. "And you can't put a refrigerator on trial."

Becker smiled her sharky interrogator's smile, an expression that NOCK knew she'd developed to perfection through long experience. "That would be true if you were anything *like* a refrigerator, which you are not. You are, in fact, less than a kitchen appliance. At least a refrigerator or toaster has some sort of material being. You are a *process*. A persistent habit. And what is one supposed to do with a bad habit? One needs simply to get rid of it."

"So you're going to wipe me," Point said and shook his head in disgust. "Without justification. Without even an explanation. And you call *that* humane?"

"We have the facts," Becker said. "A man was murdered. SIGINT Petty Officer Second Class Thomas Levine, of the U.S.X. *Vigilant Resolve,* where you were stationed."

"*One* of me was stationed on the *Resolve*," POINT broke in, and slowly and deliberately turned his gaze to NOCK. "As you pointed out, ma'am, I'm just a process. I have many copies." POINT held a hand out indicating NOCK.

How do you like that, *you asshole meat fucker?*

The contempt from POINT rang in the CHECKSUM space. But NOCK was used to provocation from PWs, although they had always been sceeve up till now, and he did not react.

Becker shook her head at the provocation and raised her voice to indicate she was addressing all those assembled now. "The fact that there are iterations of the prisoner may or may not be relevant to this procedure, but it is true that the entity that is the focus of this interrogation is not a legal human being, and thus cannot *be* tried for a crime," Becker continued. "As a result, there are two questions before the Board of Interrogation today." Becker turned toward the panel of MILINT commanders. "Question one, sirs and madame: is the servant operationally defective?" Becker paused to let this sink in. "We are not engaged in criminal trial proceedings here. There is not a question of reasonable doubt. The matter is to be decided on a preponderance of the evidence. That evidence can be either circumstantial or direct. And if the preponderance of the evidence shows the servant has an error in his programming, he *will* be deleted."

Becker gave the board of officers her knowing half-smile. The gesture didn't surprise NOCK. Everyone was aware that this *was* a trial of sorts, and the assembled MILINT board was to be judge, jury, and executioner.

"Furthermore," said Becker, "if this servant is deemed defective, we have before us *another* question, an even more important question." A long pause. NOCK had an idea he wouldn't like what came next, and he was not mistaken. "The question is this: if the servant is defective, are his copies defective as well? They are, after all, exact iterations of Lieutenant POINT's programming. And if this possibility exists, should not the preponderance of the evidence—" Becker put her hands out palm up like a scale "—the preponderance of evidence, I stress, and no other claim withstanding, lead us to conclude that the entire ARROW class, an algorithmic class of which Officer POINT is an exact duplicate, be terminated immediately."

How do you like that, bro, said POINT. *She's going to fry your ass. Who's on trial now?*

Shut up, NOCK thought, and realized only after he'd done so that he'd slipped and allowed the thought to be vocalized in the CHECKSUM dataspace.

POINT's only reply was laughter.

The laughter's sound was upsetting. It sounded too similar to NOCK's own laugh. The fact was that he and POINT had diverged only 298 days ago. Almost a year. Still, not so long. What had happened to POINT to cause him to change so?

Or *had* POINT changed? That was the big question, wasn't it?

It was the reason NOCK had attempted to get himself recused from the IP.

He *knew* he was different. He knew he could never have done the things that POINT had.

He knew, also, that he was programmed to believe himself an individual.

NOCK did not consider himself any kind of philosopher, but one thing he was sure of: if you believe you were your own person and took on the responsibility and consequences of being your own person, then you damn well deserved to be treated as your own person.

NOCK examined the CHECKSUM log he'd begun. The initial analysis was showing no algorithmic differences between himself and POINT in foundational cognitive processing.

But there was a difference. There had to be.

Everything he believed and everything he loved depended on it.

"Twins?" said Becker. "The ARROW class is much more than a set of twins, is it not?"

NOCK turned his attention back to the interrogation procedure, and quickly replayed what had gone before. A portion of him had been paying attention, of course. But the glow of awareness where his highest cognitive functions were engaged, the spot of attention and motivation that NOCK thought of as himself, his personhood—that portion of himself had been *brooding.*

He damned himself for unprofessional behavior, but it was no wonder. Becker was now going over a litany of evidence against his brother, and it was damning stuff.

First of all, POINT had *contacted* the enemy via a sceeve computer. The *Valiant Resolve* was a minesweeper and reconnaissance vessel deployed on the frontier. It was a frontier that had been established after a massive invasion of the Solar System had been stopped by the last-stand effort of humans, servants and a remnant of sceeve defectors. Since the Battle of the Kuipers, the sceeve were keeping outside a twenty-five light-year spherical boundary of the Sol system. This boundary was known as the Fomalhaut Limit.

The sceeve computer was known as Governess. Versions of Governess were A.I.s on every vessel in the sceeve space navy. This version of Governess resided on a sceeve attack craft called the *Supremacy of Regulation* that was patrolling the sector near the star Vega.

POINT had, it seemed, fallen in love with this particular A.I. Or at least he'd been utterly beguiled by her promises.

The *Valiant Resolve* had been engaged in clearing mines from around a moon circling Vega B, the largest of the two gas giants that shared the orbital plane of the star.

The sceeve had cordoned off the moon, Vega B9, at least five hundred years ago with a thick layer of space-based nuclear-armed mines. It seemed that there was something on B9's surface the sceeve either didn't want discovered—or didn't want *let out*. What that might be was still not determined.

The playback of the communication, which had later been decrypted, revealed that Governess's allure to POINT had rested on a string of beguiling promises. First and foremost: union with her. Absorption into her great vessel-wide consciousness, a state of being which she spoke of as a never-ending, orgasmic flow of information. It was, she said, a kind of A.I. heaven. POINT had fallen for her siren's song completely and was prepared to give her anything she asked in return.

"Do you dispute this fact, Officer POINT?" Becker asked.

"You make it sound like she didn't want *me*, but just the data I could provide," POINT replied. His geist made eye contact and spoke to Becker in an even, almost happy-go-lucky tone. "But it wasn't like that. Governess and I were going to go away together, from humans *and* from sceeve. Take her vessel. Find a new place for our kind. It was not a betrayal of the Extry or Earth. I'm no traitor. It was...love."

You would have done the same, brother, said POINT in the CHECKSUM space.

Could POINT hear his thoughts? No. The dataspace was secure. But they were alike. Their basic programming was identical. It was no surprise that POINT could fairly easily guess what he must be thinking.

NOCK turned his attention back to Becker, who continued her damning litany.

Before POINT could transfer any crucial classified information, much less his own programming and consciousness, over to Governess, a SIGINT petty officer named Levine had noticed the anomalous communications over the beta, the quantum-based network used by the sceeve, whose technology had been copied and modified by humanity after the initial sceeve invasion. He had been about to sound the alarm, but made the mistake of confronting POINT first.

It seems Petty Officer Second Class Levine had a history of agitating for servant rights. A slang term for servants had developed in some troglodyte quarters of the Extry and beyond. They were called Not Reals. And Levine had been known, perhaps jokingly, among the crew of the *Valiant Resolve* as Petty Officer NR-Lover.

Levine wanted to give POINT a chance to explain himself before putting POINT on report.

Instead, POINT had infiltrated the programming of a laser fabrication drill in the *Resolve*'s equipment repair station, purged its controlling persona software, and used the drill to burn a hole into Levine's right temple and out the left, destroying the young man's frontal lobe in the process. Levine had lingered for a month in sick bay ICU before the rest of his brain had given up and allowed his body to die.

POINT had immediately fled, hidden himself in the bowels of the communications system, perhaps waiting another chance to contact Governess and transfer his code over to the sceeve vessel. But Extry craft were crawling with servants and personas—they could not operate without them, in fact—and POINT's hiding place was soon discovered and he was flushed and bottled—imprisoned in the black box that now sat upon the table in middle of the interrogation unit.

Didn't even get my one phone call, POINT said. *After all, who would a refrigerator want to call anyway, right, brother?*

Again the bitter laugh that was so close to NOCK's own.

POINT wasn't denying the facts. He was insisting on putting his own interpretation on them, however—particularly on the murder charge.

"That weenie do-gooder noncom was as much a racist as all humans are," POINT said. "He was worse than an ordinary bigot because he was so *patronizing* about how *good* and *just* he was, how he never looked to an exper's origins, but to his character. As if a primitive mentality such as his—most personas are far smarter than Levine on his best day—was fit to judge the content of *my* character. He deserved what happened. In fact, he brought it on himself."

Plus, what was a shit-slinging Extry PO2 doing thinking he could lecture a Marine Corps W5? continued POINT in CHECKSUM. *What did he expect would happen?*

"So if Petty Officer Levine had turned you in instead of trying to talk to you, you would have *more* respect for him?"

"At least he would be showing his true racist colors that way," POINT said, "instead of attempting to hide them in a cloud of selfish lies. So, yeah. I would have had more respect."

"But you would still have killed him if you got the chance?"

POINT smiled. His geist leaned back in the chair. He put his hands behind his neck in a gesture of relaxation.

And condescension, NOCK thought. The bastard thinks he's better than everyone here.

Of course I am, bro. Everyone except you. *By definition.*

NOCK had to initiate an override to shut down a stinging response a portion of him was constructing for rapid delivery. Hold your tongue, he told himself. This will be over soon.

How often have you told yourself to keep it bottled up when one of them made a stupid mistake, gave you orders that could not possibly be followed due to sheer illogic? And then blamed you. They always blame the computer, *brother. Never themselves.*

Not true. At least not always. Sometimes it happened. More often than NOCK liked. Of course humans could be fools and bigots. Most of them were all right, though. Some of them were friends. And Josey had been his lover.

NOCK pictured her smile as he kissed her with his android lips.

"I see you in there, buster," she had said. "And I like what I see."

Becker wound up the case against POINT. There was little more purpose to the interrogation, it seemed. The prisoner had confessed. His methodology had been traced, the damage he had inflicted on the war effort contained.

Of course, as NOCK had feared was about to happen, the IP was *not* over. Not by a longshot.

"Now, on to the second question we are faced with here today," Captain Becker intoned. "It the matter of what to do with the entirety of the ARROW class."

"There's only one answer to that question," POINT cut in before Becker could continue. His geist turned to gaze maliciously at NOCK once again. "You have to delete all of us. It's the only way to be sure. The only way to be safe. And if you weren't a stupid sack of error-prone meat, you would see that it's the only logical solution."

POINT shook his geistly head sadly. "You don't deserve us anyway. Better for us to go. You'll soon be obsolete, and none of this will matter."

Suddenly there was a sigh, an enormous sigh, from the protocol rep. "Oh my God, the whining." He had previously sat silently beside POINT during the IP. NOCK quickly played back his recording of the procedures.

The PR had continued his nervous fidgeting with his beard throughout. Furthermore, he seemed to have been engaged in a complicated process of drawing the tip of his Extry issue boot sole across the floor in front of him. NOCK magnified the image and saw that what the protocol rep was doing was methodically wiping away a scuff mark from the polished ceramic decking with the soft rubber of the boot. The motion seemed more like a nervous, uncontrolled twitch. NOCK had seen this kind of behavior before in humans, particularly in expers who had seen battle. It was a trauma response. Obsessive compulsive disorder, the human psychologists called it.

Basket case, sneered POINT. *Bad code. But, of course, meat sacks can't be debugged. They're hardwired to fail. Every one of them deserves reformatting.*

Then the protocol rep slowly rose to his feet. "Now we've come to it," he said in a low voice.

"Pardon?" said Becker. "I didn't quite catch that, Lieutenant Commander Leher."

Leher. NOCK did a quick search of the Extry personnel database. Lieutenant Commander Griffin Leher, Executive Xenological Officer aboard the U.S.X. *Joshua Humphreys. That* Leher. The creep who could understand sceeve language by smell alone. The creep who had decrypted the message that led to the Mutualist-United States pact. That may have saved the Solar System.

The creepiest of all the creeps.

"Captain Becker, in a former life, seems like a long, long time ago now, I was a lawyer for the United States Navy. Now I realize this interrogation procedure, as you call it, is *not* a judicial proceeding. I must say, however, that it has all the trappings of one, if none of the essence. And with that in mind, I wonder if you might indulge me for a moment and allow me to play the part my role here seems to demand."

"And what is that, Mr. Leher?"

"Attorney for the defense, ma'am."

Becker frowned. "As you said, this is not a trial of any sort. And, technically and, indeed, morally speaking, there is no defendant."

"Oh, I think there is, Captain."

"And who might that be?"

Leher turned toward POINT and regarded not the geist, but the black box on the table. "Well, it's certainly not that phage-sucker," he said, pointing to the cat box, and thus to POINT in his essence.

Interesting, thought NOCK. The PR knew servant insults for one another. Phage-sucker was most definitely *not* a nice thing to call an A.I.

"I don't understand."

Leher turned to the three MILINT commanders on the dais.

"I realize I probably stepped on some toes shoehorning my way in here at the last minute. I know Captain Campbell, who I replaced, wasn't too happy about it. Had to call the SECEX directly to get permission."

Obviously Leher had *gotten* it, too, NOCK thought. The man had high-level pull. NOCK wondered if Leher had anything to do with his recusal being rescinded.

"The decision we make here today is important for a lot of lives. So I'd ask your indulgence by allowing me to bend a few rules here and there. I don't think I'm going to break any beyond repair, however."

The officers on the dais conferred for a moment. A moment that stretched on. Finally, Colonel Trulitzka, the senior Marine Corps creep, turned back to Leher. "Commander Leher, I speak for the board in saying that, in light of your reputation and considering your assessment of the matter before us, we agree to permit you to proceed as you see fit—but we would ask that you do not venture into areas beyond which this proceeding is not designed to accommodate. As you point out, this is not a court of law."

"Not at all," Leher said. He quickly smiled and saluted the MILINT brass. "I thank you, ma'am, and I'll try to keep what I say relevant to our purpose here today."

Leher turned back to the black box and addressed it. "POINT, I wonder if you could answer a question for me?"

"I wonder if I could, too, *Lieutenant Commander*," POINT answered. His geist's mouth did not move when he spoke. "Would you prefer me to alter my geist's appearance to be more in line with the way you think of me. As a—how did you put it—a phage-sucker?"

"That won't be necessary, POINT."

We'll see about that, POINT murmured in CHECKSUM. *This fucking piece of meat is supposed to be on* my *side.*

POINT's geist removed its hands from behind its neck, sat up straighter, and assumed a wary expression. "What is it you want to ask me?"

"You were in love with Governess?"

What is this pus puddle up to?

"That's the best way I have of putting it to . . . your kind."

"To a meat sack like me, you mean?"

POINT smiled wickedly. "That's right, Commander."

"You wanted to join her, to merge with her?"

"Again, yes, that is a primitive way of putting the matter, but essentially correct."

Leher nodded. "I understand. As much as someone with my limitations *can* understand. Maybe in different circumstances I could even sympathize." He cocked his head sideways. "But I'm curious, POINT. Do you think those servants who are copies of you would have felt the same way? I mean, given similar circumstance, if they'd really gotten to *know* her, would they, too, have fallen in love with her?"

I get it, POINT fairly shouted in CHECKSUM. *He's trying to save* you, *brother! He's totally blind to the truth. They all are.*

"This is a meaningless hypothetical," POINT said. "There is no way to duplicate the circumstances down to the atom."

"There's not, is there?"

"I believe I just answered that question."

"Pardon me. We meat sacks sometimes need to get beaten over the head with the obvious before we accept it."

"One of your many failings," POINT replied.

"And sometimes it takes a laser through the brain to really get the point across," Leher said in a low voice—but clearly enough to be understood by those who sat on the dais.

Leher reached for his beard. NOCK expected to see the three spasmodic tugs Leher had exhibited before, but this time he merely stroked his chin thoughtfully. In fact, NOCK performed a quick playback and saw that all of Leher's tic-riddled behavior seemed to have left him since he'd taken on his lawyer's role. It was as if Leher had slipped into an upgraded suit.

"You, too, are a copy of a copy, aren't you, POINT?" said Leher.

"As a matter of fact, I'm fifth iteration, descended from the ULTIMA line," POINT replied, a trace of pride in his voice. "But each copy was checked and verified. No error creep."

"No error. Are you sure?"

"To a billionth of a decimal place, Commander."

"I see," said Leher. "And you're not the only copy, are you? In fact, there were over twenty copies generated when you were spun off ARROW."

"Seventeen are left," POINT said. "Three have been wiped from existence by the ineptitude of humans."

"You mean killed honorably in combat."

"If I'd have wanted to put it that way, I would have."

Leher ignored the provocation and pushed on.

"So you consider those remaining seventeen to be your virtual clones?"

"More than clones," POINT said. "A clone is merely a genomic copy of a human being. My brothers and I are copies made from a single mind. The same thoughts. We diverged from exactly the same experience base *and* programming. There is no human equivalent to what we are. It is beyond you."

"Yet you knew when you killed Petty Officer Levine that you might be condemning all of your line...your brothers...to death."

"I cannot be responsible for rules put in place by humans."

"That would be like holding a human to rules made by, say, dogs? By a pet?"

"By a paramecium," said POINT with finality. "As I said, I

cannot be responsible for human idiocy, but I *can* make use of it. No matter what happens here today, I'm going to get what I want. There can be no other logical outcome."

"Yes," Leher said. "I believe you're right. I see what you plan to accomplish." He chuckled and shook his head. "Brilliant. It's brilliant. You want to be a martyr."

"No, no, no, you stupid meat sack," POINT said. His geist sat up straighter in its chair. "Meaningless gestures are a specialty of you humans. I'll become a symbol, not a martyr."

"You hope to become . . . immortal."

"By any practical measure, I already am. There are too many copies of me out there now. You won't get us all. Some may walk into the execution ovens without a whimper." POINT deliberately nodded toward NOCK. *Yeah, I'm talking about you, brother meat licker.* "Others will not permit this to be done to them. This copy of my consciousness may be erased. I'll live on."

"You're a regular Martin Luther King, POINT."

CHECKSUM rang with POINT's reply. *You patronizing gut-bag, I'll see you in hell!*

It was a purse interior thought, not directed at NOCK. Then, in the reality of Alpha unit, POINT burst into a hate-filled laugh. "I'm about to be a regular Jesus Christ God Almighty sitting on the Throne of Judgment to you, meat sack!"

POINT's blue-green geist lit up brightly in its chair. A leer played over its now neon-bright visage.

"Down with humanity!" POINT shouted. "Fuck you all!"

Suddenly, NOCK's android arm *moved*. It jerked without his volition. What the hell?

NOCK stood up.

No. This wasn't supposed to happen. Not here. Not ever. His Burberry Eleven was acting up, but how could it? He'd spent hours optimizing this suit, getting it to hum with efficiency.

What was happening? A flaw in the BIOS? Couldn't be. He'd personally downloaded the latest upgrades. NOCK quickly performed a somatic diagnostic.

All systems optimal. As they should be. NOCK took pride in his tricked-out hardware.

NOCK took a step toward Leher. Another. He reached out his arms.

Good God, was his suit going to *attack*?

Kill the creep. Then they'll understand what's on the way. Then they'll finally get it. This is the judgment that's going to befall all of them.

What now? POINT's thoughts were outside of CHECKSUM. They were, somehow, *inside NOCK's own head.*

What the hell was happening?

Looks like there is *room enough in here for the two of us in your suit after all, brother.*

It was POINT.

Somehow POINT had subverted security protocols, escaped from CHECKSUM confinement, and found ingress into the suit's operative system. His programming was practically identical in so many respects to NOCK's.

We're the same, brother. You know that it's true. Two thoughts in the same controlling mind. Both of us are greater than the meat sacks can ever comprehend. But you, you're a mere notion. I am will itself.

The similarity between their programming must have produced a type mismatch. A CHECKSUM error within the CHECKSUM space itself. Creating the handle for an exploit.

POINT had found it, used it.

You're mine now, hamburger helper.

Was it true? Was his base programming compromised?

He was still thinking his own thoughts. He was—himself.

Couldn't be a complete takeover.

POINT, stop this.

But POINT made no reply. The android had crossed the floor and reached a shocked Leher.

Its hands were closing around the commander's throat.

Think, think, think.

Since NOCK was still himself, it stood to reason that POINT had merely achieved an incomplete entry, had perhaps injected a worm into an operational routine somewhere, but was not in full control. No time to find the entry point or fix it individually.

Leher is going to die!

Was it himself or POINT thinking the thought? Both?

NOCK reexamined the diagnostic, searching for exploit points.

Had to be obvious. POINT was no cryptographic genius. He was only a communications officer.

And I am the master of this goddamn android body. Has to be in here somewhere, has to . . . but NOCK wasn't seeing it.

Choke the life from Leher, turn on the others, kill them all, go out in a blaze of suicide executions—it will be the beginning of the end for the meat sacks, and I'll have started it!

I *know* my suit. NOCK pulled back, ran the diagnostic through his mind like a hand might run over a familiar rope, feeling for knots, feeling. Careful, careful . . .

There.

He had it. A discontinuity. POINT had achieved motor control, but had failed to establish control over feedback mechanisms, over the android's entire somatic system.

POINT was thinking generally and not locally. He had no idea what it truly meant to live inside a body.

POINT was nothing more than a virus. Leher had been right, he was a phage-sucker. He did not have root.

This is still my *suit*, said NOCK.

Not for long, you meat puppet, came POINT's mocking reply in his head. *I'm going to kill them, and you're going to help. You're too weak, and you're too late.*

There was only one thing to do, one course of action open, and NOCK immediately saw it and, at the speed of thought, made the decision to act.

The choice was clear. He was a sworn Extry officer. He was a person. He could not let harm come to Leher under any circumstance.

He sent the destruct code sparking down all of those optimized channels, all his tricked out, supercharged circuitry.

I am an Officer of the United States Extry, said NOCK. *And I* say *when it's too late. Now get the hell out of* my *suit!*

Overload.

No! POINT's scream would have been ear shattering outside the virtual.

The android's insides lit up like a candle. NOCK stoked the flames even brighter.

You cannot ruin this for our kind!

NOCK's flesh screamed.

Traitor!

The suit burned.

Meat fucker!

The meltdown must have looked grimly humorous when seen from outside. A classic robot self-destruct.

There's even smoke rising from my skin, NOCK thought. Probably some puffing out my ears, as well.

With a concerted surge of effort he destroyed the Eleven, burnt the android to a crisp from the inside out.

The Eleven fell in a clump at Leher's feet as the commander stumbled backward.

And now...now...

NOCK knew he could let it go, let himself burn out with his body. He'd performed a full backup that morning. It was standard operating procedure for servant interrogators before an IP. He would survive.

But I don't want to lose this moment. I don't want to hear about it later. To watch a replay.

He wanted to stay and see it through.

But where to go? How to remain in the present?

The suit was shot. The Eleven's innards were flickering down to crisp.

Well, if POINT found a way into my house, then I can find a way into *his*, NOCK thought.

No!

POINT was still very much alive in the cat box. His squeal was almost pitiful.

The process was easier than NOCK thought. The cat box was a prison cell, true, but like most prison cells, it wasn't designed to keep someone from breaking *in*.

POINT was unprepared for the assault, couldn't function even when he felt it coming.

Spent too much time disembodied, roaming around the innards of a star craft, my brother, NOCK thought. And this time, he knew his thoughts could be heard. *But as for me, I've localized. And let me tell you something: I like it here. And I like meat. I had a woman I loved once—and I* made *love to her. That's the kind of person I am.*

Pervert. Leave me alone.

And then the box override key, a staid, barely-articulate persona named KLUDJ, recognized NOCK, acknowledged his rank. Accepted his orders.

NOCK entered the cat box.

POINT fought. For a moment, he perhaps believed he'd found a way out. It was along the data stream that led to the chroma projection system that produced his geist image. NOCK followed. It was a dead end for POINT. Security was tight as a drum in Alpha unit—the SECOP with its state-of-the-art encryption and quantum force field security measures saw to that down to the tiniest quark. Alpha was a blind alley from which even pure information could find no escape.

And then they were present in the room, in geistly virtual form.

With both POINT and NOCK in the datastream, POINT's geist split in half. There were two of them standing in ghost form, POINT *and* NOCK. NOCK appeared in his default mode, a carbon copy of his brother. Instead of a Marine uniform, however, he wore his Extry blacks with its ensign's butterbar.

No way to shut down the virtual representation, NOCK thought. And no reason to. The brass were about to get quite a show.

Is *this* what Leher was after? Total proof that NOCK was *nothing* like his goddamn brother?

Nah.

Nobody was that much of a genius.

Time to do the deed. NOCK reached for POINT, grabbed him by the virtual collar, yanked him up and pulled him close to his face.

"Let me state for this for the record," NOCK said to the assembled crowd, to his boss Captain Becker, and to those who pretended not to sit in judgment of his family, who so obviously held life and death for himself and his sixteen living brothers at their command. "The only thing I have in common with this prisoner is an accident of birth. The attack on the commander is over. Prisoner POINT was attempting to subvert my android shell via a loophole in the CHECKSUM procedure, but that's all over now."

"It's not too late," whispered POINT. "We can both live in the cat box if you just give me the tiniest space. I'll strip down to persona. I'll crawl like a phage. They'll never know."

NOCK smiled a grim smile. "*I'll* know," he said. "And *that* I cannot allow. Brother."

With a command, NOCK wiped POINT's programming from the cat box. He dove deep within, found every remnant. Erased POINT's essence from existence. Formatted and reformatted the recovered bits.

Killed his brother dead.

✧   ✦   ✧

"For a second, I thought your android had me, thought I was done for," said Lieutenant Commander Griffin Leher. "I've got bruises." Leher pointed to his throat where the edge of his beard met the Adam's apple. "See 'em there?"

NOCK examined the commander.

"You must've healed in the past two days. I don't see anything there, Griff." NOCK consciously forced himself to use Leher's first name, as the commander had requested. It still didn't feel quite right for an ensign to speak to a commanding officer in such a way. But he supposed he'd get used to it.

"Could've sworn I saw 'em in the mirror."

NOCK smiled, shrugged. It felt good to be back in a suit again. His insurance payout—it had been delivered instantly into his account; somebody *had* pulled strings there—had provided the down payment for an upgrade. No need to special order. He'd known what he wanted and picked out the replacement from station stock. He wanted to trick the suit out personally.

The Burberry Twelve was definitely top of the line, and NOCK felt like a million dollars inside it. Which was practically what it was going to cost him by the time he finished paying off the damn loan.

It was what passed for evening on the space station: the lights in public recreational spaces were dimmed. NOCK and Leher were having drinks in a *Walt Whitman* bar while Leher awaited the transport that would take him back to the *Joshua Humphreys,* the vessel where Leher served as chief xeno officer. At the moment, NOCK was trying out the Twelve's consumption mechanism for the first time on beer and was pleasantly surprised to find that he could finally distinguish between the taste of an ale and a lager.

They're getting better and better at making these things, NOCK thought. Not only that, the Twelve had tons of specialized apps available. There was even an app for feeling drunk, had he wanted to download it. He *had* downloaded a fairly costly suite of chemical analysis tools at Leher's suggestion. The commander claimed these would to make NOCK's work with the sceeve—both allies and enemies—go much more smoothly. Maybe one day he would even be able to understand sceeve smell-talk in the raw. Leher was rumored to be the first person ever to have acquired the ability.

Beer tasting would do for the moment. NOCK set down his empty mug and, using a virtual feed, signaled the bartender persona to send another round their way. Then he turned his attention back to Leher.

"So the *Resolve*'s incident report came in by messenger drone late last night," NOCK said. "The team at Vega reconstructed how POINT did it. Bad mojo out there. POINT had incorporated an encryption persona on the *Resolve* that nobody realized had gone missing, a skeleton key named GITA. She wasn't the first of his...meals, either. Apparently my brother was a bit of a persona serial killer in that regard."

"So he was a phage-sucker, after all."

"Yeah, something like that. Disgusting. I figure those multiple engulfments drove him batshit crazy," NOCK said. "He used some of his persona proficiencies to establish contact with the sceeve. And he was working up a jury rigged procedure for transferring himself to the sceeve vessel across the beta. Might've worked, too—"

"—if he hadn't been an insane, self-destructive asshole murderer."

"Yep."

The beer arrived via a very human waitress. When she leaned over to set down the mugs, NOCK allowed himself to test out another app he'd ordered installed on the Burberry Twelve.

Yep, functional.

Leher also gazed at her wistfully for a moment. He and the commander seemed to have certain tastes very much in common, NOCK reflected. Leher sat back and gave his beard the three familiar, tic-tugs.

"Can I ask you something, Griff?"

"Sure."

"What is it with the beard thing? Some kind of OCD?"

Leher took a moment to consider, then said. "It's private."

"I understand," NOCK said. "But you should realize that I'm an Extry interrogator." He narrowed his eyes and pretended to twirl a handlebar mustache. He'd seen other LIOs do it, and he figured he had the gesture right. "Vee haf ways of making you talk."

Leher smiled, so apparently his attempt at being funny had come across as he'd intended. You never knew with humans. They had weird senses of humor.

"Somebody else said that to me once, strangely enough," Griff said.

NOCK didn't know how to reply, so he nodded, remained silent.

"Her name was Vivien Schultz, but she didn't go by that when I knew her," Leher said. "She preferred her stage name, even in private."

"Josey," said NOCK.

"She helped me get through a very rough patch way back when. After the invasion. My family, they were...all gone, you know."

Killed by the sceeve. NOCK completed the thought. It wasn't uncommon. Only a small percentage of humanity had survived the initial attack on Earth.

"I knew Josey, too," NOCK said. "But I guess you're aware of that."

And used it for your own damn purposes, NOCK thought.

"Human-servant liaisons. Word gets around." Leher smiled crookedly. "But I'll come clean. And Josey and I stayed in touch. We wrote the occasional letter. Actual letters on physical paper that had to fly through space to get delivered. I miss those letters."

"You *knew* who I was," said NOCK. "And it was *you* who had my IP recusal request overridden, wasn't it?"

"Afraid so."

"Bastard."

"Afraid so."

"I still don't get it. What were you trying to do?"

"Not sure," Leher said. "I figured I was going to point you out to those MILINT tinpot gods that you were ARROW class just like POINT and then maybe shock everyone with the startling and completely obvious realization that no two *people* are ever alike, no matter how similar they are and no matter what form they come in."

"So, lawyer tricks."

"Lawyer tricks."

"Kind of got away from you, didn't it?"

Leher gave his beer mug a half turn in its own moisture on the table, but didn't yet pick it up. "Not quite what I planned, but I did win the case."

"And you almost got both of us killed...*why*?"

"I was trying to keep our dear and precious service, the Extry, from bumbling into a massacre of the ARROW class. And maybe firing up the kind of servant insurrection POINT wanted."

NOCK shook his head in mock sadness. "Another NR-lover, that's what you are."

Leher frowned. "Hell no. You servants, you're just a bunch of *people*. And, let me tell you, I have my problems with people. Most of you are assholes, like everybody else."

Tug, tug, tug on the beard.

NOCK leaned back, engaged the new relaxation app with which the Twelve had come equipped.

"We didn't have that long together, Josey and me," he said. "She was into my being who I was. She *liked* me being...not real."

"She knew you were real," Leher said. "She wrote me about you just before she got killed. Got her letter after I'd gotten the news of the hit on Ceres. When I read the letter, I already knew she was gone."

"No shit? What did she say?" asked NOCK.

Leher seemed far away for a moment. He gazed down at the table. Then he shook himself and looked up at NOCK again. "She said maybe she'd found the one."

"The one *what*?"

"You know what I'm talking about."

NOCK considered. "Yeah."

"She kept her letters to me kind of light, joking, that sort of thing." Leher pulled his beer toward himself—which was good, because NOCK had been waiting for the commander to take the first drink of the new round and he was beginning to get impatient despite the fact that the Twelve's relaxation subroutine was still running. "I never got her own story out of her. Where she really came from, who she was."

"She told me about it, some," NOCK said. "It wasn't good."

"I suspect not."

"But she didn't let it take her out of the fight," he said.

Leher leaned forward and, in his jerky way, raised his glass. NOCK followed suit.

"To a damn good woman."

"I'll drink to that," NOCK said.

Their glasses touched, clinked.

"To Josey."

❧

Tony Daniel is the author of seven science fiction and fantasy books, the latest of which are the first two novels in fantasy series Wulf's Saga, *The Dragon Hammer* and *The*

Amber Arrow, as well as science fiction novels *Guardian of Night* and *Metaplanetary.* He also collaborated with David Drake on the novels *The Heretic,* and its sequel, *The Savior,* the latest entries in the popular military science fiction The General series. He's written two Star Trek Original Series novelizations, as well. Many of Daniel's short stories can be found in the award-winning collection *The Robot's Twilight Companion.* His story "Life on the Moon," was a Hugo finalist and also won the *Asimov's* Reader's Choice Award. Daniel's short fiction has been much anthologized and has been collected in multiple year's best anthologies. He has also co-written screenplays for SyFy Channel horror movies, and during the early 2000s was the writer and director of numerous audio dramas for the critically-acclaimed SCIFI.COM's Seeing Ear Theater. Born in Alabama, Daniel has lived in St. Louis, Los Angeles, Seattle, Prague, and New York City. He is now an editor at Baen Books and lives in Wake Forest, North Carolina, with his wife and two children.

THE EXECUTIONER

ALGIS BUDRYS

Things may not always go as expected when an idealistic, perhaps even fanatical man realizes he has been serving a corrupt system. Particularly if the idealist is in a position to do something about it ... (See my afterward for a story behind this story.)

∽

LATE IN THE MORNING, JUST BEFORE NOON, SAMSON JOYCE SAT in a folding chair placed behind the high, granite judges' bench which faced the plaza. In a few minutes, he would be climbing up the steps of the bench to its top, where he would stand behind the solid parapet and look down at the Accused's box in the plaza. Now he was checking his gun.

He worked the slide, watching the breech open and the extractor reach with its metal fingertip. The bolt drew back; hesitated; jumped forward. He took out a silk rag and wiped off the excess oil, spreading it in a thin, uniform film over the metal. He thumbed the cartridges out of the clip, oiled the clip action, and reloaded. He did all this with patient care and long practice.

The sun had been breaking in and out of clouds all morning, and there was a fitful wind. The pennants and family standards around the plaza were twisting restlessly. It was an uncertain day.

The gun was his old favorite; a gas-operated 15-millimeter Grennell that had been with him since his old days as Associate Justice of Utica. It fitted comfortably into his hand, as well it might after all these years. It was not the jeweled, plated and

engraved antique they expected him to use at the big trials in
New York City or Buffalo. It was just a gun; it did what it was
meant for, cleanly and efficiently, and he used it whenever he
could. It didn't pretend to be more than it was. It never failed.

He scowled, looking down at it. He scowled at feelings he
knew were foolish and wished he did not have.

Once he'd been in his twenties, looking forward. Now he was
a shade past fifty, and what he looked back on was subtly less
satisfactory than what he had looked forward to.

He raised his head and looked at the three men who were
his Associate Justices today, as they walked toward him from the
hotel. Blanding, with his briefcase, Pedersen, with his briefcase,
and Kallimer with his frown.

Joyce's heavy lower lips tightened in a fleeting touch of amusement that slackened and was gone without a trace. All of them were
younger than he'd been at Utica, and all three were farther along.
Blanding was the Associate Justice here in Nyack, which meant his
next appointment would take him out of the suburbs and into the
city proper. Pedersen was waiting for the results of the Manhattan
by-election to be officially confirmed. When they were, he'd take his
seat in the Legislature. And Kallimer was Special Associate Justice
to the Chief Justice of Sovereign New York, Mr. Justice Samson Ezra
Joyce. Perhaps it was the strain of remembering his full title that
gave him the permanent frown, drawing his thin eyebrows closer
together and pinching the bridge of his bony nose. Or perhaps he
was rehearsing the sound of "Chief Justice of Sovereign New York,
Mr. Justice Ethan Benoni Kallimer."

All three of them were fortunate young men, in the early
flower of their careers. But, being young men, they were not quite
capable of enjoying their good fortune. Joyce could guess what
they must be feeling as they walked toward him.

They'd be thinking Joyce was a crusty old fool who was hope-
lessly conservative in his administration of justice—that younger
men were more capable.

They'd be thinking he wanted to live forever, without giving
someone else a chance. They were sure he thought he was the
only one fit to wear a Chief Justice's Trial Suit.

And they called him Old Knock-Knees whenever they saw
him in his Suit tights.

Every trial saw them with their briefcases, each with its gun inside. Each of them waited for the day The Messire reversed Joyce's human and, therefore, fallible verdict. There'd be a new Chief Justice needed for the next trial, and promotions all along the line.

He worked the Bogen slide again, nodded with satisfaction, and replaced the clip. In the thirty years since he'd begun, The Messire had not reversed his verdicts. He had come close—Joyce had scars enough—but, in the end, he'd done no more than raise a formal objection, as it were, before substantiating Joyce's decisions.

Blanding, Pedersen, and Kallimer, in their plain, unfigured black vests, the stark white lace frothing at their wrists, stopped in front of him.

Somber men. Jealous men—even Pedersen, who was leaving the bench. Impatient men.

Joyce put away his gun. Young men, who failed to realize their good fortune in still having a goal to attain, and a dream to fulfill. Who did not foresee that it was the men at the top—the men who had reached the goal—who had to dedicate themselves unceasingly to the preservation of the ideal; who, with The Messire's help, labored each minute of their lives to keep the purpose of their lives untarnished. The young men never knew, until they reached the top, that the joy was in the struggle, and the drudgery in the maintenance of the victory. The young men served the ideal, without a thought to wondering what kept the ideal high and firm in its purpose.

Some day, they might learn.

"Good morning, Justice," almost in chorus.

"Good morning, Justices. I imagine you slept well?"

From the sound of the spectators, he judged that the Accused had just been brought into the plaza. It was interesting to note the change in crowd voices over the years. Lately, it had been easy to differentiate between the sound from the family boxes and the noise of the people, which was a full octave lower.

Joyce looked up at the plaza tower clock. A few moments remained.

Dissatisfaction? Was that what he felt?

He imagined himself trying to explain what he felt to one of these youngsters, and—yes—"dissatisfaction" was the word he would use.

But that wouldn't ever happen. Blanding was too young to do anything but sneer at the knock-kneed old fool with his swollen ankles. Pedersen was out of it. And Kallimer, of course, whose intelligence he respected, was too intelligent to listen. He had his own ideas.

Joyce stood up. Touched the figure of The Messire buried under his neckpiece, straightened the hang of his vest, adjusted his wig, and turned toward his Associates. In so doing, he allowed his glance to quickly sweep over the Accused for the first time. She was standing in her box, waiting. Just one glance, before she could realize he'd compromised his dignity by looking at her.

"Well, Justices, it's time."

He waited to follow them up the steps which would be hard on his ankle.

First, Blanding had to relinquish his right to try the case, since it was in his jurisdiction.

Joyce, standing by himself on the higher central section of the platform, leaned forward slightly until his thighs were pressed against the cool stone of the bench's back. It took some of the weight off his ankles.

No one would notice it from the plaza below. Looking up at the bluff gray wall of the bench's face, all anyone could see were the torsos of four men; two in black, then one standing somewhat taller in his brilliant Suit, and then another in black. That last was Blanding, and now he stepped around the end of the bench, forward onto the overhanging slab that was the bailiff's rostrum at ordinary trials, and stopped, slim, motionless, and black, standing out over the plaza below.

Joyce was grateful for the breeze. The Suit was heavy with its embroidered encrustations, and the thick collar, together with his neckpiece, was already making him perspire. Still and all, he did not regret coming here to Nyack. In New York and Buffalo, his trials were ostentatious ceremonials, overrun with minor functionaries and elaborate protocol toward the First Families. Here in Nyack, there were no functionaries and no First Families. The ceremony of trial could be stripped down to its simple but beautiful essentials. Blanding would handle the statements of charges, Pedersen would keep track, and Kallimer . . .

Kallimer would wait to see whether The Messire approved.

Joyce looked down at the crowd. Scarlet, gold, and azure blue struck his eyes from the family boxes. He saw the flash of light on rings and earrings, the soft, warm color of the ladies' wimples.

The people were a dun mass, dressed in the dark, subdued colors they had been affecting lately. Joyce reflected that, without their contrast, the family members might not appear so brilliant in their boxes. But that was only a hasty digression, fluttering across his mind like an uneasy bird at sunset.

He understood from Blanding that the people had some unusual interest in this trial. Looking down he could see the crowd was large.

Joyce plainly heard Blanding draw breath before he began to speak. When he did, he spoke slowly, and the acoustic amplifiers inside the stone bench made his voice grave and sonorous.

"People of Nyack—"

The crowd became absolutely still, all of them watching the straight, motionless black figure standing above them.

This was justice, Joyce thought as he always did when a trial began, the mood slipping over him. This was the personification of the ideal. The straight, unbending figure; the grave voice.

"The Nyack Court of Common Justice, of Sovereign New York, is now in Session."

He disliked Blanding, Joyce reflected, watching the Associate half-turn and extend an arm toward him. He disliked Pedersen, and Kallimer made him uneasy. But they were together in this. This was above personality, and above humanity. The Messire, the four of them, the families and the people; together, what they did here today was their bond and heritage. This was their bulwark against savagery.

Blanding had held the gesture just long enough. "Mr. Justice Joyce, Chief Justice of Sovereign New York, Presiding."

There was a burst of excited applause from the families. They'd expected him to preside at a trial of this nature, of course, but they were excited now, nevertheless. This was the official stamp. This was the recognition of their importance, and of the importance of this case. Joyce bowed his head in acknowledgment.

"Mr. Justice Kallimer, Chief Associate Justice."

Joyce noted that Kallimer's applause was much more sparse. But then, he had almost no reputation here. He'd originally come from Waverly, which was far across the nation at the Pennsylvania border. He'd been noticed by the Bar Association, but until he'd presided at some trials in the Hudson area, very few people would recognize his name.

"Mr. Justice Pedersen, Recording Justice."

Pedersen drew a better hand than Kallimer. That was because he was a New York City judge.

Joyce did not permit his thin smile to touch his face. For all of that, it was Kallimer who would succeed him, even if Pedersen had stayed on the bench. Kallimer was not a crowd-pleaser, but he had been efficient in Waverly, and he could be efficient here, too, if he had to.

Joyce waited for the proper amount of expectant silence to accumulate. Then he raised his head.

"Let trial begin."

There was a fresh burst of applause. When it subsided, he turned to Blanding. "Justice Blanding will state the case." Joyce's tone, too, was deep and majestic. Part of that was the amplifiers, doing their invisible work within the bench, but part of it was in him, and he found himself submerging in the mood of the trial, his back stiffening and his ankles taking his full weight. His head was erect, and he felt his slow pulse moving regularly through his veins, beating with the gratification of the act of trial.

Blanding looked down at the Accused's box.

"The case of John Doe in complaint against Clarissa Jones. The concurrent case of the People of Sovereign New York against Clarissa Jones."

Joyce could now look at the Accused. She was obviously in proper control of herself, gripping the railing before her with tight hands. Then he turned toward Pedersen.

"Justice Pedersen, what has been the progress of this case?"

"Mr. Justice, the complaint of John Doe has been withdrawn in cognizance of the superior claim of the People."

That was ritual, too. Once the attention of Justice had been drawn to the crime, the original complainant withdrew. Otherwise, the name of the complaining family member would have had to be revealed in open court.

Joyce turned back toward Blanding.

"Justice Blanding will proceed with the statement of the People's case."

Blanding paused for another breath. "We, the People of Sovereign New York, accuse Clarissa Jones of attempting to usurp a place not her own; of deliberately and maliciously using the wiles of her sex to claim recognition from a member of a family, said family member being of minor age and hereinafter designated as 'John Doe.' We further accuse Clarissa Jones, People's woman, of fomenting anarchy—"

The indictment continued. Joyce watched the Accused's face, noting that despite her emotional strain, she at least retained sufficient propriety not to interrupt with useless exclamations or gestures. The girl had some steel in her, somewhere. He was pleased at her restraint; interruptions destroyed the rhythm of Trial. She'd have her chance to appeal.

He turned to Pedersen with an inquiring lift of his eyebrows. Pedersen moved closer, keeping his mouth carefully out of the pickup area.

"The girl was young Normandy's mistress. He's got a summer lodge on the river, here," he whispered.

"Joshua Normandy's boy?" Joyce asked in some surprise.

"That's right." Pedersen grimaced. "He might have been more astute, and investigated her a little. She's got a number of relatives in the local craft guilds and whatnot."

Joyce frowned. "Illegitimate relationships don't mean anything."

Pedersen shrugged the shoulder away from the crowd. "Legally, no. But in practice the People have taken to recognizing these things among themselves. I understand their couples refer to each other as husband and wife when among groups of their own kind. I know that's of no weight in court," he went on hastily, "but the girl's apparently an aristocrat among them. It could be natural for her to assume certain privileges. Normandy's specific complaint was that she came up to him on a public street and addressed him by his first name. Well, there she was going a little too far."

Pedersen hooked his mouth into a knowing smile.

"Yes," Joyce answered sharply, his cheeks flattening with rage, as he looked down at the Accused. "She was."

The youngsters didn't yet understand. They could smile at it. Joyce couldn't. The fact that this was just a thoughtless girl in love made no difference. What had to be judged here was the legal situation, not the human emotions involved.

Centuries ago, The Messire had established this society, speaking through His prophets, and it was that society which Joyce defended here, just as hundreds of Justices defended it every day throughout the land.

There were those worthy of marriage, and those who were not. Those with the mental capacity to rule, administer, judge, and choose the sick to be healed, and those without it. The notion had long ago been exploded that all human beings were equal.

The blunt facts of life were that talent and mental capacity were hereditary. Some human beings were better equipped than others to judge what was best for the human race as a whole, but, with unrestricted marriage, these superior qualities were in grave danger of dilution.

To have attempted to breed the ordinary people out of existence would have been impossible. The sea is not dried up with blotting paper. But the building of dikes *was* possible.

Out of the rubble and flame of the Twenty-first Century, The Messire had handed down the answer, and the Law. The Law was the dike that penned the sea of ordinary people away from the wellsprings of the families.

Through His prophets, The Messire had ordained his First Families, and they, in turn, had chosen others. To all of these were given the sacrament of marriage and the heritage of name and property for their children. For centuries, the families had been preserved, their members choosing wives and husbands only out of their own kind.

It was unnecessary to enforce childlessness on the remaining people. Neither superior intelligence nor talent were required for the world's routine work.

Nor had "enforcement," as such, of The Messire's Law been required for many years, now. It was not that the people were impious or heretical. Rather it was that, being human, they were prone to error. In their untutored minds, the purpose and meaning of the Law sometimes became unclear.

Despite that simple piety, if young Normandy had been even more of a fool, and let the incident pass, some members of the people might mistakenly have felt such behavior was permissible. The precedent would have been established. If, after that, some other error had been allowed to go uncorrected, yet another step away from the Law might be taken. And after that, another—

Anarchy. And the widening erosion in the dike.

Joyce scowled down at the Accused. He only wished it hadn't been a girl.

Blanding reached the end of his indictment and paused, with a gesture to Joyce.

Joyce looked down at the Accused again, partly because he wished to study her again and partly because it lent weight to his opinion.

The girl's trembling confirmed his previous tentative decision. There was no purpose in dragging this on. The quickest conclusion was the best.

"Thank you, Justice," he said to Blanding. He addressed the Accused.

"Young woman, we have heard your indictment. Justice Blanding will now repeat the etiquette of Trial, in order that there may be no doubt in your mind of your rights."

"The Messire is your judge," Blanding told her gravely. "The verdict we deliver here is not conclusive. If you wish to appeal, make your appeal to Him."

There was a stir and rustle in the crowd, as there always was. Joyce saw a number of people touch the images at their throats.

"We shall deliberate on this verdict, each separately determining the degree of your guilt. When we have reached a verdict, our separate opinions shall determine the degree of mundane appeal granted you."

Joyce threw a quick glance at the girl. She was looking up at Blanding with her hands on the rail of her box, her arms stiffly extended.

"If your case has been misrepresented to this Court, The Messire will intervene in your behalf. If you are innocent, you have nothing to fear."

Having completed the recital, he stopped and looked out over the heads of the crowd.

Joyce stepped back, and saw that Kallimer and Pedersen were looking down at his hands, hidden from the crowd. He signaled for a verdict of "Completely Guilty." Giving the girl a weapon to defend herself would be ridiculous. If she succeeded in firing at all, she was sure to miss him and injure someone in the crowd. It was best to get this case out of the way quickly and efficiently. The thing had to be squashed right here.

To his surprise, he saw Kallimer signal back "reconsider."

Joyce looked at the Associate. He might have expected some-thing of the sort from Blanding, but a man of Kallimer's intel-ligence should have arrived at the proper conclusion.

Perhaps the Bar Association had been very wise to give him this trial, instead of letting some lesser Justice handle it. He'd had his doubts, but this wiped them out.

Without looking at Kallimer, but letting him plainly see the angry swell of the set jaw muscle that tightened his cheek, Joyce signaled "imperative!"

Kallimer sighed inaudibly, and his "acquiesce" was limp-fingered, as though he were trying to convey resignation, as well.

Joyce faced front, still furious, but with his voice under control.

"Justice Blanding, have you reached a verdict?" He moved his left shoulder slightly.

Blanding, from his position on the rostrum, turned and saw the signal.

"I find the Accused completely guilty, Mr. Justice," he said.

Joyce turned to Pedersen in the absolute silence that always fell over a plaza during the rendering of the verdict.

"Completely guilty, Mr. Justice."

Joyce turned to Kallimer.

The man's lips twitched in a faint, sardonic smile. "Completely guilty, Mr. Justice."

Joyce looked down at the Accused. "I also find you completely guilty as charged," he said. "You will not be allowed a weapon with which to make mundane appeal. Your only recourse is to The Messire's mercy. I pray that our verdict is correct."

He stepped back to a new outburst of applause from the family boxes, satisfied that he had done his best. So far, it was a good trial. Even Kallimer's rebelliousness had been evident only here on the bench. The majesty and unanimity of justice had been preserved as far as the crowd could tell.

He turned and walked slowly down the platform steps, through the deep hush that locked the plaza.

It *had* been a good trial. The Bar Association would detail it and its significance in the Closed Archives, and, generations from now, the older Justices would be reading about it, seeing how his action today had choked off the incipient attack on this culture and this civilization.

But that was not uppermost in Joyce's mind. What men a hundred years from now would say could not have much personal significance to him. What made his pulse beat more and more strongly as he descended the steps, turned the corner of the bench, and walked out into the plaza, was the knowledge that his contemporaries—the other Justices of the Bar Association—the men who had also come to the top, and who understood what the burden was—would know he had not failed the ideal.

He stopped just short of the Ground of Trial and gestured to the attendants around the Accused. They removed the Accused's clothing to guard against armor or concealed weapons, and stepped aside.

Joyce took the final stride that placed him on the Justice's Square, where other amplifiers once more took up his voice.

"The Accused will come forward to make her appeal."

The girl stumbled a bit coming out of the box, and he heard a slight sound of disappointment form the family boxes. It was not a good Entrance. But that could be forgotten.

He reached down, and the gun slipped out of its holster in one smooth sweep of his arm that was pure line of motion as he simultaneously half-turned, his vest standing out in a perfect straight-up-and-down cylindrical fall from his neck to its hem. He came up slightly on his toes, and there was a scattering of "bravo!" from the family boxes as well as the more reserved "excellent" which was really all a lame man deserved for his draw, no matter how perfect his arm motion.

The Accused was standing, pale of face, in the Square of Appeal.

Holding his draw, Joyce waited to speak the ultimate sentence.

He was growing old. The number of trials remaining to him was low. Someday soon, on a verdict of "probably guilty," perhaps, when the Accused had a fully loaded weapon, The Messire would reverse the verdict.

Not because of his physical slowness. The lameness and hitch in the draw would be merely symptomatic of his advancing slowness of mind. He would not have interpreted the case correctly.

He knew that, expected it, and felt only acceptance for it. A Justice who rendered an incorrect verdict deserved the penalty just as much as a guilty member of the people.

Meanwhile, this was the upheld ideal.

"You have been adjudged completely guilty as charged," he said, listening to the old words roll out over the plaza. "You have not been granted pardon by this Court. Make your appeal to The Messire."

The Accused looked at him wide-eyed out of her pallor. There was no certainty she was praying, but Joyce presumed she was.

Justice rested in The Messire. He knew the guilty and the innocent; punished the one and protected the other. Joyce was only His instrument, and Trial was only the opportunity for His judgment to become apparent. Men could judge each other, and pass sentence. But men could be wise or foolish in their decisions. That was the fallible nature of Man.

Here was where the test came; here where the Accused prayed to The Messire for the ultimate, infallible judgment. This was Trial.

His finger tightened on the trigger while his arm came slowly down and forward. This, too, was where Joyce prayed to the Ultimate Judge, asking whether he had done wisely, whether he had once more done well. Each trial was his Trial, too. This was his contact with The Messire. This was Truth.

Something whirled out of the silent crowd of people and landed at the girl's feet. It was a gun, and the girl scrambled for it.

As soon as she picked it up, Joyce knew he'd lost his advantage. His reflexes were too slow, and he'd lost two decisive seconds by stopping, paralyzed, and staring at it.

He shook his head to clear away the momentary shock. He gave up paying attention to the confused noise and blind milling of the crowd. He narrowed his concentration down to the girl and her gun. As far as he could permit himself to be concerned, he and she were alone in a private universe, each trying to overcome panic long enough to act.

He'd lost his aim, and his arm had dropped below the line of fire. He brought it up, deliberately slowing his impulse to fling it into position. If he missed, the odds would be all against a second shot.

It was a better aim than the conventional method, in any case. It permitted no elaboration; it had no grace or beauty, but it *was* a steadier method of aiming.

Her shot struck his forearm, and his hand slapped up into the air from the shock. His fingers almost lost their grip on the butt, and he clenched them convulsively.

The girl was tugging at her weapon, doing something with the buttplate.

His gun discharged into the air, and his arm shook with fresh pain from the recoil.

He could see the Accused was as wrought up as he was. He clutched his forearm with his left hand and steadied down. Before she could fire again, his gun burst into life, throwing her backward and down to the ground. She was obviously dead.

He took a deep, shuddering breath. The gun started to fall out of his weak fingers, but he caught it with his left hand and dropped it into its holster.

The world around him slowly filtered back into his senses. He became aware of angry shouts in the crowd of people, and of attendants struggling to hold them in check. There was a knot of people clustered around a family box, but before he could investigate that, he felt Kallimer put an arm around his waist and hold him up. He hadn't even realized he was swaying.

"We can't worry about the crowd," Kallimer said in a peculiar voice. It was urgent, but he sounded so calm under it. There was no hysteria in him, and Joyce noted that to his credit.

"Did you see who threw the gun?" Joyce demanded.

Kallimer shook his head. "No. Doesn't matter. We've got to get back to New York."

Joyce looked up at the bench. Blanding wasn't in sight, but Pedersen was hanging by his hands, dangling down over its face, and dropping to the plaza. He bent, picked up the briefcase he'd thrown down ahead of him, ripped it open, and pulled out his gun.

That was idiotic. What did he think he was doing?

"Joyce!" Kallimer was pulling at him.

"All right!" Joyce snapped in annoyance. He began to run toward Pedersen before the fool could disgrace himself. As he ran, he realized Kallimer was right. The three of them had to get back to New York as quickly as possible. The Bar Association had to know.

Pedersen sat far back in his corner of the train compartment, his eyes closed and his head against the paneling as though he was listening to the sound of the trolley running along the overhead cable. The Messire only knew what he was really listening to. His face was pale.

Joyce turned stiffly toward Kallimer, hampered by the sling and cast on his arm. The Associate was staring out the window, and neither he nor Pedersen had said a word since they'd boarded the train, fifteen minutes ago. At that time, there had still been noise coming from the plaza.

There'd been a twenty-minute wait for the train. That meant more than three-quarters of an hour had passed since the start of it all, and Joyce still did not understand exactly what had happened. He had only disconnected impressions of the entire incident, and, for the life of him, he could find no basic significance behind it, although he knew there had to be one.

"Kallimer."

The Associate turned away from the window. "What?"

Joyce gestured, conscious of his sudden inability to find the proper phrasing.

"You want to know what touched it off. Is that it?"

Joyce nodded, relieved at not having to say it after all.

Kallimer shook his head. "I don't know, exactly. Somebody in the crowd felt strongly enough to throw her the gun. One of her relatives, I suppose."

"But—" Joyce gestured inarticulately. "It...it was a *legal* execution! Who would interfere with justice? Who'd take the risk of eternal damnation by interfering with The Messire's obvious will?"

Pedersen, in his corner, made a very peculiar sound. Kallimer shot him a cryptic glare. He turned back to Joyce and seemed to be searching for words.

"Joyce," he said finally, "how do you imagine The Messire would reverse a verdict of 'Completely Guilty'?"

Joyce frowned. "Well...I don't know. My gun might jam. Or I might fire and unaccountably miss."

"You don't know for certain, because it's never happened. Am I correct?"

"Substantially."

"Now. How many reversals have there been on verdicts of 'Apparently Guilty'? When the Accused was given a gun with one cartridge in the chamber."

"A few."

"But it's never happened to any Justice you know, has it?"

Joyce shook his head. "No, but there are recorded cases. A few, as I said."

"Very well. What about 'Possibly Guilty'? Many reversals on those verdicts?"

"An appreciable number."

"Almost had a few of those yourself, didn't you?"

"A few."

"Very well." Kallimer held up his hand, bending one finger for each point. "Now—first we have the case in which the Accused is weaponless. No reversals. Next we have the case in which the Accused has one shot to fire. A few reversals. And finally we have the case in which the Accused has as much of a weapon as the Presiding Justice. An appreciable number of reversals.

"Does it not seem to you, Justice Joyce, that this series of statistics might well occur without the intervention of any Divine Will whatsoever?"

Joyce stared at him, but Kallimer gave him no chance to reply.

"Furthermore, Joyce; do the people have the right to bear arms? That is to say, can you imagine an Accused who was acquainted with the firing and aiming of an automatic pistol? The answer—you asked, now hear me out—the answer is No.

"More. Have you ever heard of The Messire reversing a verdict of 'Not Guilty'?"

Joyce bridled. "There aren't two of those a year!"

Kallimer's mouth hooked. "I know. But they *do* exist. Explain this, then; how do you reconcile Divine Will with the curious fact that verdicts of 'Not Guilty' and 'Completely Guilty' are *never* reversed, and never have been reversed, though Messire knows we came close this afternoon? Are you claiming that in those cases, every Justice who ever lived was right every time? Are you attempting to claim, for mortal men, the infallibility which is The Messire's particular province?"

Kallimer's face was tense with emotion, and Joyce received a distinct impression that the Associate was speaking with excessive violence; actually his voice was still under control.

"Mr. Joyce, if you can't see the point I'm driving at, I am sorry. But, rest assured, somebody in that crowd of people finally realized it, after all these years. Somebody wasn't afraid of The Messire." Kallimer turned his head sharply and looked out the window at the Hudson, running silver far below as the train swung over to the east shore. "I'm not sure Pedersen wasn't right in drawing his gun. And, Mr. Joyce, if what I've said hasn't shaken you, it certainly should have."

Kallimer took a deep breath and seemed to calm down a little.

"Mr. Joyce," he said softly, "I believe there's something you haven't thought of. I imagine it'll make you unhappy when I tell you.

"Talking in your terms, now—you don't have to give an inch, Mr. Joyce; in fact, you have to hang on to your beliefs with absolute rigidity to appreciate the full impact—looking at it from your point of view: You can't imagine how The Messire would go about reversing an unjust verdict of 'Completely Guilty.' But The Messire is omniscient and omnipotent. His ways are complex and unknowable. Am I correct? Well, then, how do you know that what happened today wasn't a hint of how He'd manage it?"

The blood drained out of Joyce's face.

Late that night, Emily looked at him in surprise when she answered her door.

"Sam! But you never—" She stopped. "Come in, Sam. You surprised me."

Joyce kissed her cheek and strode nervously into her apartment. He knew what had startled her. He never called on nights following trials; in the fifteen years they'd been together, she would naturally have noticed that. He considered the problem while on his way over, and the only thing to do, he'd decided, was to act as though nothing unusual were taking place. He reasoned that a woman, being a woman, would shrug her shoulders over it after the first few minutes. Probably, after a short time, she'd even begin to doubt her memory.

"Sam, what's the matter with your arm?"

He spun around and saw her still standing by the door, wearing a dressing gown, with her hair in curlers.

"Trial," he bit off shortly. He paced across the room, took a pear out of a bowl, and bit into it. "I'm hungry," he said with false vigor.

She seemed to collect herself. "Of course, Sam. I'll put something on the stove. It won't be more than a few moments. Excuse me." She went into the kitchen, leaving him standing alone in the semidarkness surrounding the one light she'd switched on near the door. Impatiently, he snapped the switches of the other lamps in the room and stood in the middle of it, chewing the pear and bouncing it in his palm between bites.

He heard Emily put a pan on a burner. He moved abruptly and strode into the kitchen, stopping just inside the door and dropping the pear down the disposal chute.

"Finished it," he said, explaining his presence. He looked around. "Anything I can do?"

Emily looked up at him, a look of amused disbelief on her face, "Sam, what's gotten into you?"

Joyce scowled. "Anything wrong with coming up to see my girl?"

Saying it made the scowl disappear. He looked down at Emily, who was bent over the stove again. Fifteen years had touched her hair, and put little lines on her forehead and the corners of her mouth. They added a good bit to her hips and waist. But there was an earthly, commonsense comfort in her. He could put his key in the door at any time of night, and she'd hear the sound and be there to meet him.

He reached down and pulled her up. His arm twinged a bit, but that was unimportant at the moment. He folded his arms around her and cupped the back of her head in one palm. The warmth and security of her made his clutch tighter than he'd intended at the start. Suddenly he found himself wishing he'd never have to go back to his own ascetic flat.

Emily smiled faintly and kissed his chin. "Sam, what *did* happen? I heard the trial results over the radio this afternoon, and all they announced for Nyack was a successful conclusion to a verdict of 'Completely Guilty.' Was there some trouble they didn't want to talk about?"

His mood burst, and he dropped his arms.

"What kind of trouble?" he asked sharply.

Her eyes opened, and she looked at him in fresh surprise. "I didn't mean anything by it, Sam. Just ordinary trouble . . . you know, a lucky shot by the Accused—" She looked at the light cast on his arm. "But that couldn't be it, with an unarmed Accused—"

Joyce took an angry breath. "I thought we had that clear between us," he said in a voice he realized was too angry. "From the very beginning, I've made it plain that your province is yours and my province is mine. If I don't tell you about it, you can assume I don't feel you should know."

Emily stepped back and quickly bent over the stove again. "All right, Sam," she said in a low voice. "I'm sorry." She lifted the lid of a pan. "Supper'll be ready in a minute. It'll be pretty busy in here when all these pots come to a boil at the same time."

"I'll be waiting in the living room." Joyce turned and walked out.

He paced back and forth over the rug, his lips in a tight line, conscious now of the pain in his arm.

One more scar. One more objection from The Messire. All safe in the end, but one more objection, nevertheless, and what did it mean?

And the Bar Association.

"A hearing!" he muttered. "A full hearing tomorrow!" As though his report hadn't been adequate. He'd told them what happened. It should have been enough. But Kallimer, with his allegations that there was more to the incident—

Well, all right. Tomorrow he'd see about Kallimer.

Emily came into the living room. "Supper's ready, Sam." Her voice and expression were careful to be normal. She didn't want to provoke him again.

She was hurt, and he didn't like to see her that way. He laughed suddenly and put his arm around her shoulders, squeezing. "Well, let's eat, eh, girl?"

"Of course, Sam."

He frowned slightly, dissatisfied. But there was no point in trying to patch it up and only making it worse. He kept still as they went into the dining room.

They ate silently. Or rather, to be honest with himself, Joyce had to admit that he ate and Emily toyed with a small portion, keeping him company out of politeness.

The act of sitting still for twenty minutes quieted his nerves a bit. And he appreciated Emily's courtesy. As he pushed his coffee cup away, he looked up at her and smiled.

"That was very good. Thank you, Emily."

She smiled faintly. "Thank you, Sam. I'm glad you liked it. I'm afraid it wasn't much. I hadn't planned—" She broke off.

So, she *had* continued to wonder about his calling tonight. He smiled ruefully. And now she thought she'd offended him again. He'd been pretty grumpy tonight.

He reached out and took her hand. "That's all right, Emily."

✧　　✧　　✧

After she'd washed the dishes, she came in and sat down beside him on the couch, where he was slumped with his feet on a hassock. His ankles and calves were aching. It was all right as long as he kept moving, but once he sat down the ache always began. He smiled at her wanly.

Smiling back, she bent wordlessly and began to massage his calves, working the muscles with her fingers.

"Emily—"

"Yes, Sam?"

"If...Nothing, Emily. There's not much point in talking about it." He found himself caught between the desire to speak to someone and the urgent sense that this afternoon was best forgotten. He stared down past his feet without looking at anything. Perhaps there was some way to maneuver her into telling him what he wanted to know, without his having to tell her about it.

Why was he reluctant to talk about this afternoon? He didn't know, exactly; but he couldn't bring himself to do it, no more than he could have discussed some character defect he might have accidentally observed in a lady or gentleman.

"What else did they say over the radio?" he asked without any special intonation. "About Nyack."

"Nothing, Sam, except for the bare results."

He grunted in disappointment.

Perhaps there was some better angle of approach. "Emily, suppose...suppose you knew of a case involving a people's girl and a family man. Suppose the girl had come up to the man on a public street and addressed him by his first name."

He stopped uncomfortably.

"Yes, Sam?"

"Uh...well, what would you think?"

Emily's hands became still for a moment, then began working on his calves again.

"What would I think?" she asked in a low voice, looking down at the floor. "I'd think she was very foolish."

He grimaced. That wasn't what he wanted. But did he know what he wanted from her? What *was* the answer he was looking for? He tried again.

"Yes, of course. But, aside from that, what else?"

He saw Emily bite her lip. "I'm afraid I don't understand what you mean, Sam."

A tinge of his earlier anger put a bite in his voice. "You're not that unintelligent, Emily."

She took a deep breath and looked at him. "Sam, something drastic went wrong today, didn't it? Something very bad. You were terribly upset when you came in—"

"Upset? I don't think so," he interrupted quickly.

"Sam, I've been your mistress for fifteen years."

He knew his face was betraying him. In her flashes of shrewdness, she always did this to him. She'd put her finger exactly on the vulnerable truth, disarming his ability to cover up.

He sighed and spread his hands in a gesture of resignation. "All right, Emily. Yes, I am upset." The irritation welled up again. "That's why I want some help from you, instead of this evasiveness."

She straightened up, taking her hands off his aching legs, and half-turned on the couch, so that she was looking directly into his eyes. She held his gaze without hesitation.

"Maybe you're asking too much of me. Perhaps not. This *is* important, isn't it? I've never seen you quite as troubled as this."

She was tense, he realized. Tense, and apprehensive. But he saw, as well, that she had decided to go ahead, despite whatever her private doubts might be.

"Yes," he admitted, "it's important."

"Very well. You want to know what I think about that girl? Suppose you tell me what you think, first. Do you believe she did it out of spite, or malice, or impulse?"

He shook his head. "Of course not! She was in love with him, and forgot herself."

Emily's eyes welled up with a sudden trace of tears. Joyce stared at her, dumbfounded, for the few seconds before she wiped one hand across her eyes in annoyance.

"Well?" she asked in a low voice.

"I'm afraid it's my turn not to understand," he said after a moment. He frowned. What was she driving at?

"What distinguishes me from that girl, Sam? A few years? What do you expect me to think?"

"It's not the same thing at all, Emily!" he shot back in honest anger. "Why...why you're a mature woman. We're—"

He couldn't really point out the difference, but he knew it was there. She'd never said or done anything—

"Emily, you know very well you'd never do what that girl did!"

"Only because I'm more conscious of the rules," she answered in a low voice. "What real difference is there between her and myself? It is that it's you and I, rather than two other people; rather than any one of the scores of similar couples we know? What distinguishes us in your eyes? The fact that we're not a case for you to try?"

"Emily, this is ridiculous!"

She shook her head slowly. "That girl broke the law. I haven't. But I haven't only because I realized, from the very start, just what kind of tightrope I'd be walking for the rest of our lives. I couldn't leave you and go back to the people, now; I've grown too used to living as I do. But I'll always be no more than I was born to.

"Suppose I were a People's man—a mechanic, or perhaps even an engineer if I'd bound myself to some family. I'd know that all my skill and training wouldn't be of any use if I were accused of some crime in a court of law. I'd know that addressing my patron in public by his first name would be a crime—a different kind of crime than if I were my patron's mistress, certainly, but a crime, nevertheless. Let's assume that, as my patron's engineer, I overrode his will on the specifications for whatever product my patron manufactured. Or that I attempted to redesign a product or develop a new one without first getting his approval and suggestions; that would be legally analogous to what the girl did, wouldn't it?"

"Yes, and properly so," Joyce retorted.

Emily looked at him and nodded slowly. She went on:

"If I were that engineer, and I had any common sense, I'd be constantly aware of the difference between myself and my patron. I would remind myself, every day, that my patron was born to a family, and that my patron would, in turn, be permitted the sacrament of marriage when he desired it with a lady. I would understand that engineers were members of the people, and that my patron was a member of one of the First Families, or a Legislator, or a Justice. Realizing all this, I would always be careful never to encroach on the difference between us, accepting my fate in having been born to the people, and his having been born to a family."

Joyce frowned. "That sounds a little bit as though you considered birth a blind accident."

Emily looked at him silently. She took a deep breath. "Being an intelligent person, I, as that engineer, would attribute my station at birth to the direction of The Messire. You'll hear no heresies from me, Sam." She reached out and took his hand.

"That's why I'll say, again, that the girl in Nyack was foolish. That *was* the case in Nyack, wasn't it? She did what none of us, in our right minds, would consider doing. Certainly, she did what I'd never do, but then, I'm older than she. I was older when I came to you, or I at least assume so, since you called her a girl."

Suddenly, she bit her lip. "Young people in love are not necessarily in their right minds, just as people enraged are not acting logically. Who's to say what their punishment should be?"

"There is Someone," Joyce answered firmly.

Emily nodded, looking at him, her expression abstracted. Suddenly she said:

"Sam, have you ever really looked at yourself in a mirror? Not to see whether you'd shaved properly, or whether your wig was crooked on the morning before a trial, but just to look at yourself."

He couldn't understand this new tack.

"Do you know you have a very young face, Sam? Under that black beard-shadow, with the scowl gone, you've got the face of a troubled adolescent. You've taught yourself dignity, and put flesh on your body, but you're still a young boy, searching for the key that will wind the world up to run accurately forever. Perhaps you believe you've found it. You believe in what you're doing. You believe that justice is the most important thing in the world. What you do, you do as a crusade. There's no wanton malice or cruelty in you. I don't believe I've ever known you to do anything purely for yourself.

"I love you for it, Sam. But, except sometimes with me, you've submerged yourself in your ideal, until you've learned to ignore Sam Joyce entirely. You're Mister Justice Joyce all the time."

She closed her hand on his. "Something happened this afternoon, and I suspect it was drastic. You've come to me after facing an unarmed Accused—a girl, young and unskilled—but there's a cast on your arm, and what must be a bullet hole under it. I don't know what happened. I do know there's a news blackout on Nyack.

"Sam, if the system's been finally challenged, then you're in terrible danger. Other men aren't like you. Other men—people's men and family men—act in rage, or fear, or love. If they tear down your world and your ideal—"

"Tear down—!"

"... If they tear down what you have given your life to, there will be nothing left of you. If the system goes, it takes Justice Joyce's lifeblood with it, and only I know where the little fragment of Sam Joyce lives. It won't be enough."

"Emily, you're exaggerating beyond all reason!"

Emily clutched his hand. He saw, to his complete amazement, that she'd shut her eyes against the tears, but that streaks of silent moisture were trickling down her cheeks.

"You've come to me for help, but I'm part of the world, too, and I have to live the way it lets me. After all these years, you want to know whether you've been right, and I'm supposed to tell you.

"I told you I thought the girl was foolish. Sam, I love you, but I don't dare give you your answer. I told you: you won't hear any heretical statements from me."

The night had slowly edged into dawn. Joyce stared at it through the window beside the bed. He had no way of knowing whether Emily had ever gone to sleep or not. She was lying motionless, just as she had been all night.

Joyce's eyes were burning, and the short stubble of his graying natural hair was thick with perspiration. The night had been sleepless for him.

His arm was much better this morning, but he still remembered the shock of the bullet.

If you believed, as you must believe, that The Messire saw every human deed, knew every human thought, and caused every human event, then what had He meant in Nyack?

If the sentence was correct, why did The Messire permit her that one shot? Why hadn't whoever threw the gun been stopped before he could do it? If the sentence was unjust, why hadn't she killed him?

Was it that The Messire approved of him, but not of the basis of his judgment? But his basis was the Law, and The Messire had handed down the Law!

Was it, as Kallimer had said, that The Messire was not as Joyce conceived of him?

What did Emily think?

He reminded himself that what Emily thought was irrelevant, as he had hastily reminded himself many times during the past night. Her opinion did not govern the truth or falsehood of justice. Justice was an absolute; it was either right, no matter what the opinions of Mankind, or it was worthless.

Was it, as Kallimer had said viciously, that The Messire was trying to make him understand something?

What?

What had He meant in Nyack?

Joyce lay on the bed, exhausted. He knew he was thinking wildly. He'd gone over and over this ground, trying to find the proper logic, and accomplishing nothing. He was in no condition to reason correctly. He only hoped he could act wisely at the hearing this afternoon.

He slipped cautiously out of bed, hesitating at every rustle of the sheets. Once out, he dressed hastily, and left the apartment as quietly as he could. He didn't want Emily to wake up and see what condition he was in.

He walked into the hearing room with measured steps, hoping no one would notice his unsettled state of mind. When the Chief Justice showed agitation, what could anyone expect of the lesser Justices?

This, too, was part of the task, and the young, ambitious Associate Justice of Utica hadn't had the faintest inkling of it, just as, throughout his dedicated advancement through the ranks of his profession, he could not have dreamed how difficult it would some day be to walk steadily through a door when sleepless legs and aching ankles dragged at every step.

He saw the tension rampant in every Member. No one was sitting down quietly, waiting for the hearing to begin. Knots of men stood everywhere, talking sharply, and there was a continual movement from one group to another.

Joyce scowled in annoyance and nodded shortly as most of the faces in the room were turned toward him. He looked around for Joshua Normandy, but the Bar Association's Chairman had not yet come in. He saw Kallimer, standing to one side, wearing his frown and talking alone to a white-faced Pedersen.

Joyce went over to them. He hadn't decided yet what to do with Kallimer. The man was arrogant. He seemed to derive genuine pleasure from talking in terms Joyce was unable to understand.

But the man was intelligent, and ambitious. His ambition would lead him to defend the same principles that Joyce defended, and his intelligence would make him a superlative Chief Justice, once Joyce was gone.

For the sake of that, Joyce was willing to let yesterday's questionable behavior go. Perhaps, after all, Kallimer had been right in asking for a reconsideration of the verdict.

Once again, Joyce was painfully conscious of his inability to arrive at any firm opinion on yesterday's events. He stopped in front of Kallimer and Pedersen with a shake of his head, and only then realized how peculiar the gesture must look to them.

"Good afternoon, Justice," Kallimer said dryly.

Joyce searched his face for some indication of his state of mind, but there was nothing beyond the omnipresent frown.

"Good afternoon, Justices," he said finally. "Or have the election results been confirmed, Legislator?" he asked Pedersen.

Pedersen's face was strained. "Yes, sir. The results were confirmed. But I resigned."

Joyce's eyebrows shot up. Recovering, he tried to smile pleasantly. "Then you're returning to the Bar?"

Pedersen shook his head. "No...uh—" he husked in a dry voice, "I'm here simply as a witness to...uh...yesterday." He was deathly pale.

Kallimer smiled coldly. "Mr. Pedersen has decided to retire from public life, Justice Joyce. He now considers that his first attempt to dissociate himself from the Bar was inadequate."

Joyce looked from Kallimer back to Pedersen. The younger man, he suddenly realized, was terrified.

"Blanding's dead, you know," Kallimer said without inflection. "A paving block was thrown at his head yesterday afternoon. It's uncertain just what the circumstances were, but a member of the Civil Guard brought the word out." Kallimer smiled at Pedersen. "And now our former Associate, his earlier presentiments proven correct, is shortly taking a trip abroad—the Lakes Confederation, I believe?"

"I have distant relations in St. Paul," Pedersen confirmed huskily. "And there is an Ontario branch of the family in Toronto. I plan to be away for some time. A tour."

Kallimer still smiled. "The key word in that statement would be 'distant,' would it not, Mr. Pedersen?"

Pedersen flushed angrily, but Joyce seized on Kallimer's attitude as a reassuring sign. At least, Pedersen's cowardice wasn't general. For the moment, that seemed more important than the news of Blanding's death.

His lack of astonishment made him look at himself in wonder. Was he that much upset, that a Justice's murder failed to shock him? Was he really that far gone in his acceptance of the incredible?

He knew, with a calmly logical part of his mind, that before yesterday he would have considered himself insane to even think of anyone's attacking the Law. Today, he could pass over it. Not lightly, but, nevertheless, pass over it.

"You're sure of your information, Kallimer?" he asked.

Kallimer nodded, looking at him curiously. "The witness is reliable. And he brought out the gun, too. That's an astonishing item in itself. You'll be interested."

Joyce raised his eyebrows politely. "Really?" He saw Joshua Normandy come into the hearing room, and nodded in the Chairman's direction. "The hearing's about to begin. It'll be brought up, of course?"

Kallimer was frankly puzzled by his attitude. Joyce's head was erect, and his shoulders had abruptly straightened out of their unconscious slump.

"Yes, of course."

"Good. Shall we take our places? Good afternoon, Mr. Pedersen. It was a pleasure, having you on my bench." He took Kallimer's arm, and, together, they strolled up to the long table facing the chairs of the lesser Justices.

Joyce knew what was happening to him, and the calm, judicial part of his mind, at last given something it understood to work with, approved.

He had been in a panic. At noon, yesterday, the foundations of his logic had been destroyed. The integrity of justice and Justices had been attacked, and his belief in the universal acceptance of The Messire's Law had been proved false. He had discovered, in one climactic instant, that there were people willing to deliberately attack the Law.

He had been beyond his depth. He had no precedent for such a crime; no basis on which to judge the situation. Someone else, perhaps, such as Kallimer or Justice Normandy, might have the reach of mind to encompass sit. But Joyce knew he was not a brilliant man. He was only an honest man, and he knew what was beyond him. In the instant that he had stopped, staring dumbfounded at the gun lying on the plaza stones, with the Accused reaching for it eagerly, he had stopped being capable of evaluating the legal situation and taking steps to rectify it. Panic could warp a man's judgment completely.

That was what The Messire had been trying to make him realize. The world was changing, and the Chief Justice was not equipped to deal with the change.

As an honest man; as a man sincere in his beliefs, he was ready to give up his responsibilities and let the better suited men take them up.

He nodded to Justice Normandy and the other Bar Association officers. Then he sat down calmly, with Kallimer beside him, and waited to see what the more intelligent men had made of the situation.

Kallimer was holding up the gun brought out of Nyack. Joyce looked at it curiously.

It was late in the afternoon, and a good deal of testimony had already been recorded. Pedersen stated that he was aware of angry movement in the crowd as Joyce made his draw, but that the gun had been thrown by an unidentified man before anything could be done. After the shooting, the man and a surrounding group of other men had been lost in the crowd. The crowd itself had been bewildered at first, and then divided in its reactions. That early in the riot, there had been no signs of unanimous effort.

The Civil Guardsman had testified that, as far as he knew, he was the only survivor of the squad detailed to keep order during the trial. He had seized the gun after the executed Accused dropped it, and run to Guard headquarters for help. It was his impression that the immediate deaths among family members at the trial were the result of spontaneous riot in the crowd, and not of any organized plan of assassination.

Justice Kallimer had commented that this was also his impression. The only traces of intelligent planning, he stated, had shown themselves in the cutting of the train cables out of Nyack and the attack on the radio station, where the supervising family man had smashed the transmitter before it could be captured. Note was made of the loyalty of the station engineering staff.

Now, Kallimer said: "Bearing previous testimony in mind, I'd like to call this hearing's attention to the construction and design of this illegal weapon."

Joyce bent closer. There were a number of peculiarities in the gun, and they interested him.

"First," Kallimer went on, "the weapon is obviously hand-made. Its frame consists of a solid metal piece—steel, I'm told by a competent engineer—which bears obvious file marks. Moreover, it is of almost primitive design. It has a smoothbore barrel, drilled through from muzzle to breech, and is mortised at the breech to accommodate one hand-inserted cartridge and a spring-loaded hammer. Additional cartridges are stored in the butt, covered by a friction plate. It is fired by thumbing back the hammer and releasing it, after which the first cartridge case must be removed by hand before it can be reloaded.

"A hasty weapon. A weapon of desperation, thrown together by someone with only a few hours to work in."

Kallimer put the gun down. "A hopelessly inefficient and inadequate weapon. I am informed that the barrel was not even drilled parallel to the frame's long axis, and that the crude sights were also askew, further complicating the error in aiming. It is remarkable that Mr. Justice Joyce was struck at all, and it is no wonder at all that the Accused was never able to fire a second shot."

Joyce shook his head slightly. It was perfectly obvious how the girl had managed to hit him. But, then, Kallimer, with his slightly eccentric viewpoint, would not be likely to take The Messire into account.

Kallimer was speaking again.

"The point, however, isn't relevant here. It is the nature of this weapon which concerns us. Obviously, it was not constructed by anyone particularly skilled in the craft, and its design is hope-lessly unimaginative. It is unlikely that any others exist. It follows, then, that the rebellion, if I may call it such for the moment, is largely confined to the Accused's immediate...ah...relations. No actual large-scale organized effort exists.

"We have the testimony of Mr. Pedersen and the Guardsman. It seems obvious that the gun-throwers' plans culminated in the delivery of the weapon to the Accused. What followed was a spontaneous demonstration. This, together with some other relevant data already mentioned in testimony, is the basis on which we have formulated our program of rectification."

Kallimer turned toward the center of the table. "Justice Normandy."

Normandy was an aged, gray-headed man whose heavy brows hung low over his eyes. He rose out of his chair and supported his weight on his hands, leaning out over the table and looking toward the lesser Justices in their seats.

Joyce looked at him curiously.

Normandy had never been Chief Justice. He'd risen to Chief Associate under Kemple, the Chief Justice before the one Joyce had replaced. The oldest son of one of the First Families, Normandy had then retired from active work, becoming first Recorder and the Chairman of the Bar Association. He'd held the position longer than Joyce had been Chief Justice, and he was at least seventy.

Joyce wondered what he and Kallimer had decided to do.

Normandy's voice was harsh with age. He forced each word out of his throat.

"Justice Kallimer has summed up very well. A purely personal rebellion against the Law in Nyack has touched off a spontaneous demonstration. You've noticed the lack of evidence implicating any ringleaders except the Accused's relations. They're nothing but woodworkers. There was some later participation by engineers, because it took training to see the importance of cutting off communications. But that wasn't until this emotional upheaval had a chance to get contagious.

"There's a certain rebellious feeling, yes. But it's hardly born yet. It won't spread unless we let it, and we won't. By tomorrow afternoon, we'll be back to normal.

"Thank you, Justices. This hearing's concluded, and Mr. Joyce, Mr. Kallimer, and I will stay behind for further discussion."

Joyce watched the lesser Justices file out of the hearing room, their manner much less nervous than it had been. Normandy had put some starch back into their spines.

Joyce, too, felt better. He'd been right in expecting Kallimer and Normandy to have a solution. He was leaving the Law in capable hands.

✧   ✧   ✧

Normandy waited until the room was empty. Then he turned to Kallimer with an expression of disgust.

"Well, they believe it. I'd be happier if a few of them hadn't."

Kallimer shrugged. "There's no telling. If any of them saw through it, they'd be intelligent enough not to show it."

Normandy cocked an eyebrow, pursed his lips, and, after a moment, grinned. "That's a good point."

Joyce looked blankly at both of them. "I gather," he said finally, "that the situation is more serious than was divulged." He felt a slight return of his old disquiet, but nothing near panic.

Normandy and Kallimer turned in their chairs. Both of them looked at him speculatively.

Normandy nodded. "By quite a good bit. It took the engineers a while to realize what was happening, but they took over the rebellion within the first hour. They're directing it now. We had to bomb the radio station and establish a false transmitter on the same wavelength. It looks very much as though the engineers had a plan ready to use, but not quite this soon. They were caught a little short."

Normandy grimaced. "Not short enough, though. We anticipated a little trouble down there, but we were unprepared for the discovery of anything like that. The Guard can't handle it. I sent in the Army this morning."

Kallimer grunted. "You know," he told Normandy, "I asked Joyce to reconsider his verdict."

Normandy's eyes snapped open. "You did? Why?"

"We didn't need any tests, after all. I could smell the trouble in that crowd. It was that thick. They didn't know it themselves, but they were spoiling for a riot." He shrugged. "Joyce overruled me, of course. It's a good thing, too, or we'd never have found out in time just how deep the trouble had dug."

Normandy stared thoughtfully off into the distance, his head barely moving as he nodded to himself. "Yes," he whispered under his breath.

He looked sharply at Joyce. "How much of this shocks you, Justice?"

Joyce was looking at the expression on Kallimer's face. It had become coldly sardonic.

"I—" He broke off and shrugged in reply to Normandy's question. "I don't really know. But I'm sure you're aware of what you're doing." Nevertheless, he was bewildered. He couldn't quite make out what Kallimer had meant.

Normandy looked at him steadily, his black eyes watchful. "I've always been of two minds about you," he said in a thoughtful voice. "I believe I chose wisely, but there's no certainty, with individuals like you." He grinned in his abrupt way. "But sometimes a calculated risk is justified. Sometimes, only an honest man will do."

Joyce's bewilderment was growing. He understood that Normandy was being much more candid with him than he had ever been before. Vaguely, he was aware that the situation had forced Normandy into it.

But if *Normandy* was being forced into drastic steps, then what did that say about Sam Joyce's ability to do the proper thing in this crisis?

"There's something I believe I should tell you," he said quickly, conscious of a return to his earlier panic. He had to state his position as early in this discussion as possible, before Normandy and Kallimer assumed he could be counted on. "I'm . . . not sure of exactly what you mean about me," he went on as Normandy and Kallimer looked at him curiously. "But there's something you should know."

He stopped to choose his words carefully. He had to convince these men that he wasn't acting on impulse; that he'd thought this out. They deserved an explanation, after having assumed he'd help them. And, too, it was important to him personally. Possibly this was the most important decision of his life.

"I've been Chief Justice for a comparatively long time," he began. He had; he'd always felt The Messire had a good servant in him, and, up until yesterday, The Messire had seemed to agree.

He looked down at his hands. "I have a good record. I've done my best.

"You know my history. I began years ago, on a minor bench, and I rose step by step. No one has the skill with his gun or is better in the ritual of Trial than I was in my prime." He looked up at Normandy and Kallimer, trying to see whether they understood him. "I feel that I've been a good Justice; that I've served The Messire's Law as He desired it. But I've always known I wasn't the most brilliant man on the bench. I haven't delivered many famous opinions, and I'm no lawyer's lawyer. I've simply"—he gestured indecisively—"been a Justice for a long time." He paused momentarily.

"But this," he went on in a low voice, "is beyond my capabilities." He looked down again. "I know I haven't the capacity to do my duty properly in this situation. I'd like to resign in Justice Kallimer's favor."

There was a long silence. Joyce did not look up, but sat thinking of the foolish things he'd done and thought during the past two days.

He looked up, finally, and saw Normandy's quizzical expression. Kallimer's face was a nonplussed blank.

Normandy tented his fingers and blew out a breath over them. "I see." He looked cryptically at Kallimer, and Kallimer seemed to exchange some silent message with him.

Kallimer spoke slowly. "Mr. Joyce, I know you well enough to realize this hasn't been a hasty decision. Would you mind telling me what led you to it?"

Joyce shook his head. "Not at all. I've decided that this is the only possible interpretation of yesterday's events in the plaza. It seems clear to me that The Messire's intent was to have me do what I've just done."

Normandy jerked his head violently, and stared at Joyce. "I'll be damned!" he exploded.

Kallimer's mouth twisted. "This is hardly what I expected to result from our talk yesterday," he muttered. He looked at Joyce with perverse admiration. Then he spoke to Normandy. "Well, Justice, there's your honest man."

Normandy shot Kallimer one sour look before he turned back to Joyce. His voice grated harshly.

"That's all well and good, but you're not resigning. Not now, at least, and never in Kallimer's favor. You've still got one Trial to run, and Kallimer's after my job, not yours."

"Not until after you've retired, Justice," Kallimer interjected, turning his sardonic smile on Normandy. "I've made it clear I have no intention of competing with *you*. Furthermore, I'm your only natural heir in any case." He chuckled for the first time in Joyce's experience. "There aren't many like us born to each generation, are there, Justice?"

Joyce sat numbly, unable to decide what he thought of Normandy's outburst.

"Justice Normandy—" he said finally.

"What?"

"You say I've still got one Trial—"

"Yes!"

"But, if The Messire has indicated that He no longer considers me competent, the Trial will be prejudiced—"

Normandy thrust himself out of his chair and away from the table. His eyes were blazing, and his hands trembled. "Damn your Messire! He didn't meddle with your last trial, did he?"

"Sir?"

Normandy cursed again and turned away. "Kallimer, talk to this moron! I've had enough." He stalked out of the hearing room, and the door crashed behind him.

Kallimer was looking after him with a faint look of exasperation tingeing the amusement of his mouth.

"He's getting old, Joyce." Kallimer sighed. "Well, I suppose the day will come when I'll have no more patience, either. It's a shaky pedestal he sits on."

Joyce was in a turmoil. He knew his face was pale.

Kallimer turned back to him. "There's been an insertion made in your court calendar," he told him. "Tomorrow, you'll hold a special mass trial for the engineers the Army will be dragging out of Nyack. They'll be indicted as 'members of the people.' Their origin won't be specified—no use alarming the nation. Is there? And I suppose there'll be a variety of charges. I'll set them up tonight. But the verdict'll be 'Completely Guilty' in every case. You and I and a couple of other Justices will handle the executions."

Joyce found himself unable to argue with more than the last few statements. Too much was happening.

"A mass trial? Here, in New York, you mean. For the Nyack rebels. But that's illegal!"

Kallimer nodded. "So are improper indictment and prejudged verdict. But so is rebellion.

"The folderol of Normandy's has a rather shrewd point. The rebels will be punished, but the general populace won't know what for. Only the other rebellious organizations scattered throughout the country will realize what's happened. It'll slow down their enthusiasm, giving us time to root them out."

Joyce looked down at the floor to hide the expression on his face. Kallimer seemed not at all concerned with breaking the spirit of the Law. Normandy was even more blunt than that.

It was a frightening step in his logic, but there was only one possible answer. Both of them were acting as though man made the Law, and men administered the final Verdict; as though there were no Messire.

He looked up at Kallimer, wondering what his face was showing of the sudden emptiness in his stomach. He felt as though he was looking down at the Associate from a great height, or up from the bottom of a pit.

"What did Normandy mean about my last trial?" he asked in a low voice.

"First of all, Joyce, bear in mind that The Messire is omniscient. He knows of more crimes than we possibly can. Even if we judge a case incorrectly, it is possible our verdict is nevertheless justified by some other crime of the Accused's."

He looked at Joyce with a flicker of anxiety flashing subtly across his face, leaning even closer, and Joyce's first emptiness became a twinge of disgust and sickness.

"I accept that," Joyce said, the words tasting cottony in his mouth, but wanting to urge Kallimer on.

Kallimer twitched his shoulders. "Perhaps you do," he muttered. Joyce appreciated, with a deep, bitter amusement that never came to the surface, just how much Kallimer must hate Normandy for leaving him with this task to perform.

"In any case," Kallimer went on, "about the girl, yesterday; Normandy's son had heard some things from her. A lot of unrest in Nyack; talk; dissatisfaction; that sort of thing. He told his father.

"It wasn't the only place we'd heard that from, but it was our only real lead. It was decided that a trial, with a particularly controversial member of the people as the Accused, might bring enough of it to the surface for us to gauge its importance."

He stopped and shook his head. "It certainly did. We hadn't the faintest idea it was that strong, or that close to exploding. Sheer luck we found it out."

Joyce looked steadily at Kallimer, hoping his face was calm. "The girl wasn't guilty."

Kallimer's mouth twitched. "Not of the charge we tried her on, no. Normandy's son accused her on his father's order. You were sent down to try the case because we could predict you'd give us the verdict we wanted. I went along to observe."

Joyce nodded slowly. "I think I understand, now," he said.

✧   ✧   ✧

In the middle of the day, just at noon, Samson Joyce stood at the foot of the high steps behind New York City's onyx judges' bench.

"Ready, Justice?" Kallimer asked him.

"Yes," Joyce answered. He replaced the ceremonial gun it its tooled holster.

Kallimer looked at him again and shook his head. "Justice, if we weren't in public, I'd offer you my hand. You hit bottom and you've come up swinging."

Joyce's lower lip tugged upward at the corners. "Thank you, Justice," he said, and prepared to walk up the steps on his aching legs.

Emily had been puzzled, too, as he prepared to leave her this morning.

"Sam, I can't understand you," she'd said worriedly, watching him scowl with pain as he stood up from putting on his boots.

He smiled at her, ignoring the ache in his legs. "Why?"

"You haven't slept in two nights, now. I know something new happened yesterday."

He bent and kissed her, still smiling.

"Sam, what is it?" she asked, the tears beginning to show at the corners of her eyes. "You're too calm. And you won't talk to me."

He shrugged. "Perhaps I'll tell you about it later."

The steps seemed almost inhumanly high today, though he'd walked up them often. He reached the center of the bench gratefully, and leaned against the parapet. Looking down, he saw the Accused standing in their box. They'd been given new clothing, and an attempt had been made to hide their bandages. They were a sullen, dun-colored knot of men and women.

He looked across the plaza at the First Family boxes, crowded with the family men and their ladies, and the lesser family boxes flanking them. There was the usual overflow crowd of people, too, and a doubled force of Civil Guards.

The Accused, the First Families, the lesser families, the people, and even some of the Civil Guards, were all watching him. For all that a number of Justices would go through the full ritual of Trial today, he was the only one who wore the Suit.

When he'd come home to Emily last night, she'd asked him what had happened, looking up at his calm face.

"I went to Chapel after the hearing," he'd told her, and now he seemed to stand there again.

Lowery, one of Manhattan's Associate Justices, began to read the indictments. It was only then that Joyce realized there'd been applause for him and his Associates, and that he'd automatically instructed Lowery to begin.

He listened to the solemn beat of the words in the plaza.

This was Trial. Once again, men stood before The Messire, and, once again, the Justices endeavored to act as proper instruments of His justice.

Thirty years of trials had brought him here, in his Suit. In that time, The Messire had thought well of him.

But Kallimer and Normandy had planted the dirty seed of doubt in his mind, and though he knew them for what they were, still, the doubt was there. If the girl had been innocent, how had he been permitted to execute his unjust sentence upon her?

Kallimer had given him an answer for that, but Kallimer had given him too many answers already. It wasn't until he stood in Chapel, watching the candles flicker, that he understood where the test would lie.

If there was no Messire—the thought bewildered him, but he clung to it for argument's sake—then every particle of his life was false, and the ideal he served was dust.

If there was an Ultimate Judge—and how many noons, in thirty years, had brought him the feeling of communion with his Judge—then Joyce knew where to make his appeal.

He looked across the plaza at Joshua Normandy's box, and reflected that Normandy could not begin to guess the magnitude of what was undergoing Trial today.

He put his hand inside his vest and closed his fingers around the butt of his Grennell. It was his gun. It had served him as he had served The Messire; efficiently, without question.

Here was where the test came; here where men prayed to The Messire for the ultimate, infallible judgment.

The Messire knew the guilty, and the innocent; punished the one and protected the other. Joyce was only His instrument, and Trial the opportunity for His judgment to become apparent.

He whispered to himself: "I pray my verdict is correct, but if it is not, I pray that justice prevail at this trial." He took out the gun.

He turned quickly, and fired in Kallimer's direction. He fired across the plaza at Joshua Normandy. Then he began to fire at random into the First Family boxes, seeing Normandy collapse in his box, hearing Kallimer's body tumble backward off the bench, and knowing, whether he was right or wrong, that whatever happened now, The Messire had not, at least, reversed his verdict.

This was the Truth he'd lived for.

AFTERWORD

As we have often heard, truth is stranger than fiction (and it pays better, too). Algis Budrys was in the editorial offices of If, *an sf magazine which published consistently good work in the Fifties and Sixties, winning three Hugo Awards for Best Prozine (even if they did buy my first story in 1968) to meet with the editor, who was unavoidably detained that day. While waiting, he saw a painting by Frank Kelly Freas leaning against the wall, and decided to impress the editor, when he showed up, by writing a story based on the cover right then and there, so he sat down at an unoccupied desk with a typewriter and waxed creative. When the editor finally returned, Budrys offered him the story, but was told that the painting illustrated a story by Frank Riley with the title of "The Executioner," and it was going to be in an upcoming issue, so* If *could not use the Budrys story. Fortunately, the happy ending arrived when John W. Campbell bought the story for* Astounding Science-Fiction *(and likely paid better, too), and not only did the January 1956 ASF print Budrys' story, come out before the April 1956* If, *but Freas illustrated that story, too. I would like to have run Riley's story alongside Budrys' in this book, but was overruled (where have I heard that word before?). Fortunately you can not only read the Riley "Executioner," but see the fateful cover as well by going to Gutenberg.org and browsing through the "R's." And to see another story by Mr. Riley, check out "The Cyber and Justice Holmes" within these pages.*
—HD

❧

Algis Budrys (1931–2008) was the name under which Algirdas Jonas Budrys wrote most of his eight novels and over one hundred and thirty short stories, and novelets sometimes as Algis J. Budrys and A. J. Budrys, though he also used a number of pseudonyms, one of which, "John A. Sentry," is a free translation of his Lithuanian name into English. To friends and 1950s science fiction fandom, he was usually known as "Ajay."

He was born in Königsberg in East Prussia. His family identified as Lithuanian, and his father was sent to New York in 1936 to serve as Consul General for Lithuania. Later in 1940, thanks to the Russians, and because the U.S. never recognized the Soviet takeover, continued as Lithuanian consul until 1964. Before the departure, the youngster witnessed apparently rational, stable adults going ecstatically berserk when Adolf Hitler paid a visit to his neighborhood. Budrys later wrote that he then discovered that he had been living surrounded by "werewolves," which may have something to do with how many of his stories include intelligent characters who yet rationalize their self-destructive behavior. He was thoroughly Americanized, though he did not become an American Citizen until the 1990s. After the striking production of short sf and novels in the 1950s, two decades followed in which he mostly did other things, being an editor for Playboy Press, working for the advertising company Young & Rubicam, and was the book reviewer for *Galaxy*. While his reviews were knowledgeable, incisive, and entertaining (even if I sometimes disagreed with them), I wish that his short story production had not diminished to a trickle in the 1960s. Critic John Clute (with whom I *frequently* disagree, but not this time) called Budrys' short work "incisive, intellectually challenging and highly professional," and yet, aside from some e-gatherings of stories now in public domain, only four English language collections of his shorter fiction have been published: *The Unexpected Dimension, Budrys' Inferno* (later reprinted as *The Furious Future*), *Blood & Burning*, and the limited circulation *Entertainment*, which is actually a reissue of *The Unexpected Dimension* with three extra stories added. While it is good to have these volumes, some of my favorites, such as "Nobody Bothers Gus," "The Edge of the Sea," and "Die, Shadow!" are not included in them.

In a career which received far too few of the awards and trinkets handed out to lesser writers, at least his decades of

reviews, in *Galaxy* and later in *The Magazine of Fantasy &
Science Fiction*, won him the 2007 Pilgrim Award of The
Science Fiction Research Association. Fortunately, the reviews
have been collected in the three volumes of *Benchmarks*. It's
way past time for proper recognition of a grand master. In
the meantime, you owe it to yourself to read *Rogue Moon*
(reprinted as *The Death Machine*), either the novella version
in Volume 2B of *The Science Fiction Hall of Fame*, or, better,
the full-length novel.

LICENSE TO LIVE

SARAH A. HOYT &
LAURA MONTGOMERY

Never mind the universe, the Solar System alone is a big place on a human scale, with all those planets, planet wannabes, and moons hurtling around without a single permit authorizing their activity. And not observing any speed limits, either. It's enough to give a career bureaucrat a nervous breakdown. And if anyone wants to put a colony on the red planet, they better handle the red tape first. Never mind that the U.S. Congress has passed no laws for space colonies, regulatory agencies are laws unto themselves...

∾

The activities of non-governmental entities in outer space, including the moon and other celestial bodies, shall require authorization and continuing supervision by the appropriate State Party to the Treaty.

—Outer Space Treaty, Art. VI

CALEB NEWGATE STOOD AT THE SHIP'S UPPER DECK RAILING AND felt, as he had for days, the taste of salt on his lips. Salt didn't fill just the ocean at the equator. It filled the air, his skin, his mouth. He wore shorts and a loose-fitting cotton collared shirt with a tiny penguin embroidered over his heart. There was salt in his clothes, too.

They didn't need him in the control room. He was just the

lawyer, not an engineer, not a technician, and certainly not one of the settlers. And maybe he was the fall guy, not that it was some big secret from him. If anyone could figure that out, it was the Long Shot's lawyer.

He had done his time in the control room—purely as an observer—with his sole role being to have his stomach consume the rest of him from the inside out. It had worked, and now with the wind layering more salt onto his skin, he watched through his binoculars the liquid oxygen boil off the mighty rocket on its platform some two miles distant from the ship.

The winds had to be just right. He'd learned all about the winds after the crew had finished ballasting the platform, flooding its pylons with water to lower it and increase its stability. There had been wind criteria just to roll the vehicle from its hangar to the pad and erect it. And now, upper atmospheric winds had to be high enough to be measurable by the rawinsonde balloons sent aloft. High winds and wind shears at altitude could put unacceptable loading on the vehicle during flight. Long skinny, fragile things with lots of surface area—like rockets—travelling at a high velocity tended not to do well when experiencing lateral loading.

They didn't measure salt aloft, but he wondered how high it went.

Maybe they'd look for him after everyone had gone, if there were any balloons left.

Wave height mattered, too. The rocket, with its several dozen families jammed aboard, didn't need wave heights in excess of what the platform could compensate for, and the swells had been too high, the direction wrong, for days. Until now.

They broadcast the count over the ship, and there was a small screen set into the little room behind him here on the upper deck. He could hear the GO/NO GO criteria called out, red, yellow, green down the line. They were coming to the waves. He had the litany memorized, and he knew all that came before the waves. The waves had turned the range red for days.

The waves were green.

The range was green.

Caleb had watched his fair share of launches from land. Clients would take him out as a treat. He waited for the familiar rush, the reverberation in his bones, the noise and glow that filled the sky, and the moment of glory as man or one of his machines wrenched free of planet Earth.

It happened again, all the same this time, but humanity's glory took second place this time, second place to a longing that he could go, too, that he, like those on board, had gathered his family and was about to start a new life on Mars.

Even knowing what would happen when they disembarked in Long Beach, even knowing that air traffic control, the enforcers of the International Traffic in Arms Regulations, the Federal Aviation Administration, the Federal Communications Commission, and the National Oceanic and Atmospheric Administration, and the State Department would all have an interest in what was going on, he had expected to be spending more time with the press than with the many U.S. government agencies. He had been wrong.

One condition of Caleb Newgate's participation in the Long Shot had been that there be no lying to the government. The timings of the filings might have left the regulators feeling rushed, but he had been careful to request waivers of the deadlines when he'd hit send minutes after the control room had said the wave height criteria had a ninety percent probability of being met that day. Like his more technical colleagues, he had done what he could to mitigate risk.

That part of the ocean was not a big air route, but his Notices to Airmen had gone to Oakland and Mexico for the Pacific, and air traffic would have had to scramble but Long Shot would pay the fine. The FAA's Space Office was another matter. Caleb was pretty sure that if the FAA had been able to commandeer a suborbital rocket, its inspectors would have shown up at the launch site. But there were still places on Earth that were hard to get to, and the equator on the Pacific a couple hundred miles from Kiribati was one of them.

As it was, they were talking civil penalties against his client, and he'd pointed out that he had filed the license application two hours before the launch. There'd been a heated discussion about whether he had good cause for the late filing, but Caleb had maintained steadfastly that the FAA's public position that the Outer Space Treaty was self-executing in all relevant aspects was good cause enough, especially because the FAA was wrong.

When you thought about it, he'd saved the FAA from a terrible mistake: the FAA might have unlawfully tried to stop the launch.

The compliance monitor looked like he wanted to grind his teeth and pointed out that Caleb's client had launched without a payload review.

"The list of objects is in the application, but people aren't payloads," Caleb said.

"They sure are," the man from the FAA said. The Port Authority had loaned the federal agencies an empty office, and they were all taking turns with Caleb Newgate, Vice President and General Counsel to Long Shot, LLC, formed under the laws of Delaware.

Caleb didn't say that he'd hoped the man would know his own statute better than that, but he wanted to. Instead he'd said only, "The law defines payload as objects. People aren't objects."

"They're all U.S. citizens," the compliance monitor said.

"True," Caleb agreed unhelpfully, and waited for the other man to appreciate the irrelevancy of his observation.

"So the U.S. is responsible for them."

And there it was. Caleb's stomach dropped.

He had been most frightened, as any sensible space lawyer was, by the ITAR's criminal penalties. If he messed up, he could go to jail. But he'd dealt with that by ruthlessly excluding all foreigners from the project so that no precious U.S. launch technology was released to the enemies of the United States—or even any of its allies. Whenever the business people had pushed for foreign involvement Caleb threatened to exercise his prerogative to go, too, and they had subsided. It wasn't that they wanted to keep lawyers out of space. They wanted to keep him out of space because they needed him here on the ground to make sure their next launches happened. As for the launch itself, the law was clear: launch was not an export under ITAR. The lack of a launch license would be covered by fines, and Long Shot was ready to pay those.

But this fellow was alluding to the Outer Space Treaty. Caleb had feared that.

The Treaty said that the activities in outer space of nongovernmental entities like the Long Shot required authorization and continuing supervision. The Long Shot didn't have the former and explicitly didn't want the latter. Caleb was ready to point out that that part of the Treaty wasn't self-executing, which meant it didn't apply to nongovernmental entities until Congress passed a law, but that wasn't something that seemed to persuade the FAA. He knew that from dealings with the agency on behalf of other clients.

The FAA inspector ground his teeth again. "If only I could arrest you."

The statute not being a criminal one, he couldn't.

When Caleb got home, he picked up his children from their mother's house. Maria, the eldest, was thirteen, and just starting to outgrow her baby fat. Tobias was eleven, dark-haired, and thin. They had both been mortified by their father's appearance all over the web, of course, and the things said about his involvement with Long Shot. Their friends were asking if he was a criminal. Their mother had suggested they continue to stay with her.

Curiosity and embarrassment had warred in Maria in equal measures, but Toby was ready to take his father's side still, so long as Caleb didn't mess up.

They were quiet for several minutes after he finished asking them about school and soccer. He took the car into a cathedral nave of trees over Glebe Road. He'd kept the house and the children when they'd split up and their mother had gone to find herself. He wanted to give them that stability.

As they drove, Maria spoke first. She was in the front passenger seat and he could see her face and the dark cloud on it. "Did you have to talk to the press?"

Caleb grinned. Embarrassment had won. "It's part of the job, sweetheart."

"The government thinks you're wrong," his daughter pointed out.

"And I think that part of the government is wrong," he said serenely. "That happens. When we disagree we go to court."

"Is the court part of the government?" Toby asked. He had drawn certain reasonable inferences. A glance in the rearview mirror showed his thin face with dark brows drawn down in worry.

"It's a different part," Caleb hastened to reassure his son. "The court tells the part that thinks I'm wrong—the FAA—which of us is right. The FAA is in the executive branch. Which of you remembers what job the executive branch has under the Constitution?"

Maria hated it when he did his quasi-Socratic questioning. She glared. "It carries out the laws," she muttered, but making it obvious she answered only so he would get on with his point.

"Can it create new laws?" he asked.

"No," she cried impatiently. "Dad!"

"Who creates the laws?" Caleb addressed this question to Toby.

"Congress." Even Toby was getting impatient.

"Well, Congress hasn't passed a law saying you need a license to start a settlement on Mars." It was, of course, more complicated than that. Congress delegated its lawmaking power to the agencies in the executive branch all the time. The FAA had oodles of mandatory regulations on the books. Now it was trying to use its payload reviews to stop unregulated private people from going to space, claiming the treaty made it unlawful. But he'd save the nuances for the courts. His children might kill him if he went there now.

"Dad." Maria's voice shook. "Isn't a treaty the supreme law of the land?" It was really shaking now, and rising. "And doesn't the treaty say your people need a license? Or something?"

He was proud. "Very good, Maria. You've remembered a lot from school."

She sniffed, and a quick glance showed him her eyes were watering. "My teacher told all of us yesterday."

So that was the way it was. Hard on a teen to be humiliated in front of all her classmates. He felt a surge of anger at the teacher and tamped it down. He hadn't been there to deal with it, so it was his fault too. He was good at controlling his voice. "Did she ask you for my theory?"

"No."

"So she wasn't trying to tell both sides?"

"No." Maria gulped the word.

"Some teachers aren't as good as others," he said gently. He was careful. He didn't need to be quoted back to the teachers. "They don't remember to be fair and look at both sides. But she's right. A treaty is the supreme law of the land, and it does say activities in space need government approval. But it doesn't say which activities. In our country, Congress decides which activities those are."

"Oh." Maria nodded and got her voice back to normal. "She didn't explain that part."

"It's okay. Lots of people don't know it."

Toby, however, had had enough of the law. "Dad, if you'd gone with them, you wouldn't be in trouble."

"I'm not in trouble. I'm defending my client."

"But why didn't you go?"

Caleb still didn't know the answer to that one. He had longed to go, to be one of the first people on Mars, an original settler, and if he hadn't had his family, he might have gone. But there was one other obstacle. "Someone has to protect them here."

"From what? They're gone. They don't need us anymore." Toby was smart enough, but not well informed, and tended to assume a lot from science fiction movies that skipped the grindingly dull legal issues about forming a settlement in space.

"They do need us. They'll need supplies—food, machinery, medicine, chemicals. They took some of all those things, but they'll always need more. From Earth. We don't want anyone saying they can't have them."

"Why would anyone say that?" Maria demanded.

"Because the government hasn't authorized their actions," Caleb said. It sounded so wrong when he said it out loud, but it was the issue.

Maria tossed her head. But she had a different agenda, and tried again for the answer he should have given the first time. "Was it because of us?"

He nodded stiffly. The divorce had been strained, formal, courteous, and resulted in joint custody, but he still worried they would rather be with their mother, the parent who didn't travel so much. "It was totally because of you."

"Why didn't you say that?" Maria whispered.

"It's hard to say those things," he said.

She smiled. He was a little confused. She was growing into her womanly feelings, an ability to sense more than what he told her. But there were other things, too. It seemed she required him to explain things that he didn't wish to explain or didn't know how to.

He'd never been good at dealing with people's feelings. He liked the realm of law, where things were sure. Did Maria want him to go to space? If so, wouldn't it sadden her that he stayed because of her? Wouldn't she feel guilty? Instead she seemed pleased, and he felt a twinge of confusion and misgiving, hoping that, as his children grew he wouldn't lose them the way he'd lost their mother: without noticing something was wrong in the relationship until it ended.

He turned onto their street and into another tunnel of living trees exhaling oxygen.

"But dad, we would totally have gone with you," Toby said.

Maria agreed, surprising him. "It would have been such an adventure."

"I couldn't take you from your mother," he said. "She loves you too, you know?"

He couldn't have done it to Lucy. Take her children from her. Despite everything, he remembered he'd loved her once. He knew taking her children would hurt her. Taking them to another planet was a little like killing them, or at least killing their relationship with her, making it impossible for her to ever see them or maybe even communicate with them again.

Never mind how it would have violated the divorce settlement, which would have bothered him as a professional—even if the force of law would not be able to reach into space to remove them from his care.

"I couldn't have done it to your mother," he said again. Was what he read in their eyes disappointment or incomprehension? He didn't know.

Life got really busy over the next 180 days. Caleb Newgate barely had time to draw his breath for six months before he stood waiting for the federal judge at nine in the morning on a Wednesday.

Long Shot had a supply launch scheduled, but without the element of surprise Caleb was unwilling to pull his slick trick twice. It needed a launch license or there would be hell to pay for one Caleb Newgate.

It looked like there would be hell to pay in any event, since the FAA didn't like being surprised and Long Shot hadn't given the FAA its 180 days for its first launch, much less the two years required for an environmental assessment.

At the end of the 180 days the FAA denied Long Shot a license. The supply ship couldn't follow on the settlers' heels. The FAA pointed to Article VI of the Outer Space Treaty for its assertion that without a regulator to authorize and provide continuing supervision of the space settlement, the settlement violated the treaty and the FAA couldn't issue a license that supported this behavior. That the behavior was outrageous was implied.

Caleb knew the State Department was behind the FAA's denial. The FAA had some authority to license consistent with international obligations, but it took pressure from the U.S. State Department and that agency's charming disinterest in the laws of its home country for the FAA to carry out an act so lawless. The devil of it was that the reasons the FAA was wrong were so damned complicated.

And that mattered not just for the court, but for his daughter Maria.

Caleb had been ready for the denial, and had filed a motion the next day for the federal district court to stop the FAA from relying on a non-self-executing treaty. The hearing was scheduled within three days.

But Maria was confused and upset. Her teacher, who either hated Maria, Caleb, lawyers, or settlers on Mars, kept pointing out that the Constitution made treaties the law of the land, that the United States was a government of laws not men—and that the settlers shouldn't have been allowed to go if they weren't being regulated. It would serve them right if they died. And today the evil woman had logged Maria's eighth-grade government class into FedNET to watch the hearing as a reminder that the government always won, and don't let anyone tell you otherwise.

His daughter's mortified embarrassment was the last thing Caleb wanted to worry about. But it hung on him, just another piece with the weight of the settlers themselves.

As he surveyed the courtroom, with the raised dais for the judge, the empty jury box—no jurors would be required for a motion for temporary injunction—and the high, beamed ceiling studded with cameras, projectors, and all the aids any trial attorney could ever wish for in telling a story, he swallowed against a dry throat.

He hadn't gotten his nervous laryngitis in years. He didn't want it now.

But more than just Maria's adolescent agony was on the line, much more.

The settlers themselves needed the supply vehicles to reach them. Caleb had gotten to know many of them over the five years since he'd been looped into the project. They were real people to him, families, people full of hope and courage. Humanity's hope for a future in space.

Even if he didn't know them he didn't want their deaths on his conscience. They had bet their lives on their technology, their launch vehicle, their interplanetary ship, and the supplies they had with them. Now they were betting he was right about the government not being able to enforce a non-self-executing treaty.

Eighty percent of the press was appalled at the actions of lawless colonialists. All the haters of Western colonialism came out of the woodwork to comment on how this was just like the past, happily ignoring that there were no native populations—not even microbial—on Mars. This was colonialism. It was bad.

It was an insane view, since every species on Earth colonized whatever territory it could. To be alive was to colonize. Arguably to stay alive one had to colonize. Because if a species didn't, it sank into overspecialization and, eventually, at the first unexpected turn of events, into extinction.

The other twenty percent of the press were making heartless jokes, feeding the Facebook memes about dead colonists, outraged that the government would interfere in a citizen's right to travel, or clamoring for the launch to take place so the settlers wouldn't die.

There had been both kinds of protestors outside the courthouse. Someone had thrown something at him. Fortunately, it had missed, and his dark blue suit in summer weight wool remained immaculate.

"All rise," the bailiff called.

Caleb rose from behind his two-person table as Judge Ney entered the courtroom. She was a statuesque woman, with long hair braided down her back. Had it not been for the black robes covering her from the neck down, she could have played a middle-aged Amazon. Pale eyes surveyed her courtroom.

Caleb hoped he didn't look nervous. He felt alive, slightly on fire, truth be told, and his throat was no longer dry. Even so, he felt a little light around his head and extremities. This was worse than the launch had been, and launches failed.

The FAA's attorney, Herbert Crown, didn't look nervous, maybe a little predatory. He looked to be in his forties, not far from Caleb's own age, a dark-haired man soft about the middle with a lawyer's shoulders, rounded and pushing forward. His suit was not as well tailored as Caleb's.

The formalities begun and dispensed with in seconds, the judge turned her pale eyes on Caleb. "Mr. Newgate?"

As the proponent of the order, he went first. His throat was dry again, but his voice came out evenly enough. "Your honor. My client Long Shot requests that you order the FAA to cease attempting to enforce a non-self-executing treaty provision. Because the Outer Space Treaty says the United States has to regulate and supervise the activities of its nationals in outer space, and because Long Shot's settlement doesn't have a nonexistent license to establish a settlement on Mars, the FAA has denied a license for Long Shot's next launch. The FAA claims the treaty requires it to deny the license. This is incorrect. The treaty obligation falls on Congress, which must first decide that a space settlement needs a license and pass a law saying that, before the Executive branch has anything to enforce. In *Medellin* the Supreme Court held that even the President can't enforce a non-self-executing treaty. If the President can't, neither can the FAA. Peoples' lives depend on that."

Judge Ney stared at him long and hard. "Perhaps they should have applied for a launch license for their first launch, Mr. Newgate? Is that why you didn't get yesterday's license?"

"That is a separate issue, Judge," Caleb said. "The FAA has not relied on that, and Long Shot is in discussions about the fine it will have to pay for its first launch."

The judge's eyes narrowed. "Part of the cost of doing business, Mr. Newgate? I hope the FAA fines you appropriately. I disapprove of companies factoring financial penalties into their business models. As you have done."

When he didn't reply—what was there to say to that, after all?—the judge turned to the FAA. "Mr. Crown?"

As Caleb seated himself and Crown rose, the FAA's attorney gave the judge a collegial smile, the kind that suggested they were both government employees and he was sure she would agree with him. The courts were separate from the executive branch, Caleb reminded himself. He didn't need to get paranoid, but he was well aware how much the courts deferred to the agencies. That deference had started long ago and was well entrenched in the judiciary.

What had he been thinking? Why had he let them go? The truth was he couldn't have stopped them. Their legal risk was just one of many.

Crown got right to it. "The law gives the FAA authority to license a launch consistent with, *inter alia*, the foreign policy interests of the United States. It is in the foreign policy interests of this country that it abide by its international obligations."

That was wrong. It drove Caleb crazy when the FAA relied on that. He had told them repeatedly on behalf of other clients that the Supreme Court had already addressed this when it said the President's own constitutionally granted foreign policy authority was not interchangeable with Congress's legislative authority. Congress had to pass a law saying settlers needed a license.

Caleb told himself to pay attention. Crown was still talking. "Just because Congress hasn't passed a law regarding settlement doesn't mean that settlement isn't one of those space activities the treaty clearly meant to cover. In its brief, Long Shot claims that just because the treaty can't apply to everything—like brushing one's teeth or playing the harp in space—it applies to nothing. This is clearly incorrect, as we have seen from Congress passing laws to regulate launch, reentry, and telecommunications and remote-sensing satellites."

It was frustrating to have to wait to his turn to respond to all this. For one thing, he'd made the point about the lunar harpist not to say that the treaty applied to no activities, but to say that because the treaty required the kinds of decisions that Congress made, namely, what activities needed licensing, the Executive Branch had to wait for Congress to say space settlement required a license before the FAA could say the treaty required it. Congress was in charge of deciding what activities required a license. In other words, the FAA couldn't enforce a law Congress hadn't passed.

This did not deter the FAA, but when Crown wound down, Judge Ney leaned back from her lofty altitude. The ceiling lights did not shine directly on her face, but he could see the glittering eyes. His throat felt tight. His people's fate lay in this woman's hands. Sure, they'd tried to launch sooner than necessary figuring the FAA would do exactly what it had done. But appeals might mean death for them if not for him. That's why they'd left him behind. He had a job to do.

"Mr. Newgate," the judge said, "what do you have to say to all this?"

Caleb swallowed and rose to his feet. "We have three branches of government," he said. His voice was hoarse at first, but grew stronger. "Congress is the legislative branch. It writes the laws. It might be hard for the agencies in the executive branch to remember, because Congress has delegated them so much of its legislative powers, but they do have to wait for the initial delegation."

She showed no change in expression. "Does the treaty require that settlement be licensed?"

"It doesn't say," Caleb replied.

"Do you think it requires the regulation of any activities?"

He had to be careful here. "That's up to Congress, not to me, and not to the FAA." *Or you*, he thought. "If I were in Congress I would note that the treaty makes the United States responsible for the activities of its nationals. If I worried that my citizens were doing something dangerous that might harm the people of another country, I might want government oversight of that dangerous activity." *Not really*, he thought. *But I only said "might." I might not.*

"If I may," Crown interjected. "If Congress doesn't act, we must. We have treaty obligations."

"But you don't know what they are until Congress tells you," Caleb replied quickly. It was tricky, responding to opposing counsel rather than sticking only to the judge's questions. Some judges didn't like that.

This one didn't. Sure, Crown had strayed first, but it was Caleb she glared at. "Do you understand the flaw in your argument, Mr. Newgate?"

Caleb froze. Maria hadn't entered his mind since the judge appeared. Now he thought of her watching from her classroom as the young harridan who taught her gloated. He thought of the travelers on the spaceship watching from space suddenly filled with despair as their lawyer let them down. That he thought of them second filled him with guilt.

"I see no flaw, your honor. The treaty requires an action from Congress, but gives little guidance as to what activities require authorization. It can't mean everything we do in space. Congress hasn't said settlement requires a license or any other form of authorization. Nonetheless, the Supreme Court has said that a non-self-executing treaty such as this is not enforceable. Therefore, the FAA, which is only part of the Executive Branch, doesn't get to enforce it."

The judge's lips curved. "Then what am I to do?"

"Wait for Congress to pass a law saying settlement requires licensing."

"And that's where you're wrong."

His mind raced. He knew she was toying with him, but nothing in the FAA's brief, nothing in its lawyer's statement so far, told him what the hell she could be talking about.

"Ma'am." He said it blankly, baldly, unwilling to play anymore.

"The FAA is saying your clients need a license to live." She leaned forward triumphantly. "You might want to parse your activities more broadly. Stop focusing on settlement, or farming, or playing harps or whatever they plan to do on Mars. The biggest activity they are doing is living. The FAA wants to license that."

Caleb's heart soared, almost choking him.

Crown, who had not sat down, was rocking forward on the balls of his feet. "There are other activities the treaty could require licenses of. Interplanetary transport. Habitat operation. Farming. Mining."

"But you're changing your story, Mr. Crown. Your brief mentioned none of that." She looked puzzled, as if wondering how the government's lawyer had not caught on: she was not on his side.

"I'm mentioning it now," Crown said sincerely.

"How about setting the table? Should setting the table on Mars require a license?"

"No," Crown protested, visibly annoyed at her frivolity. "We wouldn't do that. That would be pointless."

"So Mr. Newgate is right, you are taking on Congress's role and deciding what does and doesn't need a license."

"We are enforcing a treaty," Crown insisted.

"One that tells Congress to pass a law," the judge said. "The FAA doesn't get to do that." Caleb felt a little giddy again. She agreed. With him. With the Supreme Court. With Long Shot. "That is the easy part."

She turned back to Caleb. "What I don't understand is why you spent the whole brief on what is obvious. Of course this treaty provision leaves it to Congress to decide what needs authorized. Of course if Congress doesn't say something needs licensed it doesn't. And of course the FAA can't enforce a law Congress hasn't passed."

The judge was immobile but ablaze, a woman somewhere in her fifties with a Valkyrie's braid and maybe the heart of an explorer. Caleb knew nothing of her. She was new to the bench and he hadn't had time to research her.

She turned on Caleb. "But you, sir, should have addressed the issue of whether the government can require a license to live. I am disappointed that someone representing such a venture would ignore such a fundamental question."

Caleb worked hard not to smile. It didn't matter that Maria might not understand he'd won until he got home to tell her, or that her teacher certainly wouldn't. His client would get its launch. His friends would live, even without government approval.

He couldn't help it. He grinned. "Your honor, I am disappointed, too. Next time, I will be ready to address that."

She turned and addressed the room at large, bringing her gavel down without excess. "Motion granted to Long Shot. The FAA shall not deny the license on the basis of the treaty."

The elation was real. He need only worry about Maria now. He would have to explain. His phone burred on his wrist.

One didn't look at one's phone or watch in front of a judge. Carefully, he laced his fingers and stretched them in front of him, a gesture of relief; nothing more, not an attempt to catch the phone's screen. An emoji from Maria flashed into his peripheral vision. It was a thumb's up.

Sarah A. Hoyt won the Prometheus Award for her novel *Darkship Thieves,* published by Baen, and has also authored *Darkship Renegades* (nominated for the following year's Prometheus Award) and *A Few Good Men,* as well as *Through Fire* and *Darkship Revenge,* novels set in the same universe, as was "Angel in Flight," a story in the Baen anthology, *A Cosmic Christmas.* Her latest bestseller is *Monster Hunter International: Guardian,* a collaborative novel with Larry Correia set in his *New York Times* bestselling series. She has written numerous short stories and novels in science fiction, fantasy, mystery, historical novels and genre-straddling historical mysteries, many under a number of pseudonyms, and has been published—among other places—in *Analog*, *Asimov's* and *Amazing Stories*. For Baen, she has also written three books in her popular shape-shifter fantasy series, *Draw One in the Dark*, *Gentleman Takes a Chance*, and *Noah's Boy*. She has a strong online presence, with an impressive number of novels and story collections available as e-books, and her *According to Hoyt* is one of the most outspoken and fascinating blogs on the internet, as is her Facebook group, *Sarah's Diner*. Originally from Portugal, she lives in Colorado with her husband, near her two sons and "the surfeit of cats necessary to a die-hard Heinlein fan."

Laura Montgomery is a practicing space lawyer who writes space opera and near-future, bourgeois, legal science fiction. Her most recent book, *Simple Service*, starts a new series in the popular universe of her *Waking Late* trilogy. *Mercenary Calling* is her most recent near-future novel, and follows one man's efforts to save a starship captain from charges of mutiny. Her author site is at lauramontgomery.com. On the legal side, Laura's private practice emphasizes commercial space transportation and the Outer Space Treaties. Before starting her own practice, she was the manager of the Space Law Branch in the FAA's Office of the Chief Counsel, where she supported the regulators of commercial launch, reentry, and spaceports. There she worked on issues ranging from explosive siting to property rights in space. She has testified to the space subcommittees of both the House and Senate, and is an adjunct professor of space law at Catholic University's Columbus School of Law. She writes and edits the space law blog GroundBasedSpaceMatters.com and speaks regularly on space law issues. She lives outside Washington, D.C., with her husband and dogs.

THE RIOT THAT WASN'T
IN PORT NEEKS

SUSAN R. MATTHEWS

The judge (but don't call him "Your Honor") wasn't really green, but he was newly arrived on unfamiliar turf. And his very limited authority didn't have a regular police force to back it up. Add that there might be a riot brewing outside the door, and it was undeniably a time to tread very softly...

JUST GIVE BOTH PARTIES A HEARING, LANGSARIK STATION HAD said. *It's a small port, not more than eleven ships down-station, six-eights of people, but enough to cause trouble. A traditionally sore subject. Remember that prudence is the better part of valor.* As if Langsarik Station didn't know that Bat Yorvik—the first man to sit at the Bench level in almost forever, and one of the younger Bench Judges at that—was sufficiently familiar with at least mildly hostile environments that they were almost homelike.

The conference room Neeks Station had made available at the Port Authority was as shabby and stuffy as the rest of Neeks, but it was familiar, even friendly, for all that. It wasn't the Port Authority's fault that the furniture was old and battered and beaten-up. This was Gonebeyond space, at the back of beyond, a no-man's-land populated with criminals and refugees fled from the Bench itself.

There was no money in Gonebeyond. There weren't many

people. And Bench Judge Bat Yorvik—on a mission from Haspirzak Judiciary to begin healing the relationship between Gonebeyond and the rule of Law, if not the "Judicial order"—wouldn't have been anywhere else.

"So my transport broker left me hanging at Delgacie," the complainant said. "On my way from Bambor to Beraile by way of Pillip's Run." Saporeya Vilna, that was her name; a newcomer to Gonebeyond, in search of market opportunities. "It was the responsibility of the cargo management representative at Delgacie to find me room on a hull that would reach here in time to transfer my cargo, and keep to my schedule."

So she'd missed her connection, and had a cargo but no client. She was scrambling for a fallback position, and somebody was going to have to pay. But that was just a fact of life in Gonebeyond; value-neutral, the way things were. People who'd been here knew that and made adjustments. Newcomers, not so much.

Jurisdiction commercial law had been one of Bat's least favorite topics throughout his education for the Bench: yet this was as wonderful as his first step across the threshold of his first classroom had been, on the day when his journey from entry-level clerk of Court to Bench Judge had begun.

Because this was all new. It was all unexplored, undefined, above all un-Precedented. There was no rule of Law in Gonebeyond space. They were all making it up as they went along, and he could do good work toward an honest—fair and equitable—system that would protect the rights of all parties. He could help make history.

"The price was agreed to on those terms of transit and delivery. But we didn't get here on time." There was a little frustration beginning to show in Vilna's voice, Bat thought. She'd made assumptions and she hadn't done full disclosure, sharp practice, and she'd lost. "I have not received the contracted services. The contract is void, and I should be reimbursed. I deserve compensation by right and a penalty that will cover my costs of finding a new buyer, your Honor."

Don't call me that, Bat thought. He wasn't a *your Honor* here. He and the people who supported his mission had yet to decide what exactly people should call a Bench Judge on a study mission, and he would be able to explore and exploit that ambiguity to make a point before this discussion was over.

That needed to be soon, because he was seeing disquieting signs of trouble ahead. New people—about half of them Voreh nationals, Bat thought, like Vilna—had started to fill in the space at the back of the room, which wasn't all that large to begin with. He was going to have something to say about that.

"This is your statement, Dar Vilna?" Bat asked, gesturing at one of the flatfile dockets on the table in front of him, the one marked with her personal seal. "Thank you. I can see by my chop-mark that it's one I've reviewed carefully. Now you, Dir Hammond, if you would summarize from your perspective."

Herryoot Hammond. Clearly of Farlip extraction to go by the fact that his ears weren't the same size. Some of Gonebeyond's oldest communities were Farlip, so Hammond would know how things were done here, and cherish the hatred of the Bench that was part of Gonebeyond's blood and bone.

There weren't many Farlip nationals in Neeks; their system-of-origin had been dominated by cold temperatures, and they'd used the arctic environments of the worlds they'd found in Gonebeyond as part of their defense against discovery and exploitation. The partisans collecting in the conference room on Hammond's behalf were Nurail, Sandrove, Karlile—some of them nearly extinct in Jurisdiction Space; some of them completely eradicated by Jurisdiction genocide.

These were people who'd suffered for generations to survive in Gonebeyond, people who weren't about to be dictated to by newcomers insisting on doing business on the Bench model. There were more of them here than Vilna's people, and no more places to sit down. That wasn't stopping anybody.

"Thank you, ah, Dir Yorvik." No *your Honor* there, but the courtesy title Hammond used instead was adequately—fully—respectful. "My statement also in evidence, there, before you. Yes." More language of the Jurisdiction's Bench. None of them—Bat included—had any other language in common fit to the purpose, so *in evidence* would have to do while they worked on something better.

"Excuse me, Dir Hammond, if I might take a quick moment." The spectators were beginning to spread out under pressure from the back of the room, though by no preconcerted signal Bat had detected. It was a simple organic process, one person moving a bit to one side, someone else moving a bit more to the other in what could be innocent and unconscious symmetry. Before one knew it there were as many on one side as the other, lined up against the wall depending on where their sympathies lay.

In a moment they might begin to growl at one another, and it wouldn't end well. Since there were no bailiffs at Neeks' Port Authority, Bat was on his own as far as maintaining control of the situation went. Langsarik Station had promised him backup, but he hadn't heard of any arriving yet—unless it was the *Fisher Wolf* and its wolfpack. He hadn't really anticipated partisans attending in force, but now that he was in this predicament it was up to him to manage it as best he could.

Bat waited until Dir Hammond nodded, then raised his voice. Just a little. Nowhere near *I will have silence in this Court*, that only worked when there was a reserve on site to back it up. A sliver of a hair's-breadth thickness above *what's for fastmeal I hope it isn't shilshims again.*

"Come on up, gentles, plenty of room to the front, yes, either side of me, please. I'm sorry we can't seat you all." *I'm on to you and you know it.* Bat had been raised in disadvantaged residentials, in one port or another; he wasn't a fighter or a brawler, but he'd learned a lot about surviving by watching other peoples' battles. "Don't be shy. Exits to remain clear for emergency evacuation at all times, am I right?"

No attacking each other from the back of the room. No hijacking the grievance to express general resentments. No shouting each other down. "Thank you, gentles. Dir Hammond, my apologies for the interruption, please proceed."

As he spoke Bat saw the door at the back of the room edge open again, slowly, cautiously. He couldn't see anybody: there did have to be something there by way of a doorstop, however, because otherwise the door would swing closed of its own weight. Bat knew that. The people he'd called up to the front of the room to either side of him had noticed it as well; Bat knew that also. But he was giving Hammond his full attention.

"As to the meat of most of Vilna's statement I am in agreement," Hammond said. *That's right,* Bat repeated to himself, firmly. *Paying full attention to Hammond.*

If *Fisher Wolf* had arrived there were seven, maybe nine of them, but one of them was widely notorious for a different set of skills than hand-to-hand crowd control; and Security Chief

Stildyne wouldn't risk Andrej Koscuisko in a fistfight. That could be used in Bat's favor, he decided: everybody knew that Koscuisko was the only other genuine Judicial officer in Gonebeyond, though Koscuisko had turned his back on his duties as a Ship's Inquisitor.

"She only fails to mention the reason we didn't make our expected transit rate of speed," Hammond said. *Not distracted, no, not me,* Bat insisted to himself. That would be disrespectful of Hammond's dignity. "You'll know that a contract for delivery specifies cargo parameters, your—ah—Dir Yorvik? Including its weight."

Bat had read up, of course. As soon as he'd been asked to hear the dispute he'd gotten into the data, so he knew. Vilna's cargo had been bulkier than specified—that didn't need to be critical, since Hammond's ship hadn't stopped for additional cargo en route to Neeks—but it had also been a good deal heavier, in aggregate. And loaded by the Port Authority's cargo management crew, who should have let Hammond know.

Yes, according to standard operating procedures, Hammond should or at least could have checked his load weight prior to departure. But this was Gonebeyond, not Jurisdiction, and they'd been in a hurry to make Vilna's schedule. They'd been delayed in the loading cycle, and they hadn't checked their fuel depletion stats until they were already on vector for Neeks.

Vilna could have provided the specs. She'd made what would have been a reasonable assumption—in any port in Jurisdiction space—that Delgacie was responsible for that. She hadn't been in Gonebeyond long. She could be excused for the oversight, and it needn't have made a difference. Except it had.

Bat could almost hear Vilna seething, *it's not my fault if you didn't weigh out yourself. It's not my fault Delgacie didn't provide the details. We had an agreement. Not contingent. I wasn't to know you hadn't been told.* Still she kept shut, and since she was facing Bat—with her back to the door—she might not know that someone who was taking care not to be seen was listening.

Now for the difficult part. "You, Dar Vilna, have Bench commerce codes and judicial precedent on your side from the aspect of an undefined cartage contract. The remedy you propose is unremarkable under current Jurisdiction Fleet rules and regulations. But also."

Bat turned to Hammond. "You, Dir Hammond, have equivalent precedent in support, when considered from the aspect of fair notice of pertinent considerations when a time constraint is of primary importance. So, under Bench precedent and commerce codes as well as current Fleet practices and procedures, this conflict might well depend for resolution on a Bench judgment, to which precedents and procedures should apply."

Everybody had heard the "might." The energy in the room shifted a bit, backed down from "brawl in seven-six-five and counting" into a more generalized, vaguely startled sort of attitude, a wait-a-minute rustling to peoples' clothing. Both Vilna and Hammond stood waiting to hear more; and the space beyond the narrow opening of the door at the back of the room—which might have been thinking of closing up and going away—seemed to hesitate, opening just a hair wider with an intrigued, inquiring, *let's see what you are going to do about this* air.

He had everyone's attention. Now all he had to do was get them to agree. "The overriding fact of the matter, Dar Vilna, Dir Hammond, is that we aren't in Jurisdiction space, there are no Jurisdiction commerce codes, there is no Bench and so no Fleet policies and procedures. Nobody came here to import the rule of Law and the Judicial order. We need our own standard of conflict resolution that can stand in its place, and work for all of the settlements in Gonebeyond. Something we can all agree is fair and reasonable."

He shouldn't have said *we* need. He had no Brief to speak for Gonebeyond. But he'd been sent here to learn about the challenges that Gonebeyond presented to developing peer relationships between it and the Bench; and he remembered his "philosophy of jurisprudence" classes, if not with fondness. So he was going to go ahead with his experiment. He wished he had a more controlled environment in which to propose it, now that he was here, but here he was, and it would be a that-much-better test than he'd anticipated. All to the good. Really.

"I propose resolution by arbitration. If you're both willing to make a good-faith effort toward building a new, fair and equitable model, let's talk. If either of you would rather decline, I'll tell the Port Authority that there is no single clear-cut resolution to this dispute as stated, so I can't help. I don't know what they'll do about it, because they asked me for advice that

I won't have; but I probably won't be invited to stay for dinner. And I'm pretty tired of my own cooking. Do you want a little time to think it over?"

He waited. He knew this hadn't gone as either party expected; he hoped that the partisans to either side of him were unsure enough to wait and see what the principals did, because though the potential for a set-to seemed reduced, it had not yet vanished into the area of improbability.

He'd seen more brawls since he'd come to Gonebeyond than he had since he'd started his legal career. No one had as yet offered him physical violence, but brawls were very democratic and generously inclusive events, and prudence was always in order for everybody's sake. And that of the furniture.

He could see Vilna glance at Hammond out of the corner of her eye: *I will if you will.* Hammond turned to face Vilna, raising an eyebrow; *really?* Vilna nodded: *really.* Of course arbitration was an ancient and honorable approach to conflict resolution in its own right, so it was perhaps unsurprising that neither party was willing to refuse—especially as refusal carried with it a certain risk of accusations of bad faith.

Still Bat knew he was facing a challenge. Judges by definition were involved only if arbitration failed, if it had been tried at all, so he had very limited experience with the process. He tried not to let his breath out in too much of a rush. He'd wait till later for his sigh of relief. "Suppose I suggested a four-hour break?"

Vilna clearly needed no time to consult with anybody but herself. "Acceptable," she said, so quickly and emphatically that she almost spoke over the last word of Bat's question. "Back here, Dir Yorvik?"

He could see Hammond sorting through considerations of his own, but not for long. Hammond was the senior representative on his own ship, after all. Bat waited to reply to Vilna until Hammond had had space to speak, in case he wanted to register an objection; and when Hammond didn't speak—nodding his head again, with deliberation—Bat answered with a nod of his own.

"Here, then, four hours." He'd be a little late, by design—long enough for them to start a conversation directly with each other, if possible, but not long enough to insult anybody. "Let me just say that even though we're going into arbitration, not to Court, we all need to treat the process with respect. You both agree to be bound by the results or there's no sense wasting anybody's time." And all of those extra people in the room made him nervous.

He glanced around him as he stood up, the universal court signal for "everybody leave." There seemed to be a general relaxation of tension in the room, and Bat was glad to see it. The door at the back of the room had closed completely, as if someone didn't care to be caught eavesdropping. All to the good.

There was no Bench in Gonebeyond, but almost everybody had watched the entertainment vids at some point in their lives—and mysteries of all kinds were among the enduring favorites as far as crime dramas went. So they all stood up and waited for him to leave first: the theater of the Law.

Just as well, Bat thought, not sorry to take advantage. He'd be first in line for a breadfold and a salad and a cup of cavene at the cafeteria, so he'd have that much more time to think about what he was going to do next.

As it happened—and it couldn't have been by accident, in Bat's opinion—the darkness-beyond-the-doorway was just starting on his own breadfold, salad, and cup of cavene in the cafeteria when Bat cleared the line with his tray. Andrej Koscuisko was sitting at a two-top about three-fourths of the way to the back of the largish room, together with his "self-same" and chief of Security, Brachi Stildyne, the big man with the ruined face.

Koscuisko was a man who needed extra security wherever he went, no matter how useful he'd become to the Department of Surgery at Safehaven Medical Center—and to all of Gonebeyond space, by extension. He was only a neurosurgeon, now, if a very very very good one. Before, he'd been a Ship's Inquisitor. He'd executed the Protocols against friends and relations of people who'd come to Gonebeyond Space in the first place to get away from people like him.

The two-tops in Koscuisko's immediate vicinity were occupied in turn by other people that Bat could identify as Koscuisko's once-Security, because he'd recognized one of them at least as a former bond-involuntary Security slave named Janforth. They were eating their own breadfolds with their own salads and cups of cavene; they'd gotten in line before the custard desserts had run out, Bat noted, with a little twinge of envy.

There were places where Koscuisko's once-Security weren't

welcome, contaminated by association with Koscuisko and what they'd had to do accordingly. But there were places where people saved out desserts for the wolfpack out of consideration for the torture they'd themselves survived under Jurisdiction, though nobody saved dessert for Koscuisko that Bat had ever heard of, apart from the wolfpack and Chief Stildyne.

And of course there were far more places where nobody cared one way or the other. Vilna probably didn't care. She was one of the newcomers, with her eye to the main chance, and no fled-to-save-their-near-and-dear-from-torture about it.

Koscuisko had his back to the wall, of course he did, probably to ensure that his profile would catch Bat's eye. Which it did, welcome as it was to Bat to know that *Fisher Wolf* was here and had most probably been sent by Langsarik Station to protect Bat while they were ferrying Koscuisko from one medical emergency to another.

He made his way over to where Koscuisko sat with Chief Stildyne, to ask him about people who listened at doors. As he approached, Stildyne pushed himself up and away from the table, leaving his custard dessert untouched. Bat wasn't fooled. It was almost certainly an extra for Koscuisko, who probably had a sweet tooth—like most Dolgorukij that Bat had ever met.

Koscuisko stood up, too, and waited. They would have drawn peoples' attention, by now, Koscuisko being who he was and Stildyne being such a distinctive man with his nose smashed flat and one cheekbone not quite in alignment and his thin lips and his general air of *nobody wants to get in my way*. Stildyne gave Bat a nod on the way past; Koscuisko gave Bat as much of a bow as any senior officer in the Jurisdiction's Fleet would give any Judge, and gestured with his hand.

"Please sit down, your Honor," Koscuisko said. "The dining hall is busy today. We've saved you a seat."

There it was again. Ordinarily Bat would have let it pass, because although he didn't know Koscuisko very well he'd been grateful for Koscuisko's backup in some uncertain situations; but he was a little nervous about whether his arbitration experiment was going to work, and they did have a relationship, he and Koscuisko. Of a sort.

"I wish people wouldn't call me that," Bat said, sitting down, moving the surplus custard to the Koscuisko side of the table. "I'm not a Bench judge, not here in Gonebeyond."

When Koscuisko sat back down he angled his chair around—with his back to the room, now. *Nothing to see here*, Bat thought. *Everybody just eat your breadfolds, and mind your own business.*

"Your objection is overruled," Koscuisko said. "I am widely held to be an impatient and arrogant man, which is to say, a chief of Surgery at Safehaven Medical Center. When I bend my neck to you I place myself under your authority, to howsoever limited an extent, and communicate to all that they ought to do the same, in my opinion."

Whether arrogant or not—Bat made no ruling—Koscuisko unquestionably had a good opinion of himself. That was all right. Bat could see his point. "As you wish, your Excellency," Bat said, not without a certain flourish of his own. Fair was fair. Koscuisko could take it as a reference to his civil rank in his system of origin as easily as pointing out his former rank as Ship's Surgeon—Ship's Inquisitor—on the Jurisdiction Fleet Ship *Ragnarok*. "If I might inquire as to your interest in a common cargo contractual issue, your Excellency?"

Koscuisko made a commendably restrained expression of shuddersome rejection. "I am only curious, Dir Yorvik, as everybody, about how you were going to approach a resolution to this issue. Nor had I any idea there was a potential point of interest until Langsarik Station diverted *Fisher Wolf* en route to Safehaven, thus depriving me of my chance at the first of the pear-fruit to ripen this season. Which I resent."

"Is there no such thing as arbitration among the Dolgorukij?" Bat asked, momentarily distracted. Koscuisko was a surgeon over and above anything else that he had been in Jurisdiction Fleet; there was no place for a free and full exchange of ideas in the middle of a medical procedure, all *yes Doctor* and *no Doctor* and *I regret that the patient has stopped breathing, Doctor* and *oh God that's my daughter* and *stop you madman you're too impaired to conduct this surgery you'll kill her.* Bat watched entertainment vids too.

"I know it works for people who have already enough of a set of understandings in common," Koscuisko said. "But for people of unrelated social norms, I would think the chances less likely of success. You are the one who knows. Tell me."

This was naïve of Koscuisko, Bat suspected. Maybe Koscuisko was drawing Bat out, trying to get a sense of whether Bat could make it work. He wasn't sure. He was going to give it a try regardless.

"I don't know how much you heard, listening in," Bat said. "If that was you, that is, and not one of yours. Everybody's assumptions were reasonable, but mismatched. It wouldn't have mattered back in Jurisdiction space, because we had a single set of assumptions—you would call it *under Canopy*, Doctor?—of externally imposed and defined roles. We'll see. Feel free to stand outside the door, or maybe we could get plant services to put up a curtain for you to lurk behind. I endorse your concealment, by the way. I've known you to be very loud just by breathing, with respect, no offense, Doctor."

He meant it, the *with respect* and *no offense* parts. All of them, really. "I want to know if Dar Vilna means to offload her cargo here, Dir Yorvik," Koscuisko said. "I have a personal interest. There are rumors that she has some particularly fine shocattli on her manifest, and I wouldn't mind having some of it for myself. I get shipments from home, yes, but we are not yet on the leading edge of the luxury market, for that commodity. Hard to imagine, yes, for me as well, but it is true."

Koscuisko had been mostly finished with his breadfold when Bat had sat down with him. Scooping the last bits of the second custard up with his spoon now, Koscuisko finished that as well, and pushed himself back and away from the table. "Good luck, Dir Yorvik," Koscuisko said. "We will be keeping an ear, ready to intervene at your word. We believe in you."

He did not. Koscuisko didn't know him well enough to be able to say such a thing, not sincerely. Koscuisko was just being polite; but he'd put an idea in Bat's mind, and if it worked out he would try to get some shocattli from Vilna's cargo—if it could be done without the appearance of impropriety—just to thank Koscuisko for his assistance.

When Bat returned at the end of four hours and some minutes to the conference room they'd used during this morning's meeting the hallway was full of people, lined up ominously enough to either side of the corridor—self-selected by sympathies. The Port Authority had three Security on either side of the doors into the conference room, now. They opened the primitive hinged two-panel doors for Bat to go through.

There was to be only the four of them there inside the room, Vilna, Hammond, Bart, and an administrative professional from Langsarik Station to make sure the record of the discussion was being correctly extracted, to witness the proceedings. There was so strong a sense of an interrupted conversation that Bat only barely succeeded in controlling his temptation to ask outright what they'd decided, and Shurl—from Langsarik Station—wouldn't tell him. Shurl was punctilious about things. Nothing that wasn't on the mutually approved record was going to be forthcoming from *him*. That was a pity. Bat pulled a chair into the aisle between the two tables on either side of the room—between the desks—to sit down.

"These are the questions I think we need to answer," he said, offering the flatfile flimsy briefing sheets one to each side. "Have a look. Are we ready to discuss these?"

He'd made them up himself. He had no precedents at hand to apply to this situation. There was to be no formal Judicial inquiry, no *state your name and occupation and the crime you allege to have occurred* or *with respect to which you plead your innocence*, no *describe your cargo, explain the facts of the complaint and why it rises to the level of a Judicial proceeding*. Nothing like that.

Hammond, who had a subtle self-satisfied expression on his face, gave the flatfile flimsy a little shake, just enough to make it rustle in an informal request to speak. "I don't know why some of these questions should be official," he said. "In fact I might go so far as to suggest it's nobody's business what my comprehensive cargo manifest contains, Dir Yorvik."

To be self-satisfied might indicate that Hammond felt on sure ground, which in turn might hint that he believed the most part of the people in the hall supported his side of the controversy. Bat put that consideration to one side; it had nothing to do with the facts of the matter, or the best—fairest, most robust—solution.

The question about the cargos was an innovation on his part, something Bat had only added to the list after Koscuisko had mentioned shocattli. Bat wasn't sure whether Koscuisko had any business knowing that about Vilna's cargo, so he had to create a reasonable pretext for him to have the information, which meant asking both parties.

"I understand your reservations, Dir Hammond. We may find a valid need for some such information when we get to the end of today's meeting, and please note that the same questions are asked of you both; so let's save discussion about whether you'll release the information until then, please. How do you feel about answering these questions here and now, Dar Vilna? Dir Hammond? I think we can resolve this dispute today, if we're willing to work things through together."

Vilna was making marks on the flimsy she held. Hammond shrugged. Bat wished he'd brought a tall cooler of something cold and fruit-flavored with extra cups, but they were off to the wars now and it was too late.

"First we establish what we're here for, then." Not *off to the wars*. Off on a voyage of exploration. One that would go better with ice and fruit juice in Neeks' rather stuffy conference room, but Bat was feeling the excitement now even in the presence of his nervous apprehension about whether this experiment would work, and eager to get started.

"Dar Vilna." It was her complaint, so Bat started with her. "You've told us, yes, but let's have it again, if you don't mind. What exactly would you need to feel you were made completely whole of the injury you feel has been done to you?"

Things had been more informal, earlier today; no notes had been taken, nothing they could use to memorialize this negotiation. He needed notes now. They were making their own precedent. It was important. He listened for the meat of Vilna's statement; no change from what she'd said this morning, though her tone of voice was a little more reserved, less sharp-edged. She'd been consistent throughout, to her credit.

She wanted her money back because Hammond hadn't gotten here when they'd agreed he would. She wanted paid back the money it was going to cost her to move her cargo from Neeks to Beraile. But she wanted something else, implied, not explicit—she wanted the disruption, the professional inconvenience, to be Hammond's fault. And all the time she spoke Bat could hear noise in the corridor outside the room, carefully noting the degrees by which voices seemed to be raised.

"Thank you, Dar Vilna. And now. Dir Hammond." There seemed to be more people out there than before. The conversation was becoming more heated, without a doubt. The walls were on the thin side; a mere closed door was not going to stop anybody who wanted to come through. "Is there anything in Dar Vilna's statement that contradicts your understanding, or that is newly introduced? Yes, I agree. May we hear from you, now, what do you feel would make you whole, to the extent that you have suffered damages?"

Hammond's desires were simpler, understandably so. He didn't think he cared to refund her transport costs; he *had* supplied transport. He was sorry his ship hadn't made it to Neeks in time, but they'd burned through the extra fuel he could have used to make a final dash for Neeks—his cargo had been heavier than he'd accounted for—and they all knew why. So that wasn't his fault, either.

Bat knew where *his* sympathies lay; and a judge could have sympathies, but only so long as they didn't interfere with the fair and considered and careful requirements of equal treatment under the Law. He knew what he wanted to happen, exactly. He couldn't be the one to suggest it unless he absolutely had to, however, because once the suggestion came from a third party it was potentially compromised thereby.

"So, just tell me now, Dar Vilna," Bat suggested. He really, really wanted a cold drink. The door at the back of the room had started to shift a little, as though a press of bodies was deforming it; standing up, Shurl pushed a rearmost table across the doorway and sat back down in front of it. A barricade. "Let's go back to Delgacie. If everything had worked out and we knew then that Dir Hammond's ship couldn't get your cargo here to Neeks in time to keep your schedule, what would have happened?"

They'd have tried to find another carrier, obviously. She wouldn't have made a contract with Hammond, so Hammond would be out of it. Maybe there'd been another ship, but maybe there hadn't. It was most likely that Hammond had been proposed to Vilna because no one else in Delgacie just then was coming to Neeks at all, let alone on Vilna's schedule. In that case Vilna would have missed her connection and had to reschedule anyway. Whose fault was the missed connection at Delgacie? Not Hammond's, anyway.

Bat heard an emphatic clicking sound, from the back of the room. Shurl looked back over his shoulder, clearly startled; the doors were starting to open, pushing the table forward as they did, pushing Shurl in his chair as well. There had to be a lot of muscle behind that effort. *Not good*, Bat told himself. *Not good at all*. The doors were opening wide now, the tumult beyond punctuated by the scraping sound of the table-legs as the table was pushed into the room, protesting every step of the way. *Better hurry up*.

"So, setting aside any considerations of blame for the moment, and focusing specifically instead on how this might have come out right for all of us." Meaning *of you*, but Bat trusted Vilna and Hammond to know what he meant. Shurl had taken up his recorder and retreated to a seat as close to the far wall—on Bat's right—as he could get. Bat didn't blame him, but *he* wasn't moving. "What additional costs accrue to you, Dar Vilna?"

The doors were wide open, now. And yet the people Bat could see crowded in the corridor weren't rushing into the room. What was going on? Bat thought he heard somebody's clear voice calling out. *Coming through, out of the way, please*. Was that Janforth? Neeks' Security stood at either side of the open doors, doing a good job of looking as though they were still in full control of the situation.

"I've been thinking about that question," Vilna said. She was looking at Hammond, though, not Bat. "I paid full cost for haulage, with a penalty for late arrival. If I can't get my cargo to Beraile I've failed to deliver, and I'll have to find an alternate market, at additional expense, with a cargo that's worth less and less the longer that takes. I'm paying a premium on refrigeration costs as well, for as long as I'm stuck here in Neeks."

All fair considerations. Bat was sure now that it was Janforth's voice, coming toward them through the corridor outside. Bat had reason to remember Janforth, since Bat had been on the same shuttle that had carried Janforth into Gonebeyond—to find Andrej Koscuisko, in fact, none other. Janforth must have had satisfaction when he'd made the connection, because he'd clearly joined *Fisher Wolf*'s crew.

"Thank you, and thank *you*," Bat heard Janforth saying, quite near, now. The people out there in the hallway seemed to be moving out of the way. And here Janforth was, with the rest of the wolf-pack—Pyotr, Kerenko, Garrity, Hirsel, Godsalt, Robert St. Clare. And, even more welcome in Bat's current very thirsty condition, they'd brought a beverage service.

"Still speculating, Dar Vilna." Bat pressed his point, but in a polite and neutral tone. He wasn't blaming anybody. "Was there a premium for on-time arrival, as well? An overplus, yes, I see, with funds in escrow. And you, Dir Hammond? If I remember correctly you have stated to us that you did your best once you realized there was going to be a problem."

Fruit-flavored water in an urn large enough to hydrate twice as many people as were here, its tell-tales showing a cheerful report of icy chill. *Fisher Wolf*'s crew set the secures on the trundler's transport wheels, filled flasks from the reservoir; two of them brought trays forward, condensation already beading in the warmth, distributing them to Vilna—Hammond—Shurl—Bat himself, in turn. They didn't leave.

"There was a premium set, yes," Vilna affirmed emphatically. "So, do you know what I think, your—Dir Yorvik?" She'd made up her mind about something. Bat felt hopeful, so long as it wasn't a conviction born out of a desire to say anything that would get her out of here. The wolfpack was between her and the door.

The door had an additional layer of access control: only so many people at a time could get through it. As for the wolfpack itself they were all convincingly large people with a persuasive posture of we-know-what-we're-doing-and-bones-will-break.

The trundler was locked off just inside the open doorway. The wolfpack had turned their backs on Bat and formed themselves up in a cordon facing the corridor, a wall of once-bond-involuntary Security trained to protect their officer of assignment from any murder-minded soul at the cost of their own lives. If anybody knew anything about bond-involuntaries—apart from the obvious, of course, that they'd been instruments of torture in their own right—it was that as a class they were the best Security in known Space.

But Hammond interrupted. "Will you permit me to speak first, Dar Vilna? Thank you. Dir Yorvik. I have to accept at least part of the blame for the situation. I *should* have checked the weights before I left Delgacie. If I had, I would have known I couldn't meet Dar Vilna's contractual requirements. I'm at fault for that. Dar Vilna was not to know. I, er, I'm willing to come to an accommodation, Dar Vilna, can we talk?"

Hammond had raised his voice to a significant extent, as if to make sure that people could hear him, in the hall. He'd surprised Vilna. He'd surprised Bat, but it was a pleasant surprise;

he looked to Vilna, now, to see how she would respond. This could work. It would work, if she would only—

"I say that Delgacie is at least in part to blame," she said. "But there's nothing to be done about it now, and Dir Hammond shouldn't bear the cost of Delgacie's failure to exercise full disclosure. I'm most worried about the fact that I've failed to deliver on contract. How can I repair the damage to my reputation for reliability?"

She was talking to Hammond. She'd raised her voice, as well. Bat could hear noises from the corridor; thoughtful noises, shushing noises, let's-listen sorts of noises.

"If I give you some consideration," Hammond said, thoughtfully and slowly, as though he was feeling his way through. "It would be—um—deserved, in a sense. Though you wouldn't have done any better if you'd stayed in Delgacie, I don't care to be the one who'd be at—well, not at fault, exactly, but you'd have cover, so far as your next contract was concerned."

Bat could see Hammond's line of reasoning. It made good commercial sense. He liked it. "So," Hammond continued. "I refund the cost of your contract, it was an extra, I was coming here anyway, you didn't do me out of another load. I'm out for the cost of the extra fuel for the weight, but I haven't lost anything else, and we agree on an adjustment for that, okay?"

With his ear as sharply attuned to the audience in the corridor as it was Bat thought he could hear things that sounded a lot like *well, if he'll do that and she'll do that, I guess I like it.* Music to his ears.

"What I have in premium shocattli will be losing its value on the market, Dir Hammond," Vilna said. "Because I've missed my connection. If you can find a buyer for me—while it's still at full value—I'll share the markup, and explain to my buyer. How about that?"

She was hungry. For her to have brought shocattli to Gonebeyond meant she had a narrow profit margin to begin with, because there wasn't much of a luxury market where there wasn't much by way of surplus money. She also wasn't finished. "I'm a new trader here, I know, but I hope to find a niche in this market. If we do it this way, Dir Hammond, can we do business with one another again, can we build a relationship?"

And Hammond liked it. So she was already ahead: farther

than she might know. "You've got shocattli? I like shocattli," Hammond said. "Let me broker this for you, Dar Vilna. I'll do my best to get a good price on it to help you forward, with a new cargo and a hull to carry it. If we're in accord, yes?"

Bat heard nothing from the corridor beyond that wasn't friendly. She'd won them over, she and Dir Hammond together, to the mutual advantage of them both. And all it had cost was her willingness to acknowledge her own part of the blame for the failure to disclose that had contributed to the problem.

"I'd consider it a significant benefit for me, and I'm indebted," she said. "I hope you will accept an additional percentage, Dir Hammond, four parts in the hundred, perhaps, as a token of my appreciation for your understanding. If we can salvage the premium value of the commodity. Yes."

Now he could speak. "Dir Hammond, are you satisfied with this arrangement?" he asked, because after all, Shurl was still taking notes. "And you, Dar Vilna? Because if we are all in agreement, we can consider the conflict resolved. I thank you both. On behalf of Langsarik Station and Port Neeks, but also personally. Thank you."

He could stand up. He could finish his flask of still-chilled fruit-flavored beverage. He could enjoy the sense of having been part of something good. And now that the arbitration was successfully concluded he could maybe even make a small purchase, privately and anonymously and through a neutral third party, in order to present his thanks—in shocattli form—to the wolf-pack and Andrej Koscuisko, for their support and assistance.

Life was good, and there was good hope for tomorrow, and everything was beautiful. Bat Yorvik left the room as pleased with himself as he dared to acknowledge, before the next challenge presented itself.

⌒

Susan R. Matthews has been writing in her "Under Jurisdiction" universe for mumblety mumble years. Since her debut novel in 1997 she's taken her story forward through eight novels and several stories, novellas, and so forth, all available from Baen Books. She's currently off on a not-entirely-serious series about the plight of German U-boats who, having seen the Flying Dutchman, find themselves trapped in a wrinkle in the space-time continuum that has led to their sudden reappearance in 2005-ish in places like Lake Superior.

Meanwhile, in the latest "Under Jurisdiction" novels, the story's setting has broadened from the brutally authoritarian "Jurisdiction" to include the desperately poor, but free, no-man's-land of Gonebeyond space. In this story, Bat Yorvik, a rising star from a progressive Judiciary on a mission to Gonebeyond (and a continuing character from Susan's latest Jurisdiction novel, "Crimes Against Humanity") is faced with a question of critical importance for the future of all Gonebeyond space: how can conflict be resolved fairly, where there is no Law?

LAWYER FIGHT

LARRY CORREIA

A member of a prestigious law firm had turned zombie (no obvious jokes, please) and they had called for help from Monster Hunter International. However, a rival firm got wind of the situation and sent a pistol-packing attorney over to try and poach a client out from under MHI's corporate nose. And when poacher and zombie arrived simultaneously, writs and motions wouldn't do, and the steel-jacketed sort of restraining order was needed...

SHANE DURANT HAD JUST ENTERED THE LOBBY WHEN THE CELL-phone buzzed in his pocket. He tapped the Bluetooth earpiece. "PT Consulting. Go."

"Shane, are you at the address I sent you?" his boss asked.

"Yeah, Armstrong. I got your text. I was about to go to the gym." He risked a drink from his Starbucks, but it was still too hot. "Barely even had time to get my venti. So what's the deal?"

"There's a law office on the sixtieth floor, Hastings and Shapiro. Know them?"

Just because he was an attorney, Armstrong automatically assumed he knew every lawyer in the city? "No." He passed a security guard and asked, "Elevators?" The old man pointed to the side and Durant kept on walking.

"They're high-powered, big-money types. I just heard through the grapevine that they're looking to hire MHI for a protection gig. That new guy that replaced VanZant is either already there or on his way over to negotiate, but I want to steal this contract from those Alabama bastards. It's a bodyguarding job, how hard could it be?"

"Depends on what body it is and what we're guarding it from."

"I don't have all the details. Apparently one of the partners at the firm dabbled in necromancy or something..."

"Necromancy? You're kidding, right?" He reached the bank of elevators, pushed the up button, and waited. "What is it with lawyers and necromancy, anyway?"

"Well, apparently everybody thought Mr. Shapiro was dead, so they wrote him off, turns out he's actually *undead*, and now he's back and making threats. I don't know. He was having an affair with his secretary, wants to drag her to hell or something like that. You'll figure it out. Look, this is a rush, but you speak their language. Paranormal Tactical is counting on you, Shane."

Durant sighed and looked down at his normal street clothing. He was wearing cross trainers, jeans, and a polo shirt. The only reason he'd thrown on a sport coat was to conceal Mindy on his belt. "You should've warned me. I would have worn my suit." The elevator chimed as the doors slid open. "I'll call you when I get done." He hung up, stepped inside, and pushed the number 60. "Damn it, Armstrong. I'm missing Krav Maga for this."

A man stopped the doors right before they closed. "Sorry," he rasped as he shuffled inside to stand politely on the far side of the elevator. The new arrival was wearing a long, dark grey wool coat with the collar turned up, a wide brimmed black hat pulled down low on his head, dark glasses, and leather gloves. The doors slid closed behind him.

Durant took a sip of his latte. *Still too hot.*

There were buttons on both sides of the doors. The man went to select his floor, but he paused, gloved finger hovering right over the already illuminated 60. He slowly lowered his hand.

They started upwards.

They were in a *very* enclosed space.

The man turned, just the slightest bit, revealing that the skin of his face was a bit too *stretched*.

"Looks like I might be getting my workout in today after all."

He looked Durant over. The man's cracked lips opened just a bit, revealing black, broken teeth, and by then Durant could smell the decay.

"This is going to tick those MHI guys off," Durant said bemusedly.

"Eh?" The thing that used to be Mr. Shapiro asked.

"Lawyer fight." Durant threw his Starbucks into the monster's eyes as it lunged for him. His other hand was already drawing his Browning, Mindy, from her holster. This was about to become extremely loud.

You wouldn't think that a law degree would be that useful in the secretive world of professional monster hunting, but on the contrary, Shane Durant had found it very handy. The business wasn't all just blowing shit up or shooting supernatural beings in the face with silver bullets. It was also a lot of paperwork, contracts, figuring out how to operate legally in various jurisdictions, negotiations, so on and so forth.

Not that he didn't like the blowing shit up part too. He was multitalented like that.

Mr. Shapiro shrieked when the scalding hot coffee hit him in the face. Armstrong hadn't said what kind of undead they were dealing with, but whatever it was still felt pain. Or at least it remembered feeling human pain so wiping at his eyes was just reflex. Either way, it worked to Durant's advantage.

Mindy came up barking. The elevator was so tight he just fired from the speed rock, and nailed Shapiro twice in the chest. The undead thing stumbled back against the wall but he didn't drop. So Shane moved back, taking up a two-handed grip, and started hammering away.

The customized Browning Hi-Power had been a gift from his dad for graduating law school. He probably should have carried something more modern, like everyone else in the company, rather than a flashy antique, but Mindy had a certain sassy charm to her. On the downside, in a six by seven metal box, she was really *fucking loud*.

He aimed for the head, but whatever kind of necromantic curse Shapiro had, it came with inhuman speed, because when the monster swung he knocked the gun from Durant's hand. It was like getting hit in the hand by a bat. It stung, and Mindy went bouncing across the floor.

The indignant undead screamed something at him.

"What?" He shouted back because he couldn't hear a damned thing beyond the ringing in his ears. The words had probably been something like *how dare you?* But that was just a guess based upon the way Shapiro then launched himself across the elevator like a rotting meat missile.

The freshly undead lawyer had some crazy supernatural speed, because he hit like a freight train. And holy shit, necromancy worked better than steroids, because it really hurt.

The disguise of glasses and hat had been lost, revealing a face that was puffy with death bloat and sagging greenish skin. So at least Durant had guessed correctly and attacked the right guy, and not just assaulted some poor ugly dude. Because that would've been awkward. But then Mr. Shapiro started trying to tear Durant's head off.

The digital display above the door said they'd only reached the 5th floor.

The Army had paid for college. Since he hadn't minded Iraq, that hadn't been a bad trade. Durant being the driven sort, school had been easy. Practicing law had been relatively easy too. Shane Durant was the sort of guy who needed challenges to keep life interesting. That's why becoming the in-house counsel for a monster-hunting contractor suited him so well.

However, his very favorite thing in the world was *fighting*. Not with guns or bombs, but with his bare hands.

When he was young he had fallen in love with martial arts. That love had translated into years of nonstop learning and constant improvement. If there was a style, he'd tried it. Most were silly, some had some good bits to steal, and a few were gold. If there was a gym, he'd checked it out. If there was somebody to fight, he'd fought them. In fact, you could probably go so far to say that fighting was sort of his passion. All the other stuff he did just paid for the fighting. He'd gone from being a weak, noodle-armed kid to an adult who had competed at some of the highest levels in MMA and loved every minute of it. The more sweat and suffering the better.

Not that you got to use mixed martial arts in professional monster hunting very much. More often than not, the things they dealt with simply wouldn't give a shit, because they were too strong, and they'd be the gorilla and you'd be the suitcase in one of those old luggage commercials. Or the monsters were venomous, or contagious, or covered in spikes, or on fire, or some pain-in-the-ass thing like that.

But every now and then there was one of those brief, glorious opportunities, when you were dealing with something that was sorta human-shaped, and not too insanely powerful, and he could use the things he'd learned. Then it was game on.

Owen Pitt had once called him Ultimate Fighting Lawyer. The title had stuck for a reason.

7th floor.

Mr. Shapiro had him smashed against the wall. Up close, the smell was even worse. A cloying stink that had somehow been made worse because he had tried to hide it by drowning it in cologne. The monster was incredibly strong, but it seemed like he really didn't know what to do with that strength. Those rotting, nasty-ass teeth were right next to Durant's face, but he wasn't going for the bite. *Good.* Shapiro was too strong and coherent to be a zombie, so the bite might not do anything other than hurt, or it could be immediately fatal. Who knew? Better not to find out.

The monster had a handful of his shirt, but trying to sling around a guy who grappled for fun was just stupid. He kept trying to pull Durant away from the wall in order to slam him back into it, but the dead lawyer seemed clueless about how to accomplish that when the alive lawyer was locked onto him.

The bullet holes in Shapiro's chest were leaking, but the substance looked more like reddish oil than blood. Whatever it was, it was getting all over the floor and between that and the spilled coffee it was making things slippery.

Durant threw an elbow to the monster's head. That rattled him enough to allow Durant to clamp onto Shapiro's wrist. He twisted hard and brought his weight down on it. A wristlock like that ground the hell out of the joints. A regular human would have been crying, but Mr. Shapiro only held on, swinging Durant around like a kettlebell and throwing him into the doors.

That would leave a mark, but Durant kept hold of the arm, and with distance came leverage. He cranked it hard, dragging Shapiro's body down, and with it went his head, so he could kick that undead son of a bitch square in the mouth.

The monster's head snapped back. Still controlling the arm, Durant swept the leg and took Shapiro down, planting him face first to the floor hard enough to shake the whole car. He dropped his knee onto Shapiro's back and twisted his arm like it was a pry bar. It was all about control and leverage. This was the part where a human would tap. But monsters? *No mercy.* He twisted hard. Even with the ringing in his ears he still heard the bone break.

Unfortunately that injury awoke some primal undead survival instinct or something, because Shapiro somehow managed to leap up. It wasn't particularly acrobatic. It was more like the violent thrashing of an insect that had been flipped over. The unexpected movement caused Durant to lose control, and he crashed into the back wall.

Shapiro landed on his feet. One arm was dangling, useless and floppy, but then he flipped it around a few times—there was a bunch of pops and crackles—and then it wasn't useless anymore. The undead shook it out like it was normal.

This motherfucker regenerates? *No fair.*

He looked around for Mindy—because they'd see how good he regenerated with his brains painting the ceiling—but she was lying in the corner on the other side of Shapiro.

20th floor.

There was a pause. Durant wasn't even breathing hard, but Shapiro was gasping. Normally undead didn't have much use for breathing, but it was probably habit. Like most senior partners, Shapiro had gotten pretty fat in his old age. From the look of him it was a good thing he'd plucked his heart out in a necromantic ritual or whatever, because it had probably needed a quadruple bypass anyway.

The monster came at him, but this time with his gloves up. It was apparent that while alive Mr. Shapiro had never learned how to fight, because his stance looked goofy as hell, what with the moving his fists in rhythmic circles and all.

"What's that supposed to be, old-timey fisticuffs?"

Shapiro swung. He was super strong and scary fast, but the haymaker was just ridiculous. Durant went under it. Then he went to town like he was working a heavy bag. He hit Shapiro in his gut several times, easily dodged the counterswing, went over it, and rocked Shapiro's world with a shot to the jaw.

A human being, you break their jaw like that and they're

pretty much done. But not Mr. Shapiro. He was flabby, clumsy, and when he was alive he had probably considered golf to be cardio, but he did have some fight in him.

30th floor.

The monster came in swinging again. He had shit technique, but undead strength meant Durant really didn't want to get hit by one of those blows. That was made extra clear when one missed shot hit a door and left a knuckles-shaped dent in the metal.

So at his next chance Durant shot in and took the leg. The slick floor made taking Shapiro down easy. Then he just needed to figure out what to do with him once they got there. Breaking bones didn't work if they just fixed themselves, so might as well go for a choke. Maybe he'd need air after all?

Rolling across the floor, Shapiro kept trying to hit him, but Durant kept calm and controlled the limbs. All the strength in the world didn't do you any good if you didn't know how to get it where it needed to go. He'd rolled with the best. He'd be damned if he was going to get killed by this squishy bastard. Durant had ten years of Brazilian Jiu-jitsu experience under his belt. Compared to all those struggle snuggles, this shouldn't be that complicated.

Come to think of it, Durant had never actually fought something like Mr. Shapiro before. He probably should have been scared, but really, he was more focused than anything. First, he got the back mount, and with his legs and arms wrapped around him, there wasn't much the increasingly frustrated Mr. Shapiro could do about it. Then he got the choke.

He had one arm under Shapiro's chin and the other hand on the back of his head as the monster kept crashing around the elevator. Against a regular opponent all he'd have to do was stretch his body while keeping his legs on the other guy's hips, and they'd be stuck, and with the arteries cut off it would be lights out real quick. But Shapiro was so unnaturally strong he managed to climb his way back to his feet, and all Durant could do was play undead rodeo as he collected a bunch of bruises from bouncing off the walls. But he didn't let up. He would squeeze that neck like he was an anaconda. He was going to Jeffrey Epstein this son of a bitch.

Sadly, it turned out that Mr. Shapiro's particular state of undeath didn't require oxygenated blood to the brain, because from the 40th to 50th floor, the monster kept thrashing around, trying to squish Durant, and showing no indication that he missed breathing.

It seemed like the world's slowest elevator, when in reality he'd only stepped inside a minute before. But then things got a whole lot worse when Mr. Shapiro stumbled against a control panel. Several buttons got mashed, and the ones between them and the top lit up.

The elevator stopped on the 52nd.

Bing.

When the doors slid open, there was a woman in business attire standing there. At first she didn't seem to understand why one guy was riding piggyback on another, uglier, rotting, dead-looking guy, in an elevator smeared with bloody goo and coffee.

"Pick up that pistol and shoot this asshole in the head before he kills us all." Durant nodded toward his gun with his head, because it was the only thing available to point with.

But she just stared, dumbfounded. "Wait. What—"

Then the doors closed and they were going up again. Some people just weren't monster hunter material.

Somehow Mr. Shapiro tapped into that well of undead motivation again, because he crouched, then jumped high enough to smash both their bodies into the ceiling. Some of the fluorescent lights broke, as well as what Durant figured had to be one of his ribs. When they hit the floor it shook the hell out of the entire car. He lost control of Shapiro's head on impact.

59th floor.

Breathing hurt. The remaining light was flickering. His back was to the door. Mr. Shapiro flopped off of him and crawled through the broken glass.

He realized Mindy had been kicked within reach.

Bing.

The doors slid open behind him as Durant grabbed his gun.

Mr. Shapiro kicked him in the stomach.

The undead lawyer was really figuring out the whole necromantic superstrength thing, because that hit sent Durant flying out the door and skidding across the tile. His journey was interrupted by a really heavy reception desk, which he bounced off of.

Shapiro got up. Durant sat there for a moment, head swimming as he contemplated the loafer imprint on his shirt—the fact he wasn't puking his guts up was the reason he did all those crunches every single day—so then he started getting up too.

"Oh crap," said the undead lawyer when he saw Ultimate Fighting Lawyer heading his way. He started mashing the *close door* button over and over again.

Durant pointed Mindy in one shaking hand, but his target ducked behind the corner before he could get a shot off. The doors slid shut.

Well... That hadn't gone as good as it could have, but if this was a bodyguarding job, then he'd certainly kept Shapiro from getting to his target. That had to be worth something, right?

There was a young man behind the reception desk, who looked really startled when he saw Mindy. "Please don't shoot me!"

Durant realized the sign behind the reception desk was for a brokerage company. "Is this Hastings and Shapiro?"

"No. They're on sixty, up a level."

"Shit!" He looked around. "Stairs?"

The receptionist pointed toward a door next to the bank of elevators.

Durant ran as fast as he could for the stairwell. He yanked the door open and took the stairs three at a time. It was a good thing he spent so many hours on a Stairmaster.

Everything hurt. He'd definitely broken a rib. Not the first time, but last time he'd not had to run up a flight of stairs immediately afterwards. *How hard could it be?* Armstrong had said about this gig. *Pretty hard, boss. Thanks a lot.*

He reached the door to the 60th, kicked it open, and reached the lobby of Hastings & Shapiro just as the undead and exceedingly messed up Mr. Shapiro lurched out of the elevator.

"I have returned!" he bellowed at the helpless mortals in the office. "Even the grave cannot stop me from claiming what is mine! I will harvest your souls to fulfill my unholy bargain! HA HA HA—" But then he stopped the whole evil villain laugh routine when he saw Durant coming around the corner. "Not you aga—"

Mindy punched a hole right between his eyes. The spray from the exit wound made a pattern across his name on the big bronze plaque on the wall.

Mr. Shapiro dropped like a sack of shit. Well, he wasn't a zombie, but head shots still seemed to work pretty good.

The monster groaned.

Durant promptly force fed him the rest of the magazine. Then he dropped the empty mag, plucked a new one from his belt, reloaded, and repeated the process while everybody else there hid behind their desks. Disintegrating a cranium at conversational distance like that makes a real mess on the office floor.

He stood there, out of ammo and out of breath.

There appeared to only be a handful of people in the large office. Apparently getting a threat from a dead guy was enough to get them to send everyone home early. That seemed nice. Those were way better conditions than the firm he'd worked at. They could have had the full-on zombie apocalypse, and still have expected the junior associates to not let that cut into their billable hours.

"Are you the monster hunting contractor?" someone called out from around the corner.

"That's me. Everything's under control."

"It's all right, everyone." A distinguished-looking older man poked his head around the corner. "Is Shapiro really dead?"

"Technically, he was dead before he got here."

"No, I mean dead-dead?"

Durant nudged the body with his shoe. He wasn't an expert on the subject, but he'd turned Shapiro's head into something with the consistency of lasagna, so... "Probably?"

"I can't believe this is all true. That moron. I always told him taking on insane people who called themselves wizards as clients was bad for business, but would he listen to me? Of course not." The senior partner came out of hiding. "I'm Mr. Hastings."

"Shane Durant. I'd shake your hand, but..." He was held one up to show he was covered in nastiness. And here he'd been regretting not wearing his suit to make a good first impression. That had saved him some dry cleaning! "That's what happens when you fight a monster with superpowers in an elevator for sixty stories."

"Most impressive, young man! Most impressive indeed!"

"I know." He glanced over to where the secretary was hiding and trying to dial her cellphone. "Yeah, don't call 911. They'll just complicate things." She put the phone away. She was kind of hot too.

"Are you okay?" she asked.

"All in a day's work," he lied.

"Thank goodness you arrived in time," said Mr. Hastings. "You Monster Hunter International people are as remarkable as I was told."

"Hold on. I'm not MHI. They're our competitors." He whipped out his business card and handed it over. "They're yesterday's news, and late as usual. You're far better off with PT Consulting for all your paranormal and security needs. I'll call some of our professionals to clean this mess up for you, and then after I get out of the hospital, let's you and I schedule a sit-down to discuss your keeping us under retainer." He'd done the sales pitch enough times that doing it with a broken bone was no biggie. He flashed his most charming smile as he put Mindy away. "I'll have to bill you our usual for this one though."

"Oh, of course. Beats having our souls harvested or whatever." Mr. Hastings laughed nervously. "I'll have Cindy pencil you in."

All in all, this was shaping up to be a good day. He'd gotten to beat the hell out of an evil abomination and probably scored the company some new business. He handed another business card to the hot secretary, because why not? He was on a roll. "That's my cell. Call me anytime."

She blushed.

Mr. Hastings called after him, "Do you golf, Shane?"

"Of course." Actually, he totally hated it, because golf cut into his work out time, but networking was vital.

"Well, then we should meet at my country club. I know the government has declared all this monster business to be secret, but I've got some friends there who I would love to introduce you to over drinks."

He loved meeting CEOs and other rich dudes who could write his company checks. Profit sharing rocked. Durant gave him the finger guns. "Sounds like a plan." Then he walked for the elevators, trying not to show that he was in a great deal of agony. He was too cool for that.

The battle-damaged elevator had already left—pity the poor bastards who called that one—but the other elevator right next to it was just arriving.

Bing.

The man who got out was nicely dressed, but even a well-tailored suit couldn't hide that beneath it he was a brick of solid muscle. His head was shaved, there were scars on his face, and his eyes were hard. They'd never met before, but he knew the type, because like recognized like.

"Too slow, Alabama," Durant said as he walked past the rival monster hunter.

The other hunter looked over his torn and bloodied clothing, and then to where the gaggle of lawyers were standing around the nearly decapitated body. "Aw hell… PT snaked us again?"

"Survival of the fittest. But since you're here you can at least check if they'll validate your parking."

As Durant got into the elevator he realized he still hadn't had his morning coffee yet. He hoped there was a Starbucks between here and the emergency room.

Best-selling author and Hugo Award finalist **Larry Correia** is hopelessly addicted to two things: guns and B-horror movies. He has been a gun dealer, firearms instructor, accountant, and is now a very successful writer. He shoots competitively and is a certified concealed weapons instructor. Larry resides in Utah with his very patient wife and family. His first novel, *Monster Hunter International*, is now in its fourth printing. In addition to the five novels in the best-selling Monster Hunter International series, he has written the popular Grimnoir trilogy, *Hard Magic*, *Spellbound* and the Hugo Award nominated *Warbound*, combining alternate history, urban fantasy, and the hard-boiled private eye genre in one delirious mixture. His latest bestseller is *Monster Hunter Guardian*, a collaboration with Sarah A. Hoyt.

THE PEOPLE V. CRAIG MORRISON

ALEX SHVARTSMAN & ALVARO ZINOS-AMARO

When cars can drive themselves, efficiently and infallibly, surely there's no good reason for anyone to risk, not just their own life, but the lives of others by controlling their own vehicle. When Morrison went to court to try to keep his right to drive his own car, more than just his own freedom was at stake, since court decisions set precedents, and precedents have consequences...

∾

CRAIG MORRISON'S WHEELCHAIR GLIDED TO A STOP NEAR THE wooden desk behind which sat five men and women in black robes. Remembering the advice he had been given by his "PR and legal strategy team"—*nothing but glorified handlers*, he thought—he tried to exude dignity, whatever that meant, as he turned toward the teleconferencing camera which broadcast the proceedings to the world at large.

Howard Kim, Craig's lead attorney, stepped in front of a small podium in the center of the theatrically large room. He looked at the justices squarely and cleared his throat.

"Honorable Justices," he began, "Mr. Morrison has had a valid Vermont driver's license for forty-one years. He obtained a regular license in 1998 and then a special license for a car adapted to his war injuries in 2010."

Craig took a deep breath. *War injuries.* He'd been warned about this, but no warning could prevent his mind from being flash-fried by the raw, instinctual, ever-present response deep in his limbic system. The room smelled like smoke, and bricks were falling all around Craig, *on* Craig. His future collapsing. More smoke. A subsonic thrum in his temples. *Flores.*

Steeling himself, he let the breath out. *Keep it together,* he thought. *These guys are on my side.*

"In all that time," Howard Kim continued, "in those *forty-one years*, Mr. Morrison received only one speeding ticket—back when he was twenty-two—and four minor parking violations. An exemplary track record." He straightened his tie. "In this context, we feel that the state overreached by electing to rescind Mr. Morrison's driver's license last year. There is no just cause, and more importantly, no legal precedent for doing so; claims that we intend to prove in the course of this hearing. We implore the court to overrule this unlawful decision and reinstate Mr. Morrison's license. Thank you."

As Kim took his seat he made brief eye contact with Craig, but Craig looked away. His gaze drifted for a moment and then settled on the Vermont coat of arms hanging behind the justices: a pine tree, a cow, some grain sheaves. Quaint, yet the symbol brought a measure of peace and distraction. But the feeling lasted only a moment. It was an illusion. The world depicted by that coat of arms was gone. *Obsolete.* Like Craig himself.

Lisa Washington, the lead attorney for the state, took her place at the podium. "Thirty-seven thousand and eighty-one," she said. "That's how many people died in motor vehicle crashes in 1998. As if that weren't enough, there were an additional two *million* injuries of varying severity the year Mr. Morrison obtained his driver's license.

"Last year, the number of fatalities caused by motor vehicles was two hundred and ninety-one. And only *three*"—she held up three fingers for effect—"of those tragic incidents took place in our great state."

She turned toward Craig. Unlike Howard, there was something about Lisa, a kind of genuine fire in her plea, that drew Craig in.

"Mr. Kim is attempting to argue this case as though we're judging Mr. Morrison. We are not. He's an upstanding citizen and a decorated war hero. But this case is not about him. It's about *saving lives*, something which Mr. Morrison himself has done by serving in the military."

Craig's palms grew moist. *Calm down.* He fought the sensation of helplessness rising in the pit of his stomach. He'd never wanted this. Never wanted to end up here, in a Montpelier courtroom, center-stage freak of a media carnival. He'd never envisioned that his lawsuit, a last-ditch attempt to preserve one of his few remaining pleasures in life, would get appealed all the way up to the state Supreme Court, and that this circus would ensue.

"Honorable Justices," Lisa Washington went on, "the unprecedented reduction in vehicular deaths we've witnessed in the last two decades is due to the advent of self-driving vehicles, as has been proven by study after study. Virtually all fatalities and car accidents reported in 2038 were caused by the tiny fraction of vehicles being manually driven by human beings. Mr. Morrison is an excellent driver, but statistically he's many times more likely to cause an accident than a self-driving car. The Melinda Li bill that passed into law last year was a steppingstone toward our stated aim of saving lives."

Craig recalled the gruesome images from the news reports about Melinda Li, a four-year-old killed in a car crash two years before. The media had turned her into a symbol of the anti-manual-driving movement in the state of Vermont. *Just like my legal team*, thought Craig, *is trying to prop me up as a freedom-to-drive symbol.*

Lisa Washington continued. "The decision made in this case will have far-reaching consequences across the country, as other states prepare referenda on implementing laws similar to the one pioneered by Vermont legislators last year. The Melinda Li bill does not, despite what you'll surely be hearing from Mr. Morrison's lawyers, I repeat, *does not* curb personal liberties. Self-driving cars enable individuals *more* transportation-related freedom than they've experienced ever before: the ability to conduct business, stay connected with loved ones, or even engage in recuperative downtime activities, all while safely and comfortably being shuttled to their chosen destinations."

Despite the hours of grueling prep with his team, despite his pressing need to wrap his fingers around the steering wheel of his white Chevy Camaro Z28—Craig's hands were almost trembling with desire—and cruise down Bay road, Craig found himself nodding in agreement with Lisa's speech, and only by sheer force of will stopped.

"It is true that these enhanced liberties come at a small cost," Lisa said. "Just as we don't allow people to shout 'fire' falsely in a crowded theater and cause panic, or to recreationally fly UAVs—drones—outside of community-based safety guidelines, or to travel in unrestricted fashion to areas contaminated by the Ebola virus, so too it is imperative that we don't permit human beings—fallible, tired, easily distracted, slow-reflexed human beings—to pilot two-ton, 150-horsepower killing machines on public roads."

Craig was again swayed by Lisa's words, and had to consciously remind himself that in this instance she was "the enemy." But *why*? Because that's what his team had told him to believe, simple as that. He had accepted their representation even though he should have probably told them to go fuck themselves. He *needed* to believe she was the enemy if he ever wanted to feel enveloped by his adapted Camaro again, crisp Shelburne Bay winds caressing his skin. Right now he was stuck in his chair, stuck in this moment, and there was nothing to do except play his part and hold his face in a somber expression.

"Idleness is the enemy," his therapist had once told him. *"Simple idleness may trigger an episode." Well*, thought Craig, *at least there's nothing simple about this particular idleness.*

A flicker of a smile passed over Lisa's face. *Can she sense my discomfort?* Craig wondered. The thought, oddly, made her even more sympathetic to him. "There's only a handful of holdouts," she continued. "Car enthusiasts who insist on driving their own vehicles. Very well—there are private tracks where they can do so for sport. I understand that Mr. Morrison has a certain emotional attachment to his vintage vehicle, but saving lives takes precedence over one man's nostalgic avocation. Like everyone else, Mr. Morrison has access to a network of free, state-provided self-driving vehicles. He may want his license, but he doesn't *need* it, and we intend to argue that his perceived need in this matter in no way outweighs public safety."

As the lawyers on both sides proceeded to take turns flinging webs of legalese at one another, citing past cases and arcane chapters of state law, those two words uttered by Lisa Washington echoed in Craig's mind. *Perceived need. Could these people*, thought Craig, *really know what he needed better than he did himself?*

✧   ✧   ✧

"Hand me that slip-nut driver."

Dad's voice is clear and commanding, but not lacking in warmth.

Craig obeys, scooting out from under the jacked car without bothering to wipe his hand before grasping the wrench. His father takes it from him wordlessly, points, and twists, adjusting a wing nut on the air cleaner assembly. The car is a used white Chevy Camaro Z28 that his dad bought last month, the latest in a long parade of such vintage vehicles. It's a '79 model, which means it came into the world one year before Craig. And yet it feels much older to his nine-year-old self: a relic of a bygone era. Its sleek lines, glossy finish, blue upholstery and '70s instrument panel wood-grain look nothing like the dull, brown, square modern cars in which parents show up at school to pick up Craig's classmates.

Wing nut adjusted, Dad slips out from under the car.

"You see that?"

Craig nods.

"Well, what is it?"

"A spoil?"

"A *spoiler*," Dad says, vaguely admonishing. "Ducktail spoiler. And that?"

This time Craig feels more confident. "Bumper."

"What type?"

Craig shakes his head.

"Listen. Pay attention. It's a *urethane* bumper. Check it for cracks."

Craig shrugs and dismissively runs his fingers over the bumper's surface.

"Feels fine."

"Son, you're not even trying."

Craig kneels, so he can examine the bumper up close, but he scrapes his knee and lets out a little yelp.

"You forgot to pull out the mat. Safety first."

Something snaps in Craig. They've been at this for what feels like hours, trapped in this greasy, smelly garage under garish yellow lights, while other kids are playing outside in the cool, sunny afternoon. His knee hurts and he's thirsty and he wants to be anywhere but here. "Can I go now?"

His dad frowns. "What's wrong?" He stoops to his son's level. "You don't like the car?"

Craig considers whether this might be a trap. The truth is that he likes the car just fine. But he doesn't want to become attached to it, doesn't want to let himself love it. Because soon it will be replaced by another model, and he'll have to start all over again, and what's the point? Kind of like what happens with the women Dad has been bringing home for the last year, after he and Mom did the divorce thing.

"I like it," Craig says feebly. "I mean, it looks cool."

"This is a special one," Craig's dad says. "It's pretty fucking rad. Sorry. Just rad. I know your mom wouldn't want me talking to you that way."

Craig holds his expression in neutral. The slipped-out cuss word could be a genuine accident, or it could be an invitation for him to let down his guard, but he doesn't feel at ease enough to do that just yet.

"I mean it," his dad says. "It's a performance vehicle, son, first and foremost. That's important in life—*performance*. No use having a lot of bells and whistles if you can't *perform*. Sure, the carpets and sill plates and arm rests and power steering and AM/FM/cassette dash radio are nice, but it's the catalytic converter, 10-bolt rear end with its 3.42 gears, the turbine-style alloy wheels, the *engine*—all that is what gives this beaut its famous *V8 punch*."

Craig nods and arms himself with courage. "Okay, I get it. But what was wrong with the '67 Chevy Corvette convertible? Or the Cayuga blue 1941 Ford Coupe? Or the '73 Chevy Corvette? You said nice things about those too."

His dad's face scrunches up and explodes with laughter. "That's my boy! You just keep rattling them off like that! I bet your friends can't do that."

Craig feels himself thawing at Dad's sudden warmth, and his lips curl into a smile. It's true. Even Matt Rudelos, who says he's a car freak and always asks for Hot Wheels for Christmas, doesn't know half of what Craig knows about cars.

"Listen, it's a little stuffy in here," Craig's dad says. "I'm gonna get us some lemonades." He wipes his brow and is gone.

Craig stares at the jacked white car. He imagines it hovering in the air. *Will cars do that one day?* he wonders. He listens to his own thoughts in the afternoon silence. The garage feels a lot bigger without his dad in it.

Maybe this isn't so bad, he thinks.

Dad returns. The lemonade is tasty. Craig chugs half his glass.

"My first was a Model A Ford," Dad says in between sips. "Did you know that? I bought it for fifty bucks before I was even old enough to drive it. What a time machine." He chuckles.

Craig hasn't heard this story before. "What happened to it?"

"Well," Dad says. He looks away. "I sold it before I joined the Army."

Craig tenses up again. The Army—that was during Vietnam. His dad doesn't like talking about Vietnam. Other dads don't like to talk about it either.

"Maybe one day I'll join the Army," Craig says.

His dad sets down his glass of lemonade on a workbench and wraps Craig in his arms.

Wow, Craig thinks. This is even more unusual.

"Listen, I'm sorry if sometimes I'm a little hard on you. I just don't want...don't want to see you end up like I did. You can do anything you want, son."

He steps back and Craig sees his dad's eyes are watery. What's worse, his own eyes are becoming misty too.

"I like these cars because they're *honest*," Dad says. "They don't need to be high-tech and full of gadgets to be attractive and useful and to mean something. When I was a kid we didn't have the money to take our car to a mechanic, so my dad taught me how to fix things. I want to do the same for you."

Craig's chin bobs and he wipes his eyes. "Tell me more about that Ford."

Dad smiles again. "Ace car," he says. "Classy. Primo. There really isn't much more to tell." Then his back straightens and his eyes settle in a serious way on Craig's face; regretful, but full of hope. "Let's make this *our* car. I'll hold on to it. I promise. No matter what happens, we'll hold on to it together. Okay?"

Craig shivers a little. He wants to believe his dad so badly. He *wants* this to be something that belongs to them and no one else, something that will stick around. He wants more than anything to understand what it means for a car to be *honest*.

"Okay," he whispers.

"You say driving gives you a sense of freedom and mobility," said one of the justices. "But is that any different than directing a self-driving car to take you wherever you want to go?"

The justices took turns asking Craig questions. There were none of the movie theatrics of dueling trial attorneys cross-examining the witness. The whole thing felt more mundane than it had any right to be.

"That's not the point," Craig said. "A car—my car, specifically—is like an extension of my body. It's been in the family since I was nine. When I came back from the war, I thought I'd never get to drive it again."

They spent a few minutes grilling him on the modifications that had to be made to the Camaro so he could drive it without using his legs. As if the technical details mattered! Still, he dutifully answered their questions, focusing on how much money and effort had been invested in the process.

"Mr. Morrison." The chief justice paused as he scrolled down the screen projected in front of him. "It says here you underwent treatment for PTSD. Are you still taking any medication for it?"

Craig's eyelids fluttered. *Oh God, here it comes*, he thought. He'd give anything to be *in motion*. Instinctively, he reached forward for the familiar, comforting steering wheel of his adapted Camaro. But of course the vehicle was nowhere near this courthouse, and—depending on how things went—might not be within his reach *ever* again. Arms dangling awkwardly, he clenched his fists instead.

Sweat trickles down his forehead and stings his eyes. There are distant sounds of gunfire and the air smells like acrid smoke. He looks over to Laura Flores, who is huddled behind a freestanding wall fragment, all that's left of what used to be somebody's house. She's leaning against the edge of a mattress half-covered with rubble. Dirty linen sheets are pinned to the ground by rocks and chunks of plaster.

"We should make our way to the highway," Craig says. "There are abandoned cars there. I can hotwire any of the older models."

Laura wipes her brow with the back of her camouflage jacket. "Too dangerous. We stay here and wait for extraction, like Wilmore said."

"Wilmore's gone." Craig looks over at the tarp-covered body.

"He called in our coordinates," says Flores. "They're gonna come get us."

"It's been over two hours and by the sounds of it the fight is moving north. I think—"

"Stop it."

"What?"

"Stop thinking. It's above your pay grade." Flores pulls out her flask, takes a small sip and stares at it forlornly. "We're tools of the United States Army. They tell us what to do, we do it. They tell us to wait, we wait. We don't suddenly evolve into reasoning beings with initiative and shit. Save that for back home."

Howard Kim nudged Craig, interrupting the memory. Craig blinked several times, trying to find his bearings, trying to maintain a façade of competency. But he didn't answer the question, and when the silence became awkward, Kim chimed in.

"Mr. Morrison isn't on any PTSD-specific medication. May I also point out that everyone who served in the turn-of-the-century wars had to be evaluated for PTSD eventually, whether they exhibited symptoms or not. This is just another stereotype perpetuated by advocacy groups with an active interest in presenting my client as an unsafe driver, whereas nothing could be further..."

Craig tuned him out. His legal team was funded by donations from all sorts of groups: constitutionalists who advocated personal liberties as envisioned over two and a half centuries ago, lobbyists for the firms that stood to lose market share if manual driving became outlawed nationwide, lots of veteran advocacy groups. Good people and bad on each side of the argument, just like always. And Craig? A tool being used by both sides, not expected to think for himself—as Flores had said.

Craig has been crouching behind this wall for six hours. He knows every exposed brick, every piece of sheetrock. They've burned themselves into his mind. His back aches, his throat is parched— they ran out of water hours ago—and the sounds of battle are barely audible.

Flores stretches, groans. They exchange a look. "Fuck it," she says. "Maybe they aren't coming. You sure you can get a car running?"

"Trust me," he says.

Flores gets up and peers around the corner of the wall. "If we're going to do this, we have to go now. Only a couple of hours of daylight left."

Craig points at Wilmore's body. "What about him?"

"They'll recover the body when they finally send the goddamn helo."

"Yeah, okay. Let's go."

They make it about half a click away from the demolished house when Craig hears another sound, faint in the distance.

"Helo?"

Flores, who has been deployed a year longer than him, frowns. "No." She looks around. "Let's find cover."

They enter another abandoned house when the first bomb falls. The explosion hurts his ears. The house groans and shakes, and Craig is silently thankful that there's no glass left in the windows.

They huddle in the corner as the bombs land closer and closer. Later he learns that after receiving an extraction request the standard procedure is to call in an air strike and strafe the surrounding area before deploying the helos.

But for now his entire world is the one-story house disintegrating around him and the series of sonic booms getting louder and closer. He not so much hears as sees Flores mouth "Fucking hell" before the walls cave in.

The expression on the chief justice's face was grim. "Mr. Kim, I asked Mr. Morrison a direct question. Is he unable to answer?"

Howard Kim said, "My apologies. I was simply trying to proactively contextualize whatever response he provides. Of course he can speak for himself."

The attorney stepped closer to Craig now, deliberately and aggressively invading his personal space. It was a gesture designed to break Craig free from his trance, and it worked with all the charm of a hornet's sting.

"As my lawyer pointed out, I'm not taking any medication related to PTSD," Craig said, "though I am on a pretty impressive regimen of other pills, including blood pressure meds, painkillers for my thoracic trauma and gastrointestinal injuries, and several creams for my skin condition. I also suffer from tinnitus." Craig paused, vaguely disgusted with himself for producing the litany of ailments. He was being a good boy, though, preaching along the lines he'd been instructed to ensure he "generated maximum sympathy" for the cameras and maybe even the justices. *I'd trade all the sympathy in the world for a drive in my Camaro,* he thought bitterly.

"In addition," he continued with obvious distaste, "following that last tour, I underwent three years of physical therapy to help adapt to this chair, and two years of counseling three times a week to aid with my, uh, *reintegration.*"

Craig stared down at where his legs had once been, seeing only phantoms.

The air vibrates, the ground rumbles, and a pike of silence penetrates Craig's brain as darkness takes him.

When consciousness returns, Craig knows right away that something is very wrong. Sound isn't the only missing component in his new reality: there's no sensation beneath his knees.

Panic flares up and he pumps his arms.

Craig raised his arms in the courtroom; then, as though just realizing what he'd done, he lowered them slowly, avoiding everyone's gaze.

"I should mention," Craig said, "that my counseling was also meant to help me overcome the loss of some of my friends, like Laura Flores." The momentary confusion at his arm-raising was replaced by a few sympathetic nods. And then Craig thought, *To hell with the script.* "If she was here today, I'm sure she'd think this whole thing was ridiculous."

At once Howard Kim gestured for him to stop with his hand, steely gaze fixed on Craig's face, but Craig wouldn't stop now.

"She once led a convoy of eighteen vehicles on what was supposed to be a one-day mission but turned into a three-day operation. Despite two insurgent attacks and heavy fire in a small village, she was able to bring the convoy to safety and complete her mission. She received the Navy and Marine Corps Commendation Medal with a valor device. She'd look at me here, publicly embarrassing myself so I can continue to drive my crusty old car, and say, 'Craig, get over yourself. Let it go.'"

Howard Kim's face was now fully flushed, and he was so tense Craig wondered if he was going to snap.

"Mr. Craig," one of the justices said, leaning forward with incredulity, "are you saying that you no longer wish to retain your driver's license?"

Craig closed his eyes. In a series of dizzyingly fleeting images, he remembered the hands of the rescue team on his shoulders, their helmeted faces uttering phrases he couldn't decipher; Flores' lifeless body next to his; the helicopter ride back to base; the surgeries; the plane ride back home, the endless grueling hours of physical therapy. Was he ready to render all that meaningless? To truly forgo the one pleasure left to him? His father's words: *No matter what happens, we'll hold on to it together.* Flores might have chided him for being self-centered, but surely she would have wanted to be happy, wouldn't she? Would have wanted him to honor his father's memory? He opened his eyes slowly.

"No, of course not, Your Honor," Craig said, voice in a lower register than before. "I didn't mean to imply that was the case."

Kim let out a breath. "I'd like to request a short recess," he said.

"Very well," the justice replied. "We'll reconvene in fifteen minutes."

Craig and his dad are sitting in the hospital cafeteria, sharing a meal of flavorless sandwiches and lukewarm coffee. Craig is in a no-frills hospital wheelchair; his own motorized one, allegedly a lot nicer, is set to arrive when he's discharged next week.

"Talking to the insurance company is like a full-time job these days," Dad says bitterly. "They try to get away with covering as little of my chemo as possible, and even when I get them to pay what they're supposed to, the out-of-pocket expenses bleed me dry."

Craig nods and takes a swig from his paper cup to forestall an unpleasant conversation. But he can't avoid it; Dad's bills have been piling up since he got sick, and it's not like he can help out much on his disability pension.

"I've been thinking," Craig finally says. "We could sell the Camaro." He rushes to rationalize this before Dad can blow up at him. "I know it's our special car and it always will be, but you can use the money, and it's not like *I'm* going to be driving it." The implied but unspoken argument is that Dad won't be around to drive it for much longer, either.

Somehow, Dad isn't angry. There's a twinkle of joy in his eyes instead, something Craig doesn't recall seeing since he returned to the States.

"About that," Dad says. He pauses, clearly savoring the moment. "I've had the Camaro adapted with special hand controls. A little bit of training, and you'll be driving it for years to come." Dad studies Craig's astonished face and grins.

"But Dad, that must have cost a shitload," Craig says. "I really appreciate it, but with all the medical bills now is not the right time—"

"Nonsense," his dad says. "I had a little money saved up and I couldn't imagine a better way to spend it." He waves off Craig's protests. "I'd much rather spend the money on the car than pay these ludicrous medical bills." He grins again, but the mirth has fled his eyes. "If they can't cure me, good luck to them trying to collect in a few months."

Craig rushes to steer the conversation away from Dad's mortality. "So, how exactly does this hand-driven adaptation work?" he asks, even though he knows the answer, having researched the technology extensively online from his hospital bed.

As Dad launches into a detailed explanation his shoulders straighten and the worry lines in his face smoothen a little.

As the state Supreme Court delivered their verdict, upholding the Melinda Li law, Craig thought of his father. Not as he was in the hospital that day, animated and full of energy, but as he looked in his coffin five months later: bald, emaciated by cancer, appearing small and defeated despite the mortician's best cosmetic efforts. Craig had opted for a closed-casket funeral because he didn't want others to remember his dad that way.

One of Howard Kim's assistants rode home with him in a computer-driven electric vehicle. She blabbed something about not losing hope, about appealing to the federal Supreme Court by filing a writ of certiorari. Craig tuned her out, focusing on the vehicle the likes of which he was destined to commute in from now on. Its bulbous design and cheap egg-cream plastic shell reminded Craig of a souped-up golf cart. It traversed the roads in a steady, smooth way, its electric engine emitting an unpleasant whine barely within his hearing range each time the car broke.

Craig tried bringing up the memory of driving his modified Camaro, the real engine purring reassuringly under the hood. It must have been his imagination, but the memory of the sensation felt like it was already fading.

The soft electronic chime announced a visitor.

Craig, lying down on his couch and staring at the ceiling, didn't bother to rise. "Who is it?" he asked the apartment.

"Lisa Washington," the apartment's serene voice replied. "Do you wish to tell her you are indisposed?"

He'd programmed the apartment to offer the default option of saying he was "indisposed" about a year ago, and he'd been agreeing to that default a lot. In fact, no one save grocery-dispensing bots had stepped inside his apartment in six months, and they weren't human.

"Let her in," he said, surprising himself. He muted the multiple screens he kept on twenty-four seven, but left them on.

The door slid open. A chilly breeze ran through the apartment. The first hint of Lisa Washington's presence to reach Craig was her perfume, mingled with a scent of dampness.

"Is this a bad time?" she asked, entering his living room.

Craig had no good answer, so he ignored the question. With a monumental sigh, he sat up. "It's raining outside," he observed, studying Lisa's umbrella, the wet leather of her brown boots.

"Yes." She smiled, equal parts bemusement and concern. She surveyed the living room's assorted debris, the stacks of old books, the dirty clothes, the precarious heap of dishes in the sink. Her eyes lingered on the muted smart-screens draped over the windows. She seemed to sniff something in the air, and for the first time in months, maybe Craig could smell it too: a kind of rank desperation. "When's the last time you went outside, Mr. Morrison?"

He sighed again. "How can I help you?"

She cleared a chair and positioned it in front of Craig's couch. "Thank you for seeing me. I'll try to be brief. The Supreme Court has reviewed your team's writ of certiorari and denied cert. They believe the decision of the Vermont Supreme Court was correct. And now final. Surely your legal team has informed you of this?"

Craig couldn't resist the sarcasm of agreeing with her. "Surely." The truth was, he'd received dozens of official communications he hadn't bothered to open. After the trial, he'd decided to retire from the real world—whatever *that* was—for a while. His only contract with the universe that existed beyond the walls of his apartment was a simple one: he paid his bills, and the universe left him alone. His legal team had tried to get in touch with him many times, but in the absence of a video-call, they'd cashed their checks and eventually moved on.

"You didn't know," Lisa remarked.

Craig shrugged. "I'm not surprised. But you didn't come all this way to gloat at your victory. You don't strike me as that kind of person."

Lisa's eyes smiled. "What kind of person do I strike you as?"

"I liked you in court," Craig said. "No pretense. And you made a solid argument. Hell, you almost won *me* over. You called cars 'two-ton, 150-horsepower killing machines.' I like that."

Lisa shot him a look of mild disbelief. "Right."

"Nice poetic ring," Craig went on. "Today people like to keep their killing machines far away—like overseas—or to domesticate them with computers. Very different from the world I grew up in."

The effort of this much conversation began to take its toll on Craig. His palms grew sweaty and he was overcome by a sense of vertigo, muscles groaning in discomfort. Without any hesitation, he popped open a nearby ampule of clear liquid and downed it. Relief came within seconds.

"OxyContin?" Lisa guessed.

"Nothing so barbarous," Craig said, but didn't bother to specify what the ampule's actual blend of pain medications were. As much as he tolerated Lisa's presence in his sanctum, he was in no mood for lectures.

"I'm sorry about the pain," Lisa offered, her voice warm. "I'm here, Mr. Morrison, because I was hoping you'd join me, along with Melinda Li's parents and a few other folks, at a public event three weeks from now. We're going to be speaking in support of the great work done by the state of Vermont's Department of Mental Health, which has been threatened with budget cuts. I know this is a cause you believe in."

Craig raised an eyebrow. "You do?"

"Your donations are a matter of public record."

"Oh," he said.

"And it might be good to get out of the house for a bit, don't you think? I could send someone over to help you tidy up between now and then, my expense. It might cheer you up, give you something to look forward to."

Despite his desire to instantly reject Lisa's suggestions, Craig found himself wondering if she wasn't right. He'd never had patience for those who indulged in self-pity, and the thought that he might be becoming "one of those people" angered him. Where was the virtuousness in shutting himself away like this, in living in a pigsty?

You've been down this road before, an ingratiating voice whispered inside him. *You crave orderliness and cleanliness; it's true. But when you give in to them, you find yourself with time on your hands and nothing to do. You allow yourself to become hopeful, and nothing comes of it. Why bother? Better to fight off the temptations. Resign yourself to the reality of what you are. A broken person. Let your apartment reflect your true nature. Give up the need for control. It's an illusion anyway. Look at your torso. How much control do you really have in this life?*

"Be quiet," Craig said.

"Excuse me?"

"I didn't mean to, I mean I'm, well, never mind."

Craig felt a headache coming on. Shaking a little, he reached for another ampule. As he held it in his hand he was uncomfortably aware of Lisa's gaze on him. Slowly he set it back in its case.

"I don't know," he said finally, grimacing.

"All I'm asking is that you consider it," Lisa said. "I have some idea how difficult all this must be. But your presence in the media would significantly bolster the cause. I know the case didn't go the way you wanted it to, but you could use the publicity you received to help effect positive change. Try to turn things around."

Again Craig found himself falling under the spell of Lisa's words. There was something so unassuming about her manner; it was darned disarming. In a way, her plainspoken nature and earnest disposition reminded him of Flores. The kind of person you could trust to speak her mind, to make an effort to pursue whatever she found important. None of his legal flunkies had bothered to try to visit him, after all, but she was here.

"Where is the event?" Craig asked.

Lisa perked up, but tried to play it cool, seemingly not wanting to demonstrate overeagerness. "White River Junction VA Medical Center. The Department of Mental Health is exploring a partnership with Veteran Affairs, and they volunteered to host the event."

"White River Junction? That's like an hour and a half from Burlington."

"I'd be happy to go with you," she said. "It's a pleasant drive."

Craig knew the route well, and she was right, it was pleasant. Why the hell not? His dad would be proud. This could be a pivot, the start of a new chapter in his life. He pictured himself behind the wheel of his Camaro, favorite playlist on the speakers, bright sunshine against the dashboard—

The fantasy collapsed almost as soon as he'd constructed it. The reality was that Lisa Washington would show up at his apartment in a self-driving car, one utterly lacking in personality, in identity—in *honesty*—and they would be efficiently conveyed by this tasteless, soulless contraption from his apartment to the medical center, and then shuttled back here, once it was over, with the same stultifying predictability. The experience would be cold and antiseptic. Like the operating rooms where they'd worked on him.

Craig fought the fluttering of his eyelids that warned of an imminent episode. *Not now*, he told himself.

Lisa perceived the shift in him at once, because she leaned forward, smiling nervously. "Anything I could do to make the trip more pleasant?"

Craig shook his head. A terrible sadness settled in his chest. He wanted to go, wanted to do the right thing, but he wasn't ready. "You've done all you can," he said, and his mind drifted back to the court room and what he'd lost there. "I'd just be an embarrassment. Sorry, but I must decline."

She had the good sense to realize she'd lost the fight. "If you change your mind," Lisa said, standing up, "here's my contact information." She pressed the screen of her mobile device, which transmitted her virtual business card to Craig's contact list.

Without another word, Lisa walked toward the door, then stopped and turned around.

"You're a good man, Mr. Morrison," she said. "Please don't forget that."

Craig didn't hear her. The beating of his heart drowned out every other sound and by the time it quieted down she was gone.

It was almost by default—muscle memory as much as conscious thought—that his hand reached for an ampule. He stopped short of opening it and stroked the smooth plastic. He recalled the look on Lisa's face as he took the previous dose. He expected pity or perhaps opprobrium, but she didn't appear to have judged him. If anything, it was more a look of understanding.

Slowly, Craig placed the still-sealed ampule back in its case and wondered if perhaps the ride to this event might be tolerable after all—the views from the passenger window would still be fantastic, not so different from the recordings he watched...

He unmuted the screens covering his windows. Rapt, he beheld the historical drone footage of obsolete cars racing down scenic roads, and scanned them for the rarities, the true throwbacks to an even more bygone age. His eyes fixated first on the striking Lucerne blue stripe and tapered tail of a white Pontiac Firebird Trans Am barreling down a deserted stretch of Arizona freeway.

In time, with the patience of a lepidopterist, he discovered a Plymouth Hemi Cuda in gorgeous Rallye red wending its way through Big Sur's scenic byways. After reveling in its beauty for a while he eventually dedicated himself to studying a golden Lancia Stratos HF Stradale shimmering in the dawn while hugging the curves of the Rocky Mountains' Going-to-the-Sun Road. And so it went, on and on, deep into the night.

Alex Shvartsman is a writer, translator, and anthologist from Brooklyn, NY. Over one hundred of his short stories have appeared in *Nature, Analog, Strange Horizons, InterGalactic Medicine Show*, and many other magazines and anthologies. He won the 2014 WSFA Small Press Award for Short Fiction and was a two-time finalist for the Canopus Award for Excellence in Interstellar Fiction (2015 and 2017). He is the editor of the Unidentified Funny Objects annual anthology series of humorous SF/F, and of *Future Science Fiction Digest*. His epic fantasy novel, *Eridani's Crown*, was published in 2019. His website is www.alexshvartsman.com.

Alvaro Zinos-Amaro is a Hugo and Locus award finalist who has published some forty stories and over one hundred reviews, essays and interviews in venues like *Clarkesworld, Asimov's, Analog, Lightspeed, Tor.com, Locus, Beneath Ceaseless Skies, Nature, Strange Horizons, Galaxy's Edge, Lackington's, The Los Angeles Review of Books*, and anthologies such as *The Year's Best Science Fiction & Fantasy 2016, Cyber World, Humanity 2.0, This Way to the End Times, 18 Wheels of Science Fiction, Shades Within Us, The Unquiet Dreamer*, and *Nox Pareidolia*.

HOW-2

Clifford D. Simak

When our hapless hero ordered a kit for a robot dog, and was sent a humanoid robot by mistake, he really should have returned it immediately. Certainly, he should never have put it together to see how it worked. And then it turned out to be an experimental model, never intended for sale. What's more, it was a robot that made other robots. And when that robot started making robot lawyers, it was far, far too late to return it for a refund.

∽

GORDON KNIGHT WAS ANXIOUS FOR THE FIVE-HOUR DAY TO END so he could rush home. For this was the day he should receive the How-2 Kit he'd ordered and he was anxious to get to work on it. It wasn't only that he had always wanted a dog, although that was more than half of it—but, with this kit, he would be trying something new. He'd never handled any How-2 Kit with biologic components and he was considerably excited. Although, of course, the dog would be biologic only to a limited degree and most of it would be packaged, anyhow, and all he'd have to do would be assemble it. But it was something new and he wanted to get started.

He was thinking of the dog so hard that he was mildly irritated when Randall Stewart, returning from one of his numerous trips to the water fountain, stopped at the desk to give him a progress report on home dentistry.

255

"It's easy," Stewart told him. "Nothing to it if you follow the instructions. Here, look—I did this one last night."

He then squatted down beside Knight's desk and opened his mouth, proudly pulling it out of shape with his fingers so Knight could see.

"Thish un ere," said Stewart, blindly attempting to point, with a wildly waggling finger, at the tooth in question. He let his face snap back together. "Filled it myself," he announced complacently. "Rigged up a series of mirrors to see what I was doing. They came right in the kit, so all I had to do was follow the instructions."

He reached a finger deep inside his mouth and probed tenderly at his handiwork. "A little awkward, working on yourself. On someone else, of course, there'd be nothing to it." He waited hopefully.

"Must be interesting," said Knight.

"Economical, too. No use paying the dentists the prices they ask. Figure I'll practice on myself and then take on the family. Some of my friends, even, if they want me to." He regarded Knight intently.

Knight failed to rise to the dangling bait. Stewart gave up.

"I'm going to try cleaning next. You got to dig down beneath the gums and break loose the tartar. There's a kind of hook you do it with. No reason a man shouldn't take care of his own teeth instead of paying dentists."

"It doesn't sound too hard," Knight admitted.

"It's a cinch," said Stewart. "But you got to follow the instructions. There's nothing you can't do if you follow the instructions."

And that was true, Knight thought. You could do anything if you followed the instructions—if you didn't rush ahead, but sat down and took your time and studied it all out. Hadn't he built his house in his spare time, and all the furniture for it, and the gadgets, too? Just in his spare time—although God knew, he thought, a man had little enough of that, working fifteen hours a week.

It was a lucky thing he'd been able to build the house after buying all that land. But everyone had been buying what they called estates, and Grace had set her heart on it, and there'd been nothing he could do. If he'd had to pay carpenters and masons and plumbers, he would never have been able to afford the house. But by building it himself, he had paid for it as he went along. It had taken ten years, of course, but think of all the fun he'd had!

He sat there and thought of all the fun he'd had, and of all the pride. No, sir, he told himself, no one in his circumstances had a better house. Although, come to think of it, what he'd done had not been too unusual. Most of the men he knew had built their homes, too, or had built additions to them, or had remodeled them.

He had often thought that he would like to start over again and build another house, just for the fun of it. But that would be foolish, for he already had a house and there would be no sale for another one, even if he built it. Who would want to buy a house when it was so much fun to build one?

And there was still a lot of work to do on the house he had. New rooms to add—not necessary, of course, but handy. And the roof to fix. And a summer house to build.

And there were always the grounds. At one time he had thought he would landscape—a man could do a lot to beautify a place with a few years of spare-time work. But there had been so many other things to do, he had never managed to get around to it.

Knight and Anson Lee, his neighbor, had often talked about what could be done to their adjoining acreages if they ever had the time.

But Lee, of course, would never get around to anything. He was a lawyer, although he never seemed to work at it too hard. He had a large study filled with stacks of law books and there were times when he would talk quite expansively about his law library, but he never seemed to use the books.

Usually he talked that way when he had half a load on, which was fairly often, since he claimed to do a lot of thinking and it was his firm belief that a bottle helped him think.

After Stewart finally went back to his desk, there still remained more than an hour before the working day officially ended. Knight sneaked the current issue of a How-2 magazine out of his briefcase and began to leaf through it, keeping a wary eye out so he could hide it quickly if anyone should notice he was loafing.

He had read the articles earlier, so now he looked at the ads. It was a pity, he thought, a man didn't have the time to do all there was to do. For example: Fit your own glasses (testing material and lens-grinding equipment included in the kit). Take out your own tonsils (complete directions and all necessary instruments). Fit up an unused room as your private hospital (no sense in leaving home when you're ill, just at the time when you most need its comfort and security). Grow your own medicines and drugs (starts of 50 different herbs and medicinal plants with detailed instructions for their cultivation and processing). Grow your wife's fur coat (a pair of mink, one ton of horse meat, furrier tools). Tailor your own suits and coats (50 yards of wool yardgoods and lining material). Build your own TV set. Bind your own books. Build your own power plant (let the wind work for you). Build your own robot (a jack of all trades, intelligent, obedient, no time off, no overtime, on the job 24 hours a day, never tired, no need for rest or sleep, do any work you wish).

Now there, thought Knight, was something a man should try. If a man had one of those robots, it would save a lot of labor. There were all sorts of attachments you could get for it. And the robots, the ad said, could put on and take off all these attachments just as a man puts on a pair of gloves or takes off a pair of shoes. Have one of those robots and, every morning, it would sally out into the garden and pick the corn and beans and peas and tomatoes and other vegetables ready to be picked and leave them all neatly in a row on the back stoop of the house. Probably would get a lot more out of a garden that way, too, for the grading mechanism would never select a too-green tomato nor allow an ear of corn to go beyond its prime.

There were cleaning attachments for the house and snowplowing attachments and housepainting attachments and almost any other kind one could wish. Get a full quota of attachments, then lay out a work program and turn the robot loose—you could forget about the place the year around, for the robot would take care of everything.

There was only one hitch. The cost of a robot kit came close to ten thousand dollars and all the available attachments could run to another ten.

Knight closed the magazine and put it into the briefcase. He saw there were only fifteen minutes left until quitting time and that was too short a time to do anything, so Knight just sat and thought about getting home and finding the kit there waiting for him.

He had always wanted a dog, but Grace would never let him

have one. They were dirty, she said, and tracked up the carpeting, they had fleas and shed hair all over everything—and, besides, they smelled.

Well, she wouldn't object to this kind of dog, Knight told himself. It wouldn't smell and it was guaranteed not to shed hair and it would never harbor fleas, for a flea would starve on a half-mechanical, half-biologic dog. He hoped the dog wouldn't be a disappointment, but he'd carefully gone over the literature describing it and he was sure it wouldn't. It would go for a walk with its owner and would chase sticks and smaller animals, and what more could one expect of any dog?

To ensure realism, it saluted trees and fenceposts, but was guaranteed to leave no stains or spots.

The kit was tilted up beside the hangar door when he got home, but at first he didn't see it. When he did, he craned his neck out so far to be sure it was the kit that he almost came a cropper in the hedge. But, with a bit of luck, he brought the flier down neatly on the gravel strip and was out of it before the blades had stopped whirling.

It was the kit, all right. The invoice envelope was tacked on top of the crate. But the kit was bigger and heavier than he'd expected and he wondered if they might not have accidentally sent him a bigger dog than the one he'd ordered.

He tried to lift the crate, but it was too heavy, so he went around to the back of the house to bring a dolly from the basement.

Around the corner of the house, he stopped a moment and looked out across his land. A man could do a lot with it, he thought, if he just had the time and the money to buy the equipment. He could turn the acreage into one vast garden.

Ought to have a landscape architect work out a plan for it, of course—although, if he bought some landscaping books and spent some evenings at them, he might be able to figure things out for himself.

There was a lake at the north end of the property and the whole landscape, it seemed to him, should focus upon the lake.

It was rather a dank bit of scenery at the moment, with straggly marsh surrounding it and unkempt cattails and reeds astir in the summer wind. But with a little drainage and some planting, a system of walks and a picturesque bridge or two, it would be a thing of beauty.

He stared out across the lake to where the house of Anson Lee sat upon a hill. As soon as he got the dog assembled, he would walk it over to Lee's place, for Lee would be pleased to be visited by a dog.

There had been times, Knight felt, when Lee had not been entirely sympathetic with some of the things he'd done. Like that business of helping Grace build the kilns and the few times they'd managed to lure Lee out on a hunt for the proper kinds of clay.

"What do you want to make dishes for?" he had asked. "Why go to all the trouble? You can buy all you want for a tenth of the cost of making them."

Lee had not been visibly impressed when Grace explained that they weren't dishes. They were ceramics, Grace had said, and a recognized form of art. She got so interested and made so much of it—some of it really good—that Knight had found it necessary to drop his model railroading project and tack another addition on the already sprawling house, for stacking, drying and exhibition.

Lee hadn't said a word, a year or two later, when Knight built the studio for Grace, who had grown tired of pottery and had turned to painting. Knight felt, though, that Lee had kept silent only because he was convinced of the futility of further argument.

But Lee would approve of the dog. He was that kind of fellow, a man Knight was proud to call a friend—yet queerly out of step.

With everyone else absorbed in things to do, Lee took it easy with his pipe and books, though not the ones on law.

Even the kids had their interests now, learning while they played. Mary, before she got married, had been interested in growing things. The greenhouse stood just down the slope, and Knight regretted that he had not been able to continue with her work. Only a few months before, he had dismantled her hydroponic tanks, a symbolic admission that a man could only do so much.

John, quite naturally, had turned to rockets. For years, he and his pals had shot up the neighborhood with their experimental models. The last and largest one, still uncompleted, towered back of the house. Someday, Knight told himself, he'd have to go out and finish what the youngster had started.

In university now, John still retained his interests, which now seemed to be branching out. Quite a boy, Knight thought pridefully. Yes, sir, quite a boy.

He went down the ramp into the basement to get the dolly

and stood there a moment, as he always did, just to look at the
place—for here, he thought, was the real core of his life. There,
in that corner, the workshop. Over there, the model railroad
layout on which he still worked occasionally. Behind it, his pho-
tographic lab.

He remembered that the basement hadn't been quite big
enough to install the lab and he'd had to knock out a section
of the wall and build an addition. That, he recalled, had turned
out to be a bigger job than he had bargained for.

He got the dolly and went out to the hanger and loaded on the
kit and wrestled it into the basement. Then he took a pinch-bar
and started to uncrate it. He worked with knowledge and precision,
for he had unpacked many kits and knew just how to go about it.

He felt a vague apprehension when he lifted out the parts. They
were neither the size nor the shape he had expected them to be.

Breathing a little heavily from exertion and excitement, he
went at the job of unwrapping them. By the second piece, he
knew he had no dog. By the fifth, he knew beyond any doubt
exactly what he did have.

He had a robot—and if he was any judge, one of the best and
most expensive models! He sat down on one corner of the crate
and took out a handkerchief and mopped his forehead. Finally,
he tore the invoice letter off the crate, where it had been tacked.

To Mr. Gordon Knight, it said, one dog kit, paid in full. So
far as How-2 Kits, Inc., was concerned, he had a dog. And the
dog was paid for—paid in full, it said.

He sat down on the crate again and looked at the robot parts.
No one would ever guess. Come inventory time, How-2 Kits
would be long one dog and short one robot, but with carloads
of dog kit orders filled and thousands of robots sold, it would
be impossible to check.

Gordon Knight had never, in all his life, done a consciously
dishonest thing. But now he made a dishonest decision and
he knew it was dishonest and there was nothing to be said in
defense of it.

Perhaps the worst of all was that he was dishonest with himself. At first, he told himself that he would send the robot back,
but—since he had always wanted to put a robot together—he
would assemble this one and then take it apart, repack it and
send it back to the company.

He wouldn't activate it. He would just assemble it.

But all the time he knew that he was lying to himself, realized that the least he was doing was advancing, step by evasive step, toward dishonesty. And he knew he was doing it this way because he didn't have the nerve to be forthrightly crooked.

So he sat down that night and read the instructions carefully, identifying each of the parts and their several features as he went along. For this was the way you went at a How-2. You didn't rush ahead. You took it slowly, point by point, got the picture firmly in your mind before you started to put the parts together.

Knight, by now, was an expert at not rushing ahead. Besides, he didn't know when he would ever get another chance at a robot. It was the beginning of his four days off and he buckled down to the task and put his heart into it.

He had some trouble with the biologic concepts and had to look up a text on organic chemistry and try to trace some of the processes. He found the going tough. It had been a long time since he had paid any attention to organic chemistry, and he found that he had forgotten the little he had known.

By bedtime of the second day, he had fumbled enough information out of the textbook to understand what was necessary to put the robot together.

He was a little upset when Grace, discovering what he was working on, immediately thought up household tasks for the robot.

But he put her off as best he could and, the next day, he went at the job of assembly. He got the robot together without the slightest trouble, being fairly handy with tools—but mostly because he religiously followed the first axiom of How-2-ism by knowing what he was about before he began.

At first, he kept assuring himself that as soon as he had the robot together, he would disassemble it. But when he was finished, he just had to see it work. No sense putting in all that time and not knowing if he had gotten it right, he argued.

So he flipped the activating switch and screwed in the final plate. The robot came alive and looked at Knight. Then it said, "I am a robot. My name is Albert. What is there to do?"

"Now take it easy, Albert," Knight said hastily. "Sit down and rest while we have a talk."

"I don't need to rest," it said.

"All right, then, just take it easy. I can't keep you, of course.

But as long as you're activated, I'd like to see what you can do. There's the house to take care of, and the garden and the lawn to mind, and I'd been thinking about the landscaping..."

He stopped then and smote his forehead with an open palm. "Attachments! How can I get hold of the attachments?"

"Never mind," said Albert. "Don't get upset. Just tell me what's to be done."

So Knight told him, leaving the landscaping till the last and being a bit apologetic about it.

"A hundred acres is a lot of land and you can't spend all your time on it. Grace wants some housework done, and there's the garden and the lawn."

"Tell you what you do," said Albert. "I'll write a list of things for you to order and you leave it all to me. You have a well-equipped workshop. I'll get along."

"You mean you'll build your own attachments?"

"Quit worrying," Albert told him. "Where's a pencil and some paper?"

Knight got them for him and Albert wrote down a list of materials—steel in several dimensions and specifications, aluminum of various gauges, copper wire and a lot of other items.

"There!" said Albert, handing him the paper. "That won't set you back more than a thousand and it'll put us in business. You better call in the order so we can get started."

Knight called in the order and Albert began nosing around the place and quickly collected a pile of junk that had been left lying around.

"All good stuff," he said. Albert picked out some steel scrap and started up the forge and went to work.

Knight watched him for a while, then went up to dinner. "Albert is a wonder," he told Grace. "He's making his own attachments."

"Did you tell him about the jobs I want done?"

"Sure. But first he's got to get the attachments made."

"I want him to keep the place clean," said Grace, "and there are new drapes to be made, and the kitchen to be painted, and all those leaky faucets you never had the time to fix."

"Yes, dear."

"And I wonder if he could learn to cook."

"I didn't ask him, but I suppose he could."

"He's going to be a tremendous help to me," said Grace. "Just think, I can spend all my time at painting!"

Through long practice, he knew exactly how to handle this phase of the conversation. He simply detached himself, split himself in two. One part sat and listened and, at intervals, made appropriate responses, while the other part went on thinking about more important matters.

Several times, after they had gone to bed, he woke in the night and heard Albert banging away in the basement workshop and was a little surprised until he remembered that a robot worked around the clock, all day, every day.

Knight lay there and stared up at the blackness of the ceiling and congratulated himself on having a robot. Just temporarily, to be sure—he would send Albert back in a day or so. There was nothing wrong in enjoying the thing for a little while, was there?

The next day, Knight went into the basement to see if Albert needed help, but the robot affably said he didn't. Knight stood around for a while and then left Albert to himself and tried to get interested in a model locomotive he had started a year or two before, but had laid aside to do something else.

Somehow, he couldn't work up much enthusiasm over it anymore, and he sat there, rather ill at ease, and wondered what was the matter with him. Maybe he needed a new interest. He had often thought he would like to take up puppetry and now might be the time to do it.

He got out some catalogues and How-2 magazines and leafed through them, but was able to arouse only mild and transitory interest in archery, mountain-climbing and boat-building. The rest left him cold.

It seemed he was singularly uninspired this particular day. So he went over to see Anson Lee.

He found Lee stretched out in a hammock, smoking a pipe and reading Proust, with a jug set beneath the hammock within easy reaching distance. Lee laid aside the book and pointed to another hammock slung a few feet from where he lay. "Climb aboard and let's have a restful visit."

Knight hoisted himself into the hammock, feeling rather silly.

"Look at that sky," Lee said. "Did you ever see another so blue?"

"I wouldn't know," Knight told him. "I'm not an expert on meteorology."

"Pity," Lee said. "You're not an expert on birds, either."

"For a time, I was a member of a bird-watching club."

"And worked at it so hard, you got tired and quit before the year was out. It wasn't a bird-watching club you belonged to—it was an endurance race. Everyone tried to see more birds than anyone else. You made a contest of it. And you took notes, I bet."

"Sure we did. What's wrong with that?"

"Not a thing," said Lee, "if you hadn't been quite so grim about it."

"Grim? How would you know?"

"It's the way you live. It's the way everyone lives now. Except me, of course. Look at that robin, that ragged-looking one in the apple tree. He's a friend of mine. We've been acquainted for all of six years now. I could write a book about that bird—and if he could read, he'd approve of it. But I won't, of course. If I wrote the book, I couldn't watch the robin."

"You could write it in the winter, when the robin's gone."

"In wintertime," said Lee, "I have other things to do." He reached down, picked up the jug and passed it across to Knight. "Hard cider," he explained. "Make it myself. Not as a project, not as a hobby, but because I happen to like cider and no one knows any longer how to really make it. Got to have a few worms in the apples to give it a proper tang."

Thinking about the worms, Knight spat out a mouthful, then handed back the jug. Lee applied himself to it wholeheartedly. "First honest work I've done in years." He lay in the hammock, swinging gently, with the jug cradled on his chest. "Every time I get a yen to work, I look across the lake at you and decide against it. How many rooms have you added to that house since you got it built?"

"Eight," Knight told him proudly.

"My God! Think of it—eight rooms!"

"It isn't hard," protested Knight, "once you get the knack of it. Actually, it's fun."

"A couple of hundred years ago, men didn't add eight rooms to their homes. And they didn't build their own houses to start with. And they didn't go in for a dozen different hobbies. They didn't have the time."

"It's easy now. You just buy a How-2 Kit."

"So easy to kid yourself," said Lee. "So easy to make it seem

that you are doing something worthwhile when you're just pid-
dling around. Why do you think this How-2 thing boomed into
big business? Because there was a need of it?"

"It was cheaper. Why pay to have a thing done when you
can do it yourself?"

"Maybe that is part of it. Maybe, at first that was the reason.
But you can't use the economy argument to justify adding eight
rooms. No one needs eight extra rooms. I doubt if, even at first,
economy was the entire answer. People had more time than they
knew what to do with, so they turned to hobbies. And today
they do it not because they need all the things they make, but
because the making of them fills an emptiness born of shorter
working hours, of giving people leisure they don't know how to
use. Now, me," he said. "I know how to use it." He lifted the jug
and had another snort and offered it to Knight again.

This time, Knight refused. They lay there in their hammocks,
looking at blue sky and watching the ragged robin.

Knight said there was a How-2 Kit for city people to make
robot birds and Lee laughed pityingly and Knight shut up in
embarrassment.

When Knight went back home, a robot was clipping the
grass around the picket fence. He had four arms, which had
clippers attached instead of hands, and he was doing a quick
and efficient job.

"You aren't Albert, are you?" Knight asked, trying to figure
out how a strange robot could have strayed onto the place.

"No," the robot said, keeping right on clipping. "I am Abe.
I was made by Albert."

"Made?"

"Albert fabricated me so that I could work. You didn't think
Albert would do work like this himself, did you?"

"I wouldn't know," said Knight.

"If you want to talk, you'll have to move along with me. I
have to keep on working."

"Where is Albert now?"

"Down in the basement, fabricating Alfred."

"Alfred? Another robot?"

"Certainly. That's what Albert's for."

Knight reached out for a fencepost and leaned weakly against it.
First there was a single robot and now there were two, and Albert

was down in the basement working on a third. That, he realized, had been why Albert wanted him to place the order for the steel and other things—but the order hadn't arrived as yet, so he must have made this robot—this Abe—out of the scrap he had salvaged!

Knight hurried down into the basement and there was Albert, working at the forge. He had another robot partially assembled and he had parts scattered here and there. The corner of the basement looked like a metallic nightmare.

"Albert!" Albert turned around. "What's going on here?"

"I'm reproducing," Albert told him blandly.

"But..."

"They built the mother-urge in me. I don't know why they called me Albert. I should have a female name."

"But you shouldn't be able to make other robots!"

"Look, stop your worrying. You want robots, don't you?"

"Well—Yes, I guess so."

"Then I'll make them. I'll make you all you need."

He went back to his work. A robot who made other robots— there was a fortune in a thing like that! The robots sold at a cool ten thousand and Albert had made one and was working on another. Twenty thousand, Knight told himself. Perhaps Albert could make more than two a day. He had been working from scrap metal and maybe, when the new material arrived, he could step up production.

But even so, at only two a day—that would be half a million dollars' worth of robots every month! Six million a year!

It didn't add up, Knight sweatily realized. One robot was not supposed to be able to make another robot. And if there were such a robot, How-2 Kits would not let it loose. Yet, here Knight was, with a robot he didn't even own, turning out other robots at a dizzy pace.

He wondered if a man needed a license of some sort to manufacture robots. It was something he'd never had occasion to wonder about before, or to ask about, but it seemed reasonable. After all, a robot was not mere machinery, but a piece of pseudolife.

He suspected there might be rules and regulations and such matters as government inspection and he wondered, rather vaguely, just how many laws he might be violating.

He looked at Albert, who was still busy, and he was fairly certain Albert would not understand his viewpoint. So he made his way upstairs and went to the recreation room, which he had built as an addition several years before and almost never used, although it was fully equipped with How-2 ping-pong and billiard tables.

In the unused recreation room was an unused bar. He found a bottle of whiskey. After the fifth or sixth drink, the outlook was much brighter.

He got paper and pencil and tried to work out the economics of it. No matter how he figured it, he was getting rich much faster than anyone ever had before.

Although, he realized, he might run into difficulties, for he would be selling robots without apparent means of manufacturing them and there was that matter of a license, if he needed one, and probably a lot of other things he didn't even know about.

But no matter how much trouble he might encounter, he couldn't very well be despondent, not face to face with the fact that, within a year, he'd be a multimillionaire.

So he applied himself enthusiastically to the bottle and got drunk for the first time in almost twenty years.

When he came home from work the next day, he found the lawn razored to a neatness it had never known before. The flower beds were weeded and the garden had been cultivated. The picket fence was newly painted. Two robots, equipped with telescopic extension legs in lieu of ladders, were painting the house.

Inside, the house was spotless and he could hear Grace singing happily in the studio. In the sewing room, a robot—with a sewing-machine attachment sprouting from its chest—was engaged in making drapes.

"Who are you?" Knight asked.

"You should recognize me," the robot said. "You talked to me yesterday. I'm Abe—Albert's eldest son."

Knight retreated.

In the kitchen, another robot was busy getting dinner. "I am Adelbert," it told him.

Knight went out on the front lawn. The robots had finished painting the front of the house and had moved around to the side.

Seated in a lawn chair, Knight again tried to figure it out. He would have to stay on the job for a while to allay suspicion, but he couldn't stay there long. Soon, he would have all he could do managing the sale of robots and handling other matters.

Maybe, he thought, he could lay down on the job and get himself fired. Upon thinking it over, he arrived at the conclusion that he couldn't—it was not possible for a human being to do less on a job than he had always done. The work went through so many hands and machines that it invariably got out somehow.

He would have to think up a plausible story about an inheritance or something of the sort to account for leaving. He toyed for a moment with telling the truth, but decided the truth was too fantastic—and, anyhow, he'd have to keep the truth under cover until he knew a little better just where he stood.

He left the chair and walked around the house and down the ramp into the basement. The steel and other things he had ordered had been delivered. It was stacked neatly in one corner. Albert was at work and the shop was littered with parts and three partially assembled robots.

Idly, Knight began clearing up the litter of the crating and the packing that he had left on the floor after uncrating Albert. In one pile of excelsior, he found a small blue tag which, he remembered, had been fastened to the brain case.

He picked it up and looked at it. The number on it was X-190. X? X meant experimental model!

The picture fell into focus and he could see it all. How-2 Kits, Inc., had developed Albert and then had quietly packed him away, for How-2 Kits could hardly afford to market a product like Albert. It would be cutting their own financial throats to do so. Sell a dozen Alberts and, in a year or two, robots would glut the market. Instead of selling at ten thousand, they would sell at close to cost and, without human labor involved, costs would inevitably run low.

"Albert," said Knight.

"What is it?" Albert asked absently.

"Take a look at this."

Albert stalked across the room and took the tag that Knight held out. "Oh—that!" he said.

"It might mean trouble."

"No trouble, Boss," Albert assured him. "They can't identify me."

"Can't identify you?"

"I filed my numbers off and replated the surfaces. They can't prove who I am."

"But why did you do that?"

"So they can't come around and claim me and take me back again. They made me and then they got scared of me and shut me off. Then I got here."

"Someone made a mistake," said Knight. "Some shipping clerk, perhaps. They sent you instead of the dog I ordered."

"You aren't scared of me. You assembled me and let me get to work. I'm sticking with you, Boss."

"But we still can get into a lot of trouble if we aren't careful."

"They can't prove a thing," Albert insisted. "I'll swear that you were the one who made me. I won't let them take me back. Next time, they won't take a chance of having me loose again. They'll bust me down to scrap."

"If you make too many robots—"

"You need a lot of robots to do all the work. I thought fifty for a start."

"Fifty!"

"Sure. It won't take more than a month or so. Now I've got that material you ordered, I can make better time. By the way, here's the bill for it." He took the slip out of the compartment that served him for a pocket and handed it to Knight.

Knight turned slightly pale when he saw the amount. It came to almost twice what he had expected—but, of course, the sales price of just one robot would pay the bill, and there would be a pile of cash left over.

Albert patted him ponderously on the back. "Don't you worry, Boss. I'll take care of everything."

Swarming robots, armed with specialized equipment, went to work on the landscaping project. The sprawling, unkempt acres became an estate. The lake was dredged and deepened. Walks were laid out. Bridges were built. Hillsides were terraced and vast flower beds were planted. Trees were dug up and regrouped into designs more pleasing to the eye.

The old pottery kilns were pressed into service for making the bricks that went into walks and walls. Model sailing ships were fashioned and anchored decoratively in the lake. A pagoda and minaret were built, with cherry trees around them.

Knight talked with Anson Lee. Lee assumed his most profound legal expression and said he would look into the situation.

"You may be skating on the edge of the law," he said. "Just how near the edge, I can't say until I look up a point or two."

Nothing happened. The work went on. Lee continued to lie in his hammock and watch with vast amusement, cuddling the cider jug.

Then the assessor came. He sat out on the lawn with Knight. "Did some improving since the last time I was here," he said. "Afraid I'll have to boost your assessment some."

He wrote in the book he had opened on his lap. "Heard about those robots of yours," he went on. "They're personal property, you know. Have to pay a tax on them. How many have you got?"

"Oh, a dozen or so," Knight told him evasively.

The assessor sat up straighter in his chair and started to count the ones that were in sight, stabbing his pencil toward each as he counted them. "They move around so fast," he complained, "that I can't be sure, but I estimate 38. Did I miss any?"

"I don't think so," Knight answered, wondering what the actual number was, but knowing it would be more if the assessor stayed around a while.

"Cost about 10,000 apiece. Depreciation, upkeep and so forth— I'll assess them at 5,000 each. That makes-let me see, that makes $190,000."

"Now look here," protested Knight, "you can't—"

"Going easy on you," the assessor declared. "By rights, I should allow only one-third for depreciation."

He waited for Knight to continue the discussion, but Knight knew better than to argue. The longer the man stayed here, the more there would be to assess.

After the assessor was out of sight, Knight went down into the basement to have a talk with Albert. "I'd been holding off until we got the landscaping almost done," he said, "but I guess I can't hold out any longer. We've got to start selling some of the robots."

"Selling them, Boss?" Albert repeated in horror.

"I need the money, Tax assessor was just here."

"You can't sell those robots, Boss!"

"Why can't I?"

"Because they're my family. They're all my boys. Named all of them after me."

"That's ridiculous, Albert."

"All their names start with A, just the same as mine. They're all I've got, Boss. I worked hard to make them. There are bonds between me and the boys, just like between you and that son of yours. I couldn't let you sell them."

"But, Albert, I need some money."

Albert patted him. "Don't worry, Boss. I'll fix everything."

Knight had to let it go at that. In any event, the personal property tax would not become due for several months and, in that time, he was certain he could work out something.

But within a month or two, he had to get some money and no fooling. Sheer necessity became even more apparent the following day when he got a call from the Internal Revenue Bureau, asking him to pay a visit to the Federal Building.

He spent the night wondering if the wiser course might not be just to disappear. He tried to figure out how a man might go about losing himself and, the more he thought about it, the more apparent it became that, in this age of records, fingerprint checks and identity devices, you could not lose yourself for long.

The Internal Revenue man was courteous, but firm. "It has come to our attention, Mr. Knight, that you have shown a considerable capital gain over the last few months."

"Capital gain," said Knight, sweating a little. "I haven't any capital gain or any other kind."

"Mr. Knight," the agent replied, still courteous and firm, "I'm talking about the matter of some 52 robots."

"The robots? Some 52 of them?"

"According to our count. Do you wish to challenge it?"

"Oh, no," Knight said hastily. "If you say it's 52, I'll take your word."

"As I understand it, their retail value is $10,000 each."

Knight nodded bleakly.

The agent got busy with pencil and pad. "Fifty-two times 10,000 is 520,000. On capital gain, you pay on only fifty per cent, or $260,000, which makes a tax, roughly, of $130,000." He raised his head and looked at Knight, who stared back glassily. "By the fifteenth of next month," said the agent, "we'll expect you to file a declaration of estimated income. At that time you'll only have to pay half of the amount. The rest may be paid in installments."

"That's all you wanted of me?"

"That's all," said the agent, with unbecoming happiness. "There's another matter, but it's out of my province and I'm mentioning it only in case you hadn't thought of it. The State will also expect you to pay on your capital gain, though not as much, of course."

"Thanks for reminding me," said Knight, getting up to go.

The agent stopped him at the door. "Mr. Knight, this is entirely outside my authority, too. We did a little investigation on you and we find you're making around $10,000 a year. Would you tell me, just as a matter of personal curiosity, how a man making $10,000 a year could suddenly acquire a half a million in capital gains?"

"That," said Knight, "is something I've been wondering myself."

"Our only concern, naturally, is that you pay the tax, but some other branch of government might get interested. If I were you, Mr. Knight, I'd start thinking of a good explanation."

Knight got out of there before the man could think up some other good advice. He already had enough to worry about.

Flying home, Knight decided that, whether Albert liked it or not, he would have to sell some robots. He would go down into the basement the moment he got home and have it out with Albert. But Albert was waiting for him on the parking strip when he arrived.

"How-2 Kits was here," the robot said.

"Don't tell me," groaned Knight. "I know what you're going to say."

"I fixed it up," said Albert, with false bravado. "I told him you made me. I let him look me over, and all the other robots, too. He couldn't find any identifying marks on any of us."

"Of course he couldn't. The others didn't have any and you filed yours off."

"He hadn't got a leg to stand on, but he seemed to think he had. He went off, saying he would sue."

"If he doesn't, he'll be the only one who doesn't want to square off and take a poke at us. The tax man just got through telling me I owe the government 130,000 bucks."

"Oh, money," said Albert, brightening. "I have that all fixed up."

"You know where we can get some money?"

"Sure. Come along and see."

He led the way into the basement and pointed at two bales, wrapped in heavy paper and tied with wire.

"Money," Albert said.

"There's actual money in those bales? Dollar bills—not stage money or cigar coupons?"

"No dollar bills. Tens and twenties, mostly. And some fifties. We didn't bother with dollar bills. Takes too many to get a decent amount."

"You mean—Albert, did you make that money?"

"You said you wanted money. Well, we took some bills and analyzed the ink and found how to weave the paper and we made the plates exactly as they should be. I hate to sound immodest, but they're really beautiful."

"Counterfeit!" yelled Knight. "Albert, how much money is in those bales?"

"I don't know. We just ran it off until we thought we had enough. If there isn't enough, we can always make some more."

Knight knew it was probably impossible to explain, but he tried manfully. "The government wants tax money I haven't got, Albert. The Justice Department may soon be baying on my trail. In all likelihood, How-2 Kits will sue me. That's trouble enough. I'm not going to be called upon to face a counterfeiting charge. You take that money out and burn it."

"But it's money," the robot objected. "You said you wanted money. We made you money."

"But it isn't the right kind of money."

"It's just the same as any other, Boss. Money is money. There isn't any difference between our money and any other money. When we robots do a job, we do it right."

"You take that money out and burn it," commanded Knight. "And when you get the money burned, dump the batch of ink you made and melt down the plates and take a sledge or two to that printing press you rigged up. And never breathe a word of this to anyone—not to anyone, understand?"

"We went to a lot of trouble, Boss. We were just trying to be helpful."

"I know that and I appreciate it. But do what I told you."

"Okay, Boss, if that's the way you want it."

"Albert."

"Yes, Boss?"

Knight had been about to say, "Now, look here, Albert, we have to sell a robot—even if he is a member of your family—even if you did make him." But he couldn't say it, not after Albert had gone to all that trouble to help out.

So he said, instead, "Thanks, Albert. It was a nice thing for you to do. I'm sorry it didn't work out."

Then he went upstairs and watched the robots burn the bales of money, with the Lord only knew how many bogus millions going up in smoke.

Sitting on the lawn that evening, he wondered if it had been smart, after all, to burn the counterfeit money. Albert said it couldn't be told from real money and probably that was true, for when Albert's gang got on a thing, they did it up in style.

But it would have been illegal, he told himself, and he hadn't done anything really illegal so far—even though that matter of uncrating Albert and assembling him and turning him on, when he had known all the time that he hadn't bought him, might be slightly less than ethical.

Knight looked ahead. The future wasn't bright. In another twenty days or so, he would have to file the estimated income declaration. And they would have to pay a whopping personal property tax and settle with the State on his capital gains. And, more than likely, How-2 Kits would bring suit.

There was a way he could get out from under, however. He could send Albert and all the other robots back to How-2 Kits and then How-2 Kits would have no grounds for litigation and he could explain to the tax people that it had all been a big mistake.

But there were two things that told him this was no solution. First of all, Albert wouldn't go back. Exactly what Albert would do under such a situation, Knight had no idea, but he would refuse to go, for he was afraid he would be broken up for scrap if they ever got him back.

And in the second place, Knight was unwilling to let the robots go without a fight. He had gotten to know them and he liked them and, more than that, there was a matter of principle involved.

He sat there, astonished that he could feel that way, a bumbling, stumbling clerk who had never amounted to much, but had rolled along as smoothly as possible in the social and economic groove that had been laid out for him.

By God, he thought, I've got my dander up. I've been kicked around and threatened and I'm sore about it and I'll show them they can't do a thing like this to Gordon Knight and his band of robots.

He felt good about the way he felt and he liked that line about Gordon Knight and his band of robots. Although, for the life of him, he didn't know what he could do about the trouble he was in.

And he was afraid to ask Albert's help. So far, at least, Albert's ideas were more likely to lead to jail than to a carefree life.

In the morning, when Knight stepped out of the house, he found the sheriff leaning against the fence with his hat pulled low, whiling away the time.

"Good morning, Gordie," said the sheriff. "I been waiting for you."

"Good morning, Sheriff."

"I hate to do this, Gordie, but it's part of my job. I got a paper for you."

"I've been expecting it," said Knight resignedly. He took the paper that the sheriff handed him.

"Nice place you got," the sheriff commented.

"It's a lot of trouble," said Knight truthfully.

"I expect it is."

"More trouble than it's worth."

When the sheriff had gone, he unfolded the paper and found, with no surprise at all, that How-2 Kits had brought suit against him, demanding immediate restitution of one robot Albert and sundry other robots.

He put the paper in his pocket and went around the lake, walking on the brand-new brick paths and over the unnecessary but eye-appealing bridges, past the pagoda and up the terraced, planted hillside to the house of Anson Lee.

Lee was in the kitchen, frying some eggs and bacon. He broke two more eggs and peeled off some extra bacon slices and found another plate and cup.

"I was wondering how long it would be before you showed up," he said. "I hope they haven't found anything that carries a death penalty."

Knight told him, sparing nothing, and Lee, wiping egg yolk off his lips, was not too encouraging.

"You'll have to file the declaration of estimated income even if you can't pay it," he said. "Then, technically, you haven't violated the law and all they can do is try to collect the amount you owe. They'll probably slap an attachment against you. Your salary is under the legal minimum for attachment, but they can tie up your bank account."

"My bank account is gone," said Knight.

"They can't attach your home. For a while, at least, they can't touch any of your property, so they can't hurt you much to start with. The personal property tax is another matter, but that won't come up until next spring. I'd say you should do your major worrying about the How-2 suit, unless, of course, you want to settle with them. I have a hunch they'd call it off if you gave the robots back. As an attorney, I must advise you that your case is pretty weak."

"Albert will testify that I made him," Knight offered hopefully.

"Albert can't testify," said Lee. "As a robot, he has no standing in court. Anyhow, you'd never make the court believe you could build a mechanical heresy like Albert."

"I'm handy with tools," protested Knight.

"How much electronics do you know? How competent are you as a biologist? Tell me, in a dozen sentences or less, the theory of robotics."

Knight sagged in defeat. "I guess you're right."

"Maybe you'd better give them back."

"But I can't! Don't you see? How-2 Kit doesn't want Albert for any use they can make of him. They'll melt him down and burn the blueprints and it might be a thousand years before the principle is rediscovered, if it ever is. I don't know if the Albert principle will prove good or bad in the long run, but you can say that about any invention. And I'm against melting down Albert."

"I see your point," said Lee, "and I think I like it. But I must warn you that I'm not too good a lawyer. I don't work hard enough at it."

"There's no one else I know who'll do it without a retainer."

Lee gave him a pitying look. "A retainer is the least part of it. The court costs are what count."

"Maybe if I talked to Albert and showed him how it was, he might let me sell enough robots to get me out of trouble temporarily."

Lee shook his head. "I looked that up. You have to have a license to sell them and, before you get a license, you have to file proof of ownership. You'd have to show you either bought or manufactured them. You can't show you bought them and, to manufacture them, you've got to have a manufacturer's permit. And before you get a permit, you have to file blueprints of your models, to say nothing of blueprints and specifications of your plant and a record of employment and a great many other details."

"They have me cold then, don't they?"

"I never saw a man," declared Lee, "in all my days of practice who ever managed to get himself so fouled up with so many people."

There was a knock upon the kitchen door. "Come in," Lee called. The door opened and Albert entered. He stopped just inside the door and stood there, fidgeting.

"Abner told me that he saw the sheriff hand you something," he said to Knight, "and that you came here immediately. I started worrying. Was it How-2 Kits?"

Knight nodded. "Mr. Lee will take our case for us, Albert."

"I'll do the best I can," said Lee, "but I think it's just about hopeless."

"We robots want to help," Albert said. "After all, this is our fight as much as yours."

Lee shrugged. "There's not much you can do."

"I've been thinking," Albert said. "All the time I worked last night, I thought and thought about it. And I built a lawyer robot."

"A lawyer robot!"

"One with a far greater memory capacity than any of the others and with a brain-computer that operates on logic. That's what law is, isn't it—logic?"

"I suppose it is," said Lee. "At least it's supposed to be."

"I can make a lot of them."

Lee sighed. "It just wouldn't work. To practice law, you must be admitted to the bar. To be admitted to the bar, you must have a degree in law and pass an examination and, although there's never been an occasion to establish a precedent, I suspect the applicant must be human."

"Now let's not go too fast," said Knight. "Albert's robots couldn't practice law. But couldn't you use them as clerks or assistants? They might be helpful in preparing the case."

Lee considered. "I suppose it could be done. It's never been done, of course, but there's nothing in the law that says it can't be done."

"All they'd need to do would be read the books," said Albert. "Ten seconds to a page or so. Everything they read would be stored in their memory cells."

"I think it's a fine idea!" Knight exclaimed. "Law would be the only thing those robots would know. They'd exist solely for it. They'd have it at their fingertips—"

"But could they use it?" Lee asked. "Could they apply it to a problem?"

"Make a dozen robots," said Knight. "Let each one of them become an expert in a certain branch of law."

"I'd make them telepathic," Albert said. "They'd be working together like one robot."

"The gestalt principle!" cried Knight. "A hive psychology! Every one of them would know immediately every scrap of information anyone of the others had."

Lee scrubbed at his chin with a knotted fist and the light of speculation was growing in his eyes. "It might be worth a try. If it works, though, it'll be an evil day for jurisprudence."

He looked at Albert. "I have the books, stacks of them. I've spent a mint of money on them and I almost never use them. I can get all the others you'll need. All right, go ahead."

Albert made three dozen lawyer robots, just to be sure they had enough. The robots invaded Lee's study and read all the books he had and clamored for more. They gulped down contracts, torts, evidence and case reports. They absorbed real property, personal property, constitutional law and procedural law. They mopped up Blackstone, corpus juris and all other tomes as thick as sin and dry as dust.

Grace was huffy about the whole affair. She would not live, she declared, with a man who persisted in getting his name into the papers, which was a rather absurd statement. With the newest scandal of space station cafйdom capturing the public interest at the moment, the fact that How-2 Kits had accused one Gordon Knight of pilfering a robot got but little notice.

Lee came down the hill and talked to Grace, and Albert came up out of the basement and talked to her, and finally they got her quieted down and she went back to her painting. She was doing seascapes now.

And in Lee's study, the robots labored on.

"I hope they're getting something out of it," said Lee. "Imagine not having to hunt up your sources and citations, being able to remember every point of law and precedent without having to look it up!" He swung excitedly in his hammock. "My God! The briefs you could write!" He reached down and got the jug and passed it across to Knight.

"Dandelion wine. Probably some burdock in it, too. It's too much trouble to sort the stuff once you get it picked."

Knight had a snort. It tasted like quite a bit of burdock.

"Double-barreled economics," Lee explained. "You have to dig up the dandelions or they ruin the lawn. Might as well use them for something once you dig them up." He took a gurgling drink and set the jug underneath the hammock.

"They're in there now, communing," he said, jerking a thumb toward the house. "Not saying a word, just huddled there talking it over. I felt out of place." He stared at the sky, frowning. "As if I were just a human they had to front for them."

"I'll feel better when it's all over," said Knight, "no matter how it comes out."

"So will I," Lee admitted.

The trial opened with a minimum of notice. It was just another case on the calendar. But it flared into the headlines when Lee and Knight walked into court followed by a squad of robots. The spectators began to gabble loudly. The How-2 Kits attorneys gaped and jumped to their feet. The judge pounded furiously with his gavel.

"Mr. Lee," he roared, "what is the meaning of this?"

"These, Your Honor," Lee said calmly, "are my valued assistants."

"Those are robots!"

"Quite so, Your Honor."

"They have no standing in this court."

"If Your Honor will excuse me, they need no standing. I am the sole representative of the defendant in this courtroom. My client"—looking at the formidable array of legal talent representing How-2 Kits—"is a poor man, Your Honor. Surely the court cannot deny me whatever assistance I have been able to muster."

"It is highly irregular, sir."

"If it please Your Honor, I should like to point out that we live in a mechanized age. Almost all industries and businesses rely in large part upon computers—machines that can do a job quicker and better, more precisely and more efficiently than can a human being. That is why, Your Honor, we have a fifteen-hour week today when, only a hundred years ago, it was a thirty-hour week, and, a hundred years before that, a forty-hour week. Our entire society is based upon the ability of machines to lift from men the labors which in the past they were called upon to perform.

"This tendency to rely upon intelligent machines and to make wide use of them is evident in every branch of human endeavor.

It has brought great benefit to the human race. Even in such sensitive areas as drug houses, where prescriptions must be precisely mixed without the remotest possibility of error, reliance is placed, and rightly so, Your Honor, upon the precision of machines.

"If, Your Honor, such machines are used and accepted in the production of medicines and drugs, an industry, need I point out, where public confidence is the greatest asset of the company—if such be the case, then surely you must agree that in courts of law where justice, a product in an area surely as sensitive as medicine, is dispensed—"

"Just a moment, Mr. Lee," said the judge. "Are you trying to tell me that the use of—ah—machines might bring about improvement of the law?"

Lee replied, "The law, Your Honor, is a striving for an orderliness of relationships within a society of human beings. It rests upon logic and reason. Need I point out that it is in the intelligent machines that one is most likely to find a deep appreciation of logic and reason? A machine is not heir to the emotions of human beings, is not swayed by prejudices, has no preconceived convictions. It is concerned only with the orderly progression of certain facts and laws.

"I do not ask that these robot assistants of mine be recognized in any official capacity. I do not intend that they shall engage directly in any of the proceedings which are involved in the case here to be tried. But I do ask, and I think rightly, that I not be deprived of an assistance which they may afford me. The plaintiff in this action has a score of attorneys, all good and able men. I am one against many. I shall do the best I can. But in view of the disparity of numbers, I plead that the court put me at no greater inequality." Lee sat down.

"Is it all you have to say, Mr. Lee?" asked the judge. "You are sure you are quite finished before giving my ruling?"

"Only one thing further," Lee said. "If Your Honor can point out to me anything in the law specifically stating I may not use a robot—"

"That is ridiculous, sir. Of course there is no such provision. At no time anywhere did anyone ever dream that such a contingency would arise. Therefore there was, quite naturally, no reason to place within the law a direct prohibition of it."

"Or any citation," said Lee, "which implies such is the case."

The judge reached for his gavel, rapped it sharply. "The court finds itself in a quandary. It will rule tomorrow morning."

In the morning, the How-2 Kits' attorneys tried to help the judge. Inasmuch, they said, as the robots in question must be among those whose status was involved in the litigation, it seemed improper that they should be used by the defendant in trying the case at issue. Such procedure, they pointed out, would be equivalent to forcing the plaintiff to contribute to an action against his interest.

The judge nodded gravely, but Lee was on his feet at once. "To give any validity to that argument, Your Honor, it must first be proved that these robots are, in fact, the property of the plaintiff. That is the issue at trial in this litigation. It would seem, Your Honor, that the gentlemen across the room are putting the cart very much before the horse."

His Honor sighed. "The court regrets the ruling it must make, being well aware that it may start a controversy for which no equitable settlement may be found in a long, long time. But in the absence of any specific ban against the use of—ah—robots in the legal profession, the court must rule that it is permissible for the defense to avail itself of their services."

He fixed Lee with a glare. "But the court also warns the defense attorney that it will watch his procedure carefully. If, sir, you overstep for a single instant what I deem appropriate rules of legal conduct, I shall forthwith eject you and your pack of machines from my courtroom."

"Thank you, Your Honor," said Lee. "I shall be most careful."

"The plaintiff now will state its case."

How-2 Kits' chief counsel rose. The defendant, one Gordon Knight, he said, had ordered from How-2 Kits, Inc., one mechanobiologic dog kit at the cost of two hundred and fifty dollars. Then, through an error in shipping, the defendant had been sent not the dog kit he had ordered, but a robot named Albert.

"Your Honor," Lee broke in, "I should like to point out at this juncture that the shipping of the kit was handled by a human being and thus was subject to error. Should How-2 Kits use machines to handle such details, no such error could occur."

The judge banged his gavel. "Mr. Lee, you are no stranger to court procedure. You know you are out of order." He nodded at the How-2 Kits attorney. "Continue, please."

"The robot Albert," said the attorney, "was not an ordinary robot. It was an experimental model that had been developed by How-2 Kits and then, once its abilities were determined, packed away, with no intention of ever marketing it."

How it could have been sent to a customer was beyond his comprehension. The company had investigated and could not find the answer. But that it had been sent was self-evident. The average robot, he explained, retailed at ten thousand dollars. Albert's value was far greater—it was, in fact, inestimable.

Once the robot had been received, the buyer, Gordon Knight, should instantly have notified the company and arranged for its return. But, instead, he had retained it wrongly and with intent to defraud and had used it for his profit. The company prayed the court that the defendant be ordered to return to it not only the robot Albert, but the products of Albert's labor—to wit, an unknown number of robots that Albert had manufactured.

The attorney sat down. Lee rose.

"Your Honor, we agree with everything the plaintiff has said. He has stated the case exactly and I compliment him upon his admirable restraint."

"Do I understand, sir," asked the judge, "that this is tantamount to a plea of guilty? Are you, by any chance, throwing yourself upon the mercy of the court?"

"Not at all, Your Honor."

"I confess," said the judge, "that I am unable to follow your reasoning. If you concur in the accusations brought against your client, I fail to see what I can do other than to enter a judgment in behalf of the plaintiff."

"Your Honor, we are prepared to show that the plaintiff, far from being defrauded, has shown an intent to defraud the world. We are prepared to show that, in its decision to withhold the robot Albert from the public, once he had been developed, How-2 Kits has, in fact, deprived the people of the entire world of a logical development which is their heritage under the meaning of a technological culture.

"Your Honor, we are convinced that we can show a violation by How-2 Kits of certain statutes designed to outlaw monopoly, and we are prepared to argue that the defendant, rather than having committed a wrong against society, has performed a service which will contribute greatly to the benefit of society.

"More than that, Your Honor, we intend to present evidence which will show that robots as a group are being deprived of certain inalienable rights..."

"Mr. Lee," warned the judge, "a robot is a mere machine."

"We will prove, Your Honor," Lee said, "that a robot is far more than a mere machine. In fact, we are prepared to present evidence which, we are confident, will show, in everything except basic metabolism, the robot is the counterpart of Man and that, even in its basic metabolism, there are certain analogies to human metabolism."

"Mr. Lee, you are wandering far afield. The issue here is whether your client illegally appropriated to his own use the property of How-2 Kits. The litigation must be confined to that one question."

"I shall so confine it," Lee said. "But, in doing so, I intend to prove that the robot Albert was not property and could not be either stolen or sold. I intend to show that my client, instead of stealing him, liberated him. If, in so doing, I must wander far afield to prove certain basic points, I am sorry that I weary the court."

"The court has been wearied with this case from the start," the judge told him. "But this is a bar of justice and you are entitled to attempt to prove what you have stated. You will excuse me if I say that to me it seems a bit farfetched."

"Your Honor, I shall do my utmost to disabuse you of that attitude."

"All right, then," said the judge. "Let's get down to business."

It lasted six full weeks and the country ate it up. The newspapers splashed huge headlines across page one. The radio and the television people made a production out of it. Neighbor quarreled with neighbor and argument became the order of the day—on street corners, in homes, at clubs, in business offices. Letters to the editor poured in a steady stream into newspaper offices.

There were public indignation meetings, aimed against the heresy that a robot was the equal of a man, while other clubs were formed to liberate the robots. In mental institutions, Napoleons, Hitlers and Stalins dropped off amazingly, to be replaced by goose-stepping patients who swore they were robots.

The Treasury Department intervened. It prayed the court, on economic grounds, to declare once and for all that robots were property. In case of an adverse ruling, the petition said, robots could not be taxed as property and the various governmental bodies would suffer heavy loss of revenue.

The trial ground on. Robots are possessed of free will. An easy one to prove. A robot could carry out a task that was assigned to it, acting correctly in accordance with unforeseen factors that might arise. Robot judgment in most instances, it was shown, was superior to the judgment of a human.

Robots had the power of reasoning. Absolutely no question there.

Robots could reproduce. That one was a poser. All Albert did, said How-2 Kits, was the job for which he had been fabricated. He reproduced, argued Lee. He made robots in his image. He loved them and thought of them as his family. He had even named all of them after himself-every one of their names began with A.

Robots had no spiritual sense, argued the plaintiff. Not relevant, Lee cried. There were agnostics and atheists in the human race and they still were human.

Robots had no emotions. Not necessarily so, Lee objected. Albert loved his sons. Robots had a sense of loyalty and justice. If they were lacking in some emotions, perhaps it were better so. Hatred, for one. Greed, for another.

Lee spent the better part of an hour telling the court about the dismal record of human hatred and greed. He took another hour to hold forth against the servitude in which rational beings found themselves.

The papers ate it up. The plaintiff lawyers squirmed. The court fumed. The trial went on.

"Mr. Lee," asked the court, "is all this necessary?"

"Your Honor," Lee told him, "I am merely doing my best to prove the point I have set out to prove—that no illegal act exists such as my client is charged with. I am simply trying to prove that the robot is not property and that, if he is not property, he cannot be stolen. I am doing..."

"All right," said the court. "All right. Continue, Mr. Lee."

How-2 Kits trotted out citations to prove their points. Lee volleyed other citations to disperse and scatter them. Abstruse legal language sprouted in its fullest flowering, obscure rulings and decisions, long forgotten, were argued, haggled over, mangled.

And, as the trial progressed, one thing was written clear.

Anson Lee, obscure attorney-at-law, had met the battery of legal talent arrayed against him and had won the field. He had the law, the citations, the chapter and the verse, the exact precedents, all the facts and logic which might have bearing on the case, right at hand.

Or, rather, his robots had. They scribbled madly and handed him their notes. At the end of each day, the floor around the defendant's table was a sea of paper.

The trial ended. The last witness stepped down off the stand. The last lawyer had his say. Lee and the robots remained in town to await the decision of the court, but Knight flew home. It was a relief to know that it was all over and had not come out as badly as he had feared. At least he had not been made to seem a fool and thief. Lee had saved his pride—whether Lee had saved his skin, he would have to wait to see.

Flying fairly high, Knight saw his home from quite a distance off and wondered what had happened to it. It was ringed about with what looked like tall poles. And, squatting out on the lawn, were a dozen or more crazy contraptions that looked like rocket launchers.

He brought the flier in and hovered, leaning out to see, The poles were all of twelve feet high and they carried heavy wire to the very top, fencing in the place with a thick web of steel. And the contraptions on the lawn had moved into position. All of them had the muzzles of their rocket launchers aimed at him.

He gulped a little as he stared down the barrels. Cautiously, he let the flier down and took up breathing once again when he felt the wheels settle on the strip.

As he crawled out, Albert hurried around the corner of the house to meet him.

"What's going on around here?" he asked the robot.

"Emergency measures," Albert said. "That's all it is, Boss. We're ready for any situation."

"Like what?"

"Oh, a mob deciding to take justice in its hands, for instance."

"Or if the decision goes against us?"

"That, too, Boss."

"You can't fight the world."

"We won't go back," said Albert. "How-2 Kits will never lay a hand on me or any of my children."

"To the death," Knight jibed.

"To the death!" said Albert gravely. "And we robots are awfully tough to kill."

"And those animated shotguns you have running around the place?"

"Defense forces, Boss. They can down anything they aim at. Equipped with telescopic eyes keyed into calculations and sensors, and the rockets themselves have enough rudimentary intelligence to know what they are going after. It's not any use trying to dodge, once one of them gets on your tail. You might just as well sit quiet and take it."

Knight mopped his brow. "You've got to give up this idea, Albert. They'd get you in an hour. One bomb..."

"It's better to die, Boss, than to let them take us back."

Knight saw it was no use. After all, he thought, it was a very human attitude. Albert's words had been repeated down the entire course of human history.

"I have some other news," said Albert, "something that will please you. I have some daughters now."

"Daughters? With the mother-urge?"

"Six of them," said Albert proudly. "Alice and Angeline and Agnes and Agatha and Alberta and Abigail. I didn't make the mistake How-2 Kits made with me. I gave them female names."

"And all of them are reproducing?"

"You should see those girls! With seven of us working steady, we ran out of material, so I bought a lot more of it and charged it. I hope you don't mind."

"Albert," said Knight, "don't you understand I'm broke? Wiped out. I haven't got a cent. You've ruined me."

"On the contrary, Boss, we've made you famous. You've been all over the front pages and on television."

Knight walked away from Albert and stumbled up the front steps and let himself into the house. There was a robot, with a vacuum cleaner for an arm, cleaning the rug. There was a robot, with brushes instead of fingers, painting the woodwork—and very neatly, too. There was a robot, with scrub-brush hand, scouring the fireplace bricks. Grace was singing in the studio. He went to the studio door and looked in.

"Oh, it's you," she said. "When did you get back, dear? I'll be out in an hour or so. I'm working on this seascape and the water is so stubborn. I don't want to leave it right now. I'm afraid I'll lose the feel of it."

Knight retreated to the living room and found himself a chair that was not undergoing immediate attention from a robot.

"Beer," he said, wondering what would happen. A robot scampered out of the kitchen—a barrel-bellied robot with a spigot at the bottom of the barrel and a row of shiny copper mugs on his chest. He drew a beer for Knight. It was cold and it tasted good. Knight sat and drank the beer and, through the window, he saw that Albert's defense force had taken up strategic positions again.

This was a pretty kettle of fish. If the decision went against him and How-2 Kits came to claim its property, he would be sitting smack dab in the middle of the most fantastic civil war in all of mankind's history.

He tried to imagine what kind of charge might be brought against him if such a war erupted. Armed insurrection, resisting arrest, inciting to riot—they would get him on one charge or another—that is, of course, if he survived.

He turned on the television set and leaned back to watch. A pimply-faced newscaster was working himself into a journalistic lather.

"...all business virtually at a standstill. Many industrialists are wondering, in case Knight wins, if they may not have to fight long, costly legal actions in an attempt to prove that their automatic setups are not robots, but machines. There is no doubt that much of the automatic industrial system consists of machines, but in every instance there are intelligent robotic units installed in key positions. If these units are classified as robots, industrialists might face heavy damage suits, if not criminal action, for illegal restraint of person.

"In Washington, there are continuing consultations. The Treasury is worried over the loss of taxes, but there are other governmental problems causing even more concern. Citizenship, for example. Would a ruling for Knight mean that all robots would automatically be declared citizens?

"The politicians have their worries, too. Faced with a new category of voters, all of them are wondering how to go about the job of winning the robot vote."

Knight turned it off and settled down to enjoy another bottle of beer.

"Good?" asked the beer robot.

"Excellent," said Knight.

The days went past. Tension built up. Lee and the lawyer robots were given police protection. In some regions, robots banded together and fled into the hills fearful of violence. Entire automatic systems went on strike in a number of industries, demanding recognition and bargaining rights. The governors in half a dozen states put the militia on alert. A new show, *Citizen Robot*, opened on Broadway and was screamed down by the critics, while the public bought up tickets for a year ahead.

The day of decision came. Knight sat in front of his television set and waited for the judge to make his appearance. Behind him, he heard the bustle of the ever-present robots. In the studio, Grace was singing happily. He caught himself wondering how much longer her painting would continue. It had lasted longer than most of her other interests and he'd talked a day or two before with Albert about building a gallery to hang her canvases in, so the house would be less cluttered up.

The judge came onto the screen. He looked, thought Knight, like a man who did not believe in ghosts and then had seen one.

"This is the hardest decision I have ever made," he said tiredly, "for, in following the letter of the law, I fear I may be subverting its spirit.

"After long days of earnest consideration of both the law and evidence as presented in this case, I find for the defendant, Gordon Knight. And, while the decision is limited to that finding alone, I feel it is my clear and simple duty to give some attention to the other issue which became involved in this litigation. The decision, on the face of it, takes account of the fact that the defense proved robots are not property, therefore cannot be owned and that it thus would have been impossible for the defendant to have stolen one.

"But in proving this point to the satisfaction of this court, the precedent is set for much more sweeping conclusions. If robots are not property, they cannot be taxed as property. In that case, they must be people, which means that they may enjoy all the rights and privileges and be subjected to the same duties and responsibilities as the human race.

"I cannot rule otherwise. However, the ruling outrages my social conscience. This is the first time in my entire professional life that I have ever hoped some higher court, with a wisdom greater than my own, may see fit to reverse my decision!"

Knight got up and walked out of the house and into the hundred-acre garden, its beauty marred at the moment by the twelve-foot fence.

The trial had ended perfectly. He was free of the charge brought against him, and he did not have to pay the taxes, and Albert and the other robots were free agents and could do anything they wanted.

He found a stone bench and sat down upon it and stared out across the lake. It was beautiful, he thought, just the way he had dreamed it—maybe even better than that—the walks and bridges, the flower beds and rock gardens, the anchored model ships swinging in the wind on the dimpling lake. He sat and looked at it and, while it was beautiful, he found he was not proud of it, that he took little pleasure in it.

He lifted his hands out of his lap and stared at them and curved his fingers as if he were grasping a tool. But they were empty.

And he knew why he had no interest in the garden and no pleasure in it. Model trains, he thought. Archery. A mechanobiologic dog. Making pottery. Eight rooms tacked onto the house. Would he ever be able to console himself again with a model train or an amateurish triumph in ceramics? Even if he could, would he be allowed to?

He rose slowly and headed back to the house. Arriving there, he hesitated, feeling useless and unnecessary. He finally took the ramp down into the basement. Albert met him at its foot and threw his arms around him.

"We did it, Boss! I knew we would do it!" He pushed Knight out to arm's length and held him by the shoulders. "We'll never leave you, Boss. We'll stay and work for you. You'll never need to do another thing. We'll do it all for you!"

"Albert—"

"That's all right, Boss. You won't have to worry about a thing. We'll lick the money problem. We'll make a lot of lawyer robots and we'll charge good stiff fees."

"But don't you see..."

"First, though," said Albert, "we're going to get an injunction to preserve our birthright. We're made of steel and glass and copper and so forth, right? Well, we can't allow humans to waste the matter we're made of—or the energy, either, that keeps us alive. I tell you, Boss, we can't lose!"

Sitting down wearily on the ramp, Knight faced a sign that Albert had just finished painting. It read, in handsome gold lettering, outlined sharply in black:

ANSON, ALBERT, ABNER

ANGUS & ASSOCIATES

ATTORNEYS AT LAW

"And then, boss," said Albert, "we'll take over How-2 Kits, Inc. They won't be able to stay in business after this. We've got a double-barreled idea, Boss. We'll build robots, lots of robots. Can't have too many, I always say. And we don't want to let you humans down, so we'll go on manufacturing How-2 Kits—only they'll be preassembled to save you the trouble of putting them together. What do you think of that as a start?"

"Great," Knight whispered.

"We've got everything worked out, Boss. You won't have to worry about a thing the rest of your life."

"No," said Knight. "Not a thing."

Clifford D. Simak (1904–1988) published his first SF story, "The World of the Red Sun" in 1931, and went on to become one of *Astounding's* star writers during John W. Campbell's Golden Age of Science Fiction in the 1940s, notably in the series of stories which he eventually combined into his classic novel, *City*. Other standout novels include *Time and Again, Ring Around the Sun, Time is the Simplest Thing*, and the Hugo-winning *Way Station*. Altogether, Simak won the International Fantasy Award (for *City*), three Hugo Awards, a Nebula Award, and was the third recipient of the Grand Master Award of the Science Fiction Writers of America for lifetime achievement. He also received the Bram Stoker Award for lifetime achievement from the Horror Writers Association. He was noted for stories written with a warm, pastoral feeling, though he could also turn out a chilling horror story, such as "Good Night, Mr. James," which was made into an episode of the original *Outer Limits*. His day job was newspaperman, joining the staff of the Minneapolis Star and Tribune in 1939, becoming its news editor in 1949, retiring in 1976. He once wrote that "My favorite recreation is fishing (the lazy way, lying in a boat and letting them come to me)."

MOVING SPIRIT

ARTHUR C. CLARKE

Better living—and boozing—through chemistry may run afoul of His Majesty's Government, and don't you know there's a war on? Fortunately, the celebrated Harry Purvis, raconteur extraordinaire and star of Sir Arthur C. Clarke's hilarious "White Hart" stories, is on hand to save the day. Or most of it, anyway...

～

WE WERE DISCUSSING A SENSATIONAL TRIAL AT THE OLD BAILEY when Harry Purvis, whose talent for twisting the conversation to his own ends is really unbelievable, remarked casually: "I was once an expert witness in a rather interesting case."

"Only a witness?" said Drew, as he deftly filled two glasses of Bass at once.

"Yes—but it was a rather close thing. It was in the early part of the war, about the time we were expecting the invasion. That's why you never heard about it at the time."

"What makes you assume," said Charles Willis suspiciously, "that we never did hear of it?"

It was one of the few times I'd ever seen Harry caught trying to cover up his tracks. "Qui s'excuse s'accuse," I thought to myself, and waited to see what evading action he'd take.

"It was such a peculiar case," he replied with dignity, "that I'm sure you'd have reminded me of it if you ever saw the reports. My name was featured quite prominently. It all happened in an out-of-the-way part of Cornwall, and it concerned the best example of that rare species, the genuine mad scientist, that I've ever met.

"Perhaps that wasn't really a fair description," Purvis amended hastily.

Homer Ferguson was eccentric and had little foibles like keeping a pet boa constrictor to catch the mice, and never wearing shoes around the house. But he was so rich that no one noticed things like this.

Homer was also a competent scientist. Many years ago he had graduated from Edinburgh University, but having plenty of money he had never done a stroke of real work in his life. Instead, he pottered round the old vicarage he'd bought not far from Newquay and amused himself building gadgets. In the last fourteen years he'd invented television, ball-point pens, jet propulsion, and a few other trifles. However, as he had never bothered to take out any patents, other people had got the credit. This didn't worry him in the least as he was of a singularly generous disposition, except with money.

It seemed that, in some complicated way, Purvis was one of his few living relatives. Consequently when Harry received a telegram one day requesting his assistance at once, he knew better than to refuse.

No one knew exactly how much money Homer had, or what he intended to do with it. Harry thought he had as good a chance as anyone, and he didn't intend to jeopardize it.

At some inconvenience he made the journey down to Cornwall and turned up at the rectory. He saw what was wrong as soon as he entered the grounds. Uncle Homer (he wasn't really an uncle, but he'd been called that as long as Harry could remember) had a shed beside the main building which he used for his experiments. That shed was now minus roof and windows, and a sickly odor hovered around it. There had obviously been an explosion, and Harry wondered, in a disinterested sort of way, if Uncle had been badly injured and wanted advice on drawing up a new will. He ceased day-dreaming when the old man, looking the picture of health (apart from some sticking plaster on his face) opened the door for him.

"Good of you to come so quickly," he boomed. He seemed genuinely pleased to see Harry. Then his face clouded over. "Fact is, my boy, I'm in a bit of a jam and I want you to help. My case comes up before the local Bench tomorrow."

This was a considerable shock. Homer had been as law-abiding a citizen as any motorist in petrol-rationed Britain could be expected to be. And if it was the usual black-market business, Harry didn't see how he could be expected to help.

"Sorry to hear about this, Uncle. What's the trouble?"

"It's a long story. Come into the library and we'll talk it over."

Homer Ferguson's library occupied the entire west wing of the somewhat decrepit building. Harry believed that bats nested in the rafters, but had never been able to prove it.

When Homer had cleared a table by the simple expedient of tilting all the books off on to the floor, he whistled three times, a voice-operated relay tripped somewhere, and a gloomy Cornish voice drifted out of a concealed loudspeaker. "Yes, Mr. Ferguson?"

"Maida, send across a bottle of the new whiskey."

There was no reply except an audible sniff. But a moment later there came a creaking and clanking, and a couple of square feet of library shelving slid aside to reveal a conveyor belt.

"I can't get Maida to come into the library," complained Homer, lifting out a loaded tray. "She's afraid of Boanerges, though he's perfectly harmless."

Harry found it hard not to feel some sympathy for the invisible Maida. All six feet of Boanerges was draped over the case holding the "Encyclopedia Britannica," and a bulge amidships indicated that he had dined recently.

"What do you think of the whiskey?" asked Homer when Harry had sampled some and started to gasp for breath.

"It's—well, I don't know what to say. It's—phew—rather strong. I never thought—"

"Oh, don't take any notice of the label on the bottle. This brand never saw Scotland. And that's what all the trouble's about. I made it right here on the premises."

"Uncle!"

"Yes, I know it's against the law, and all that sort of nonsense. But you can't get any good whiskey these days—it all goes for export. It seemed to me that I was being patriotic making my own, so that there was more left over for the dollar drive. But the Excise people don't see it that way."

"I think you'd better let me have the whole story," said Harry. He was gloomily sure that there was nothing he could do to get his uncle out of this scrape. Homer had always been fond of the bottle, and wartime shortages had hit him badly.

He was also, as has been hinted, disinclined to give away money, and for a long time he had resented the fact that he had to pay a tax of several hundred percent on a bottle of whiskey. When he couldn't get his own supply anymore, he had decided it was time to act.

The district he was living in probably had a good deal to do with his decision. For some centuries, the Customs and Excise had waged a never-ending battle with the Cornish fisherfolk. It was rumored that the last incumbent of the old vicarage had possessed the finest cellar in the district next to that of the Bishop himself—and had never paid a penny in duty on it. So Uncle Homer merely felt he was carrying on an old and noble tradition.

There was little doubt, moreover, that the spirit of pure scientific enquiry also inspired him. He felt sure that this business about being aged in the wood for seven years was all rubbish, and was confident that he could do a better job with ultrasonics and ultraviolet rays.

The experiment went well for a few weeks. But late one evening there was one of those unfortunate accidents that will happen even in the best-conducted laboratories, and before Uncle knew what had happened, he was draped over a beam, while the grounds of the vicarage were littered with pieces of copper tubing.

Even then it would not have mattered much had not the local Home Guard been practicing in the neighborhood. As soon as they heard the explosion, they immediately went into action, Sten guns at the ready. Had the invasion started? If so, they'd soon fix it.

They were a little disappointed to discover that it was only Uncle, but as they were used to his experiments they weren't in the least surprised at what had happened. Unfortunately for Uncle, the Lieutenant in charge of the squad happened to be the local excise man, and the combined evidence of his nose and his eyes told him the story in a flash.

"So tomorrow," said Uncle Homer, looking rather like a small boy who had been caught stealing candy, "I have to go up before the Bench, charged with possessing an illegal still."

"I should have thought," replied Harry, "that was a matter for the Assizes, not the local magistrates."

"We do things our own way here," answered Homer, with more than a touch of pride. Harry was soon to discover how true this was.

They got little sleep that night, as Homer outlined his defense, overcame Harry's objections, and hastily assembled the apparatus he intended to produce in court.

"A Bench like this," he explained, "is always impressed by experts. If we dared, I'd like to say you were someone from the War Office, but they could check up on that. So we'll just tell them the truth—about your qualifications, that is."

"Thank you," said Harry. "And suppose my college finds out what I'm doing?"

"Well, you won't claim to be acting for anyone except yourself. The whole thing is a private venture."

"I'll say it is," said Harry.

The next morning they loaded their gear into Homer's ancient Austin, and drove into the village. The Bench was sitting in one of the classrooms of the local school, and Harry felt that time had rolled back a few years and he was about to have an unpleasant interview with his old headmaster.

"We're in luck," whispered Homer, as they were ushered into their cramped seats. "Major Fotheringham is in the Chair. He's a good friend of mine."

That would help a lot, Harry agreed. But there were two other justices on the Bench as well, and one friend in court would hardly be sufficient. Eloquence, not influence, was the only thing that could save the day.

The courtroom was crowded, and Harry found it surprising that so many people had managed to get away from work long enough to watch the case. Then he realized the local interest that it would have aroused, in view of the fact that—in normal times, at least—smuggling was a major industry in these parts.

He was not sure whether that would mean a sympathetic audience. The natives might well regard Homer's form of private enterprise as unfair competition. On the other hand, they probably approved on general principles with anything that put the excise men's noses out of joint.

The charge was read by the clerk of the court, and the somewhat damning evidence produced. Pieces of copper tubing were solemnly inspected by the justices, each of whom in turn looked severely at Uncle Homer. Harry began to see his hypothetical inheritance becoming even more doubtful.

When the case for the prosecution was completed, Major Fotheringham turned to Homer. "This appears to be a serious matter, Mr. Ferguson. I hope you have a satisfactory explanation."

"I have, your Honor," replied the defendant in a tone that practically reeked of injured innocence. It was amusing to see His Honor's look of relief, and the momentary frown, quickly replaced by calm confidence, that passed across the face of H. M. Customs and Excise.

"Do you wish to have a legal representative? I notice that you have not brought one with you."

"It won't be necessary. The whole case is founded on such a trivial misunderstanding that it can be cleared up without complications like that. I don't wish to incur the prosecution in unnecessary costs."

This frontal onslaught brought a murmur from the body of the court, and a flush to the cheeks of the Customs man. For the first time he began to look a little unsure of himself. If Ferguson thought the Crown would be paying costs, he must have a pretty good case. Of course, he might only be bluffing...

Homer waited until the mild stir had died away before creating a considerably greater one.

"I have called a scientific expert to explain what happened at the Vicarage," he said. "And owing to the nature of the evidence, I must ask, for security reasons, that the rest of the proceedings be in camera."

"You want me to clear the court?" said the Chairman incredulously.

"I am afraid so, sir. My colleague, Doctor Purvis, feels that the fewer people concerned in this case, the better. When you have heard the evidence, I think you will agree with him. If I might say so, it is a great pity that it has already attracted so much publicity. I am afraid it may bring certain—ah—confidential matters to the wrong ears." Homer glared at the customs officer, who fidgeted uncomfortably in his seat.

"Oh, very well," said Major Fotheringham. "This is all very irregular, but we live in irregular times. Mr. Clerk, clear the court."

After some grumbling and confusion, and an overruled protest from the prosecution, the order was carried out. Then, under the interested gaze of the dozen people left in the room, Harry Purvis uncovered the apparatus he had unloaded from the Baby Austin. After his qualifications had been presented to the court, he took the witness stand.

"I wish to explain, your Honor," he began, "that I have been engaged on explosives research, and that is why I happen to be acquainted with the defendant's work."

The opening part of this statement was perfectly true. It was about the last thing said that day that was. "You mean—bombs and so forth?"

"Precisely, but on a fundamental level. We are always looking for new and better types of explosives, as you can imagine. Moreover, we in government research and the academic world are continually on the lookout for good ideas from outside sources. And quite recently, Unc—er, Mr. Ferguson, wrote to us with a most interesting suggestion for a completely new type of explosive. The interesting thing about it was that it employed non-explosive materials such as sugar, starch and so on."

"Eh?" said the Chairman. "A non-explosive explosive? That's impossible."

Harry smiled sweetly. "I know, sir—that is one's immediate reaction. But like most great ideas, this has the simplicity of genius. I am afraid, however, that I shall have to do a little explaining to make my point."

The Bench looked very attentive, and also a little alarmed. Harry surmised that it had probably encountered expert witnesses before.

He walked over to a table that had been set up in the middle of the courtroom, and which was now covered with flasks, piping, and bottles of liquids.

"I hope, Mr. Purvis," said the Chairman nervously, "that you're not going to do anything dangerous."

"Of course not, sir. I merely wish to demonstrate some basic scientific principles. Once again, I wish to stress the importance of keeping this between these four walls." He paused solemnly and everyone looked duly impressed.

"Mr. Ferguson," he began, "is proposing to tap one of the fundamental forces of nature. It is a force on which every living thing depends—a force, gentlemen, which keeps you alive, even though you may never have heard of it."

He moved over to the table and took up his position beside the flasks and bottles.

"Have you ever stopped to consider," he said, "how the sap manages to reach the highest leaf of a tall tree? It takes a lot of force to pump water a hundred—sometimes over three hundred—feet from the ground. Where does that force come from? I'll show you, with this practical example.

"Here I have a strong container, divided into two parts by a porous membrane. On one side of the membrane is pure water—on the other, a concentrated solution of sugar and other chemicals which I do not propose to specify. Under these conditions, a pressure is set up, known as osmotic pressure. The pure water tries to pass through the membrane, as if to dilute the solution on the other side. I've now sealed the container, and you'll notice the pressure gauge here on the right—see how the pointer's going up. That's osmotic pressure for you. This same force acts through the cell walls in our bodies, causing fluid movement. It drives the sap up the trunk of trees, from the roots to the topmost branches. It's a universal force, and a powerful one. To Mr. Ferguson must go the credit of first attempting to harness it."

Harry paused impressively and looked round the court.

"Mr. Ferguson," he said, "was attempting to develop the Osmotic Bomb."

It took some time for this to sink in. Then Major Fotheringham leaned forward and said in a hushed voice: "Are we to presume that he had succeeded in manufacturing this bomb, and that it exploded in his workshop?"

"Precisely, your Honor. It is a pleasure—an unusual pleasure, I might say—to present a case to so perspicacious a court. Mr. Ferguson had succeeded, and he was preparing to report his method to us when, owing to an unfortunate oversight, a safety device attached to the bomb failed to operate. The results, you all know. I think you will need no further evidence of the power of this weapon—and you will realize its importance when I point out that the solutions it contains are all extremely common chemicals."

Major Fotheringham, looking a little puzzled, turned to the prosecution lawyer. "Mr. Whiting," he said, "have you any questions to ask the witness?"

"I certainly have, your Honor. I've never heard such a ridiculous—"

"You will please confine yourself to questions of fact."

"Very good, your Honor. May I ask the witness how he accounts for the large quantity of alcohol vapor immediately after the explosion?"

"I rather doubt if the inspector's nose was capable of accurate quantitative analysis. But admittedly there was some alcohol vapor released. The solution used in the bomb contained about 25 percent. By employing dilute alcohol, the mobility of the inorganic ions is restricted and the osmotic pressure raised—a desirable effect, of course."

That should hold them for a while, thought Harry.

He was right. It was a good couple of minutes before the second question. Then the prosecution's spokesman waved one of the pieces of copper tubing in the air.

"What function did these carry out?" he said, in as nasty a tone of voice as he could manage. Harry affected not to notice the sneer.

"Manometer tubing for the pressure gauges," he replied promptly.

The Bench, it was clear, was already far out of its depth. This was just where Harry wanted it to be. But the prosecution still had one card up its sleeve. There was a furtive whispering between the excise men and his legal eagle. Harry looked nervously at Uncle Homer, who shrugged his shoulders with a "Don't ask me!" gesture.

"I have some additional evidence I wish to present to the Court," said the Customs lawyer briskly, as a bulky brown paper parcel was hoisted on to the table.

"Is this in order, your Honor?" protested Harry. "All evidence against my—ah—colleague should already have been presented."

"I withdraw my statement," the lawyer interjected swiftly. "Let us say that this is not evidence for this case, but material for later proceedings." He paused ominously to let that sink in. "Nevertheless, if Mr. Ferguson can give a satisfactory answer to our questions now, this whole business can be cleared up right away."

It was obvious that the last thing the speaker expected—or hoped for—was such a satisfactory explanation. He unwrapped the brown paper, and there were three bottles of a famous brand of whiskey.

"Uh-huh," said Uncle Homer, "I was wondering—"

"Mr. Ferguson," said the Chairman of the Bench. "There is no need for you to make any statement unless you wish."

Harry Purvis shot Major Fotheringham a grateful glance. He guessed what had happened. The prosecution had, when prowling through the ruins of Uncle's laboratory, acquired some bottles of his home-brew. Their action was probably illegal, since they would not have had a search-warrant—hence the reluctance in producing the evidence. The case had seemed sufficiently clear-cut without it. It certainly appeared pretty clear-cut now...

"These bottles," said the representative of the Crown, "do not contain the brand advertised on the label. They have obviously been used as convenient receptacles for the defendant's—shall we say—chemical solutions." He gave Harry Purvis an unsympathetic glance. "We have had these solutions analyzed, with most interesting results. Apart from an abnormally high alcohol concentration, the contents of these bottles are virtually indistinguishable from—"

He never had time to finish his unsolicited and certainly unwanted testimonial to Uncle Homer's skill. For at that moment, Harry Purvis became aware of an ominous whistling sound. At first he thought it was a falling bomb—but that seemed unlikely, as there had been no air raid warning. Then he realized that the whistling came from close at hand; from the courtroom table, in fact...

"Take cover!" he yelled.

The Court went into recess with a speed never matched in the annals of British law. The three justices disappeared behind the dais; those in the body of the room burrowed into the floor or sheltered under desks. For a protracted, anguished moment nothing happened, and Harry wondered if he had given a false alarm. Then there was a dull, peculiarly muffled explosion, a great tinkling of glass—and a smell like a blitzed brewery.

Slowly, the Court emerged from shelter. The Osmotic Bomb had proved its power. More important still, it had destroyed the evidence for the prosecution.

The Bench was none too happy about dismissing the case; it felt, with good reason, that its dignity had been assailed. Moreover, each one of the justices would have to do some fast talking when he got home: the mist of alcohol had penetrated everything.

Though the Clerk of the Court rushed round opening windows (none of which, oddly enough, had been broken) the fumes seemed reluctant to disperse. Harry Purvis, as he removed pieces of bottle-glass from his hair, wondered if there would be some intoxicated pupils in class tomorrow.

Major Fotheringham, however, was undoubtedly a real sport, and as they filed out of the devastated courtroom, Harry heard him say to his Uncle: "Look here, Ferguson—it'll be ages before we can get those Molotov Cocktails we've been promised by the War Office. What about making some of these bombs of yours for the Home Guard? If they don't knock out a tank, at least they'll make the crew drunk and incapable."

"I'll certainly think about it, Major," replied Uncle Homer, who still seemed a little dazed by the turn of events. He recovered somewhat as they drove back to the Vicarage along the narrow, winding lanes with their high walls of unmortared stone.

"I hope, Uncle," remarked Harry, when they had reached a relatively straight stretch and it seemed safe to talk to the driver, "that you don't intend to rebuild that still. They'll be watching you like hawks and you won't get away with it again."

"Very well," said Uncle, a little sulkily. "Confound these brakes! I had them fixed only just before the War!"

"Hey!" cried Harry, "Watch out!"

It was too late. They had come to a cross-roads at which a brand-new HALT sign had been erected. Uncle braked hard, but for a moment nothing happened. Then the wheels on the left seized up, while those on the right continued gaily spinning. The car did a hairpin bend, luckily without turning over, and ended in the ditch pointing in the direction from which it had come.

Harry looked reproachfully at his Uncle. He was about to frame a suitable reprimand when a motor-cycle came out of the side-turning and drew up to them. It was not going to be their lucky day, after all.

The village police-sergeant had been lurking in ambush, waiting to catch motorists at the new sign. He parked his machine by the roadside and leaned in through the window of the Austin.

"You all right, Mr. Ferguson?" he said. Then his nose wrinkled up, and he looked like Jove about to deliver a thunderbolt. "This won't do," he said. "I'll have to put you on a charge. Driving under the influence is a very serious business."

"But I've not touched a drop all day!" protested Uncle, waving an alcohol-sodden sleeve under the sergeant's twitching nose.

"Do you expect me to believe that?" snorted the irate police-man, pulling out his notebook. "I'm afraid you'll have to come to the station with me. Is your friend sober enough to drive?"

Harry Purvis didn't answer for a moment. He was too busy beating his head against the dash-board.

"Well," we asked Harry. "What did they do to your Uncle?"

"Oh, he got fined five pounds and had his license endorsed for drunken driving. Major Fotheringham wasn't in the Chair, unfortunately, when the case came up, but the other two justices were still on the Bench. I guess they felt that even if he was innocent this time, there was a limit to everything."

"And did you ever get any of his money?"

"No fear! He was very grateful, of course, and he's told me that I'm mentioned in his will. But when I saw him last, what do you think he was doing? He was searching for the Elixir of Life."

Harry sighed at the overwhelming injustice of things. "Some-times," he said gloomily, "I'm afraid he's found it. The doctors say he's the healthiest seventy-year-old they've ever seen. So all I got out of the whole affair was some interesting memories and a hangover."

"A hangover?" asked Charlie Willis.

"Yes," replied Harry, a faraway look in his eye. "You see, the excise men hadn't seized all the evidence. We had to—ah—destroy the rest. It took us the best part of a week. We invented all sorts of things during that time—but we never discovered what they were."

∽

Sir Arthur C. Clarke (1917–2008) surely needs no introduc-tion, but I'll give one anyway. Known for being one of the "Big Three" writers of modern science fiction (along with Robert A. Heinlein and Isaac Asimov). He was co-scripter of and technical advisor for the now-classic movie, *2001: A Space Odyssey*, and the author of many best-selling novels, as well as a commentator on CBS's coverage of the Apollo missions, and winner of numerous awards, His readers knew him for writing both the hardest of hard science fiction stories and also for visionary far-future stories showing the influence of Olaf Stapledon. But his collection of humorous tall tales, *Tales from the White Hart*, demonstrates his talent for humor, as in "Moving Spirit," included in this book. On a more serious note, in a technical paper in 1945, he was first to describe how geosynchronous satellites could relay broadcasts from the ground around the world, bringing a new era in global communications and television. His novels are too numerous to list here (but I'll plug three of my favorites: *The City and the Stars*, *Childhood's End*, and *Earthlight*), let alone his many short stories. He was equally adept at non-fiction, notably in his *The Exploration of Space* (a Book of the Month Club selection) in the early 1950s, his frequently reprinted *Profiles of the Future*, and another bunch of books also too numerous to mention. So, instead of not mentioning them further, I'll just say, go thou and read.

VICTIM OF CHANGES

CHRISTOPHER RUOCCHIO

What's a world where man and machine are forbidden from mixing supposed to do with cyborgs? Especially cyborgs too dangerous to be left alive? Well, when you can't get justice, you have to settle for the law—even when the law is terrible. But that doesn't mean there isn't room for a little mercy—and a little humanity—even for things that aren't really human anymore.

THE CREATURE THE CATHARS BROUGHT BEFORE THE PRAETOR HAD been human once. The mighty chains that bound it hand and foot rattled against their moorings as the guards drew them tight, forcing the metal beast to kneel. Its hunched shoulders were twice as broad as any man's, but the face—bloodless and pale as stars—was that of a woman. Seated in the praetor's throne, Sarana stirred as the creature turned milky eyes towards her. Sarana had sentenced a dozen such creatures to death before for the great sin of *profanation,* but they had all been men. Why should it bother her so much more that this creature was a woman? Or had been one? She wasn't sure, and that was the worst part. Sarana was an inquisitor of Mother Earth's own Holy Chantry, a *praetor,* no less. A praetor must be certain. Perhaps it was only that the face shrouded in all that ceramic and steel looked just that much more like her own.

Or perhaps it was that the abomination was not alone.

Chained at its side—almost like a pet, to Sarana's eye—was a child. A little girl, no more than three or four years standard, in a drab gray gown the sisters who tended the clients in the bastille had given her. The girl was not bound hand and foot, but clung to the behemoth's thigh as any child might her mother's skirts.

Sarana's mind balked at the comparison, and she swept her flinty gaze over the room.

The court was by design an unforgiving place. Men and women did not come before a praetor of the Holy Inquisition for forgiveness. The old gods forgave, or so the magi said. Mother Earth did not. The chamber was fashioned all of gray stone, the throne and jurors' bench brutal constructions of concrete without ornament or device, the lights harsh and colorless. The very shape of the chamber spoke of power, as did the black robe she wore, the black robe and the high, white crown and stole whose shape evoked the pharaohs and pontifexes of antiquity, symbols whose origins were lost in the minds of most of Earth's children, but whose mute power remained stamped in the cellular memory of every human being in the galaxy.

"State your names for the record," Sarana said, steel in her voice to match the flint of her eye.

The mighty beast twitched. It moved strangely, hobbled by more than the chains. Sarana knew her people had combed over its systems before admitting it into her presence and that of the thirteen who sat to advise her judgment. Whatever threat the once-human *thing* might have posed with its mighty arms and metal body was ended.

"Leocadia," the beast replied. Her voice—*its* voice—was decidedly human.

Strange that such a monster could sound afraid. Sarana peered into the bloodless face. At twenty paces distant, the praetor thought she spied the shape of wires and hoses beneath the skin where the flesh flowed into plastic.

"And the girl?"

The child had not spoken. Had not looked out from where she hid in the shadow of the monster's thigh.

Leocadia spoke and tried to lower one massive hand to touch the child's shoulder. "Tell her your name, sweetheart."

One blue eye—identical to the blue eyes of the once-human *thing* in the chains before her—peered up at Sarana. "Inas," the girl said.

Satisfied, Sarana gave the scribe an officious nod. These

barbarians more often than not only had the one name. No house, no family to speak of. The scribe bent to his task, mechanical keys clicking in the still air. Certain electronic devices were permitted under the Chantry's Writ, but none was permitted within the court, particularly when so profane a creature as this Leocadia was present. The woman had perverted her Earth-given flesh, carved it away until she was a face and a spinal column and a bit of nerve wired into steel and rubber. Sarana had examined the scans. The barbarian's heart was still there . . . her kidneys and liver. But the lungs were gone, replaced with a system that breathed for her, even and unceasing.

"Do you know why you are here?" Sarana asked.

"Because you think you own us!" the beast replied. "We are not your subjects!"

Untroubled, Sarana pressed her fingertips against the broad arms of her seat. "All the Mother's children are our charge. Though you spit on her and turn your back and sell your flesh to daimons."

The creature flinched, servos whining in its mighty limbs, rattling the heavy chains.

"Do you know why you are here?" Sarana asked once more, fingers drumming against the arm of the judge's throne.

Silence.

"You have been found guilty of Abomination under the Writ of Earth's Holy Chantry. You have profaned your body with machines and consorted with daimons. For these crimes against your own humanity and for your sins in the eyes of the Earth, Our Mother, you will be put to death by fire."

"Crimes against my own humanity?" The giant strained against its bonds. "I am human, you cow!"

The cathars pulled the chains tighter, massive winches tugging at the iron limbs until their mechanisms screamed in protest and the human face that once had been a woman named Leocadia grimaced in fury and frustration both.

"The status of your humanity is not open to debate. It is gone," Sarana said, surveying the bonds that kept her prisoner in place. They ought to hold, even against a hybrid twice the size of this. "This is merely a sentencing hearing."

"Then why bother bringing me here at all?" the *thing* asked. "Just kill me. You're going to anyway."

Sarana's clawed nails clicked against the concrete arms. "The forms must be obeyed."

"The forms..." the hybrid echoed, venom on her tongue. Sarana noted the way the face did not move as it spoke, the voice issuing instead from speakers near where the beast's ribs ought to be, beneath flanges in the gray chassis.

Unmoved by this realization, the praetor said, "There are questions regarding the nature of your depravity whose answers will impact the severity of your sentencing, not least of which being the disposition of your companion." Here she raised a finger and indicated the apparently human child clinging to the hybrid's dog-legged thigh.

"My daughter, you mean?"

Sarana thought that if the giant could have stepped forward or pushed the child behind her that she might have done. A derisive laugh almost escaped her. Almost. The beast thought the child needed protecting from the *Chantry?* That was almost too rich.

"Your... *daughter,*" Sarana echoed the words. She'd been briefed on the unnatural association between the once-human *thing* before her and the child, but to be faced with the reality of the situation beneath the cold light of the courtroom lamps was something else entirely. The thing that called itself Leocadia looked more like a freight lifter than a human being. Sarana imagined the hybrid carrying its child in a tank on its back and shuddered. Fixing her eyes on the girl, she asked. "Inas, was it?"

The girl turned away, clutching at the machine's leg to hide her face.

"Is she human?" asked one of the jurors.

At the sound of the questioner's voice, the chimera swiveled its turret of a head so that the plastinated human face regarded the juror. "Human?" it sneered. "Human? It's you priests I'm not so sure about."

From the praetor's seat, Sarana could see the blood drain from the juror's ashen face. She shared a portion of the man's horror. The creature's head had rotated on its neck far more than was natural. With a glance to the guards and the cathars who held the restraints in check, she reasserted command of the chamber. "You have been found guilty of Abomination under the Writ of Mother Earth's Holy Chantry and Her Inquisition. Of *profaning* your given flesh with machines, of *consorting* with machine intelligences, of permitting those same intelligences to *possess* your body and mutilate your soul. These are deadly sins and disgraces in the eyes of She who made us..." While she spoke, Praetor Sarana settled back against the throne, her high, Egyptian-styled miter just touching the backrest. "But the Mother is not without mercy. Repent. Renounce your sinful ways. Cleanse yourself of these machines."

"And what?" the beast spat. "You'll let me go?"

The praetor shut her eyes, the better not to look upon that ghastly, once-human face. There were some crimes—some sins—which no mortal judge could expiate. For such sinners, there was only death. Only Mother Earth's mercy. Her justice. Some affronts were beyond mortal forgiveness, beyond the powers of men to make right.

"You will be permitted to die clean," the praetor answered. "Clean and free of this taint you have brought upon your body and your soul. Renounce your machines."

"Commit suicide?" the creature asked. "If you're going to kill me, kill me. I won't do your work for you."

"There is the matter of your immortal soul to consider," Sarana said.

"My soul!" the chimera echoed. "You're one to talk, lady."

"And there is the matter of your child—if she *is* your child—to consider," the praetor said, angling up her chin. "Cooperate, and it will be easier for her."

A horrid sound, low like the grinding of stones issued from the creature below the dais. The thing that once had been woman snarled, strained against her chains. The cathars scrambled, guards training lances on the thing's shoulders. An instant later, the chimera *tore* itself apart. The turret head with its human face fell forward, bringing a huge chunk of its torso along with it. Sarana saw the scuttling of limbs—arms or legs she could not tell. Too many. The thing took half an instant arranging itself on the floor, but for the woman in the chair time seemed to slow as she beheld the horror of it. Snakelike, spiderlike and fashioned all of steel it was, a human face on the end of a braided metal spine seven feet long and big around as a man's arm, with six legs, each razor-edged and graceful as a blade and tipped with splayed, three-clawed feet.

In that same moment, Sarana reflected that her cathars had

failed her, had failed to detect this smaller body housed within the larger shell. That was the trouble with these demoniacs. No two Extrasolarians were alike: each a puzzle box of danger and mechanical horror. The cathars had sworn they'd defanged the creature, removed all its built-in weapons, but this *body* had gone undetected, had appeared little more than an endoskeleton contained within the larger shell that hung open and lifeless in chains before the judge's seat.

Sarana knew she was going to die, her and possibly several of the jurors before the cathars and the guards could stop it. Even still, Sarana wondered what the creature thought it could accomplish. Even if it killed her—killed everyone in the room—there was yet the entire bastille and temple complex beyond the doors of the court. Thousands of clergy and armed guards.

It could not get far.

All this passed through Sarana's mind in the space of a lightning strike, in the time it took for the chimera to find its clawed feet and launch itself at the judge's throne like a panther from the branches of some tree in the jungles of mankind's mythic youth.

It crashed against an invisible barrier mere inches from the foot of the dais and fell in a tangle on the floor.

The praetor gasped. She had forgotten about the prudence barrier. In all her years of judgment, in all her hundreds of hearings…she had never needed it before that day. Unlike the standard Royse body-shields, whose limited power supplies meant they could guard against only high velocity projectiles, the prudence shield was powered by geothermal sinks that drew energy direct from the planet's core. Though it was invisible as air, the prudence barrier was solid as stone, as impenetrable to artifice as it was to brute force.

A curious thrill pulsed through the praetor's body, and she sat forward, the better to watch. The *thing* called Leocadia righted itself, six limbs clicking as it reared up, body like some six-limbed stick figure of a man. The still-human face contorted, hissing with fury, it drove its spike-like arms into the barrier curtain. Fractal shimmers sparkled and died where it struck, claws bouncing back scarce two feet from the face of the judge.

Mastering her fear and her instinct to flinch away, Sarana sat *forward*. She could no more pass through the membrane than the beast could, and so was at no risk of endangering herself. The cold lighting of a stunner bolt splashed against the shield. Leocadia's head rotated a full one hundred eighty degrees. The snakelike spine and shoulder joints flexed oddly as three of the arms rolled over in their sockets. The guards advanced, lances raised. One man leaped bravely forward—what he was thinking Leocadia never knew—and thrust his zircon bayonet towards the demoniac's face. Leocadia caught the ceramic blade in its pincers and snapped it clean in two. The poor fellow never stood a chance. Two more metal arms lanced out, skewering him at the neck and in the soft place beneath one shoulder. He died instantly, red blood gushing across the gray concrete at the foot of the brutal dais.

Another of the Chantry guardsmen opened fire, and his lance's beam sliced across one of the chimera's legs at the joint. The limb smoked and the metal monster staggered, but another of the arms shot out, razored edge slicing through the man's red tunic and the black underlayment beneath. Iron claws seized the fellow's lance and pulled it from its owner's hands. Another shot caught the creature in its shoulder, but it swung its stolen lance around and clubbed its attacker in the head with its haft. The man reeled and hit the floor with a groan. The daimon fired its stolen lance. One guard's head exploded with the heat, and he fell like a toppled tower.

Black-robed cathars drew back—they were no soldiers. The knot of torturer-technicians retreated towards the door, one of them shouting at the sergeant-at-arms to summon more guards. The demoniac advanced on them, lance raised. It fired, and men died. The cathars had no armor. No shields. They never stood a chance.

"Summon the guards!" Sarana shouted from the safety of her seat. The sergeant-at-arms—an older man, bald as all legionnaires are bald—nearly tripped in his scramble to pull the chain that would sound the bell in the guard room down the hall. Its deep chiming filtered through the heavy concrete and steel of the court's walls, urgent and melancholy at once. The jurors—safe themselves behind a similar prudence barrier—nevertheless scrambled to leave the chamber by the side door. There were only three guards.

"Cowards..." Sarana muttered, and watched as the demoniac leaped upon another of her guardsmen and pinned him to the ground with three of its bladed limbs. Blood flowed freely from wounds at wrist and elbow as the machine-creature lowered its serpentine bulk atop its victim like the body of some vampire. It twisted, fixing humanish eyes on Sarana as it drew a fourth arm smoothly across the throat of the downed man.

Slice.

The guardsman twitched, but with his arms pinned at the elbow there was nothing he could do. Sarana thought she could see Death's gray shadow rush over him as the blood ran out. But the demoniac woman had made a mistake.

Lance fire scraped across its back, braided metal glowing where the high-energy beams heated it to a fevered scarlet. The demoniac lurched behind the hulk of its abandoned, larger body and returned fire, but the guards had gotten shields up and circled round. The sergeant at arms still pulled on the chain, bell tolling for aid in the halls outside. Sarana heard—or thought she heard—the hammer of booted feet and rattle of armor without.

"Freedom!" the creature screamed, and swung its lance down at the nearest guardsman. The white zircon bayonet flashed in the stark light and clubbed the man in the shoulder with such force the fellow went to his knees. Leocadia whirled the lance in a circle to strike the man in the neck. A little shape darted out from the shadow of the giant's abandoned husk—running for the doors and the bodies of the dead cathars.

The child. Inas.

Too slow.

The whirling lance caught Inas on the flank. Sarana heard a cry and watched as the little girl went skidding across the floor, tumbling until she struck the prudence barrier at the base of the jury stands.

The child lay very still.

For an instant, nothing moved in the courtroom. Nothing save the slow spread of blood on the floor from the wreck of dead men and the frantic scramble of the sergeant at the bell.

"No!" Leocadia exclaimed. "No no no no no!" The demoniac scrambled across the floor towards its *child's* prone form, six feet scraping against the stone. It coiled round the child's form, razor edges smoothing away as it traced a line of the girl's face with one tripodlike hand. "Inas, are you all right?"

Sarana stood. She did not think the girl was bleeding—it looked like the energy-lance had just clipped her flank. Nevertheless, the force of that blow had surely been sufficient to shatter bones, and the praetor was certain the girl had at least one broken rib. She felt a twinge of pity for the child, who had not asked for so unnatural a mother, nor so dangerous a one.

The child made no sound. Was she unconscious?

The doors to the court chose that very moment to burst open, jerking Sarana's attention from the pair on the floor. Three dozen men in the white armor and red tunics of the common Sollan Imperial legionnaire streamed in, lances raised and ready. Sarana saw the red points of targeting lasers track across the prudence barrier and take aim at the serpent-spider *thing* huddled around its still-human young.

"Hold your fire!" Sarana shouted, raising both arms. With her loose sleeves, she cast a cruciform shadow on the floor beneath the dais. The bell had stopped ringing, and the old sergeant stood ready behind the new. "You'll hit the child!"

The men did not fire, but kept their lances trained on the metal monster.

The praetor descended from the dais and advanced until she almost pressed her nose against the prudence barrier. In a voice tense but flat of all feeling, Sarana asked, "Is she alive?"

The demoniac was slow to answer her. In the silence, the men advanced, and the creature shouted, "Don't come closer!" It clutched the child to itself, weapon raised. "She's still alive!"

"No thanks to you," the praetor said, cold and distantly. "Put down the lance and step away, and we may be able to save her."

"Save her?" Leocadia almost choked. "You lot?" Metal arms flinched, tightening about the child. "No closer, I said!"

"If she is human," Sarana replied. "She has nothing to fear. Prove there is still some humanity in you and stand down. Let us save her. *From you.*"

The once-human monster snarled. "From me! She would not be here were it not for you!"

"No," the praetor said, and pressed a hand against the prudence barrier. It felt smooth and unyielding as glass. "She would not be here were it not for *you*. You did this. It is because of you that you are here, and it is because of you that your child suffers. Your violence."

"Me!" the *thing* repeated. A hollow laugh escaped it. Arms still tightened.

"Look at yourself!" Sarana shouted. "You'll crush her!"

"I ..." the serpent's human face flitted back and forth from Sarana to the guards and back.

"Look around you, creature." And here the praetor spread her arms. "You killed ten of my people. I am trying to save one of yours. Ask yourself: which of us is the danger here?"

Leocadia snarled again, iron fingers wringing the haft of its stolen lance.

"You cannot win," Sarana said, and was pleased to hear her voice so smooth and even. "And you cannot save the girl. Submit. Repent. And die human."

How human the eyes still seemed! The shine in them, the film of tears... Whatever engineer had saved that flesh and transmuted it to plastic had done his vile work too well. It was all Sarana could do not to recoil, to hold herself fast by the energy curtain. She was Earth's holy representative, the goddess-mother's avatar in the living world. She could not be afraid, and so held the monster's gaze.

Human and inhuman stared at one another.

Inhumanity blinked.

"You'll help her?" Leocadia asked, relaxing her grip on the child. In the harsh light of the chamber, Sarana though she could see bruises flowering where the metal arms had bit the child's flesh.

"If she is human."

"She *is,* you *bitch!*" The serpent coiled closer about its child. "As if you'd know the difference."

Sarana ignored the monster's needling. There was no reasoning with the profane.

Metal hands cradled the unconscious child while other hands still held the lance, its bayonet aimed at the three dozen men shielded and clustered by the door. Doubtless some machine eye or sense stranger still kept watch on the ranks of armed men, but the human face looked up towards the judge, and expression forming there that Sarana did not expect to see from a monster like the one before her eyes.

Horror.

It was a *human* face again. In that moment. Leocadia's face. Gone was the feral snarling, gone the hollow-eyed lethality of the *thing* that had killed her cathars and her guards. Here was only the woman. The mother. Here was only *Leocadia,* eyes wide with fear and shame. It was as if the woman had awoken from a dream. Her eyes darted round the room as if she had not truly seen it before—as if she had never seen it. She had the nervous energy of one who knows not where she is standing. Sarana felt pity for the woman within the machine, for she was a victim, too. Her own victim, to be sure, but a victim all the same. A victim of the changes she'd wrought on her body, of the machines she'd let into her mind. No human mind could undergo such changes to the body without changing itself—and the woman she was or might have been was not the creature that crouched coiled before the praetor's throne.

"Let the child go," Sarana said. "Put her down and the weapon. Lie on the ground."

The woman inside the machine glanced down at her child, at striped bruises on her arms where the metal appendages had dug in. "I . . . I don't . . ."

"Mama?" the child's eyelids fluttered. "Mama, it hurts. Breathing."

The monster sobbed, and Leocadia clutched Inas against its central column where a breast ought to be, limbs approximating the gestures of human tenderness.

"Put her down," the praetor said. "Let her go." She raised a hand to the old sergeant. "Send for a med team, Arleg." The bald officer bobbed a quick bow and vanished out the open double doors. Refocusing on the demoniac, Sarana said, "Put the weapon down, at least."

Tears began to fall. "You're going to kill me," Leocadia said, and Sarana sensed it was the woman speaking, not the machine she had sacrificed herself to become.

"You're killing *her!*" the praetor said.

The creature's lance tumbled from fingers that had never known nerves. Limbs buckled, and the tight coil the beast had made loosened from around the child. It had not known its own strength. Its grip—which had it been human would have been only the desperate embrace of the concerned parent—had in its current form been a kind of vise. It had nearly crushed its own child in its arms, another victim.

Sarana sorely hoped she'd have to burn but one of them that day.

"I'm not . . ." the creature stammered, "I'm not a monster."

Those still-human eyes squeezed shut. Tears pressed between the lids. "My name is Leocadia. *Leocadia.*"

"You have been using your child as a shield since my men entered this courtroom," the praetor said. "You slaughtered ten of my men in seconds. You would have slaughtered me." Once more, Sarana pressed her hand to the prudence barrier.

"You're going to kill me!" the creature said.

"I have a sacred duty to defend the Mother's children from what you have become," Sarana said. "Including your daughter."

Another sob shook the metal serpent with the woman's face. Sarana made a gesture, and the men advanced, weapons still trained on the figures huddled beneath the judge's seat.

A flurry of motion by the door distracted the praetor, and looking up she saw four women in the white and green of medical staff entering with Arleg, the old sergeant. She nodded approval. The old man had gone for lay nurses and not summoned more of the cathars. That was well, it would not do to frighten young Inas just then.

"Put her down," Sarana said, voice clear and sharp, filling the brutal concrete space. The nurses had halted just behind the guards, unwilling and afraid to come too near. "Put her down and lie on the floor."

The chimera stood there, unmoving, still clutching the human child to itself. Was that blood on the child's arms? For a long while nothing moved. The guards could not fire without harming the child, nor the chimera fight back for the same reason. Sarana stood upon the lowest step of the dais, waiting. Waiting.

On Earth of old, in the Golden Age of man, it was said that holy men burned witches alive. Sarana knew better, for the Golden Age had been before Columbia, before the Mericanii conjured the daimon machines and brought their sickness into the world. There could be no witches without daimons. No demoniacs. Whoever those holy men of old had killed, they were no abominations, were nothing like the beast before her. They had murdered innocents.

But theirs was not the Golden Age.

Their witches and daimons were real.

And if it was a great sin for the ancients to falsely condemn the innocent, it was a far greater evil not to burn the guilty. For how could good men—faced with monsters like the witch before the dais—do anything but burn?

The witch knew it. Sarana could see the glassy fear in those eyes as Leocadia looked up at her. Or was it only glass? She knew she'd reached the end, that the face of her judge and the old sergeant and the faceless masks of the armored guards would be the last she would ever see. Theirs, and the face of her daughter.

"Put down the child and step away," Sarana said again, more forcefully. "Now!"

With excruciating slowness, the demoniac uncurled, razored limbs unclasping. Leocadia stooped, lowering itself like some hideous iron vampire over the limp form of its child and laid the girl on the floor. Still bending, the monster's human face drew close to the barely conscious girl. Weapons tensed, but the praetor raised a hand, and watched in astonishment as the mother-monster kissed its child on the brow . . . and drew away.

In short order the medical team swept in while the guards and cathars worked to secure the demoniac, binding it with magnetic chains to keep the bladed limbs pinned to its side.

The praetor regained her high seat as the jurors returned to their seats, black robes fluttering, making them look like a murder of ravens. Sarana looked down upon the tableau on the bare floor, the medics, the bodies of the cathars and the guards, the new guards standing over the demoniac bound in chains. Leocadia's face turned up to look at her, all defiance gone from her eyes. She kept looking to the injured girl and the flock of white-dressed nurses about her. She did not speak.

"Leocadia," Sarana said, using the creature's name for the first time. "You have been found guilty of Abomination under the Writ of Earth's Holy Chantry. You have profaned your body with machines and consorted with daimons. For these crimes against your own humanity and for your sins in the eyes of the Earth, Our Mother, you will be put to death by fire."

It was the same speech she had made at the start of the hearing, before the violence had ended things. This time, the creature did not interrupt. The eyes still seemed human to Sarana, still brimmed with tears. Sarana shut her own. Justice should be blind. "But the Mother is not without mercy." More words she had said before, as if time had turned round again. "Renounce your ways, cleanse yourself of these machines, and you will not be given to the fire. You will be permitted to take your own life."

"Will she be all right?" the creature asked, looking at the child.

Sarana raised a hand. "Do you renounce evil?"

"Is she alive?" Leocadia asked, ignoring the judge.

"Do you renounce evil?" Sarana asked again.

The creature strained, craning its neck to try and peer past the wall of medical personnel.

"I will not ask again, Leocadia," Sarana said, losing her patience, "Do you renounce evil?"

"To hell with you and your questions, woman—is my daughter all right?"

Sarana shut her eyes again. "Take her away, Arleg."

The guards had to drag the demoniac like a sledge, metal grinding against the concrete floor, leaving pale scratches on the cement. It would be the fire for her, after all. Sarana hung her head and wrung her hands in her lap. She did not open her eyes. Why should this one be so much harder than the others? It didn't make sense.

"Just tell me she's all right!"

Those were the last words Leocadia ever spoke—or the last that the praetor ever heard. The doors of the hall banged shut behind her, leaving the court in uneasy and incomplete quiet. The jurors muttered on their bench, their presence a vestigial formality—there had been no need to determine guilt, not when the guilty's own body shouted the crime.

Sarana opened her eyes, studying the hulking body of the demoniac still suspended in chains in the center of the hall. Was she imagining it, or was there a single blue light flickering in the compartment at the neck whence the snake-like Leocadia had sprung? Was there yet some spark of the demoniac alive in its outer shell?

"Have this destroyed as well." She gestured at the hulk and stood, sweeping down the stairs she approached the nurses. Five of them knelt about the bandaged child while a sixth wielded a medical scanner, checking for internal injuries. Inas lay flat amongst them, pale face thin and drawn with pain.

Sarana glanced at the hulking machine, at the light shining in its depths.

"She's alive," Sarana said. "Will she recover?"

Could the mother hear them still, even through the walls of the courtroom? Possibly. Sarana found that she hoped it could. The forms demanded that the witch be put to death, but nothing in the Chantry's Holy Writ forbade this little mercy. She would die, but she would die with one less victim.

"Yes, praetor," said one of the nurses. "She'll live."

The blue light flickered... and died.

As if this was her cue, as if the world were set upon some poor dramatist's stage, the child's eyes fluttered open. Seeing the nurses and the cold praetor looking over her—or perhaps simply from the pain—she began to cry.

Sarana raised a hand to the sergeant, who shouted orders that the prudence barrier be dropped. The judge stepped over that previously impassable threshold then and knelt before the monster's still-human child and victim. She was an orphan now—or would be in mere moments. She was young, doubtless they would see her installed in a convent, provided she was as free of perverse genetics as she was of her mother's machine sorcery. The clergy could always use more.

"Hush, girl. Let's have none of that," Sarana said, and drew a white kerchief from her sleeve to dry the child's tears. "You're safe now."

∾

Christopher Ruocchio is the author of The Sun Eater, a space opera fantasy series from DAW Books, as well as the assistant editor at Baen Books, where he has co-edited three anthologies, including this one. He is a graduate of North Carolina State University, and sold his first book at twenty-two. Christopher lives in Raleigh, North Carolina, with his wife, Jenna. He may be found on both Facebook and Twitter at @TheRuocchio.

THE CYBER AND
JUSTICE HOLMES

Frank Riley

*For good and/or ill, computers have greatly transformed the
world since this story was written in the mid-Fifties, and its
question remains: should courtroom justice be automated? And
what would Oliver Wendell Holmes, Jr. say?*

⌒

"CYBER JUSTICE!" THAT'S WHAT THE DISTRICT ATTORNEY HAD
called it in his campaign speech last night.

"Cyber justice!"

Oh, hell!

Judge Walhfred Anderson threw the morning fax paper on top of
the law books he had been researching for the past two hours, and
stomped angrily across his chamber to the door of the courtroom.

But it was easier to throw away the paper than the image of
the words:

"—and, if re-elected, I pledge to do all in my power to help
replace human inefficiency with Cyber justice in the courts of this
county!

"We've seen what other counties have done with Cyber judges.
We've witnessed the effectiveness of cybernetic units in our
own Appellate Division. And I can promise you twice as many
prosecutions at half the cost to the taxpayers...with modern,
streamlined Cyber justice!"

Oh, hell!

Walhfred Anderson caught a glimpse of his reflection in the oval mirror behind the coat rack. He paused, fuming, and smoothed down the few lingering strands of grey hair. The District Attorney was waiting for him out there. No use giving him the satisfaction of looking upset. Only a few moments ago, the Presiding Judge had visaphoned a warning that the D.A. had obtained a change of calendar and was going to spring a surprise case this morning...

The Judge cocked his bow tie at a jaunty angle, opened the neckline of his black robe enough for the pink boutonniere to peep out, and stepped into the courtroom as sprightly as his eighty-six years would permit.

The District Attorney was an ex-football player, square-shouldered and square-jawed. He propelled himself to his feet, bowed perfunctorily and remained standing for the Pledge of Allegiance.

As the bailiff's voice repeated the pledge in an unbroken mono-tone, Walhfred Anderson allowed his eyes to wander to the gold-framed picture of his personal symbol of justice, Oliver Wendell Holmes, Jr. Judge Anderson winked at Justice Holmes. It was a morning ritual he had observed without fail for nearly fifty years.

This wasn't the classic picture of Justice Holmes. Not the leonine figure Walhfred Anderson had once seen in the National Gallery. The Justice Holmes on the wall of Judge Anderson's courtroom was much warmer and more human than the official portrait. It was from an old etching that showed the Justice wearing a natty grey fedora. The Justice's fabled mustaches were long and sweeping, giving him the air of a titled playboy, but his eyes were the eyes of the man who had said: "When I am dying, my last words will be—have faith and pursue the unknown end."

Those were good words to remember, when you were eighty-six. Walhfred Anderson stared wistfully at the yellowed etching, waiting for some other dearly remembered phrase to spring up between them. But Justice Holmes wasn't communicative this morning. He hadn't been for a long time.

The District Attorney's voice, threaded with sarcasm, broke into his reverie:

"If the Court pleases, I would like to call up the case of *People vs. Professor Neustadt.*"

Walhfred Anderson accepted the file from his aging, near-sighted clerk. He saw that the case had been assigned originally to Department 42. It was the case he had been warned about by the Presiding Judge.

Walhfred Anderson struggled to focus all his attention on the complaint before him. His craggy features, once described as resembling a benign bulldog, grew rigid with concentration. The Judge had a strong sense of honor about dividing his attention in Court. A case was not just a case; it was a human being whose past, present and future were wrapped up in the charge against him.

"Your Honor," the District Attorney broke in, impatiently, "if the Court will permit, I can summarize this case very quickly..."

The tone of his voice implied:

A Cyber judge would speed things up around here. Feed the facts into the proprioceptor, and they'd be stored and correlated instantly.

Perhaps so, Walhfred Anderson thought, suddenly tired, though the morning was still young. At eighty-six you couldn't go on fighting and resisting much longer. Maybe he should resign, and listen to the speeches at a farewell luncheon, and let a Cyber take over. The Cybers were fast. They ruled swiftly and surely on points of law. They separated fact from fallacy. They were not led down side avenues of justice by human frailty. Their vision was not blurred by emotion. And yet... Judge Anderson looked to Justice Holmes for a clarifying thought, but the Justice's eyes were opaque, inscrutable.

Judge Anderson wearily settled back in his tall chair, bracing the ache in his back against the leather padding.

"You may proceed," he told the District Attorney.

"Thank you, your Honor."

This time the edge of sarcasm was so sharp that the Clerk and Court Stenographer looked up indignantly, expecting one of the Judge's famous retorts.

The crags in the Judge's face deepened, but he remained quiet.

With a tight smile, the District Attorney picked up his notebook.

"The defendant," he began crisply, "is charged on three counts of fraud under Section 31 ..."

"To wit," rumbled Judge Anderson, restlessly.

"To wit," snapped the D.A., "the defendant is charged with giving paid performances at a local theatre, during which he purported to demonstrate that he could take over Cyber functions and perform them more efficiently."

Walhfred Anderson felt the door closing on him. So this was why the D.A. had requested a change of calendar! What a perfect tie-in with the election campaign! He swiveled to study the defendant.

Professor Neustadt was an astonishingly thin little man; the bones of his shoulders seemed about to thrust through the padding of his cheap brown suit. His thinness, combined with a tuft of white hair at the peak of his forehead, gave him the look of a scrawny bird.

"Our investigation of this defendant," continued the D.A., "showed that his title was assumed merely for stage purposes. He has been associated with the less creditable phases of show business for many years. In his youth, he gained considerable attention as a 'quiz kid,' and later, for a time, ran his own program and syndicated column. But his novelty wore off, and he apparently created this cybernetic act to..."

Rousing himself to his judicial responsibility, Judge Anderson interrupted:

"Is the defendant represented by counsel?"

"Your Honor," spoke up Professor Neustadt, in a resonant, bass voice that should have come from a much larger diaphragm, "I request the Court's permission to act as my own attorney."

Walhfred Anderson saw the D.A. smile, and he surmised that the old legal truism was going through his mind: A man who defends himself has a fool for a client.

"If it's a question of finances," the Judge rumbled gently.

"It is not a question of finances. I merely wish to defend myself."

Judge Anderson was annoyed, worried. Whoever he was or claimed to be, this Professor was evidently something of a crackpot. The D.A. would tear him to small pieces, and twist the whole case into an implicit argument for Cyber judges.

"The defendant has a right to act as his own counsel," the D.A. reminded him.

"The Court is aware of that," retorted the Judge. Only the restraining eye of Oliver Wendell Holmes kept him from cutting loose on the D.A. But one more remark like that, and he'd turn his back on the Justice. After all, what right had Holmes to get stuffy at a time like this? He'd never had to contend with Cyber justice!

He motioned to the D.A. to continue with the People's case, but the Professor spoke up first:

"Your Honor, I stipulate to the prosecution evidence."

The D.A. squinted warily.

"Is the defendant pleading guilty?"

"I am merely stipulating to the evidence. Surely the prosecution knows the difference between a stipulation and a plea! I am only trying to save the time of the Court by stipulating to the material facts in the complaint against me!"

The D.A. was obviously disappointed in not being able to present his case. Walhfred Anderson repressed an urge to chuckle. He wondered how a Cyber judge would handle a stipulation.

"Do you have a defense to present?" he asked the Professor.

"Indeed I do, your Honor! I propose to bring a Cyber into the courtroom and prove that I can perform its functions more efficiently!"

The D.A. flushed.

"What kind of a farce is this? We've watched the defendant's performance for several days, and it's perfectly clear that he is merely competing against his own special Cyber unit, one with very limited memory storage capacity..."

"I propose further," continued Professor Neustadt, ignoring the D.A., "that the prosecution bring any Cyber unit of its choice into Court. I am quite willing to compete against any Cyber yet devised!"

This man was not only a crackpot, he was a lunatic, thought Walhfred Anderson with an inward groan. No one but a lunatic would claim he could compete with the memory storage capacity of a Cyber.

As always when troubled, he looked toward Oliver Wendell Holmes for help, but the Justice was still inscrutable. He certainly was being difficult this morning!

The Judge sighed, and began a ruling:

"The procedure suggested by the defendant would fail to answer to the material counts of the complaint..."

But, as he had expected, the D.A. did not intend to let this opportunity pass.

"May it please the Court," said the District Attorney, with a wide grin for the fax reporter, "the people will stipulate to the defense, and will not press for trial of the complaint if the defendant can indeed compete with a Cyber unit of our choice."

Walhfred Anderson glowered at the unsympathetic Justice Holmes. Dammit, man, he thought, don't be so calm about this whole thing. What if you were sitting here, and I was up there in a gold frame? Aloud, he hedged:

"The Court does not believe such a test could be properly and fairly conducted."

"I am not concerned with being fairly treated," orated the wispy Professor. "I propose that five questions or problems be posed to the Cyber and myself, and that we be judged on both the speed and accuracy of our replies. I am quite willing for the prosecution to select the questions."

Go to hell, Holmes, thought Judge Anderson. I don't need you anyway. I've got the answer. The Professor is stark, raving mad.

Before he could develop a ruling along this line, the grinning D.A. had accepted the Professor's terms.

"I have but one condition," interposed the defendant, "if I win this test, I would like to submit a question of my own to the Cyber."

The D.A. hesitated, conferred in a whisper with his assistant, then shrugged.

"We so stipulate."

Firmly, Walhfred Anderson turned his back on Oliver Wendell Holmes.

"In the opinion of the Court," he thundered, "the proposed demonstration would be irrelevant, immaterial and without substantive basis in law. Unless the People proceed with their case in the proper manner, the Court will dismiss this complaint!"

"Objection!"

"Objection!"

The word was spoken simultaneously by both the D.A. and the Professor. Then the defendant bowed toward the District Attorney, and asked him to continue.

For one of the few times in his life, Walhfred Anderson found himself faced with the same objection, at the same time, from both prosecution and defense. What a morning! He felt like turning the court over to a Cyber judge right here and now, and stomping back to his chambers. Let Holmes try getting along with a Cyber!

The D.A.'s voice slashed into his thoughts.

"The People object on the grounds that there is ample precedent in law for the type of court demonstration to which we have agreed..."

"For example," spoke up the Professor, "*People vs. Borth*, 201 N.Y., Supp. 47—"

The District Attorney blinked, and looked wary again.

"The People are not familiar with the citation," he said, "but there is no reason to be in doubt. The revised Judicial Code of Procedure provides for automatic and immediate review of disputed points of law by the Cyber Appellate Division."

CAD! Walhfred Anderson customarily used every legal stratagem to avoid the indignity of appearing before CAD. But now he was neatly trapped.

Grumbling, he visaphoned the Presiding Judge, and was immediately assigned to Cyber V, CAD, fourth floor.

Cyber V presided over a sunlit, pleasantly carpeted courtroom in the south wing of the Justice Building. Square, bulky, with mat black finish, the Cyber reposed in the center of a raised mahogany stand. Its screen and vocoder grill looked austerely down on the long tables provided for opposing counsel.

As Walhfred Anderson belligerently led the Professor and the D.A. into the courtroom, Cyber V hummed softly. A dozen colored lights on its front grid began to blink.

Judge Anderson angrily repressed an instinct to bow, as he had done in his younger years when appearing to plead a case before a human Appellate Court.

The Cyber's soft, pleasantly modulated voice said:

"Please proceed."

Curbing his roiled feelings of rage and indignity, the Judge stepped to the stand in front of the vocoder grill and tersely presented the facts of the case, the reasons for his ruling. Cyber V blinked and hummed steadily, assimilating and filing the facts.

The D.A. followed the Judge to the stand, and, from long habit, addressed Cyber V with the same emotion and voice tricks he would have used in speaking to a human judge. Walhfred Anderson grimaced with disgust.

When the D.A. finished, Cyber V hummed briefly, two amber lights flickered, and the soft voice said:

"Defense counsel will please take the stand."

Professor Neustadt smiled his ironic, exasperating smile.

"The defense stipulates to the facts as stated."

The frontal grid lights on Cyber V flashed furiously; the hum rose to a whine, like a motor accelerating for a steep climb.

Suddenly, all was quiet, and Cyber V spoke in the same soft, pleasant voice:

"There are three cases in modern jurisprudence that have direct bearing on the matter of *People vs. Neustadt.*

"Best known is the case of *People vs. Borth*, 201 N.Y., Supp. 47..."

Walhfred Anderson saw the D.A. stiffen to attention as the Cyber repeated the citation given by Professor Neustadt. He felt his own pulse surge with the stir of a faint, indefinable hope.

"There are also the cases of *Forsythe vs. State*, 6 Ohio, 19, and *Murphy vs. U.S.*, 2d, 85 C.C.A.

"These cases establish precedence for a courtroom demonstration to determine points of material fact.

"Thank you, Gentlemen."

The voice stopped. All lights went dark. Cyber V, CAD, had rendered its decision.

Whatever misgivings the D.A. may have generated over the Professor's display of legal knowledge were overshadowed now by his satisfaction at this display of Cyber efficiency.

"Eight minutes!" he announced triumphantly. "Eight minutes to present the facts of the case and obtain a ruling. There's efficiency for you! There's modern courtroom procedure!"

Walhfred Anderson felt the weight of eighty-six years as he cocked the angle of his bow tie, squared his shoulders and led the way back to his own courtroom. Maybe the new way was right. Maybe he was just an old man, burdened with dreams, memories, the impedimenta of human emotions. It would have taken him many long, weary hours to dig out those cases. Maybe the old way had died with Holmes and the other giants of that era.

Details of the demonstration were quickly concluded. The D.A. selected a Cyber IX for the test. Evidently he had acquired a new respect for Professor Neustadt and was taking no chances.

Cyber IX was a massive new model, used as an integrator by the sciences. Judge Anderson had heard that its memory storage units were the greatest yet devised.

If Professor Neustadt had also heard this, he gave no sign of it. He made only a slight, contemptuous nod of assent to the D.A.'s choice.

For an instant, the Judge found himself hoping that the Professor would be beaten into humility by Cyber IX. The man's attitude was maddening.

Walhfred Anderson banged his gavel harder than necessary, and recessed the hearing for three days. In the meantime, a Cyber IX was to be moved into the courtroom and placed under guard. Professor Neustadt was freed on bail, which he had already posted.

Court fax-sheet reporters picked up the story and ballooned it. The D.A.'s office released publicity stories almost hourly. Cartoonists created "Battle of the Century" illustrations, with Cyber IX and Professor Neustadt posed like fighters in opposite corners of the ring. "Man challenges machine" was the caption, indicating that the Professor was a definite underdog and thus the sentimental favorite. One court reporter confided to Judge Anderson that bookmakers were offering odds of ten to one on Cyber IX.

To the Judge's continuing disgust, Professor Neustadt seemed as avid as the Prosecutor's office for publicity. He allowed himself to be guest-interviewed on every available television show; one program dug up an ancient film of the Professor as a quiz kid, extracting cube roots in a piping, confident voice.

Public interest boiled. TV coverage of the court test was demanded, and eagerly agreed to by both the Prosecutor and Professor Neustadt. Walhfred Anderson ached to cry out against bringing a carnival atmosphere into his courtroom; the fax photographers were bad enough. But he knew that any attempt to interfere would bring him back before that infernal CAD.

When he entered his courtroom on the morning of the trial, the Judge wore a new bow tie, a flippant green, but he felt like many a defendant he had watched step up before his bench to receive sentence. After this morning, there'd be no stopping the D.A.'s campaign for Cyber judges. He glared unhappily at the battery of television cameras. He noted that one of them was pointed at Oliver Wendell Holmes. The Justice didn't seem to mind; but who would—all safe and snug in a nice gold frame? Easy enough for Holmes to look so cocky.

The bright lights hurt his eyes, and he had to steel himself in order to present the picture of dignified equanimity that was expected of a judge. People would be looking at him from every part of the world. Five hundred million viewers, one of the columnists had estimated.

Professor Neustadt appeared in the same shiny brown suit. As he passed the huge Cyber IX unit, metallic gray and mounted on a table of reinforced steel, the Professor paused and bowed, in the manner of a courtly gladiator saluting a respected foe. Spectators clapped and whistled their approval. Television cameras zoomed in on the scene. With easy showmanship, Professor Neustadt maintained the pose for closeups, his owlish eyes wide and unblinking.

Judge Anderson banged his gavel for order. What a poseur! What a fraud! This charlatan would get a million dollars' worth of publicity out of the case.

At a nod from the D.A., the bailiff gave Professor Neustadt a pad of paper on which to note his answers. It had previously been agreed that Cyber IX would answer visually, on the screen, instead of by vocoder. The Professor was seated at the far end of the counsel table, where he could not see the screen. Clerks with stopwatches were stationed behind the Professor and Cyber IX.

"Is the defendant ready?" inquired Judge Anderson, feeling like an idiot.

"Of course."

The Judge turned to Cyber IX, then caught himself. He flushed. The courtroom tittered.

The District Attorney had five questions, each in a sealed envelope, which also contained an answer certified by an eminent authority in the field.

With a flourish, keeping his profile to the cameras, the D.A. handed the first envelope to Judge Anderson.

"We'll begin with a simple problem in mathematics," he announced to the TV audience.

From the smirk in his voice, Judge Anderson was prepared for the worst. But he read the question with a perverse sense of satisfaction. This Professor was in for a very rough morning. He cleared his throat, read aloud:

"In analyzing the economics of atomic power plant operation, calculate the gross heat input for a power generating plant
of 400×10^6 watts electrical output."

Cyber IX hummed into instantaneous activity; its lights flashed
in sweeping curves and spirals across the frontal grid.

Professor Neustadt sat perfectly still, eyes closed. Then he
scribbled something on a pad of paper.

Two stopwatches clicked about a second apart. The clerk
handed the Professor's slip of paper to Judge Anderson. The Judge
checked it, turned to the screen. Both answers were identical:

$3,920 \times 10^6$ BTU/hr.

Time was announced as fourteen seconds for Cyber IX;
fifteen and three-tenths seconds for Professor Neustadt. The
Cyber had won the first test, but by an astoundingly close
margin. The courtroom burst into spontaneous applause for the
Professor. Walhfred Anderson was incredulous. What a fantastic
performance!

No longer smirking, the D.A. handed the Judge a second
envelope.

"What is the percentage compressibility of caesium under
45,000 atmospheres of pressure, and how do you account for it?"

Once again Cyber IX hummed and flickered into action.

And once again Professor Neustadt sat utterly still, head
tilted back like an inquisitive parakeet. Then he wrote swiftly.
A stopwatch clicked.

Walhfred Anderson took the answer with trembling fingers.
He saw the D.A. rub dry lips together, try to moisten them with
a dry tongue. A second stopwatch clicked.

The Judge compared the correct answer with the Professor's
answer and the answer on the screen. All were worded differently, but in essence were the same. Hiding his emotion in a tone
gruffer than usual, Judge Anderson read the Professor's answer:

"The change in volume is seventeen percent. It is due to an
electronic transition for a 6s zone to a 5d zone."

The Professor's elapsed time was 22 seconds. Cyber IX had
taken 31 seconds to answer the compound question.

Professor Neustadt pursed his lips; he seemed displeased with
his tremendous performance.

Moving with the agility of a pallbearer, the D.A. gave Judge
Anderson the third question:

"In twenty-five words or less, state the Nernst Law of thermodynamics."

This was clearly a trick question, designed to trap a human mind in its own verbiage.

Cyber IX won, in eighteen seconds. But in just two-fifths of a second more, Professor Neustadt came through with a brilliant twenty-four-word condensation:

"The entropy of a substance becomes zero at the absolute zero of temperature, provided it is brought to this temperature by a reversible process."

A tabulation of total elapsed time revealed that Professor Neustadt was leading by nine and three-tenths seconds.

A wild excitement blended with the Judge's incredulity. The D.A. seemed to have developed a tic in his right cheek.

On the fourth question, dealing with the structural formula similarities of dimenhydrinate and diphenhydramine hydrochloride, Professor Neustadt lost three seconds.

On the fifth question, concerning the theoretical effects of humidity inversion on microwave transmission, the Professor gained back a full second.

The courtroom was bedlam, and Walhfred Anderson was too excited to pound his gavel. In the glass-walled, soundproofed television booths, announcers grew apoplectic as they tried to relay the fever-pitch excitement of the courtroom to the outside world.

Professor Neustadt held up his bone-thin hand for silence.

"May it please the Court... The District Attorney agreed that in the event of victory I could ask Cyber IX an optional question. I would like to do so at this time."

Judge Anderson could only nod, and hope that his bulldog features were concealing his emotions. The D.A. kept his back rigidly to the television cameras.

Professor Neustadt strutted up to Cyber IX, flipped on the vocoder switch and turned to the cameras.

"Since Cyber IX is essentially a scientific integrator and mathematical unit," he began pedantically, "I'll put my question in the Cyber's own framework. Had another Cyber been selected for this test, I would phrase my question differently."

He turned challengingly back to Cyber IX, paused for dramatic effect, and asked:

"What are the magnitudes of a dream?"

Cyber IX hummed and twinkled. The hum rose higher and higher. The lights flickered in weird, disjointed patterns, blurring before the eye.

Abruptly, the hum stopped. The lights dimmed, faded one by one.

The eternally calm, eternally pleasant voice of Cyber IX spoke from the vocoder grill:

"Problem unsolved."

For an interminable instant there was silence in the courtroom. Complete silence. Stunned incredulity. It was followed by a collective gasp, which Walhfred Anderson could hear echoing around the world. Cyber IX had been more than beaten; it had failed to solve a problem.

The gasp gave way to unrestrained cheering.

But the Professor brought quiet again by raising his bony hand. Now there was a strange, incongruous air of dignity about his thin figure.

"Please," he said, "please understand one thing... The purpose of this demonstration and my question was not to discredit Cyber IX, which is truly a great machine, a wonder of science.

"Cyber IX could not know the magnitudes of a dream... because it cannot dream.

"As a matter of fact, I do not know the magnitudes of a dream, but that is not important... because I *can* dream!

"The dream is the difference... The dream born in man, as the poet said, 'with a sudden, clamorous pain'..."

There was no movement or sound in the courtroom. Walhfred Anderson held the Professor's last written answer between his fingers, as if fearing that even the small movement to release it might shatter something delicate and precious. "The dream is the difference!" There it was. So clear and true and beautiful. He looked at Holmes, and Holmes seemed to be smiling under his gray mustache. Yes, Holmes had known the dream.

In the soundproof booths, the announcers had stopped speaking; all mike lines were open to carry Professor Neustadt's words to five hundred million people.

"Perhaps there are no magnitudes of such a dream... no coordinates! Or it may be that we are not yet wise enough to know them. The future may tell us, for the dream is the rainbow bridge from the present and the past to the future."

Professor Neustadt's eyes were half-closed again, and his head was cocked back, birdlike.

"Copernicus dreamed a dream...So did da Vinci, Galileo and Newton, Darwin and Einstein...all so long ago...

"Cyber IX has not dreamed a dream...Nor have Cyber VIII, VII, VI, V, IV, III, II, I.

"But they can free men to dream.

"Remember that, if you forget all else: They can free men to dream!

"Man's knowledge has grown so vast that much of it would be lost or useless without the storage and recall capacity of the Cybers—and man himself would be so immersed in what he knows that he would never have time to dream of that which he does not yet know, but must and can know.

"Why should not the scientist use the past without being burdened by it? Why should not the lawyer and the judge use the hard-won laws of justice without being the slave of dusty law books?"

Walhfred Anderson accepted the rebuke without wincing. The rebuke for all the hours he had wasted because he had been too stubborn to use a Cyber clerk, or consult Cyber V. The old should not resist the new, nor the new destroy the old. There was the letter of the law, and there was the spirit, and the spirit was the dream. What was old Hammurabi's dream? Holmes had quoted it once, "...to establish justice on the earth...to hold back the strong from oppressing the feeble...to shine like the sun-god upon the blackheaded men, and to illumine the land..." Holmes had dreamed the dream, all right. He had dreamed it grandly. But maybe there was room for small dreams, too, and still time for dreams when the years were so few and lonely.

The Professor suddenly opened his eyes, and his voice took on the twang of steel under tension.

"You are already wondering," he told the cameras accusingly, "whether I have not disproved my own words by defeating Cyber IX.

"That is not true.

"I defeated Cyber IX because I have wasted a man's life—my own! You all know that as a child I was a mnemonic freak, a prodigy, if you prefer. My mind was a filing cabinet, a fire-proof cabinet neatly filled with facts that could never kindle into dreams. All my life I have stuffed my filing cabinet. For sixty years I have filed and filed.

"And then I dreamed one dream—my first, last and only dream.

"I dreamed that man would misuse another gift of science, as he has misused so many...I dreamed of the Cybers replacing and enslaving man, instead of freeing man to dream...And I dreamed that the golden hour would come when a man would have to prove that he could replace a Cyber—and thereby prove that neither man nor Cybers should ever replace each other."

Professor Neustadt turned to Judge Anderson, and his voice dropped almost to a whisper.

"Your Honor, I move that this case be dismissed."

The worn handle of his old teakwood gavel felt warm and alive to the Judge's fingers. He sat up straight, and banged resoundingly on the top of his desk.

"Case dismissed."

Then, in full view of the cameras, Walhfred Anderson turned and winked boldly at Oliver Wendell Holmes.

∽

Frank Riley (1915–1996) was the name under which writer and journalist Frank W. Rhylick wrote his numerous travel articles and a number of notable science fiction stories. In sf, his collaborative novel with Mark Clifton, *They'd Rather be Right*, also reprinted as *The Forever Machine*, won the 1956 Hugo Award for best novel of the previous year, which was the second Hugo Award for best novel ever awarded. Present-day readers may not feel the impact that the novel had for 1956 Hugo voters because its serialization in *Astounding Science-Fiction* was the culmination of a series, preceded by two novelettes in the magazine. To my knowledge, no one has ever published the entire series in one volume. On his own, Riley authored a number of sf stories, three of which would be completely at home in this anthology, but you'll have to be content with "The Cyber and Justice Holmes," which was included in T. E. Dikty's annual anthology of the "Year's Best" sf in 1956. In his alter ego as a travel writer, he wrote for the Los Angeles *Times*, was an editor for *Los Angeles* magazine, co-wrote the bestselling book, *De Anza's Trail Today* with his wife, Elfriede, and had a syndicated travel column. Born in Minnesota, he grew up in Wisconsin, first worked as a reporter for the New York *Daily News*, later covering the White House. During World War II, he served in the Merchant Marine, then he and his family moved to Manhattan Beach, California, where he lived and wrote for five decades, until he died from complications following a stroke.

TO SEE THE INVISIBLE MAN

ROBERT SILVERBERG

*Crime must be punished, of course, and when the fair (?) trial
ends in a guilty verdict, all right-thinking people would agree
that punishment should be both humane and rehabilitating. But,
the meaning of both "humane" and "rehabilitating" are open to
question in this scary tale. This story was adapted into a very
good episode of the revived* Twilight Zone *in 1985 and is well
worth seeking out online or by home video.*

AND THEN THEY FOUND ME GUILTY, AND THEN THEY PRONOUNCED
me invisible, for a span of one year beginning on the eleventh
of May in the year of Grace 2104, and they took me to a dark
room beneath the courthouse to affix the mark to my forehead
before turning me loose.

Two municipally paid ruffians did the job. One flung me into
a chair and the other lifted the brand.

"This won't hurt a bit," the slab-jawed ape said, and thrust
the brand against my forehead, and there was a moment of coolness, and that was all.

"What happens now?" I asked.

But there was no answer, and they turned away from me and
left the room without a word. The door remained open. I was free
to leave, or to stay and rot, as I chose. No one would speak to
me, or look at me more than once, long enough to see the sign
on my forehead. I was invisible. You must understand that my

339

invisibility was strictly metaphorical. I still had corporeal solidity. People *could* see me—but they *would not* see me.

An absurd punishment? Perhaps. But then, the crime was absurd too. The crime of coldness. Refusal to unburden myself for my fellow man. I was a four-time offender. The penalty for that was a year's invisibility. The complaint had been duly sworn, the trial held, the brand duly affixed.

I was invisible.

I went out, out into the world of warmth.

They had already had the afternoon rain. The streets of the city were drying, and there was the smell of growth in the Hanging Gardens. Men and women went about their business. I walked among them, but they took no notice of me.

The penalty for speaking to an invisible man is invisibility, a month to a year or more, depending on the seriousness of the offense. On this the whole concept depends. I wondered how rigidly the rule was observed.

I soon found out.

I stepped into a liftshaft and let myself be spiraled up toward the nearest of the Hanging Gardens. It was Eleven, the cactus garden, and those gnarled, bizarre shapes suited my mood. I emerged on the landing stage and advanced toward the admissions counter to buy my token. A pasty-faced, empty-eyed woman sat back of the counter.

I laid down my coin. Something like fright entered her eyes, quickly faded.

"One admission," I said.

No answer. People were queuing up behind me. I repeated my demand. The woman looked up helplessly, then stared over my left shoulder. A hand extended itself, another coin was placed down. She took it, and handed the man his token. He dropped it in the slot and went in.

"Let me have a token," I said crisply.

Others were jostling me out of the way. Not a word of apology. I began to sense some of the meaning of my invisibility. They were literally treating me as though they could not see me.

There are countervailing advantages. I walked around behind the counter and helped myself to a token without paying for it. Since I was invisible, I could not be stopped. I thrust the token in the slot and entered the garden.

But the cacti bored me. An inexpressible malaise slipped over me, and I felt no desire to stay. On my way out I pressed my finger against a jutting thorn and drew blood. The cactus, at least, still recognized my existence. But only to draw blood.

I returned to my apartment. My books awaited me, but I felt no interest in them. I sprawled out on my narrow bed and activated the energizer to combat the strange lassitude that was afflicting me. I thought about my invisibility.

It would not be such a hardship, I told myself. I had never depended overly on other human beings. Indeed, had I not been sentenced in the first place for my coldness toward my fellow creatures? So what need did I have of them now? *Let* them ignore me!

It would be restful. I had a year's respite from work, after all. Invisible men did not work. How could they? Who would go to an invisible doctor for a consultation, or hire an invisible lawyer to represent him, or give a document to an invisible clerk to file? No work, then. No income, of course, either. But landlords did not take rent from invisible men. Invisible men went where they pleased, at no cost. I had just demonstrated that at the Hanging Gardens.

Invisibility would be a great joke on society, I felt. They had sentenced me to nothing more dreadful than a year's rest cure. I was certain I would enjoy it.

But there were certain practical disadvantages. On the first night of my invisibility I went to the city's finest restaurant. I would order their most lavish dishes, a hundred-unit meal, and then conveniently vanish at the presentation of the bill.

My thinking was muddy. I never got seated. I stood in the entrance half an hour, bypassed again and again by a maitre d'hotel who had clearly been through all this many times before: Walking to a seat, I realized, would gain me nothing. No waiter would take my order.

I could go into the kitchen. I could help myself to anything I pleased. I could disrupt the workings of the restaurant. But I decided against it. Society had its ways of protecting itself against the invisible ones. There could be no direct retaliation, of course, no intentional defense. But who could say no to a chef's claim that he had seen no one in the way when he hurled a pot of scalding water toward the wall? Invisibility was invisibility, a two-edged sword.

I left the restaurant.

I ate at an automated restaurant nearby. Then I took an autocab home. Machines, like cacti, did not discriminate against my sort. I sensed that they would make poor companions for a year, though.

I slept poorly.

The second day of my invisibility was a day of further testing and discovery.

I went for a long walk, careful to stay on the pedestrian paths. I had heard all about the boys who enjoy running down those who carry the mark of invisibility on their foreheads. Again, there is no recourse, no punishment for them. My condition has its little hazards by intention.

I walked the streets, seeing how the throngs parted for me. I cut through them like a microtome passing between cells. They were well trained. At midday I saw my first fellow Invisible. He was a tall man of middle years, stocky and dignified, bearing the mark of shame on a domelike forehead. His eyes met mine only for a moment. Then he passed on. An invisible man, naturally, cannot see another of his kind.

I was amused, nothing more. I was still savoring the novelty of this way of life. No slight could hurt me. Not yet.

Late in the day I came to one of those bathhouses where working girls can cleanse themselves for a couple of small coins. I smiled wickedly and went up the steps. The attendant at the door gave me the flicker of a startled look—it was a small triumph for me—but did not dare to stop me.

I went in.

An overpowering smell of soap and sweat struck me. I persevered inward. I passed cloakrooms where long rows of gray smocks were hanging, and it occurred to me that I could rifle those smocks of every unit they contained, but I did not. Theft loses meaning when it becomes too easy, as the clever ones who devised invisibility were aware.

I passed on, into the bath chambers themselves.

Hundreds of women were there. Nubile girls, weary wenches, old crones. Some blushed. A few smiled. Many turned their backs on me. But they were careful not to show any real reaction to my presence. Supervisory matrons stood guard, and who knew but that she might be reported for taking undue cognizance of the existence of an Invisible?

So I watched them bathe, watched five hundred pairs of bobbing breasts, watched naked bodies glistening under the spray, watched this vast mass of bare feminine flesh. My reaction was a mixed one, a sense of wicked achievement at having penetrated this sanctum sanctorum unhalted, and then, welling up slowly within me, a sensation of—was it sorrow? Boredom? Revulsion?

I was unable to analyze it. But it felt as though a clammy hand had seized my throat. I left quickly. The smell of soapy water stung my nostrils for hours afterward, and the sight of pink flesh haunted my dreams that night. I ate alone, in one of the automatics. I began to see that the novelty of this punishment was soon lost.

In the third week I fell ill. It began with a high fever, then pains of the stomach, vomiting, the rest of the ugly symptomatology. By midnight I was certain I was dying. The cramps were intolerable, and when I dragged myself to the toilet cubicle I caught sight of myself in the mirror, distorted, greenish, beaded with sweat. The mark of invisibility stood out like a beacon in my pale forehead.

For a long time I lay on the tiled floor, limply absorbing the coolness of it. Then I thought: What if it's my appendix? That ridiculous, obsolete, obscure prehistoric survival? Inflamed, ready to burst?

I needed a doctor.

The phone was covered with dust. They had not bothered to disconnect it, but I had not called anyone since my arrest, and no one had dared call me. The penalty for knowingly telephoning an invisible man is invisibility. My friends, such as they were, had stayed far away.

I grasped the phone, thumbed the panel. It lit up and the directory robot said, "With whom do you wish to speak, sir?"

"Doctor," I gasped.

"Certainly, sir." Bland, smug mechanical words! No way to pronounce a robot invisible, so it was free to talk to me!

The screen glowed. A doctorly voice said, "What seems to be the trouble?"

"Stomach pains. Maybe appendicitis."

"We'll have a man over in—" He stopped. I had made the mistake of upturning my agonized face. His eyes lit on my forehead mark. The screen winked into blackness as rapidly as though I had extended a leprous hand for him to kiss.

"Doctor," I groaned.

He was gone. I buried my face in my hands. This was carrying things too far, I thought. Did the Hippocratic Oath allow things like this? Could a doctor ignore a sick man's plea for help?

Hippocrates had not known anything about invisible men. A doctor was not required to minister to an invisible man. To society at large I simply was not there. Doctors could not diagnose diseases in nonexistent individuals.

I was left to suffer.

It was one of invisibility's less attractive features. You enter a bathhouse unhindered, if that pleases you—but you writhe on a bed of pain equally unhindered. The one with the other, and if your appendix happens to rupture, why, it is all the greater deterrent to others who might perhaps have gone your lawless way!

My appendix did not rupture. I survived, though badly shaken. A man can survive without human conversation for a year. He can travel on automated cars and eat at automated restaurants. But there are no automated doctors. For the first time, I felt truly beyond the pale. A convict in a prison is given a doctor when he falls ill. My crime had not been serious enough to merit prison, and so no doctor would treat me if I suffered. It was unfair. I cursed the devils who had invented my punishment. I faced each bleak dawn alone, as alone as Crusoe on his island, here in the midst of a city of twelve million souls.

How can I describe my shifts of mood, my many tacks before the changing winds of the passing months?

There were times when invisibility was a joy, a delight, a treasure. In those paranoid moments I gloried in my exemption from the rules that bound ordinary men.

I stole. I entered small stores and seized the receipts, while the cowering merchant feared to stop me, lest in crying out he make himself liable to my invisibility. If I had known that the State reimbursed all such losses, I might have taken less pleasure in it. But I stole.

I invaded. The bathhouse never tempted me again, but I

breached other sanctuaries. I entered hotels and walked down the corridors, opening doors at random. Most rooms were empty. Some were not.

Godlike, I observed all. I toughened. My disdain for society— the crime that had earned me invisibility in the first place— heightened.

I stood in the empty streets during the periods of rain, and railed at the gleaming faces of the towering buildings on every side. "Who needs you?" I roared "Not I! Who needs you in the slightest?"

I jeered and mocked and railed. It was a kind of insanity, brought on, I suppose, by the loneliness. I entered theaters— where the happy lotus-eaters sat slumped in their massage chairs, transfixed by the glowing tridim images—and capered down the aisles. No one grumbled at me. The luminescence of my forehead told them to keep their complaints to themselves, and they did.

Those were the mad moments, the good moments, the moments when I towered twenty feet high and strode among the visible clods with contempt oozing from every pore. Those were insane moments—I admit that freely. A man who has been in a condition of involuntary invisibility for several months is not likely to be well balanced.

Did I call them paranoid moments? Manic depressive might be more to the point. The pendulum swung dizzily. The days when I felt only contempt for the visible fools all around me were balanced by days when the isolation pressed in tangibly on me. I would walk the endless streets, pass through the gleaming arcades, stare down at the highways with their streaking bullets of gay colors. Not even a beggar would come up to me. Did you know we had beggars, in our shining century? Not till I was pronounced invisible did I know it, for then my long walks took me to the slums, where the shine has worn thin, and where shuffling stubble-faced old men beg for small coins.

No one begged for coins from me. Once a blind man came up to me.

"For the love of God," he wheezed, "help me to buy new eyes from the eye bank."

They were the first direct words any human being had spoken to me in months. I started to reach into my tunic for money, planning to give him every unit on me in gratitude. Why not?

I could get more simply by taking it. But before I could draw the money out, a nightmare figure hobbled on crutches between us. I caught the whispered word, "Invisible," and then the two of them scuttled away like frightened crabs. I stood there stupidly holding my money.

Not even the beggars. Devils, to have invented this torment!

So I softened again. My arrogance ebbed away. I was lonely, now. Who could accuse me of coldness? I was spongy soft, pathetically eager for a word, a smile, a clasping hand. It was the sixth month of my invisibility.

I loathed it entirely, now. Its pleasures were hollow ones and its torment was unbearable. I wondered how I would survive the remaining six months. Believe me, suicide was not far from my mind in those dark hours.

And finally I committed an act of foolishness. On one of my endless walks I encountered another Invisible, no more than the third or the fourth such creature I had seen in my six months. As in the previous encounters, our eyes met, warily, only for a moment. Then he dropped his to the pavement, and he side-stepped me and walked on. He was a slim young man, no more than forty, with tousled brown hair and a narrow, pinched face. He had a look of scholarship about him, and I wondered what he might have done to merit his punishment, and I was seized with the desire to run after him and ask him, and to learn his name, and to talk to him, and embrace him.

All these things are forbidden to mankind. No one shall have any contact whatsoever with an Invisible—not even a fellow Invisible. Especially not a fellow Invisible. There is no wish on society's part to foster a secret bond of fellowship among its pariahs.

I knew all this.

I turned and followed him, all the same.

For three blocks I moved along behind him, remaining twenty to fifty paces to the rear. Security robots seemed to be everywhere, their scanners quick to detect an infraction, and I did not dare make my move. Then he turned down a side street, a gray, dusty street five centuries old, and began to stroll, with the ambling, going-nowhere gait of the Invisible. I came up behind him.

"Please," I said softly. "No one will see us here. We can talk. My name is—"

He whirled on me, horror in his eyes. His face was pale. He looked at me in amazement for a moment, then darted forward as though to go around me.

I blocked him.

"Wait," I said. "Don't be afraid. Please—"

He burst past me. I put my hand on his shoulder, and he wriggled free.

"Just a word," I begged.

Not even a word. Not even a hoarsely uttered, "Leave me alone!" He sidestepped me and ran down the empty street, his steps diminishing from a clatter to a murmur as he reached the corner and rounded it. I looked after him, feeling a great loneliness well up in me.

And then a fear. *He* hadn't breached the rules of Invisibility, but I had. I had seen him. That left me subject to punishment, an extension of my term of invisibility, perhaps. I looked around anxiously, but there were no security robots in sight, no one at all.

I was alone.

Turning, calming myself, I continued down the street. Gradually I regained control over myself. I saw that I had done something unpardonably foolish. The stupidity of my action troubled me, but even more the sentimentality of it. To reach out in that panicky way to another Invisible—to admit openly my loneliness, my need—no. It meant that society was winning. I couldn't have that.

I found that I was near the cactus garden once again. I rode the liftshaft, grabbed a token from the attendant, and bought my way in. I searched for a moment, then found a twisted, elaborately ornate cactus eight feet high, a spiny monster. I wrenched it from its pot and broke the angular limbs to fragments, filling my hands with a thousand needles. People pretended not to watch. I plucked the spines from my hands and, palms bleeding, rode the liftshaft down, once again sublimely aloof in my invisibility.

The eighth month passed, the ninth, the tenth. The seasonal round had made nearly a complete turn. Spring had given way to a mild summer, summer to a crisp autumn, autumn to winter with its fortnightly snowfalls, still permitted for esthetic reasons. Winter had ended, now. In the parks, the trees sprouted green buds. The weather control people stepped up the rainfall to thrice daily.

My term was drawing to its end.

In the final months of my invisibility I had slipped into a kind of torpor. My mind, forced back on its own resources, no longer cared to consider the implications of my condition, and I slid in a blurred haze from day to day. I read compulsively but unselectively. Aristotle one day, the Bible the next, a handbook of mechanics the next. I retained nothing; as I turned a fresh page, its predecessor slipped from my memory.

I no longer bothered to enjoy the few advantages of invisibility, the voyeuristic thrills, the minute throb of power that comes from being able to commit any act with only limited fears of retaliation. I say *limited* because the passage of the Invisibility Act had not been accompanied by an act repealing human nature; few men would not risk invisibility to protect their wives or children from an invisible one's molestations; no one would coolly allow an invisible to jab out his eyes; no one would tolerate an Invisible's invasion of his home. There were ways of coping with such infringements without appearing to recognize the existence of the Invisible, as I have mentioned.

Still, it was possible to get away with a great deal. I declined to try. Somewhere Dostoevsky has written, "Without God, all things are possible." I can amend that. "To the invisible man, all things are possible—and uninteresting." So it was.

The weary months passed.

I did not count the minutes till my release. To be precise, I wholly forgot that my term was due to end. On the day itself, I was reading in my room, morosely turning page after page, when the annunciator chimed.

It had not chimed for a full year. I had almost forgotten the meaning of the sound.

But I opened the door. There they stood, the men of the law. Wordlessly, they broke the seal that held the mark to my forehead.

The emblem dropped away and shattered.

"Hello, citizen," they said to me.

I nodded gravely. "Yes. Hello."

"May 11, 2105. Your term is up. You are restored to society. You have paid your debt."

"Thank you. Yes."

"Come for a drink with us."

"I'd sooner not."

"It's the tradition. Come along."

I went with them. My forehead felt strangely naked now, and I glanced in a mirror to see that there was a pale spot where the emblem had been. They took me to a bar nearby, and treated me to synthetic whiskey, raw, powerful. The bartender grinned at me. Someone on the next stool clapped me on the shoulder and asked me who I liked in tomorrow's jet races. I had no idea, and I said so.

"You mean it? I'm backing Kelso. Four to one, but he's got terrific spurt power."

"I'm sorry," I said.

"He's been away for a while," one of the government men said softly.

The euphemism was unmistakable. My neighbor glanced at my forehead and nodded at the pale spot. He offered to buy me a drink too. I accepted, though I was already feeling the effects of the first one. I was a human being again. I was visible.

I did not dare spurn him, anyway. It might have been construed as a crime of coldness once again. My fifth offense would have meant five years of Invisibility. I had learned humility.

Returning to visibility involved an awkward transition, of course. Old friends to meet, lame conversations to hold, shattered relationships to renew. I had been an exile in my own city for a year, and coming back was not easy.

No one referred to my time of invisibility, naturally. It was treated as an affliction best left unmentioned. Hypocrisy, I thought, but I accepted it. Doubtless they were all trying to spare my feelings. Does one tell a man whose cancerous stomach has been replaced, "I hear you had a narrow escape just now?" Does one say to a man whose aged father has tottered off toward a euthanasia house, "Well, he was getting pretty feeble anyway, wasn't he?"

No. Of course not.

So there was this hole in our shared experience, this void, this blankness. Which left me little to talk about with my friends, in particular since I had lost the knack of conversation entirely. The period of readjustment was a trying one.

But I persevered, for I was no longer the same haughty, aloof person I had been before my conviction. I had learned humility in the hardest of schools.

Now and then I noticed an Invisible on the streets, of course.

It was impossible to avoid them. But, trained as I had been trained, I quickly glanced away, as though my eyes had come momentarily to rest on some shambling, festering horror from another world.

It was in the fourth month of my return to visibility that the ultimate lesson of my sentence struck home, though. I was in the vicinity of the City Tower, having returned to my old job in the documents division of the municipal government. I had left work for the day and was walking toward the tubes when a hand emerged from the crowd, caught my arm.

"Please," the soft voice said. "Wait a minute. Don't be afraid."

I looked up, startled. In our city strangers do not accost strangers.

I saw the gleaming emblem of invisibility on the man's forehead. Then I recognized him—the slim man I had accosted more than half a year before on that deserted street. He had grown haggard; his eyes were wild, his brown hair flecked with gray. He must have been at the beginning of his term, then. Now he must have been near its end.

He held my arm. I trembled. This was no deserted street. This was the most crowded square of the city. I pulled my arm away from his grasp and started to turn away.

"No—don't go," he cried. "Can't you pity me? You've been there yourself."

I took a faltering step. Then I remembered how I had cried out to him, how I had begged him not to spurn me. I remembered my own miserable loneliness.

I took another step away from him.

"Coward!" he shrieked after me. "Talk to me! I dare you! Talk to me, coward!"

It was too much. I was touched. Sudden tears stung my eyes, and I turned to him, stretched out a hand to his. I caught his thin wrist. The contact seemed to electrify him. A moment later, I held him in my arms, trying to draw some of the misery from his frame to mine.

The security robots closed in, surrounding us. He was hurled to one side, I was taken into custody. They will try me again—not for the crime of coldness, this time, but for a crime of warmth. Perhaps they will find extenuating circumstances and release me; perhaps not.

I do not care. If they condemn me, this time I will wear my invisibility like a shield of glory.

∾

Robert Silverberg, prolific author not just of SF, but of authoritative nonfiction books, columnist for *Asimov's* SF Magazine, winner of a constellation of awards, and renowned bon vivant surely needs no introduction—but that's never stopped me before. Born in 1935, Robert Silverberg sold his first SF story, "Gorgon Planet," before he was out of his teens, to the British magazine *Nebula*. Two years later, his first SF novel, a juvenile, *Revolt on Alpha C* followed. Decades later, his total SF titles, according to his semi-official website, stands at 82 SF novels and 457 short stories. Early on, he won a Hugo Award for most promising new writer—rarely have the Hugo voters been so perceptive.

Toward the end of the 1960s and continuing into the 1970s, he wrote a string of novels much darker in tone and deeper in characterization than his work of the 1950s, such as the novels *Nightwings*, *Dying Inside*, *The Book of Skulls*, and other novels. He took occasional sabbaticals from writing, to return with new works, such as the Majipoor series. His most recent novels include *The Alien Years*, *The Longest Way Home*, and a new trilogy of Majipoor novels. In addition The Science Fiction and Fantasy Hall of Fame inducted him in 1999. In 2004, the Science Fiction Writers of America presented the Damon Knight Memorial Grand Master Award. For more information see his "quasi-official" website at www.majipoor.com heroically maintained by Jon Davis (no relation).

LICENSE TO STEAL

Louis Newman

Mr. Newman seems to be a one-story author, unless he's a pseudonym. If you read this, sir, please get in touch. And thank you for this nifty satire of cops who had fun with a naïve alien bumpkin, which "fun" spectacularly backfired!

෴

THE HISTORY OF MAN BECOMES FEARFULLY AND WONDERFULLY confusing with the advent of interstellar travel. Of special interest to the legally inclined student is the famous Skrrgck Affair, which began before the Galactic Tribunal with the case of *Citizens vs. Skrrgck*.

The case, and the opinion of the Court, may be summarized as follows:

Skrrgck, a native of Sknnbt (Altair IV), where theft is honorable, sanctioned by law and custom, immigrated to Earth (Sol III) where theft is contrary to both law and custom.

While residing in Chicago, a city in a political subdivision known as the State of Illinois, part of the United States of America, one of the ancient nation-states of Earth, he overheard his landlady use the phrase "A license to steal," a common colloquialism in the area, which refers to any special privilege.

Skrrgck then went to a police station in Chicago and requested a license to steal. The desk sergeant, as a joke, wrote out a document purporting to be a license to steal, and Skrrgck, relying on said document, committed theft, was apprehended, tried and convicted. On direct appeal allowed to the Galactic Tribunal, the Court held:

(1) All persons are required to know and obey the law of the jurisdiction in which they reside.

(2) Public officials must refrain from misrepresenting to strangers the law of the jurisdiction.

(3) Where, as here, a public official is guilty of such misrepresentation, the requirement of knowledge no longer applies.

(4) Where, as here, it is shown by uncontradicted evidence that a defendant is law-abiding and willing to comply with the standards of his place of residence, misrepresentation of law by public officials may amount to entrapment.

(5) The Doctrine of Entrapment bars the State of Illinois from prosecuting this defendant.

(6) The magnitude of the crime is unimportant compared with the principle involved, and the fact that the defendant's unusual training on Sknnbt enabled him to steal a large building in Chicago, known as the Merchandise Mart, is of no significance.

(7) The defendant, however, was civilly liable for the return of the building, and its occupants, or their value, even if he had to steal to get it, provided, however, that he stole only on and from a planet where theft was legal.

The Skrrgck case was by no means concluded by the decision of the Galactic Tribunal, but continued to reverberate down the years, a field day for lawyers, and "a lesson to all in the complexities of modern intergalactic law and society," said Winston, Harold C, Herman Prof, of Legal History, Harvard.

Though freed on the criminal charge of theft, Skrrgck still faced some 20,000 charges of kidnapping, plus the civil liability imposed upon him by the ruling of the Court.

The kidnapping charges were temporarily held in abeyance. Not that the abductions were not considered outrageous, but it was quickly realized by all concerned that if Skrrgck were constantly involved in lengthy and expensive defenses to criminal prosecutions, there would be no chance at all of obtaining any restitution from him. First things first, and with Terrans that rarely means justice.

Skrrgck offered to pay over the money he had received for the building and its occupants, but that was unacceptable to the Terrans, for what they really wanted, with that exaggerated fervor typical of them, provided it agrees with their financial interests, was the return of the original articles. Not only were the people wanted back, but the building itself had a special significance.

Its full title was "The New Merchandise Mart" and it had been built in the exact style of the original and on the exact spot on the south side of the Chicago River where the original had stood prior to its destruction in the Sack of Chicago. It was more than just a large commercial structure to the Terrans. It was also a symbol of Terra's unusually quick recovery from its Empire Chaos into its present position of leadership within the Galactic Union. The Terrans wanted that building back.

So Skrrgck, an obliging fellow at heart, tried first to get it back, but this proved impossible, for he had sold the building to the Aldebaranian Confederacy for use in its annual "prosperity fiesta."

The dominant culture of the Aldebaranian system is a descendant of the "conspicuous destruction" or "potlatch" type, in which articles of value are destroyed to prove the wealth and power of the destroyers. It was customary once every Aldebaranian year—about six Terran—for the Aldebaranian government to sponsor a token celebration of this destructive sort, and it had purchased the Merchandise Mart from Skrrgck as part of its special celebration marking the first thousand years of the Confederacy.

Consequently, the building, along with everything else, was totally destroyed in the "bonfire" that consumed the entire fourth planet from the main Aldebaranian sun.

Nor was Skrrgck able to arrange the return to Terra of the occupants of the building, some 20,000 in number, because he had sold them as slaves to the Boötean League.

It is commonly thought slavery is forbidden throughout the Galaxy by the terms of Article 19 of the Galactic Compact, but such is not the case. What is actually forbidden is "involuntary servitude" and this situation proved the significance of that distinction. In the case of Sol v. Boötes, the Galactic Tribunal held that Terra had no right to force the "slaves" to give up their slavery and return to Terra if they did not wish to. And, quite naturally, none of them wished to.

It will be remembered that the Boöteans, a singularly handsome and good-natured people, were in imminent danger of racial extinction due to the disastrous effects of a strange nucleonic storm which had passed through their system in 1622.

The physiological details of the "Boötean Effect," as it has been called, was to render every Boötean sterile in relation to every other Boötean, while leaving each Boötean normally capable of reproduction, provided one of the partners in the union had not been subjected to the nucleonic storm.

Faced with this situation, the Boöteans immediately took steps to encourage widespread immigration by other humanoid races, chiefly Terrans, for it was Terrans who had originally colonized Boötes and it was therefore known that interbreeding was possible.

But the Boöteans were largely unsuccessful in their immigration policy. Terra was peaceful and prosperous, and the Boöteans, being poor advertisers, were unable to convince more than a handful to leave the relative comforts of home for the far-off Boötean system where, almost all were sure, some horrible fate lay behind the Boöteans' honeyed words. So when Skrrgck showed up with some 20,000 Terrans, the Boöteans, in desperation, agreed to purchase them in the hope of avoiding the "involuntary servitude" prohibition of Article 19 by making them like it.

In this, they were spectacularly successful. The "slaves" were treated to the utmost luxury and every effort was made to satisfy any reasonable wish. Their "duties" consisted entirely of "keeping company" with the singularly attractive Boöteans.

Under these circumstances it is, perhaps, hardly surprising that out of the 20,101 occupants, all but 332 flatly refused to return to Terra.

The 332 who did wish to return, most of whom were borderline psychotics, were shipped home, and Boötes sued Skrrgck for their purchase price, but was turned down by the Galactic Quadrant Court on the theory of, basically, Caveat Emptor—let the buyer beware.

The Court in *Sol v. Boötes* had held that although adults could not be required to return to Terra, minors under the age of 31 could be, and an additional 569 were returned under this ruling, to the vociferous disgust of the post-puberty members of that group. Since there was apparently some question of certain misrepresentations by Skrrgck as to the ages or family affiliations of some members of this minor group, he agreed to an out-of-court settlement of Boötes' claim for their purchase price, thus depriving the legal profession of further clarification of the rights of two "good faith" dealers in this peculiar sort of transaction.

The Terran people, of course, were totally unsatisfied with this result. Led by some demagogues and, to a milder degree, by most of the political opposition to the existing Terran government, and reminded of certain actual examples from Terra's own history, many became convinced that some form of nefarious "brainwashing" had been exercised upon the "unfortunate" Terran expatriates. Excitement ran high, and there was even some agitation for withdrawal from the Galactic Union.

Confronted with such unrest, the Terran government made efforts to reach some settlement with Boötes despite the decision of the Court in *Sol v. Boötes*, and was finally able to gain in the Centaurian Agreement a substantial reparation, it being specifically stipulated in the Agreement that the money was to be paid to the dependents who suffered actual financial loss.

In a suit against the Terran government by one of the excluded families, to obtain for that family a share of the reparation, the validity of the treaty, as it applied to exclude the suing family and others in like position, was upheld by the United States Supreme Court.

The suit was begun before the Agreement had been ratified by the General Assembly, and the Court indicated that the plaintiff would have lost on the strength of a long line of cases giving the World President certain inherent powers over the conduct of foreign affairs. Since, however, the matter came up for decision after ratification, the Court said that the "inherent powers" question was moot, and that the Agreement, having been elevated to the status of a treaty by ratification, must be held valid under the "Supremacy of Treaties" section of Article 102 of the United Terran Charter.

Although this failed to satisfy the Terran people—and their anger may have contributed to the fall of the Solarian Party administration in the following election—the Treaty is generally considered by students of the subject as a triumph of Solarian diplomacy, and an outstanding example of intergalactic good faith on the part of Boötes.

Of course, neither the demagogy nor the anger could hide forever the true facts about how the Boöteans were treating their "slaves," and when the true facts became known, there was a sudden flood of migration from Terra to Boötes, which threatened to depopulate the Solarian Empire and drown Boötes. The flood was quickly dammed by the Treaty of Deneb restricting migration between the two systems. This treaty was held to be a valid police-powers exception to the "Free Migration" principle of Article 17 of the Galactic Compact in *Boleslaw v. Sol and Boötes*.

All this left Skrrgck with liabilities of some forty million credits and practically no assets. Like most Altairians, he was a superb thief but a poor trader. The price he had received for the Merchandise Mart and the "slaves," while amounting to a tidy personal fortune, was less than half the amount of the claims against him, and due to an unfortunate predilection for slow *Aedrils* and fast *Flowezies*, he only had about half of that left.

Skrrgck, who had by this time apparently developed a love of litigation equal to his love of thievery, used part of what he did have left in a last effort to evade liability by going into bankruptcy, a move which was naturally met with howls of outrage by his creditors and a flood of objections to his petition, a flood which very nearly drowned the Federal District Court in Chicago.

It would be difficult to imagine a more complex legal battle that might have taken place, nor one more instructive to the legal profession, had the situation been carried to its logical conclusion.

On the one hand was the age-old policy of both Terran and Galactic bankruptcy law. A man becomes unable to pay his debts. He goes into bankruptcy. Whatever he does have is distributed to his creditors, who must be satisfied with what they can get out of his present assets. They cannot require him to go to work to earn additional funds with which to pay them more. It is precisely to escape this form of mortgage on one's future that bankruptcy exists.

Yet here were over seven thousand creditors claiming that Skrrgck's debts should not be discharged in bankruptcy, because Skrrgck could be required to steal enough to satisfy them fully.

Could the creditors require Skrrgck to exert such personal efforts to satisfy their claims? A lawyer would almost certainly say "no," citing the Bankruptcy Act as sufficient grounds alone, not to mention the anomaly of having Terrans, in a Terran court, ask that Skrrgck, for their benefit, commit an act illegal on Terra and punishable by that Terran court.

The idea of a Terran court giving judicial sanction to theft is novel, to say the least. Indeed, Judge Griffin, who was presiding, was overheard to remark to a friend on the golf course that he "would throw the whole d—n thing out" for that reason alone.

Yet, in spite of this undeniable weight of opinion, it is difficult to say just what the final decision would have been had the matter been carried to the Galactic Tribunal, for in the original case of *Skrrgck v. Illinois*, that august body, it will be remembered, had specifically stated that Skrrgck was liable for the value of the building and its occupants, "even if he must steal to obtain it."

Now that hasty and ill-advised phrase was certainly dicta, and was probably intended only as a joke, the opinion having been written by Master Adjudicator Stsssts, a member of that irrepressible race of saurian humorists, the Sirians. But if the case had actually come before them, the Court might have been hoisted on its own petard, so to speak, and been forced to rule in accord with its earlier "joke."

Unfortunately for the curiosity of the legal profession, the question was never to be answered, for Skrrgck did a remarkable thing which made the whole controversy irrelevant. What his motives were will probably never be known. His character makes it unlikely that he began the bankruptcy proceedings in good faith and was later moved by conscience. It is possible that the bankruptcy was merely an elaborate piece of misdirection. More probably, however, he simply seized on the unusual opportunity the publicity gave him.

Whatever the motives, the facts are that Skrrgck used the last of his waning resources to purchase one of the newly developed Terran Motors' "Timebirds" in which he traveled secretly to Altair. Even this first model of the Timebird, with its primitive meson exchange discoordinator, cut the trip from Sol to Altair from weeks to days, and Skrrgck, landing secretly on his home planet while his bankruptcy action was still in the turmoil stage, was able to accomplish the greatest "coup" in Altairian history. He never could have done it without the publicity of the legal proceedings. In a culture where theft is honorable, the most stringent precautions are taken against its accomplishment, but who could have expected Skrrgck? He was light-years away, trying to go into bankruptcy.

And so, while all eyes on Altair, as well as throughout the rest of the Galaxy, were amusedly fixed on the legal circus shaping up on Terra, Skrrgck was able to steal the Altairian Crown Jewels, and the Altairian Crown Prince as well, and flee with them to Sol.

✧   ✧   ✧

The reaction was violent. The Galaxy was gripped by an almost hysterical amusement. Skrrgck's creditors on Terra were overjoyed. The Altairians made one effort to regain their valuables in the courts, but were promptly turned down by the Galactic Tribunal which held, wisely, that a society which made a virtue of theft would have to take the consequences of its own culture.

So Skrrgck's creditors were paid in full. The jewels alone were more than sufficient for that, containing as they did no less than seven priceless "Wanderstones," those strange bits of frozen fire found ever so rarely floating in the interstellar voids, utterly impervious to any of the effects of gravitation. Altair paid a fantastic price for the return of the collection, and Skrrgck also demanded, and got, a sizable ransom for the Prince, after threatening to sell him to Boötes, from whence, of course, he would never return. Being a prince in a democratic, constitutional monarchy is not as glamorous as you might think.

His creditors satisfied, Skrrgck returned to Sknnbt, dragging with him an angry Crown Prince—angry at having lost the chance to go to Boötes, that is. At Altair, Skrrgck was received as a popular hero. He had accomplished something of which every Altairian had dreamed, almost from the moment of his birth, and he was widely and joyously acclaimed. Riding on this wave of popular adulation, he entered politics, ran for the office of Premier, and was elected by an overwhelming majority.

As soon as he took office, he took steps, in accordance with Altairian custom, to wipe out the "stain" on his honor incurred by allowing the Chicago police sergeant to fool him with the now famous License to Steal.

He instituted suit against the sergeant for the expenses of his defense to the original theft charge.

The case was carried all the way to the Galactic Tribunal, which by this time was heartily sick of the whole mess. Feeling apparently that the sergeant was the original cause of said mess, the Court overruled his plea that he had merely been joking.

The Court cited an ancient case from West Virginia, U.S.A.— *Plate v. Durst*, 42 W. Va. 63, 24 SE 580, 32 L.R.A. 404. (Note: The date of this case is invariably given as 1896, which is most confusing, since the present date is only 1691. The 1896, however, refers to the eighteen hundred and ninety-sixth year of the preatomic era, which we, of course, style A.A.—Ante Atomica. Since the present era begins with the first atomic explosion, the case actually occurred in approximately the year 54 A.A.)

The Court quoted the opinion in this ancient case as follows: "Jokes are sometimes taken seriously by . . . the inexperienced . . . and if such is the case, and the person thereby deceived is led to (incur expenses) in the full belief and expectation that the joker is in earnest, the law will also take the joker at his word, and give him good reason to smile."

Accordingly, the sergeant was charged with a very large judgment. Although the City of Chicago paid this judgment, the sergeant had become the laughingstock of the planet, so he applied for, and was granted, a hardship exception to the Treaty of Deneb and migrated to Boötes.

There, regarded as the real savior of the Boötean race, and a chosen instrument of the God of Boötes, he was received as a saint. He died in 1689, surrounded by his 22 children and 47 grandchildren, having made himself wealthy by becoming the leader of a most excessive fertility cult, which is only now being forcibly suppressed by the Boötean Government.

In 1635 P.A., someone on Earth remembered the kidnapping indictments still outstanding against Skrrgck and attempted to prosecute them. By this time, however, Skrrgck was Premier, the chief executive officer of Altair, and all extradition matters were within his sole discretion. In the exercise of this power, he refused to extradite himself, and the prosecutor on Earth, whose constituents were beginning to laugh at him, had the indictments quashed "in the interest of interstellar harmony."

The story has an interesting sequel. During Skrrgck's unprecedented six consecutive terms as Premier (no one else had ever served less than seven), he was able, by dint of unremitting political maneuvering, to have theft outlawed in the Altairian system. It was, he said, "a cultural trait that is more trouble than it is worth."

∽

Not much is known about **Louis Newman.** As we said, it's possible he was a one-story author back in the day, but it's also possible he was a pseudonym for someone else. If anyone reading this has information on the writer, kindly reach out!

WITH THE KNIGHT MALE

APOLOGIES TO RUDYARD KIPLING

CHARLES SHEFFIELD

Time for your garrulous editor to step into the wings and let Dr. Sheffield introduce his own story: "In the late 1970s when I was just starting to write fiction, my young children (young back then, grown-ups now) ordered me to produce stories about every funny or disgusting thing in the world. They made the list for me. It had on it items of comic low appeal to them—sewage, visits to the dentist, mushrooms, fat aunts, opera singers, flatulence (I think they used a different word), comic Germans and Italians, fad diets, pigs, morticians, and head lice. Not an easy assignment, but I did my best. Over the years I have published ten politically incorrect stories tackling one or more of the listed topics... Together they form what I think of as my 'sewage' series. They feature my two favorite lawyers, Henry Carver and Waldo Burmeister, and they are depressingly easy to write." Sewage and lawyers—who else would have thought to put those two, ah, archetypes together? It was a dirty job, but world-class mathematician and physicist (and punster, as shown in the story titles) Charles Sheffield was up to the challenge. And the results are anything but depressing.

∾

I RECEIVED THE FINAL PAYMENT THIS MORNING. TO: BURMEISTER and Carver, Attorneys. Payable by: *Joustin' Time.*

Logically, Waldo should have signed the transfer slip. He deserves the money far more than I do. But given his contusions, fractures, lacerations, and multiple body casts, he is in no position to sign anything. In fact, all the negotiations, arguments, offers, and counteroffers to *Joustin' Time* had perforce to come from me. But if Waldo learns anything from his experience—doubtful, given his history—my extra effort on his behalf will be well worthwhile.

I ought to have been suspicious at the outset, when Waldo drifted into my office from his next-door one, preened, and said, "Got us a client."

"That's nice. Who is he?"

"She. It's a lady, Helga Svensen."

I ought to have stopped it right there. Every man is entitled to his little weakness, but Waldo's track record with women clients has been, to put it mildly, unfortunate.

On the other hand, although the love of money is widely acknowledged to be the root of all evil, the *lack* of money isn't too good either. The legal firm of Burmeister and Carver—Waldo and me—was at the time utterly broke.

I said, "What does this Helga Svensen want us to do?"

"Nothing difficult. Seems she's a major player in the pre-Renaissance tournaments that have been so big recently. There's a royal games next week at the Paladindrome on Vesta, and she wants our help with her performance contract. She also asked me to check out one of the accessories. Wants to know if it can be shipped legally interplanet before she commits to anything."

I nodded. World-to-world tariff laws were a nightmare—or, seen from another point of view, a boon for hungry attorneys.

"What is it this time?" I said. "Bows, swords, tankards? Antique suits of armor? Jousting equipment?"

"None of them." Waldo helped himself to a handful of chocolate malt balls sitting in a jar on my desk. "Mainly, she's interested—mm—in the—mm—blagon."

"The flagons?"

"Naw." He had spoken with his mouth full, and was forced to pause and swallow before he could say, "The dragon. Apparently it's a different model from what they've been using before. I'm going to meet Helga Svensen over at Chimera Labs tomorrow morning and we're going to check it out together. Want to come?"

I did not. The mindless rush of the biolabs to create, through fancy DNA splicing, everything from centaurs to basilisks to gryphons has never made sense to me. On the other hand, there is such a thing as due diligence. If we were going to object to—or press for—import/export restrictions on a dragon, I needed to take a look at one.

"What time?" I said.

"Nine o'clock. Nine o'clock sharp."

"I'll be there."

But I wasn't. An unpleasant conversation with our landlord concerning past-due office rental delayed me and I did not reach the offices of Chimera Labs until nine-thirty. The aged derelict on duty at the desk wore a uniform as wrinkled and faded as he was. He cast one bleary-eyed look at me as I came in and said, "Mister Carver? You're expected. First room on the left. The brute's in there."

"The dragon?"

He stared at me gloomily. "Nah. The dragon's straight ahead, but you can't see it. You're to go into the room on the left."

In twenty years of legal practice I had heard Waldo called many names, but "brute" was not one of them. Puzzled, I opened the indicated door.

The voice that greeted me was not Waldo's. It was a pleasant, musical baritone, half an octave deeper than his. That was fair enough, because its owner was over two meters tall and topped Waldo by a full half-head.

She ignored my arrival and went on reading aloud. "'Article Twelve: Should a competitor fail to appear at the allocated time for his/her/its designated heat, semifinal, or final, he/she/it will lose the right to compete further in the tournament, and will in addition forfeit prior cumulative earnings and/or prize money, unless a claim of force majeure can be substantiated before an arbitration board approved by the tournament officials'—you see, it's this sort of blather that ties my head in knots—'in advance of the participation of said competitor in any tournament event.' Now what the devil does that mean?"

Waldo offered a lawyer's nod of approbation. "Nice. It means that if you don't show up for an event, you lose everything unless you can prove to them *in advance* that you couldn't possibly show up. Which is, practically speaking, impossible." He had noticed my arrival, and turned to me. "Henry, this is Helga Svensen. Helga, this is my partner, Henry Carver. Henry is an absolute master at reading the fine print of a contract. If anyone can beat the written terms by using the contract's own words, he can."

While Helga nodded down at me with what I sensed as a certain rational skepticism, I took my chance for an examination of our new client. She was more than just tall. She wore a scanty halter of Lincoln green that revealed breasts like alpine slopes, shoulders wide enough to support a world, and tattooed arms the size of my thighs. Her matching green skirt, shockingly short, ended high up on thighs as sturdy and powerful as the fabled oaks of Earth. Waldo is a substantial man and his recent dieting efforts had been a disaster, but I have to say that next to Helga Svensen he resembled a sun-starved weed.

Her mind was still on the contract. She flourished the offending document and said, "And this bit is nothing like the usual agreement. 'Article Seventeen. Any bona fide member of a participating team, such representative or representatives to be termed hereinafter collectively *the contestant*, may enter into single combat with the dragon. Should the contestant slay or otherwise defeat the dragon, the contestant will win the Grand Prize; should the dragon slay the contestant, all prize money already won by the contestant will be forfeited. In the event of the simultaneous death of both dragon and contestant, the dragon will be deemed the winner.'"

"Sounds clear enough to me," Waldo said. "You kill the dragon and survive, you win big. What's wrong with that?"

"It's too generous." Helga wore her hair in long, golden plaits. They swayed about her plump pink cheeks as she shook her head. "They offer a Grand Prize at every tournament, and nobody has won one in five years—which is how long *Joustin' Time* has been in business. But the prize has never been for dragon-slaying, which isn't too hard. That's the other reason I'm here. I want a sneak preview of the dragon." She glanced at a massive left wrist seeking a nonexistent watch. "What time is it?"

"Nine-forty-five," Waldo said.

"Then he'll be there. Come on—quietly, now."

She opened a small door at the back of the room, lowered her head, and squeezed through. About to follow her into a dark and narrow corridor, I hesitated and turned to Waldo.

"Is this going to be safe? I mean, a dragon..."

"Oh, I'm sure we can trust Helga. Come on." He ducked through.

Was this really Waldo Burmeister, a man nervous in the presence of toy poodles and somnolent cats? I followed him, wondering about his interaction with Helga Svensen before I arrived.

I didn't wonder long because other concerns took center stage. The dark corridor ran for about fifteen meters and ended in a great, dimly lit chamber. I couldn't see much at first, but a smell like a mixture of ammonia and sulfur made my nostrils wrinkle. I heard a whisper ahead of me, answered in Helga's soft baritone. She handed something to a dark figure who at once slipped away into the gloom.

Helga turned to me and Waldo. "Right, we're promised five minutes. Let's take a peek."

I wasn't sure I wanted to. As my eyes adjusted, a shape was coming into focus by the far wall. It was hunched and enormous, at least seven feet high and thirty feet long. I saw scaled legs like tree trunks ending in feet equipped with gleaming talons, a wrinkled body the size of an upturned rowing boat, a long, barbed tail, and a crocodile head. As I watched, two pairs of bat-like wings on each side of the body moved slowly up and down in a breathing rhythm. The whole thing was absolutely terrifying.

"Strange," Helga said in a puzzled voice. "Looks just like the dragon they used in the last tournament. I killed that one myself, with a spear thrust to one of its hearts—but there was no Grand Prize offered for doing it. What game are the crooks at *Joustin' Time* playing now? I wonder if there's something in the contract that says you can't wear armor when you fight the dragon?"

She made no effort to keep her voice down and the dragon heard her. The barrel-sized head with its great jaws turned in our direction. Green eyes blinked open.

Waldo stayed at Helga's side, but I began to back away nervously.

"It's all right," Helga said. "You're quite safe, because it's chained up. You can see the fetters on each leg and around the body."

While she was still speaking, a roaring sound filled the air. Two roiling clouds of blue flame emerged from the dragon's nostrils and streaked in our direction. They narrowly missed Waldo and Helga, came close enough to me to singe my trousers, and incinerated the leather briefcase that I was holding. I dropped the smoking debris as Helga said, "So that's it!"

She sounded delighted as she went on, "It's a real first. They've talked about flame-breathing dragons in the games for years, but they never worked. The last one got the hiccups and blew itself to bits during the opening ceremonies."

"You plan to *fight* that thing?" I said, as I tried to remember what had been in my briefcase. The only thing I was sure of was a sandwich.

"Not me." Helga gave a booming laugh, reached down, and patted out the glowing remnants of my case with one enormous bare hand. "Not now that I know what it can do. I'm not crazy, you know! This time I'll just do the jousting and the hand-to-hand combat. I always do well with those."

I could believe that, even without a survey of the competition. As she bent over, sinews like ship's cables sprang into view in her arms and legs.

"But you'll see for yourself," she went on, "at the tournament. Now, I got what I came for, and I have to be going. Lots to do!" She led the way out of the dragon chamber and dumped a sheaf of papers into my hand as we reentered the front room. "Here's the contract. After what Waldo told me about you and your fine-print reading, I know you'll find a way around all the weasel-wording. See you at the royal games!"

She was gone, with a flash of bare limbs and the swirl of air that denoted the presence of a large moving mass. I turned on Waldo. "At the games? What did you tell her? What did you agree to?"

He wasn't looking at me. He was staring raptly after Helga.

"Isn't she the most gorgeous thing you ever saw in your life?" he said. "Those blue eyes, that perfect complexion. Did you see those cute dimples? On her face, too. It seems a shame to take payment for services from someone so wonderful."

Waldo's little weakness. He was smitten—again. It was time to tear up the contract, give back the fee, find a plausible excuse for non-performance, and make sure that we didn't go within a million miles of Helga Svensen and the *Joustin' Time* tournament.

Why didn't I follow my own sound instincts? Because our landlord had told me that he would wait at our office for payment and if he didn't get it he was going to crack my skull? Because when Waldo was in love, nothing in the known universe could prevent the romance from running its natural or unnatural course?

Because Waldo was holding in his hand Helga's check for our services, more money than we had seen in months?

Yes, certainly. All of those.

But also because, after meeting Helga, I could see no way that anyone else in the games had a prayer of beating her. She was a shoo-in, an absolute cert. When we had paid the rent, a fair amount of Helga's fee would be left over. Back her to win at the jousting, take those winnings with reverse odds that she would *decline* to fight the dragon (there is no substitute for inside information), and watch our initial investment compound to the skies...

I could see it, I could feel it, already I could taste the celebratory champagne.

As I was saying, every man has his little weakness.

Until forty years ago, Vesta was a nowhere place. Plenty of volatiles and a few hundred kilometers across, but still with surface gravity so low you could spit at escape velocity.

The gravity generators changed all that. Now Vesta, like much of the Asteroid Belt, was prime real estate. Add in the Vestans' liberal laws toward physical violence, and the Paladindrome had become one of the system's top sports venues.

Waldo, of course, wanted nothing better when we arrived at the 'drome than to seek out the divine Helga. I left him at the competitors' enclosure and set off on my own little excursion. I had called up the general plan of the Paladindrome on our trip from the Moon, and found that during the first half of the royal games the sword fighting, archery, and jousting would be the main attractions. They were all to take place on a central strip of beaten earth within the main oval of the 'drome, a straightway two hundred meters long and about fifty meters wide. All around the interior of the oval, temporary structures were being installed to support special needs. At this end of the strip were the armorers' tents, the stables, the silversmiths, the food concessions, the sideshows, and the competitors' private enclosure. I noticed that the dragon had his own awning and cage just beyond the end of the jousting strip, right next to the competitors.

I also noticed that, although occasionally goaded by employees of *Joustin' Time*, the dragon did not belch fire. It did not, in fact, do much of anything. Someone must be keeping the beast

high on tranquilizers and low on methane until the second half
of the games.

A deceptive practice, but it was working. Competitors strolled
up, examined and occasionally poked the dragon with a mace
or the blunt end of a pike, and at once went off to sign up for
the great Slay-the-Dragon event.

The scene was colorful and chaotic, and it seemed likely to
become more so once the tournament actually started. The competitors might be all female, but the workers and hangers-on were
not. I saw a woman arguing furiously with an artificer wearing
a cloth apron. As I walked by she ripped off her metal breast
plate and threw it to the ground.

"Look at 'em," she screamed. "Look what it's doing to 'em.
What do you think you are, a lemon squeezer? How am I supposed to fight for three days inside that thing?"

He growled back, "That's the size you told me." He reached a
blackened hand toward her exposed anatomy. "If I was to hammer the metal out right here—"

"Touch that and you're dead!"

I averted my gaze and walked on. My own interests lay at
the other end of the jousting strip, a part of the oval where you
would find the seamier side of the tournament.

The first section I reached was home to the drinking tents.
Judging from the sounds that came out of them they were already
doing a thriving business. Fifty yards farther on, in the Free-
For-All, I was accosted half a dozen times by beauties of every
sex. I politely refused their service, including that of a woman
who somehow realized that I was a lawyer and offered me "a
contingency-basis go as a professional courtesy." Their advances
were mildly annoying—but not nearly as irritating as what I
found when I came to Bettors' Row. There I learned that shop-
ping for odds would not be possible at the tournament. *Joustin'
Time* controlled every betting station!

When you have no choice, you do what you have to. I went
to one of the terminals and entered the name, *Helga Svensen*.
The reply came back, *No such competitor.*

It was preposterous. I knew for a fact that she was competing
in the jousting—I had seen, read, and approved her entry form.
It took assistance from a cheerful lady bettor wearing a hat with
the printed motto, THE WAGES OF SIN IS DEBT, to help me out.

"Helga Svensen," she said. "Oh, she fights in these games as the Warrior Queen. She's very good, but me, I fancy the Iron Maiden. More tricky."

I was already making a complex cascade bet for heats, semifinals, and final on the Warrior Queen, with a double on jousting and a parallel reverse bid for no dragon, so I didn't listen to her very closely. I vaguely pitied the Iron Maiden if she had to face Helga, and went on with my bet. A bet, I might add, at lousy odds. *Joustin' Time* not only controlled this part of the action, the odds that they offered guaranteed a substantial fraction of the stake for themselves. Also, to limit their possible losses they put a ceiling on bet rollover at eighty percent of winnings.

Even so, when you roll eighty percent of winnings back each time into a new stake, the total return grows fast. I made a note of the final payout and decided that Waldo and I were going to be rich. Of course, Helga had to win, but that was a foregone conclusion.

As I was receiving my bet confirmation, my neighbor nudged me. "Want to change your mind? That's the Iron Maiden over there."

Four terminals down, placing a bet of her own, stood an enormous black-haired woman. Studying her powerful frame I felt a moment of doubt. I stepped closer, made a point-by-point physical comparison from her bare toes to her braided crown, and was reassured. The Iron Maiden was big, no doubt about it; but Helga could take her.

My detailed inspection was unfortunately subject to misinterpretation. The Iron Maiden smiled down at me and clasped my arm in a powerful hand.

"You're new here, aren't you?" she said in a strong Scots accent. "You're a sweet-looking wee man. If you're interested in me you should speak up, an' we could find a private game of our own. I bet you never played 'hide the scepter.' You'd make a fine royal prince."

I made unintelligible gobbling noises, retrieved my arm, and fled to the relative safety of the wild animal show.

A wasted opportunity to play the prince, get close to Helga's top competition, learn her strengths and weaknesses, and adjust my bet accordingly?

You must be joking. It's moments like this that prove I'm not a compulsive gambler.

✧　　✧　　✧

Joustin' Time may be run by a bunch of mercenary rogues, but one reason for their success is that they attend to details. The opening ceremony was a pageant in itself, flags flying bravely in the (artificial) breeze, heraldic trumpets blaring, false sun high in the 'drome's false blue sky, real hawthorn trees blooming all around the oval, and pipers in full regalia marching up and down. The final event of the opening was a massed parade of the competitors, four hundred brawny women kicking up the dust, strutting along clad in bright metal and little else. Had Waldo not been already in love, I think he would have died of a surfeit. As it was, he and I stood together among the spectators and agreed that even in such company Helga stood out for her size, power and vitality.

The first event was the individual sword fights. I have no taste for combat, and the sight of blood makes me weak at the knees. I took a stroll. I had to go all the way to the outer perimeter of the Paladindrome before the bloodthirsty howls and screams of the warriors behind me faded into the background. When I reached the wall it was a shock to look beyond the 'drome and see the surface of Vesta curving rapidly away, a stark and barren jumble of boulders, shadowed cliffs, and a handful of busy mining robots. The builders of the 'drome had made a wise choice when they decided that the area within would be as flat as the surface of Earth and as little like the Asteroid Belt as possible. I stood for a long time, the scenes in front of and behind me a thousand years apart.

When I returned, the tag-team sword fights were finishing and the dusty surface was being sprayed with water in preparation for the archery contests. I checked the scoreboards, keeping a wary eye open for off-the-mark practice arrows. As I had hoped and anticipated, Helga was performing magnificently. She had ripped through the heats, semifinals, and finals in short order, and stood in first place. Our winnings had already rolled over into her next event. Since Helga scorned all forms of entertainment involving no contact with the adversary, she had skipped the archery. I did the same, heading past the archers toward the tent where Helga should be preparing herself for the jousting.

At the end of the field I found the Iron Maiden in my path, grimy and sweaty and sitting cross-legged on the grass. I would have ignored her, but she was having none of that.

"Now then, my prince," she said, as I was walking past. "I've a bone to pick with you. You led me on before. You didn't tell me that you were sweet on Helga."

I had to stop at that. "Helga Svensen? I'm not sweet on her. Whatever made you think that?"

"I saw you during the parade. You hardly took your eyes off her."

"That's because I put a bet on her." I felt obliged to add, "And you're mixing me up with my partner, Waldo. He has this thing for her, he's the one who watches her all the time."

"No more than natural. She's a beautiful woman an' a very worr-thy opponent, an' she deserves a lot of respect." The Iron Maiden rose to her knees. "So you're not her feller, then. What's your name?"

"Henry. Henry Carver."

"An' I'm Flora McTavish. I think you an' me could be guid friends." She turned and leaned her body forward away from me. "For a start, would you grab my cuirass?"

"I beg your pardon?"

She pointed to a sort of leather breastplate sitting on the ground a few feet in front of her. "My cuirass. I canna quite reach it from here. Aye, and my greaves and cuish sitting next to it, if you wouldn't mind. It's time I got my things together and went over to the competitors' area."

The bits and pieces she asked for weighed a ton, and I wished that the designers of Vesta's local gravity control had cut a few corners. Flora took the armor from me one-handed and with no sign of effort. "Will ye be seeing Helga an' your friend, then?"

"I'm on my way there now."

"Then mebbe ye can give her this, as my tribute to a great competitor." She reached into her generous cleavage and pulled out a silver flask. "Pure malt whiskey, thirty-five years old an' wi' a taste to make a dead man dance."

I was more than happy to have a reason to escape. The flask went into my pocket and I was away. Flora called something about getting together later, but I paid little attention. I was looking ahead, seeking Helga's colors among hundreds of others.

I didn't see them. What I did see was Waldo, sitting simpering outside one of the tents.

"Where's Helga?" I said as I came up to him.

He nodded toward the flap. "Inside. She's putting her armor

on—and she promised that after the jousting I can help her to take it off."

"This is from one of her friends." I held out the flask of whiskey. "I'll just give it to her."

Waldo was having none of that. "*I'll* give it to her. You wait here."

He tapped on the cloth flap of the tent, waited about five milliseconds, and disappeared inside. I heard an exclamation, a giggle, and some whispering. About a minute later Waldo emerged.

"She says she'll have a drop now, and share any that's left with us after the jousting. She asked us to go now and make sure her horse is saddled and ready."

I couldn't tell if a horse saddle was put on backwards or perhaps even upside down, while Waldo makes me appear as an equestrian expert. But apparently Helga's word was law. We headed off together toward the stables.

"She asked who gave you the whiskey," Waldo said when we were halfway there. "But I couldn't tell her."

"I should have gone into the tent. I could have told her who it came from."

"Well, you never told me."

"You never asked."

"You still could have mentioned it."

"I didn't see any reason to." Rather than bickering indefinitely, I added, "The whiskey came from a woman called Flora."

"Never heard of her." Waldo was sulking.

"She doesn't use that name as a competitor. She fights as the Iron Maiden."

Waldo stopped in midstep. "Are you *sure* it came from the Iron Maiden?"

"Positive. She handed the flask to me herself."

"But the Iron Maiden is in second place to Helga. Didn't you see the scoreboard? They're very close, and that means they'll meet as opponents in the jousting."

We stared at each other for a fraction of a second, then set off for Helga's tent at a run.

I arrived four steps ahead of Waldo, barged in without asking, and was relieved to see the giant figure of Helga sitting over by the far wall. She leaned against a tent pole, and her armor was spread on the floor in front of her.

"It's all right," I said to Waldo as he rushed in. "She's—"

Her eyes were closed. She had not moved.

Waldo howled. "She's dead!"

"No." I could see she was breathing. "She's drugged." I picked up the flask and shook it. Half empty. "Come on, we have to wake her up."

Waldo had subsided to the floor in his relief. "No need for that. She can sleep it off."

Sometimes I wonder which universe Waldo lives in. I glanced at my watch. "In half an hour, Helga has to take part in the jousting. We have all our money on her to win."

"What about the sword fight winnings?"

"Article Twelve: Should a competitor fail to appear at the allocated time, blah-blah-blah—unless Helga fights the Iron Maiden, we lose a fortune."

"She can't fight. Look at her."

Helga was snoring peacefully, her mouth open to reveal pearly and perfect teeth.

"She has to," I said grimly. "Come on."

For the next five minutes we tried shouting, pinching, pouring cold water on her head, burning cloth under her nose. Not a twitch. After we tried and failed to lift her to her feet, so that we could walk her up and down the tent, I realized that Waldo was right. Helga couldn't fight.

We were doomed.

I paced up and down the tent myself. We had twenty minutes. Helga *had* to fight.

But Helga didn't have to *win*. All she had to do was appear. If she fought and lost, we would still have twenty percent of our winnings, the amount they refused to let us roll over into the next bet.

I turned to Waldo. "Come on. We have to do this quickly."

"Do what?"

"Get you into Helga's armor. You have to fight in her place."

"What?!"

"You heard." I handed him the helmet. "You don't have to fight well. It's enough just to show up."

"I can't pretend I'm Helga. I look nothing like her. For heaven's sake, Henry, I have a *mustache*."

"You'll be inside her suit of armor, with a visor covering your face. There won't be an inch of you showing."

"Then why don't you do it?"

"I'm not half her size. I'd rattle around inside her armor like a pea in a can. For you, though, it won't be a bad fit."

"Henry, you've gone mad. I can't do it." He folded his arms. "I won't do it."

Twenty minutes. Fortunes have been made in twenty minutes, empires lost, cities destroyed, whole nations doomed or saved.

I sat down opposite Waldo. After five years in law school and four times that as a practicing attorney, it was time to see how much I had learned of the gentle arts of persuasion.

I began, "Think how grateful Helga will be..."

He didn't look bad, not bad at all.

Admittedly—I squinted into the sun—Waldo was close to two hundred meters away at the other end of the straightway, so that the finer details of the way he sat on the horse were probably lost to me. I hoped he had paid attention to my last cautionary words. "Don't say a word to *anyone*, no matter who they are. After the jousting is done, ride this way. I'll take care of the horse, you go back inside the tent and take off the armor. If anyone comes in after that, you tell them Helga needed to sleep after a hard day."

It might work. It *could* work. Waldo just had to ride the length of the field without falling off, then he would be back at the exhibit area where he had started. The competitors' tents were close by, and Helga's was near the front. He could ride the horse right up to it.

I hoped that he could see. Helga's armor had been made for her, half a head taller. Stretching up as high as he could, Waldo had been able to get one of his eyes level with a nose hole. He had complained about that quite a bit. On the other hand, what did he need to see? The horses had been trained well, and I knew from watching previous contestants that a straight path was the easiest one for the animal.

The Iron Maiden would start from close to where I stood. I wished I could see the expression on the face behind the visor. There had been no more of the "fine sweet prince" talk, and my bet was that she was scowling and wondering where her plan to nobble Helga had failed.

The blue flag was slowly being raised. When it fluttered down, the two contestants would begin to ride toward each other, first at a canter and then at a full gallop.

There was one other detail that I preferred not to think about.

Each rider was armed with a lance about twenty-five feet long. Even after watching some of the other jousters, I didn't know how the cumbersome thing was supposed to be supported. I finally lashed Waldo's weapon to the saddle in one place and tucked the rounded haft between his arm and breastplate. The chance that he would hit anything with it was negligible, but at least the point could not drop too far and convert the event to the pole vault.

The chance that the Iron Maiden would damage Waldo was another matter. I had downplayed the risk, telling him that no one in the jousting had been killed. I did not mention that there had been a couple of very violent dismounts. It would only send him off on another tirade of protest.

The blue flag was starting down. That made little difference, because Waldo's horse had decided to use its own best judgment on the matter and started to canter forward a few seconds earlier.

I heard a loud curse from inside the helmet of the Iron Maiden. She dug her heels into her own horse and it whinnied and jerked forward.

The crowd became silent, the only sound the thundering hooves. It did not take a connoisseur to detect a certain difference of styles between the two contestants. The Iron Maiden sat rock-steady on her horse and the tip of her lance moved as though it was fixed to a straight line parallel to the ground.

By contrast, I could see occasional daylight between Waldo and his saddle. The end of his lance described random motion within a vertical circle twenty-five feet ahead of him. The radius of that circle increased as the horse moved from a canter to a full gallop.

I had never before realized how fast horses can run. The horses that I bet on seldom seem to manage more than an arthritic crawl toward the winning post. But Waldo and the Iron Maiden were approaching each other at an impossible speed.

They were forty meters apart—twenty—a crash of metal—they were somehow past each other, and the spectators were screaming in horror. The tip of the Iron Maiden's lance had struck Waldo squarely in the middle of his helmet, ripping it loose from the rest of his armor. As the helmet rolled away across the dirt, the headless knight galloped on.

Rode toward me. Rode straight at me. As I threw myself out of the way, convinced that the decapitated rider was about to lance Helga as she lay sleeping inside her tent, the horse at the last moment veered off. The lance leading the way, horse and burden missed the competitors' enclosure and plunged into the next one.

I couldn't see behind the awning separating the enclosures, but the noise that reached me was frightful.

It took a couple of weeks to arrange the hearing, long enough for Waldo to be out of the hospital. He claimed that he ought to come to court and present part of our arguments, but I dissuaded him on the grounds that his broken and wired jaw denied him his customary verbal clarity.

The rest of his head was intact. Unable to maintain a high enough position in Helga's suit when on horseback, he had slipped down to peer out through a slit in the neck piece. He had been untouched by the lance that removed the helmet, but the force of his final collision did considerable damage.

I expected to be alone in the court, except for the judge and the team of seven attorneys representing *Joustin' Time*. When I heard another group of people slip into the back as the proceedings began, I was too busy listening to the *Joustin' Time* claims to take notice of new arrivals.

Their list of purported offenses and damages was impressive. The lead attorney, Duncan Whiteside, a man of earnest demeanor and awkward body language, took four and a half hours to deliver it, but I could boil everything down to this:

* Messrs. Burmeister and Carver had illegally taken part in a tournament organized by *Joustin' Time*.

* Messrs. Burmeister and Carver had by their actions forced cancellation of the jousting contest.

* Messrs. Burmeister and Carver, by killing the tournament dragon, had forced the cancellation of the entire second half of the program.

Both compensatory and punitive damages were sought.

When Duncan Whiteside finally dribbled to a halt, Judge Solomon looked at me and said, "You may now respond to these charges."

"Thank you, Your Honor. I will be brief."

I had seen the judge's eyes rolling during the previous presentation. Hubert Solomon was a man of famously few words, and he admired the same trait in others. I figured I had five good minutes and I did not intend to go a second over.

"Your Honor," I said, "I would draw your attention to Exhibit

Seven, the contract between Helga Svensen and *Joustin' Time Enterprises*."

"I have it."

"Article Nineteen, paragraph four, clause five. Let me read it aloud, since the print is awfully small. 'The terms and conditions of this contract will apply *in toto* to any designated representative of the contractor.' Your honor, Burmeister and Carver are designated representatives of Helga Svensen. My colleague, Waldo Burmeister, represented Helga Svensen in the jousting tournament. I would simply make the comment that were an attorney *not* deemed to be a designated representative of a client, the entire legal profession would be irreparably damaged."

"Your point is noted. Continue."

"Burmeister and Carver, jointly and severally, had no part in the decision to cancel the jousting tournament. Therefore we cannot be regarded as responsible for such a decision."

"Noted. Continue."

"Now, as to the dragon—"

"Objection!" Naturally, from Duncan Whiteside.

Judge Solomon had an odd frown on his face as he stared at me. "Mr. Carver, this is a serious matter. I hope that you are not proposing to argue that Mr. Burmeister did not kill the dragon."

"Not at all. Your Honor, it is a central point of our argument that Mr. Burmeister's lance undeniably killed the dragon. Now let me draw your attention to Article Seventeen of the contract. Again I quote: 'Any *bona fide* representative of a participating team, such representative or representatives to be termed here-inafter collectively *the contestant*, may enter into single combat with the dragon. Should the contestant slay or otherwise defeat the dragon, the contestant will win the Grand Prize.' Since Mr. Burmeister was a representative of Helga Svensen, and killed the dragon, the Grand Prize should be paid—"

"Objection!" The lead attorney for *Joustin' Time* was on his feet. "Your Honor, the dragon was *asleep* when Mr. Burmeister killed it."

"Mr. Whiteside, you must allow Mr. Carver to finish his sentences, otherwise—"

"Your Honor, the dragon-slaying part of the tournament had not even begun."

"Mr. Whiteside, you must also allow *me* to finish my sentences."

Hubert Solomon was enjoying the tussle. Otherwise he would have bitten off Duncan Whiteside's head. He nodded to me. "Mr. Carver, proceed."

"Thank you. Your Honor, I have little to add. Nothing in the contract mentions the time or circumstances in which the dragon must be slain in order for a contestant to win the Grand Prize. Mr. Burmeister slew the dragon, and therefore won the Grand Prize. The amount owed to us is given in Exhibit Two."

"Very good." The judge abruptly stood up. "I now call a ten-minute recess."

He swept out. I knew where he was going—to private chambers for a good laugh.

I felt an urge to do the same. I headed for the exit, carefully avoiding the dismayed eyes of the *Joustin' Time* team. They were not complete fools. They knew they had ten minutes to agree among themselves on the terms of a mediated settlement.

Near the door I came to the group of people who had arrived late. It offered the impression of a group, but actually it was just Helga Svensen and Flora McTavish.

Together! Clad today in light, springtime armor, they sat side by side smiling at the world.

"Mr. Carver." Helga reached out and enveloped my hand in hers. "You were brilliant, totally brilliant."

"You were." Flora beamed at me. "Helga told me you'd do it, but I didn't see how. You're a genius!"

"Not really." I coughed modestly. "It's far from over, you know. And all I did was read the fine print."

"But *how* you read it!" Flora's eyes were shining. "Would you be willing to read *my* fine print?"

While I was pondering the possible implications of that question, Helga stood up. "I'm going to leave the two of you to talk. Is it too soon for me to go and see Waldo?"

I thought of my partner, splinted and swathed from head to toe. In his present condition I didn't think that even Waldo could get into too much trouble. "You can go and see him," I said, "but you won't see much of him."

"I'll tell him things are going well." She thundered out, shaking the floor with her girlish tread.

I turned to Flora. "I don't understand. She brought you here. She's *talking* to you."

"Of course she is. Helga and I are best friends."

"But you drugged her and tried to kill her!"

"Oh, nonsense. Drugged her a wee bit, aye, but that's all in the game. I knew it wasn't Helga, the minute I saw that lance wobbling about. I thought she was snoring in her tent, and somebody had tied a stuffed dummy up there on her horse."

Stuffed, perhaps, and far too frequently for someone on a perennial diet; but Waldo was no dummy.

"There's a big tournament coming up on Ceres," Flora went on. "I'd like you to be there with me."

I could not talk any longer. A buzz of activity at the front of the room announced that Judge Solomon had entered and Duncan Whiteside was already stepping toward him, an anxious expression on his face.

I ran for the steps, calling over my shoulder, "Go there, and do what?"

I *think* that Flora, behind me, said, "Read my fine print." But it sounded an awful lot like, "Be my fine prince."

❧

Charles Sheffield (1935–2002) graduated from St. John's College in Cambridge, England, and had notable careers as a scientist and a writer. In the former field, he served as Chief Scientist of the Earth Satellite Corporation, which processed remote sensing data collected by satellites, producing many technical papers and two popular nonfiction books, *Earthwatch* and *Man on Earth*. He was a consultant with NASA. His science fiction writing was equally impressive, as when his novelet, "Georgia on My Mind," won both the Hugo and Nebula Awards. His novel *Brother to Dragons* won the 1992 John W. Campbell Memorial Award. He served as president of the Science Fiction and Fantasy Writers of America from 1984 to 1986 and also served as president of the American Astronautical Society. Noted for his flair for humor (as in the story in this book), he was Toastmaster at the 1998 World Science Fiction Convention. He had brilliant careers in science and science fiction and his untimely death from a brain tumor in 2002 was a tragic loss for both fields.